Okay, Skeeter, just stay calm. You've been in worse spots. Just get back to the Time Tours Inn and hide out until the gate cycles open and you'll be fine.

Then the sound of nightmare: "Hey! Hey, odds maker!" It was the lean, grizzled Roman who'd placed the bet, about a hundred yards behind him. Even from here, Skeeter could see the blood spattered on his clothes.

Skeeter did the only logical, honorable thing he could: he ran like hell.

"Stop! Stop, you—" The rest was Latin Skeeter hadn't learned yet.

Skeeter dodged and ran with everything in him. Given his skill at vanishing in the places he'd lived as a child, losing himself in Rome ought to be a piece of cake.

But his pursuer was faster than he looked. The man was gaining. Thunderstorms rolling across the vast plains of Outer Mongolia had looked friendlier than that Roman's face. And he had a knife in his hand. A *really* long one.

Skeeter cut around another corner, dashed down a long straight-way, zipped around another corner—

And yelled, even as he tried to stop. The street ended abruptly in a drop-off straight in the Tiber river....

WAGERS OF SIN

ROBERT ASPRIN
LINDA EVANS

WAGERS OF SIN

Copyright © 1996 by Bill Fawcett & Associates

A Baen Books Original

Baen Publishing Enterprises
P.O. Box 1403
Riverdale, NY 10471

ISBN: 0-671-87730-5

Cover art by Gary Ruddell

First printing, July 1996

Distributed by Simon & Schuster
1230 Avenue of the Americas
New York, NY 10020

Printed in the United States of America

CHAPTER ONE

Skeeter Jackson was a scoundrel.

A dyed-in-the-wool, thieving scoundrel.

He knew it, of course; knew it as well as anyone else in La-La Land (at least, anyone who'd been on Shangri-La Station longer than a week). Not only did he know it, he was proud of it, the way other men were proud of their batting averages, their cholesterol counts, their stock portfolios.

Skeeter was *very* careful to rub shoulders with men of the latter type, who not only boasted of *large* 'folios, but carried enormous amounts of cash in money belts declared through ATF at Primary (so they wouldn't be charged taxes for any money they'd brought with them). Skeeter rarely failed to get hold of at least *some* of that money, if not the whole money belt. Ah, the crisp, cool feel of cash in hand . . .

But he wasn't just a thief. Oh, no. Skeeter was a master *con artist* as well, and *those* skills (ruthless cunning, serpentine guile, the ability to radiate innocent enthusiasm) were among the best.

So—in honor of Yesukai the Valiant and for the very practical reason of survival—he worked hard at being the very best scoundrel he could make himself. Once he'd arrived (freshly scrubbed to get the New York filth off his hide and out of his soul), it hadn't taken Skeeter long to create a life uniquely

1

his own on a time terminal unique among time terminals.

There was only *one* La-La Land. He loved it fiercely.

On this particular fine morning, Skeeter rose, stretched, and grinned. *The game's afoot, Watson!* (He'd heard that in a movie someplace and liked the sound of it.) The glow coming in beneath his door told him Residence lights were on, not in their dimmed "night" mode. That was really the only way to tell, unless you had an alarm clock with a PM indicator light; Skeeter's had burned out long ago, the last time he'd heaved it at the wall for rudely awakening him with yet another hangover to regret.

Showered and shaved with minimal time wasted, he dressed for the day—and the next two glorious weeks. After some of the things he'd worn, the costume he now donned felt almost natural. Whistling absently to himself, Skeeter—working hard as ever on his chosen vocation—contemplated his brilliant new scheme. And the one gaping hole in it.

Surprisingly, the station's excellent library hadn't been much help. To minimize information leakage, Skeeter *had* searched the computers, gleaning bits of valuable information here and there (and managing to tot up more than a week's worth of earnings against the computer-access account belonging to a scout currently out in the field). *That* little scam was actually worth the otherwise wasted effort, as the scout had once maligned Skeeter in public—wrongly, as it happened; Skeeter hadn't even been involved. Skeeter, therefore felt free to indulge his natural urge to cause the scout the greatest amount of distress possible in the shortest amount of time, all without leaving behind any proof the s.o.b. could use to prosecute.

Irritatingly elusive, the one piece of the puzzle Skeeter needed most just wasn't *in* any pilfered file.

The *only* place to find what he needed was inside someone's head. Brian Hendrickson, the librarian, would know, of course—he knew, just as sharply as though he'd learned it mere moments previously, everything he'd ever seen, read, or heard (and probably more—lots more), but Brian's dislike of Skeeter was La-La Land Legend. After ruling out Brian, who was left?

Just needing one more piece of expert advice, Skeeter was running out of time to find it—and had never had many friends to find it from. Well, hell, folks with his chosen vocation *wouldn't* have many friends, now would they? Trust just didn't come with the territory. Having accepted that years ago, Skeeter continued to mentally rummage through the list of people he *might* be able to ask, tossed out all scouts, most guides (Agnes Fairchild was willing—mmm, was she ever!—she just didn't *know*). He hesitated—again—on Goldie Morran. She'd be motivated, all right, and she'd probably *know*, too; but he wasn't about to share potentially enormous profits by confiding his plan to *any* of the other scoundrels who made La-La Land their permanent home. To make the score himself, Goldie-the-heartless-Morran, TT-86's leading authority on rare coins and gems, was out.

What he *needed* was someone who'd *been* there, first-hand.

Other than a handful of rich visitors who'd been through the Porta Romae multiple times—most of whom Skeeter had "liberated" from the burden of their cash and were therefore to be avoided at any cost—Skeeter finally came up with a single, qualified man in the whole of TT-86: Marcus.

A startled grin passed across his face. As it happened, Marcus was probably better suited to give Skeeter advice on this particular scheme than all the so-called experts in La-La Land. *Should've just gone to Marcus in the first place and saved myself a heap of time and trouble*. But he'd been embarrassed, feeling a pang of inexplicable guilt at the thought of conning his best (and practically his only) friend into helping him. Of course, he'd also have missed racking up all those on-line hours against that asshole of a scout. . . .

By coincidence rare and somewhat miraculous, Marcus actually *liked* Skeeter. *Why*, Skeeter had not a single clue. Downtimers often came up with the strangest ideas, many of them quaintly useless, others so eccentric they passed beyond the understandable into the misty, magical realm of things like what made the gates work and what did women really want, anyway? He'd given up on both, long ago, avoiding stepping through any more gates than absolutely necessary and taking his flings where he could find them, not very discontented when he couldn't. He didn't feel proud about his ignorance; business, however, was business.

So Skeeter finished the last touches on his "business uniform" then headed for Commons to hunt down Marcus, then meet Agnes and her group for the tour.

Skeeter liked the open airy feeling of Commons. Not only did it compensate (a little) for the loss of vast, open plains of his teenage years, but more importantly, it *always* smelled to Skeeter like *money*. Vast sums of cold, hard currency changed hands here. It wasn't too much to ask of the gods, was it, that some small trickle of that vast amount fall blissfully into his deserving hands?

Theology aside (and only the many gods knew what Skeeter's was: he certainly didn't), Commons was just plain fun. Particularly at this time of year. As he strode out into the body-jammed floor, picking his way through multiple festivals and reenactments in progress, Skeeter had to shake his head and grin.

What a madhouse! There were, of course, the usual tourist gates with their waiting areas, ramps, and platforms; ticket booths for those who'd waited to arrive before deciding on a destination—fine, if you could afford the hotel bills waiting for your tour to leave; timecard automated dispensers (hooked into the station's database and set up to match retinal scans and replace the original's temporal-travel data for those idiots who'd lost theirs); and of course, timecard readers (at the entrance and exit of every gate, to scan where and when you'd already been in a desperate effort to prevent some fool tourist from shadowing him- or herself).

There were also shops and restaurants, on multiple levels, many with entrances by balcony only; bizarre stairways to nowhere; balconies and girder-supported platforms suspended three and four stories above the floor; barricaded and fenced-off areas marking either unevenly recurring, unstable gates or stable but unexplored gates; and—the *piece de resistance*—multiple hundreds of costumed, laughing, drinking, quarreling, fighting, kissing, hugging, *gullible* tourists. With fat wallets just waiting for someone's light-fingered touch . . .

Just now Commons looked exactly like the North Pole might if Santa's elves had gone quietly mad on LSD in the process of decorating the workshop. He breathed in the smell of celebration and money and grinned up at the whole, gaudy, breathtaking length of Commons, loving every bit of the craziness that always overtook Shangri-La Station this time of year.

"And what," a woman's voice said practically at his elbow, "are *you* grinning about, Skeeter Jackson?"

He looked up—then down—and found Ann Vinh Mulhaney, TT-86's resident projectile weapons instructor. Ann was so petite she was smaller than her teenaged son. Barely came up to Skeeter's biceps. She was, however, the second or third deadliest person on station, depending on whether Kit Carson had showed up at the range for some shooting practice most recently, or whether Ann had (since Kit's last target practice) hit the gym mats for a series of sweat-building katas and bone-pounding sparring sessions against Sven Bailey, the station's widely known Number One deadliest individual.

Skeeter felt ridiculous, towering over a woman who terrified him down to his cockles. *Uh-oh. What'd I do now?*

Oddly, Ann was smiling up at him, like that famous painting of the Mona Lisa. Like good old Mona, Ann revealed absolutely nothing in dark, knowing eyes. The strange little smile on her lips did not touch them. For a moment, he was actually cold-sweating scared of her, despite at least a foot and several inches height advantage and a good chance at outsprinting her, even in this crowd.

Then something altered subtly and he realized the smile had just turned friendly. *What does she want? Does she want to hire me to steal something, maybe, or bring her back a special souvenir as a surprise for somebody?* Skeeter not only couldn't understand how Ann's husband could actually *live* with that deadly little viper, he honestly could find no sane reason why Ann would even talk to him.

She looked him up and down, then met his gaze. "Heard you were going through the Porta Romae."

Uh-oh. He answered very carefully, "Uh, yeah, that was sorta the plan. Me and Agnes, you know."

She just nodded, as though confirming the cinching of a wager with someone about what Skeeter Jackson was up to now.

He relaxed. Settling a wager was all right. Ann was certainly entitled to ask him questions if the answers won her a tidy sum in some bet.

But she was still smiling, friendly-like. *The Christmas season, maybe? Manifesting itself in a determined "do unto others" even if it killed her?*

She took the initiative once again. "So, what *were* you grinning about? Misadventures, schemes, and scams downtime?"

"Ann! You wound me!"

She just laughed, eyes and the twist of her mouth clearly skeptical.

"Honestly, I was just taking in all of . . . *that*."

She followed his gaze and her eyes softened. "It is, um, overwhelming, isn't it? Even crazier than *last* year's contest."

Skeeter grinned again. "At least I don't see any three-story, arm-waving Santas to catch fire this year."

She shared his laugh. "No, thank goodness! I thought Bull Morgan was going to fall into a fit of apoplexy when he saw the smoke and flames. Good thing Pest Control's good at putting out fires, too."

"Yeah. They were good, that day. You know," Skeeter said thoughtfully, "I think the holiday season is my very favorite time of year on station. All of that," he waved a hand toward the insanity surrounding them, "cheers a guy up. You know?"

Ann studied him minutely. "So, the holidays cheer you up, do they? Rachel's hands are always full this time of year with half-suicidal people who don't do holidays well. But with you, well, I think I can guess why."

"Yeah?" Skeeter asked with interest, wondering how transparent he'd become since leaving Yesukai's camp.

"Let's see . . . I'm betting—figuratively," she added hastily, "that the holiday season is usually the closest you ever come to getting *rich*. True or false?"

He had to laugh, even while wincing. "Ann, with triple the ordinary number of tourists jamming Commons, how can a guy lose? 'Course I'm happiest this time of year!" He didn't add that the pain of five missed Christmases—holidays that had nothing to do with the expensive bribes his parents piled under the tree each year—were also responsible for his determined merrymaking as he caught up on all the childhood holidays he'd been alone.

Ann just sighed. "Skeeter, you are an irrepressible scoundrel." She caught his gaze, then, and shocked him speechless. "But you know, I think if you ever got caught and kicked off TT-86, La-La Land would be a lot less fun. You're . . . intriguing, Skeeter Jackson. Like a puzzle, where all the pieces don't quite fit right." With an odd little smile, she said, "Maybe I ought to ask Nally Mundy about it." Skeeter groaned inwardly. Not too many people knew. Skeeter's had been a fleeting, fifteen-second sound-byte's worth of fame, jammed between a triple homicide and a devastating hotel fire on the evening news, years ago. But Nally Mundy knew. Skeeter hadn't quite forgiven him for discovering that juicy little tidbit to hound him about.

Before he could lodge a protest, though, Ann said, "Well, anyway, good hunting—whatever you're up to. See you 'round in a couple of weeks."

She left before he could open his mouth.

And Ann Vinh Mulhaney wishes me good hunting, no less. La-La Land felt like it had turned upside down.

Skeeter glanced up, more than halfway expecting to see crowds of people thronging the Commons' floor, rather than the distant, girdered ceiling.

"Huh," was his only comment.

Skeeter glanced at the gate-departure board suspended from the ceiling and whistled silently. He would have to stretch his legs if he wanted to catch Marcus before he went off-shift at the Down Time Bar & Grill. But he still had several minutes' leeway until he had to catch up with Agnes for the Porta Romae Gate departure.

He picked his way cautiously through a horde of "medieval" damsels, knights in handcrafted chain-mail armor, and throngs of pages and squires, even "authentic" vendors and friars, all headed for Tournament down the newest of TT-86's active gates, the "Anachronism" as 'eighty-sixers called it after the name of the organization that used it most. It led, of all places, to North America prior to the coming of the paleo-Indian population that would eventually cross the Bering Strait and settle two empty continents. Several times a year, hordes—masses— of medieval loons flooded TT-86, every one of them just dying to step through the Anachronism to play at war, medieval style.

Skeeter shook his head. From the realities of war as he'd seen it, Skeeter couldn't find much in wholesale slaughter that *should* be turned into any kind of game. For him, it smacked a little of heresy (whatever that might be) to mock the brave dead they pretended to emulate. Clearly, they got something from it they badly needed, or they wouldn't keep doing it. Especially with the cost so high.

Not only did they have every other tourist's normal expenses, they had to get permission to take their own horses and hunting falcons along, with *stiff* penalties if any of the uptime animals got loose and started a breeding colony millennia before they should have existed; they had to haul fodder and cut-up mice for their animals; then had to find a place to *keep* said animals until Anachronism's departure date—and then, of course, they *all* had to get through the gate in time, balking horses, screeching falcons, their own provisions

as well as the animals', in short, everything required
for a one-month, downtime Tournament and the honor
to have fought in or attended one.

The single thing he understood about them was their
detestation of nosey newsies. It was rumored that *no*
newsie had ever gotten through with them. Or if they
had, they hadn't survived to tell the tale. North America
was a bad place, that long ago. Sabre cats, dire wolves—
you name it. Meaning, of course, that Skeeter's
intention of stepping through the Anachronism was
right up there with his intention of walking up to Mike
Benson and holding out his hands to be cuffed.

Skeeter watched with admiration as hawkers of
"medieval wares" counted up their sales and tourists
pushed to hand over cash for "MAGIC POTIONS!";
crystals mounted as necklaces or stand-alone little
trinkets, attuned to the buyer's aura by placing it under
the pillow for seven consecutive full moons; charms
for wealth, health, harmony, courage, and beauty;
exquisite, illuminated calligraphy with even more
exquisite prices; plus relatively cheap jewelry that
commanded top-rate prices because it was "handmade
in the most ancient methods known to our medieval
ancestors."

In Skeeter's educated estimation, they were as much
con artists as Skeeter himself. They even kept back
the good stuff (he knew; he'd pilfered a coveted item
or two for his quarters, to liven it up a bit), keeping it
hidden to sell *at* the Tournament, bringing along a
supply of junk to sell to gullible tourists, to help defray
expenses a little. They were con men and women, all
right. They just had a different angle on the art than
Skeeter did.

Ianira Cassondra—who had occasionally made
Skeeter's hair stand on end, just with a simple word
or two—called them fakes, charlatans, and even worse,

because they had neither the training to dabble in such things, nor the proper attitude for it.

"They will inadvertently hurt people one day. Just wait. Station management will do nothing about them *now*; but when people start falling down sick with all manner of strange illnesses, their trade *will* be banished." She'd sighed, dark eyes unhappy. "And Management will most likely outlaw *my* booth as well, as I doubt Bull Morgan is capable of telling the difference."

Skeeter had wanted to contradict her, but not only was he half scared she *was* reading the future, in the back of his own mind, Skeeter knew perfectly well that Bull Morgan wouldn't know the difference, and wouldn't care, either, just so long as the crummy tourists were protected.

Skeeter thought dark, vile thoughts at bureaus and the bureauc-rats that ran 'em, and skittered through long lines in Edo Castletown waiting for the official opening of the new Shinto Shrine that was nearly finished. He dashed past Kit Carson's world-famous hotel, past extraordinary gardens with deep streams where colored fish kept to the shadows, trying to avoid becoming a sushi lunch for some *Ichthyornis* or a *Sordes fritcheus* diving down from the ceiling.

Skeeter smiled reminiscently, recalling the moment Sue Fritchey had figured out what their crow-sized "pterosaurs" really were: "My God! They're a new species of *Sordes*! They shouldn't be living at the same time as a *sternbergi* at all. My God, but this is . . . it's revolutionary! A warm-blooded, fur-covered *Sordes*— and a *fish* eater, not an insectivore, but it's definitely a *Sordes*, there's no mistaking that!—and it survived right up until the end of the Cretaceous. All along, we've thought *Sordes* died out right at the end of the Jurassic! What a paper this is going to be!" she'd laughed, eyes shining. "Every paleontological journal uptime is going to be begging me for the right to publish it!"

For Sue Fritchey, *that* was heaven.

Grapevine or not, Skeeter *still* hadn't heard what Sue had decided about the pair of eaglelike, toothed birds that had popped through an unstable gate months ago. But whatever they were, they were going to make Sue Fritchey famous. He wished her luck.

Reaching the edge of Urbs Romae, with its lavishly decorated Saturnalia poles and cut evergreen trees, also boasting paid actors to reenact the one day a year Roman slaves could give orders to their masters— orders that had to be obeyed and often had the watching audience laughing so hard, both men and women had to wipe their eyes dry just to see the show—Skeeter slowed to a walk, whistling cheerfully to himself, winking at pretty girls he passed, girls who sometimes blushed, yet always followed his departure with their eyes.

Skeeter ducked beneath the sea of paper umbrellas tourists and residents alike carried—protection against droppings from aforementioned wild prehistoric birds and pterosaurs—and finally hunted out the Down Time Bar & Grill where Marcus worked as a bartender.

The Down Time, tucked away in the "Urbs Romae" section of Commons, was a favorite haunt of 'eighty-sixers. Among other things, it was a great place to pick up gossip.

And in Skeeter's line of work, gossip usually meant profit.

So he ducked under the girders which half hid the bar's entryway (another reason 'eighty-sixers liked it: the place didn't advertise) and crossed the threshold, already savoring the anticipation of setting his newest scheme into delightful motion.

The first person to see him, however, was none other than Kenneth "Kit" Carson, retired time scout. *Uh-oh* . . . Skeeter gulped and tried on a bright grin, the one he'd learned to use as a weapon of self-defense long, long ago. He'd been avoiding Kit's company for weeks, ever since he'd tried to sweet-talk that penniless, gorgeous little redhead, Margo, into bed with him by pretending to be a scout—only to learn to his terror that she was Kit's only grandkid. Kit's *underage* only grandkid.

What Kit had casually threatened to do to him . . .

"Hi, Skeeter. How they hangin'?" Kit—long and lean and tough as a grizzled bear—grinned up at him and took a slow sip from a cold glass of Kirin.

"Uh . . . fine, Kit. Just fine . . . How's, uh . . . Margo?" He wanted to bite off his tongue and swallow it. *Idiot!*

"Oh, fine. She'll be visiting soon. School vacation."

As one very small predator in a very large pond, Skeeter knew a bigger predator's smile when he saw one. Skeeter took a vow to make himself scarce from *anyplace* Margo decided to visit. "Good, that's real good, Kit. I, uh, was just looking for Marcus."

Kit chuckled. "He's in back, I think."

Skeeter shot past Kit's table, heading for the billiard and pool tables in the back room. Very carefully, he did *not* reach up and wipe sweat from his damp brow. Kit Carson scared him. And not just because the retired time scout had survived more, even, than Skeeter had. Mostly, Skeeter Jackson had a healthy fear of the older male relatives of *any* girl he'd tried to get into bed. Most of them took an extremely dim view of his chosen vocation.

Going one on one with a man who could break major bones as casually as Skeeter could lift a wallet was not Skeeter's idea of fun.

Fortunately, Marcus was exactly where Kit had said

he'd be: serving drinks in the back room. Skeeter
brightened at once. Running into Kit like that—on
the eve of launching his new adventure—was *not* a
bad omen, he told himself. Marcus would be Skeeter's
good luck charm for this venture. The old, familiar
itch between his shoulderblades was never wrong.
Skeeter grinned happily.

Look out, suckers. Ready or not, here I come!

Marcus had just set drinks down on a newly occupied
table in the back pool room when Skeeter Jackson
made a grand entrance and grinned in his direction.
Marcus smiled, very nearly laughing aloud. Skeeter
was dressed for business, which in this case meant a
short, flamboyant tunic, more of a Greek Ionian-style
chiton, really, with knobby knees showing naked below
the hem and legs that were far more heavily muscled
and powerful-looking than most people would have
guessed from the whipcord-lean rest of him. Judging
by his costume, Skeeter must be working the crowds
that always gathered to watch the famous Porta Romae
cycle again.

The god Janus—Roman deity of doorways and
portals—had for some unknown reason decreed that
the Porta Romae would cycle open yet again in less
than an hour, moving the gate inexorably along to
the next opening two weeks hence. Marcus hid a
shiver, remembering his single trip through that portal
to arrive here. He had never really believed in Rome's
strange gods until his final master had dragged him,
terrified and fainting, through the Porta Romae into
La-La Land. Now he knew better and so never failed
to give the powerful Roman gods their proper
libations.

"Marcus! Just the person I'm dying to see." Skeeter's
grin was infectious and genuine. Very little else about

Skeeter Jackson was, which made him one of the loneliest people Marcus knew.

"Hello, Skeeter. You wish your favorite beer?" Marcus was so uncomfortable with Skeeter's lifestyle he tried hard not to mention it, in the probably vain hope he could save the young up-and downtimer from the life he led. Marcus was, in fact, doubtless the only one in the whole of The Found Ones who offered the odd young man his friendship. To be raised in two times, then set adrift in a third . . .

Skeeter Jackson was greatly in need of a friend. So Marcus, busy as he was with demanding work at the bar and an equally demanding—but more fun—job as the father of two little girls, added a third Herculean task to his life: the eventual conversion of Skeeter Jackson from Scoundrel to Honest Man, deserving of the title Found One.

Skeeter's grin widened. "Sure. I won't turn down a beer, you know that." Both men laughed. "But mostly, I wanted to talk to you. Got a minute?"

Marcus glanced out at the other tables. Most were empty. Nearly everyone was out on the Commons, watching the fun as La-La Land's Roman gate prepared to open into the past. Between now and then, a whole series of antics would unfold as tourists and Time Tours guides and baggage handlers tried to get through the portal with all their baggage, money purses, and assorted children still intact, waiting impatiently while much of the previous tour exited the Porta Romae in staggering, white-faced clumps. The rest coming back through were fine, swaggering down the ramp like aloof, supremely self-confident Roman Senators.

Marcus shook off his mental astonishment that *every* tour came back like this, some pleased as kittens with a bowl of cream and others . . . Well, the drawings circulating amongst The Found Ones said it all, didn't they?

Marcus smiled at Skeeter, who waited hopefully. "Of course. Let me get the beer for you, please."

"Get one for yourself, too. I'm buying."

Oh-oh. Marcus hid a grin. Skeeter wanted something. He was a thoroughgoing scoundrel, was Skeeter Jackson, but Marcus understood why, something most 'eighty-sixers didn't. Not even most Found Ones knew. Marcus hadn't even told Ianira, although with his beautiful Ianira, what she did or did not know was always a complete mystery to Marcus.

Skeeter had been so drunk that night, he probably didn't remember everything he'd said. But Marcus did. So he kept trying, hope against hope, to befriend Skeeter Jackson, asking the gods who had watched over his own life to help his friend finally figure it all out—and do something about it besides swindle, cheat, and steal his way toward the grave.

Marcus set down Skeeter's beer first, then took a chair opposite and seated himself, waiting as was appropriate for Skeeter to drink first. Skeeter had always been a free man, born into a good family, raised by another good man. Even with the eventual understanding Marcus had reached that *no one* here could call him slave, Skeeter was still Marcus' social superior in every way Marcus had ever heard of.

"Oh, I'm gonna miss that," Skeeter said after a long pull. "Now . . . You were born in Rome, right?"

"Well, no, actually, I was not."

Skeeter blinked. "You weren't?"

"No. I was born in Gallia Comata, in a very small village called Cautes." He couldn't help the pride that touched his voice. A thousand years and his little village was still there—changed a great deal, but still standing beneath the high, sharp mountains of his childhood, beautiful as ever under their mantles of snow and cloud. The same wild, rushing stream still cut through the heart of the village, just as it always had, clear and cold enough to shock a grunt from even the stoutest man.

"Cautes? Where the hell is that?"

Marcus grinned. "I once asked Brian Hendrickson, in the library, about my village. It is still there, but the name is different, just a little. Gallia Comata no longer exists at all. My village, called now Cauterets, is in the place you would know as France, but it is still famous for the sacred warm springs that cure women who cannot bear children."

Skeeter started to grin, then didn't. "You're serious."

"Yes, why would I not be? I cannot help that I was born in conquered territory and—"

"About the women, I mean?" Skeeter's expression was priceless: another scheme was taking shape visibly on his unguarded face.

Marcus laughed. "I do not know, Skeeter. I was only a child when I was taken away, so I cannot be sure, but all the villagers said it. Roman women came there from all southern Gaul to bathe in the waters, so they could get a child."

Skeeter chuckled in turn, his thoughts still visible in his eyes. "They'd have done better to sleep with their husbands—or somebody's husband, anyway—a little more often."

"Or drink less lead," Marcus added, proud of what he had learned in his few years in La-La Land. Rachel Eisenstein, the head physician in the time terminal, had told Marcus the levels of dissolved lead in his own blood *were* dropping, which was the only reason he'd been able to father little Artemisia and Gelasia.

"Touché." Skeeter lifted his glass and drained half the brew. "Aren't you going to drink any of that beer?"

Marcus carefully poured a libation to the gods—just a few drops spilled onto the wooden floor—then tasted his own beer. He'd be scrubbing the floor later, anyway, so a little worship wouldn't anger his employers. They groused more about the free drinks Marcus sometimes gave away to those in need than they did about a little spillage.

"Okay," Skeeter took another swig, "you were born in France, but lived in Rome most of your life, right?"

"Yes. I was sold as a young boy to a slave trader coming down the Roman highway from Aqua Tarbellicae." Marcus shivered. "The first thing he did was change my name. He said mine was not pronounceable."

Skeeter blinked. "Marcus isn't your real name?"

He tried to smile. "It has been for more than eighteen years. And you probably could not pronounce my own name any more than the Romans could. I have grown accustomed to 'Marcus' and so I am content to keep it."

Skeeter was staring at him as though he couldn't believe what he was hearing. Marcus shrugged. "I have tried to explain, Skeeter. But no one here understands."

"No, I, uh, guess not." He cleared his throat, the expression in his eyes making Marcus wonder what *Skeeter* remembered. "Anyway, you were saying about Rome . . ."

"Yes. I was taken to the city of Narbo on the coast of the Mediterranean Sea, where I was put on a slave ship and sent to Rome, where I was kept in an iron cage until the time came for me to be auctioned on the block." Marcus gulped beer hastily to hide the tremors in his hands. Those particular memories were among the ones that woke him up nights, shaking inside a layer of cold sweat. "I lived in Rome from the time I was eight years of age."

Skeeter leaned forward. "Great. See, Agnes got me a free ticket through Porta Romae, she's guiding on the tour this trip, and it's a pretty quiet two weeks, only one day of public games, on the very last day. That's why she could get me through as a guest."

Marcus shook his head. Poor Agnes. She hadn't been in La-La Land very long. "You are shameful, Skeeter. Agnes is a nice girl."

"Sure is. I never could afford a ticket to Rome on my own. So anyway, I got this great idea, see, but I've never been there, so I thought maybe you could help me out?"

Marcus fiddled with his beer glass. "What is the idea?" He was always cautious not to commit himself to any of Skeeter's perpetually shady schemes.

"It's perfect," Skeeter enthused, eyes sparkling with glee. "I wanted to do a little betting—"

"*Betting?* On the games?" If that were all Skeeter wanted, he saw no harm in it. It was strictly illegal, of course; but Marcus didn't know of a single tourist who hadn't tried it. And it was so much less worse than what it might have been, all Marcus felt was a kind of giddy relief. Maybe Agnes was a good influence on Skeeter? "Very well, what did you want to ask me?"

Skeeter's grin revealed relief and triumph. "Where do I go? To make the bets, I mean?"

Marcus chuckled. "The Circus Maximus, of course."

"Yeah, but *where?* The damned thing's a *mile long!*"

Ahh . . .

"Well . . . The best place is on the Aventine side of the Circus, near the spot where the gladiators enter the arena. They come in through the starting boxes, of course, at the square end of the Circus, closest to the Tiber River. But the public entrances closest to there are very popular betting sites, as well. There are the professional gambling stalls, of course,"

Marcus mused, "but I would stay away from them. Most will find an excuse to cheat a colonial blind. Of course, much of the betting takes place in the stands themselves, while the bouts are underway." He wondered what Skeeter's reaction would be to watching men butcher one another. Many tourists came back physically ill.

"That's great, Marcus! Thanks! If I win, I'll cut you in on the deal."

If Skeeter Jackson remembered that generous offer two weeks from now—and followed through on it— Marcus mused, he would have done more for Marcus than he could possibly know. Ever-present worry over finances swiftly captured Marcus' attention and swept his thoughts far away from the table where his friend was drinking his beer. Ianira, despite his protests and pride, had insisted on contributing to his "debt-free" fund a sizeable chunk of her earnings—made by giving historians whatever information she could for the "primary research source" fees. Ianira also sold genuine ancient Greek recipes for all manner of cheesecakes— though she had paid for learning to make every single variety under the whip (and more) in her first husband's house downtime.

The cheesecakes' delightful flavors and characteristics, Marcus now knew, had once been discussed in the Athenian Agora as seriously as any philosophy by the most important men in Athens. Their recipes had been lost for centuries, but Ianira, hurting still from her husband's brutality, knew them all by heart, had memorized them in a terror to survive. Now, with amusement healing old scars, she sold the recipes one by one to Arley Eisenstein, who gave her a percentage of his profits—substantial, given the cheesecakes' reborn stunning success.

Ianira made money faster than Marcus had ever

believed possible, particularly after she became the proud owner of a free-standing stall that catered to the strange and increasingly bizarre "acolytes" who sought her out as though on pilgrimage. Some of them had paid the price of the Primary Gate just to look at her, praying she would say something to them. Some even gave her money, as though she were the most revered being in the world and their money was the only offering they could give.

Ah, money. When Marcus had tried to refuse her money, out of pride and dignity, she'd caught his hand and forced him to look at her. "You are my chosen, my beloved!" Dark eyes held his, burdened with so much he wanted to erase forever. Neither money nor Marcus could erase the past: brutal marriage or, worst of all, Ianira's terrifying, heavy, close-held secret knowledge of the rituals (both public and carefully hidden private), of the many-breasted Artemis of Ephesus, where she had grown to maidenhood in the world-famous temple. At that moment, those bottomless eyes flashed with what must have been the same look that had prompted the rash Trojan prince Paris to risk everything to flee to the windy plains of Troy with the much-sought-after Helen as his mistress.

Even in memory, Marcus' head spun hopelessly under the onslaught of that look. He had, of course, melted utterly at the winning smile that followed, not to mention the touch of her hands. "I am desperately selfish of you, Marcus. I do not understand this 'honor' of yours, so stubborn to pay off an illegal debt; but if this money will help fulfill that demand inside you, then I will be sure never to allow you to deny my help." In a rare gesture of emotion, she clutched him tight as if afraid to let go. Her uptilted face revealed a sea of tears bravely held brimming on her eyelashes. Still holding him, she said in roughened voice, "Please. I know you are proud and I love you for it. But if I lose you . . ."

He had crushed her close, trying with everything in him to promise that he was hers forever, not just the way things were now, with no formal words spoken, but the correct way, the way of formally taking her as his public wife—just as soon as he could rid himself of hated debt to the man who had brought him here and set him the task of learning—and keeping secret records of—which men travelled the gates to Rome and Athens and what they brought back.

He didn't understand his one-time master's orders, any more than he understood how beautiful, highborn Ianira could love a man who had been a slave nearly all his life. So he simply kept the records, considering it a challenging puzzle to be solved, a clue to what made his former master's brain work while slowly gathering the money to pay his slave debt. He took Ianira's money, little as he wanted to, because he was desperate to get out from under such debt, to gain at least a little of the status that would put him on something approaching her own level.

Marcus' bittersweet thoughts were rudely interrupted by the unmistakable voice of Goldie Morran. Instant irritation made his skin shudder, like a horse's when big, biting flies descended to slake their thirst. Marcus sometimes wondered, looking at Goldie Morran, if she had been called Goldie for the shining, golden hair Roman women had once so coveted they'd had wigs made from the tresses of their slaves (impossible to tell now—Goldie's hair was, at present, a peculiar shade of Imperial Purple, leaving little clue as to its original color), or because she was an avaricious old gargoyle who wanted nothing in the world more than cold, hard cash—preferably in the form of gold—

coinage, dust, nugget, whatever she could get her claws on.

Harpy-eyes glanced his way. "Marcus, get me a beer."

Then she sank down into one of the chairs beside Skeeter, inviting herself into their private conversation. As Marcus poured beer from the tap, seething and manfully holding it back—Goldie Morran was a regular customer—she glanced at Skeeter. "Hear you're going downtime. Isn't that new, even for you?"

Marcus set the beer in front of Goldie. She took a long, slow pull while waiting for Skeeter's usual outburst.

Skeeter surprised them both.

"Yes, I'm going to Rome. I'm taking a slow two-week vacation so I can get better acquainted with Agnes Fairchild. She and I have become rather close over the last week or so and, besides, she has the right to take a guest with her on slow tours." He spread his hands. "Who am I to turn down a free trip to ancient Rome?"

"And what," Goldie glanced up coyly, the neon lights in the bar doing strange things to her sallow face and genuinely purple-silver hair, "what exactly is it you intend to steal?"

Skeeter laughed easily. "I'm a scoundrel and you know it, but I'm not planning to steal anything, except perhaps Agnes' heart. I might have tried for yours, Goldie, if I thought you had one."

Goldie made an outrageous sound, glaring at him, clearly at a loss for words—perhaps a Down Time Bar & Grill first. Then, turning her back to him, Goldie gulped down the remains of her beer and slammed down a scattering of coins to pay for it. They jounced, slid, and rolled in circles; one even fell to the hardwood floor with a musical ringing sound.

Silver, a part of Marcus' mind said, having become

intimately acquainted with Roman coinage and its forgeries.

Goldie, leaning over Skeeter's chair very much like a harpy sent by the gods to punish evildoers, said, "You will live to regret that, Skeeter Jackson." The chill of a glacier filled her voice. And underlying the frozen syllables, Marcus heard plainly a malice thick as unwatered Roman wine. It hung on the air between them for just an instant. Then she whirled and left, flinging over her shoulder, "Why you choose to become friends with uneducated, half-wild downtimers who can scarce bathe themselves properly is beyond me. It will be your ruin."

Then she was gone.

Marcus discovered he was shaking with rage. His dislike of Goldie Morran and her sharp tongue and prejudices had just changed in a way that frightened him. Dislike had flared like a fire in high wind, smoldering from a half-burnt lump of coal to a roaring conflagration consuming his soul—and everything foolish enough to come too close.

Marcus was proud of his recently acquired education, which included several languages, new and wonderful sciences that seemed like the magical incantations that made the world run its wandering course through the stars—rather than the stars wandering their courses around it—even mathematics explained clearly enough that he had been able to learn the new ways of counting, multiplying, dividing, learning the basics of multicolumn bookkeeping along with the new tools—all of it adding up to something no scribe or mathematician in all of Ancient Rome could do.

Perhaps a boy from Gallia Comata could be considered half-wild, but even as a chained, terrified boy of eight, he had known perfectly well how to bathe—and had amused his captors by requesting a basin each night to wash the dirt and stinking fear sweat off his skin.

He actually jumped when Skeeter spoke.

"Vicious old harpy," Skeeter said mildly, his demeanor as perfectly calm as his person was neat and eternally well groomed. "She'll do anything to throw her competition off form." He chuckled. "You know Marcus—here, sit down again—I would dearly love to see someone scam *her*."

Marcus sat down and managed to hold his sudden laughter to a mere grin, although he could not keep it from bubbling in his eyes. "That would be something to witness. It's interesting, you know, watching the two of you circle, probe defenses, finally sending darts through chinks in one another's armor."

Skeeter just stared at him.

Marcus added, "You both are strong-willed, Skeeter, and generally get exactly what you want from life, same as Goldie. But I will tell you something important." In this one particular case, at least, Ianira was not the only "seer" in his family. The story was there, plain to witness for anyone who simply bothered to look, and knowing people as he did, the future was not difficult to predict. He finished his beer in one long swallow, aware that Skeeter's gaze had never left his face.

"Goldie," Marcus said softly, "has declared war upon you, Skeeter, whether you welcome it or no. She reminds me of the Mediterranean sharks that followed the slave ship, feeding off those who died. No . . . the sharks did only what they were made to do. *Goldie* is so far gone in the enjoyment of her evil deeds, there is no hope of salvaging anything good from her."

He returned Skeeter's unblinking gaze for several moments. Then his friend spoke, almost coldly as Goldie had. "Meaning you think *me* worth salvaging. Is that it, *friend*?"

Marcus went ice-cold all through. "You are a good man, Skeeter," he said earnestly, leaning forward to try and make his friend understand. "Your heart is as generous as your laughter. It is merely my hope that you might mend your morals to match. You are a dear friend to me. I do not enjoy seeing you suffer."

Skeeter blinked. "Suffer?" He began to laugh. "Marcus, you are truly the wonder of the ages." His grin melted a little of the icy fear in Marcus' heart. "Okay, I'll promise I'll try to be a good little tourist in Rome, all right? I still want to do that betting, but nothing more devious than that. Satisfied?"

Marcus sagged a little in his chair. "Yes, Skeeter. I am." Feeling more hopeful than he had in months, he was forced to apologize for having to abandon his friend so soon after coming to a somewhat uneasy understanding of one another's intentions in this odd friendship. "I am most sorry, my friend, but I must return to work, before the manager returns from watching the Porta Romae cycle, and I have not yet finished all the chores he set me to do. Go with the gods when you step through Porta Romae, Skeeter. Thank you for the beer. And the company."

Skeeter's grin lit up his face again. "Sure. Thank *you*. See you in a couple of weeks, then."

Marcus smiled, then busied himself cleaning vacated tables and wiping down the bar. Skeeter Jackson strolled out like a man about to own the world.

CHAPTER TWO

Agnes Fairchild was a nice girl. Not too pretty, but sweet and generous. And great in bed. By Skeeter's standards, the shy, academic types were often the most fun: overcoming their inhibitions and showing them a thing or two about mad, wet sex was as good as getting a stunning "10" into bed. He often regretted the fact that his lovers never stayed with him long, but, hey, there were new women coming through La-La Land all the time. And after Skeeter's childhood experiences, he was *not* choosy about looks. Willingness and sincerity were what counted. A knockout in your *own* bed was great. But a bombshell in somebody else's bed was no fun at all.

So when Agnes Fairchild walked into Skeeter's life, he was more than pleased. And when she opened up the chance to do some scheming *outside* the time terminal, he showered her with every charm at his command. She even taught him enough Latin to get by in case they were separated—which he wouldn't— and did not—allow to happen—not until the day of the games. Agnes was good at her job, too. Skeeter enjoyed tagging along with her tour group almost as much as he enjoyed a passionate lover willing to share intimacy during sultry Roman nights. The ancient city come to life was like a Hollywood movie set to Skeeter—but a movie set full of real people with real money he could pry loose from real hands that wouldn't miss a few pilfered coins, because they were all dead already.

Of course, he didn't tell Agnes that. He just enjoyed her company and sights like Augustus' giant sundial and the huge Emporium of market stalls that backed the wharves and warehouses of the Porticus Aemelia—where he picked up a bit of profit with light-fingered skill—and bided his time while charming everyone from the richest billionaire in the group—whose money pouch Skeeter coveted—to the smallest, wide-eyed little girl who called him "Unk Skeeter." He even liked tickling and teasing her when she tickled and teased him. She was cute. Skeeter had discovered to his surprise that he liked kids. There'd been a time when the sight of another child—particularly boys—had made his blood run cold.

Long time ago, Skeeter. Long, long time ago. You're not everybody's bogda *any more. You're not* anybody's bogda *anymore.* And that was the best part of all. As long as he kept up the con games, the swindles, the mastery of skills a bitter, deadly childhood had taught him, Skeeter Jackson would never again be anybody's isolated, lonely, private tribal spirit-in-the-flesh, a position that had, much of the time, amounted to that of victim, unable to retaliate when teased, taunted, or hooted at in careful privacy by the other boys, because it was unseemly behavior for a *bogda* to roughhouse, no matter what the provocation. So he'd developed the knack of endurance and remained a victim because that was the only thing he *could* do, other than steal the belongings of certain tormentors and plant them in the yurts of other tormentors. He'd grown skilled at the game and enjoyed the results with bitter, malicious glee.

And all of that was something few people understood,

or ever could understand, because Skeeter would sooner die than admit *any* of it to those who hadn't already figured it out for themselves.

He wondered, sometimes, if his friend Marcus carried memories as frightening as his own? After two weeks in Rome, he was convinced of it. After witnessing what went on casually on the streets, he deliberately asked Agnes to take him to see the slave markets. What he found there . . . well, if Skeeter had harbored any shred of scruple, it was erased by the sights and sounds of that place.

Anything he stole from *any* rich Roman bastard was money the wretch deserved to lose. The more, the better. For a moment, Marcus' words about him and his standing with Goldie Morran made sense. There were levels and *levels* of depravity. Compared to these pros, Skeeter was a saint. He watched through narrowed eyes endless parades of rich, arrogant Roman men carried through the streets in fancy sedan chairs and recalled the bitter cold winds which swept endlessly across the steppes where he'd grown to teenhood.

He recalled, too, the glint of winter sunlight on sharp steel and the myriad ways of killing a man the people who'd raised him had taught their sons. And as he remembered, Skeeter watched wealthy Romans abuse helpless people and bitterly wished he could introduce the two groups for an intimate little get-together: Roman to Yakka Mongol, steel to steel.

Because that would never happen in Skeeter's sight, he elected himself the Yakka Clan's sole emissary in this city of marble and misery and money. He could hardly wait to start depriving them of *serious* amounts of gold earned on blood, not just a purse here and there just begging to be lifted by nimble fingers. His long-awaited chance finally came the morning of their last day in Rome. The entire tour group left the inn near dawn.

"Form up in your groups," Agnes called, echoed by other Time Tours guides and even a freelancer or two hired for guiding their employers safely to places not on the main tour, then safely back again. Since Skeeter was closest to Agnes, it was her voice he paid most attention to as they formed up in the silvery, pearl-hued morning. "We'll be taking seats together in the upper tier, which is reserved for slaves and foreigners. Be sure you have the proper coinage with you to purchase admission tickets and don't forget to collect a colored handkerchief to cheer on your favorite racing team. The gladiatorial games will begin after midday, once the racing is completed . . ."

Skeeter wasn't really listening. He was planning his scheme and trying to recall Marcus' instructions. He had a pouch half full of copper coins, mostly *unciae*, or one-twelfth of an *as*, the *as* being a pound of copper divided into twelve "ounces" (the first coins Romans had minted, according to Agnes). They were mixed with a few silver *denarii* and *sestercii*, plus a few gold *aurii* on top just to make it look good. Agnes had loaned him the silver and gold coins so he could—as he'd explained it—impress local merchants that he really did have money. That way, they'd be less likely to gyp him. "Agnes, I don't want them to think I'm some provincial rube not worth wasting their time on."

And like the sweet girl she was, she'd believed every word.

He wondered how long she'd be able to stomach watching what Romans did to non-Romans. Two weeks was more than enough for him, even *without* watching the games, and he'd spent five years in the yurts of the Yakka clan.

"Skeeter?"

He glanced up and found Agnes smiling at him. "Yeah?"

"Ready?"

"Am I ever!"

Her smile was so enchanting, he kissed her, earning hoots and whistles from half the crowd. She blushed to the roots of her mouse-brown hair.

"All right, people, let's go!"

Skeeter followed eagerly as Agnes led the first group away from the inn Time Tours owned on the Aventine Hill and ushered her charges into the narrow, winding streets of an already crowded, noisy Rome. *Games day*, Skeeter identified the electric difference from the tours' previous mornings. Skeeter hung back, letting Agnes gain distance. Tourists eager for their first—and for many of them, only—look at genuine Roman games surged ahead. Skeeter grinned, then slipped quietly away from the group and headed for the Circus Maximus by the route Marcus had given him two weeks previously.

He knew the entrance he wanted was near the starting gates of the mile-long structure. Shops selling food, wine, commemorative mugs with scenes of chariot racing molded into them, even shops selling baskets and seat cushions did brisk business despite the early hour. The morning air was clear and golden as dawn brightened the hot, Latin sky. The scents of frying peas and sausages mingled with the smell of wine, the stink of caged animals, and the sweat of several thousand men and women pushing their way toward the entrances. A few betting stalls did even brisker business, a sight that made Skeeter all but salivate.

Yesukai, your wandering bogda *has done found hisself in paradise!*

The streets were confusing, though, and so were

the entrances. There were more archways into the great Circus than he'd expected. And crowds jammed each one. Which entrance, exactly, had Marcus meant? He walked all the way to the squared-off end of the Circus, down by the stinking Tiber, which flowed past the starting gates just beyond a couple of little temples he recognized from photos. The scream of caged cats and the bleating of zebras assaulted Skeeter's ears. Down here, too, were men stripped to the waist, hauling the great cages into place from barges tied up at the river. Teams of high-strung racing horses fought their handlers, while collared slaves rolled tiny, tea-cup chariots of wicker and wood into place for the first races. Men and boys who must be charioteers, given the colors of their tunics, stood around in groups, looking deadly earnest as they discussed what must have been last-minute strategy.

Well, Skeeter decided, *I'll just pick the nearest entrance to all this and hope for the best. This* ought *to be just about where Marcus meant*.

He found a likely looking spot and prepared to launch his scheme. Although Agnes had taught him some "survival phrases" he hadn't known, Skeeter had begun work several weeks previously. Through that pilfered library account, he'd learned as many Latin phrases as he could, aware he'd need them for his patter, as well as understanding the likeliest responses he'd get back from potential customers. And if he didn't understand something, Skeeter had carefully learned, "Please, I'm just a poor foreigner, your Latin is too complicated. Would you say it more simply?" He'd even researched what kind of markers to give out to those who placed bets. No need to learn how to make payouts . . .

Since the gladiatorial fights wouldn't take place until

afternoon, Skeeter had a simple plan—collect a ransom in betting money, then simply vanish while the races were on. He'd hightail it back to the inn, apologize to Agnes later this afternoon by claiming he hadn't been feeling well, then tonight when Porta Romae cycled, he'd step back into La-La Land a rich man. And an *untouchable* rich man, so long as he didn't try to step uptime with any of his winnings.

Rubbing metaphorical hands, Skeeter Jackson looked over the crowd, reined in an impish grin of anticipation, took a deep breath . . . and shouted, "Bets, place your bets, gladiatorial combats only, best odds in town. . . ."

Within half an hour, Skeeter had begun to wonder if his scheme were going to pan out, after all. Most of the people who approached him declined to wager at all. Those who did were mostly poor people who wagered a copper *as*, or more likely, one of the cheaper copper coins based on a fraction of an *as*. *Great. Must've picked the wrong damned entrance*. He was just about to try a different arched entryway when a lean, grizzled man in his early forties, sporting a short-trimmed head of reddish-blond hair, sauntered over, trailed by a collared slave.

"Bets, eh?" the man said, eying Skeeter appraisingly. "On the combats?"

"Yes, sir," Skeeter grinned, trying to hide the sudden pounding of his pulse. Judging by the gold the man wore and the embroidery on his tunic, this guy was *rich*.

"Tell me, what odds do you place on the bout with Lupus Mortiferus?"

"To win or lose?"

A flicker of irritation ran through dark amber, lupine eyes. "To win, of course."

Skeeter didn't know a damned thing about Lupus Mortiferus or his track record. He'd simply been quoting made-up odds all morning. He smiled and said cheerfully, "Three to one."

The lean man's eyes widened. "Three to one?" Startlement gave way to sudden, intense interest. "Well, now. Those are interesting odds, indeed. You're a stranger, I think, by your accent."

Skeeter shrugged. "If I am?"

His mark grinned. "I'll place a bet with you, stranger. How about fifty *aurii*? Can your purse handle that big a bite?"

Skeeter was stunned. Fifty gold *aurii*? That was . . . that was five thousand silver *sestercii*! When he thought of the money he'd get exchanging fifty gold *aurii* at Goldie Morran's shop back in Shangri-La Station . . .

"Of course, friend! Of course. I may be a foreigner, but I am not without resources. You just surprised me." Skeeter prepared the marker.

"Stellio," the grizzled Roman addressed his slave, "fetch fifty *aurii* from my money box." The man produced a key from a pouch at his waist and handed it over.

The slave dashed into the crowd.

"I have pressing business elsewhere," the Roman said with a smile, tucking the marker into his pouch, "but I assure you my slave is trustworthy. He was a complete knave when I bought him, which is why he bears that name, but sufficient correction can cure any man's bad habits." The Roman laughed. "A slave without a tongue is much more docile. Not to mention silent. Don't you agree?"

Skeeter nodded, but felt a little sick. Once, as a boy, he'd seen a man's tongue cut out . . .

The Roman strolled off into the crowd. Clearly, Skeeter had quoted the wrong odds on Lupus whatever. But on the bright side, he wouldn't be around when this guy came to collect his hundred-fifty *aurii*. Skeeter repressed a shiver. Just as well. He wondered with a pang of genuine pity what that poor slave had done to merit having his tongue cut out.

No wonder Marcus didn't want to come back here. Ever.

Skeeter continued taking bets, filling his money pouch and giving out markers while waiting for Stellio to return. Shrill notes from Roman trumpets, sounding the beginning of the opening parade, floated on the clear morning air. A roar went up from the crowd. Skeeter took a few last bets, then spotted Stellio running toward him. The man was panting, mouth hanging open with exertion from his run. Skeeter swallowed hard. He *didn't* have a tongue.

"Nrggahh," the poor man said, shoving the pouch into Skeeter's hands.

He ran off again before Skeeter could say a word in response. Feeling a little queasy still, Skeeter opened the pouch and tipped shining gold into his hand. The slave hadn't cheated him. Fifty gold *aurii* . . . They glittered in the sunlight, striking glints like lightning against the dark Gobi sky. Skeeter grinned as he counted them back into the pouch, then tightened the drawstring and secured it to his waist. *Just wait until Goldie sees* these!

A few stragglers placed bets, mostly with copper coins ranging from full *asses* through the whole spectrum of its fractions: the *sextans*, the *quadrans* and *triens*, a *quincunx*, several *semis* coins, the cheaper *septunx*, the *bes*, and *dodrans*, one *dextans* and *deunx* each, and of course, the inevitable and popular *uncia*. He even got a couple more silver *sestercii*—then the trumpets signalling the start of the first chariot race sang out.

Time to leave.

He decided to buy a little wine to cool his throat

and used some of his takings to purchase it from a nearby shop which nestled under the stands, one of several hundred other little stalls, from the look of it. He noticed some shrimp set delicately on grape leaves and decided to try some. *Mmm! The Romans know how to cook a shrimp!* That finished, Skeeter noticed some cheesecakes along the back shelf. Several were molded into the shape of a woman's breast.

He asked and was told, "Almond cheesecake. Whole is all I sell."

Well, that one in the corner looked pretty small. He gestured toward it and the proprietor duly placed it in front of him, then collected the coins Skeeter produced from his "winnings." One bite and he knew that, good as this was, Ianira Cassondra's were so much superior it was like comparing caviar to potted meat. As he munched contentedly, a roar went up inside the stadium. "First race, huh?" Skeeter asked conversationally, proud of his acquired Latin.

The man looked startled. "Race? You hadn't heard? The Emperor requested a special opening to the day's games."

Paying only half attention, Skeeter said, "Really?" He was hungrier than he'd thought and this cheesecake wasn't bad, washed down with the last of his wine.

"Yes," the shopkeeper told him, considerable surprise running through dark eyes. "A special exhibition bout by the Emperor's favorite gladiator."

"*What?*" He nearly strangled on cheesecake and wine.

"Yes. Bout to first blood in honor of Lupus Mortiferus' hundredth appearance in the arena." The man chuckled. "What a champion. Haven't been better'n one to four odds on him since his eightieth victory. Bout ought to be finished any minute—"

Skeeter didn't wait to hear more. He didn't *have* a

hundred-fifty *aurii* to pay off that idiotic bet. *Damn, damn, damn!* He shot out of the shop, leaving the half-eaten cheesecake behind. He headed down the long facade of the Circus, toward town. The River Tiber ran its merry way somewhere behind him. He kept his pace at a fast walk, not wanting to draw attention to himself by running. As much money as he was carrying, someone might mistake him for a thief.

Okay, Skeeter, just stay calm. You've been in worse spots. He's not going to come collecting that money right away, even if the bout is going on right now. Just get back to the Time Tours Inn and hide out until the gate cycles and you'll be just fine. You've gotten through worse. Lots worse.

Another roar broke from the high tiers of seats. Skeeter winced. Then silence fell over the great arena. Skeeter wanted to break into a run, but held himself to a brisk walk, like some businessman intent on important business.

Then, the sound of nightmare: "Hey! Hey, odds maker!"

He glanced around—and *felt* his cheeks go cold.

It was the lean, grizzled Roman who'd placed the bet, about a hundred yards behind him. Even from here, Skeeter could see the blood spattered on his clothes and arms.

Oh, man, I gotta bad feeling that IS Lupus Mortiferus.

Skeeter did the only logical, honorable thing he could.

He ran like hell.

"Stop! Stop, you—"

The rest of it was Latin Skeeter hadn't learned yet.

He ducked around the first corner he came to and picked up speed. The money pouches at his belt swung and bruised his thighs with every stride. The streets near the Circus were a maze of narrow alleys and crooked, twisting passageways. Skeeter dodged and ran with everything in him, convinced he could outrun the heavier Roman with ease. Given his skill at vanishing in the places he'd lived as a child, losing himself in Rome ought to be a piece of cake.

But his pursuer was faster than he looked.

Skeeter glanced back and bit back a yelp of terror. The man was still with him—and gaining. Thunderstorms rolling across the vast plains of Outer Mongolia had looked friendlier than that Roman's face. And he had a *long* knife in his hand. A *really* long one.

Skeeter skidded around another corner, crashed through a group of women who shrieked curses at him, and kept going. *Can't just go to the inn. He'd track me there and carve me up into little bits of Skeeter. Where, then?* Clearly, he hadn't studied the layout of the city adequately. Skeeter cut around another corner, dashed down a long straight-way, zipped around another corner—

And yelled, even as he tried to stop.

The street ended abruptly in a drop-off straight into the Tiber. Momentum carried him over the edge. Skeeter sucked in air, knowing the gold would weigh him down. Then he splashed feet-first into the muddy river and sank toward the bottom. Skeeter swam frantically for the surface, holding his breath and kicking with every bit of strength he had left. His face broke water. He gulped air into burning lungs.

Something hard grazed his shoulder. Skeeter yelled, went under, strangled . . . then caught at something that splashed down right in front of him. He was lifted completely out of the water. For an instant, he was face-to-face with an astonished slave rowing a large boat. The man was so shocked, he dropped the oar. Skeeter plunged like a rock back into the river. A tremendous backwash sent water into his sinuses. But he hung onto the oar and managed to drag his head above water again. He blinked river water and hair out of his eyes, coughing weakly and drawing in shuddering lungfuls of air that only set him coughing harder.

The boat above him was a shallow-draft thing that looked like a pleasure yacht of some sort. Rowers all along the side leaned over to stare at him. Several oars fouled badly, cracking into one another like gunshots. The whole yacht slewed in the water.

Great. Talk about not attracting attention.

A glance over one shoulder revealed Lupus Mortiferus on the bank, shaking his fist and cursing inaudibly. *Just get me out of this one, God, and I swear I'll never come back to Rome again. I'll stick to obnoxious tourists and government bureaucrats and other deserving UPtimers.* Skeeter clung to the oar, pulled along by the yacht's momentum for a couple of moments, allowing him to regain his breath; then an overseer stalked to the gunwales to see what was fouling the oars.

"What the—"

Skeeter lost most of the curse in the translation, but the general gist seemed to be, "Get the hell off my oar!"

Skeeter was about to marshall a sob story to convince the guy to let him climb aboard when the s.o.b. snaked out a whip that caught Skeeter right across the hands. Pain blossomed like acid. He yelled and let go involuntarily—and plunged back into the river. Skeeter snorted a noseful of water before he managed to kick his way back to the surface.

Gotta get to shore . . . before I . . . wear out and drown. That gold was *heavy*. But the few minutes' rest clinging to the oar had helped. Skeeter struck out for the nearest bank, which thankfully was opposite the Circus and the wrathful Lupus Mortiferus. By the time he reached the riverbank and crawled out, sodden tunic clinging to his thighs and back, Skeeter was shaking with exhaustion. But he still had the gold. And he was still alive.

He'd just begun to celebrate those two facts with a shaky grin when a terrifying, familiar voice shouted, "There! He's there!"

Lupus Mortiferus had crossed a bridge Skeeter hadn't even noticed.

And he had friends with him.

Big, mean, ugly-looking ones.

Skeeter swore shakily under his breath and shoved himself to his feet. *Can't possibly outrun 'em.* Hell, he could scarcely stand up. Out-talk 'em? Convince 'em the whole scam had been a simple miscommunication? In English, he could probably have pulled it off. But not in Latin. The language handicap made that impossible. Wondering what Romans *did* with confidence men they caught—a roar of voices from the Circus gave him a clue—Skeeter looked wildly around for some way out of this.

What he saw was a group of horse handlers loading racing teams onto a barge for the trip across to the Circus. The horses were between him and the group of enraged gladiators. Skeeter didn't have many skills, but living in a yurt of the Yakka Clan, one thing he *had* learned to do was *ride*. If it had four legs and hooves, Skeeter could ride it.

So he ran straight *toward* the men hunting him and caught a glimpse of shocked amazement on Lupus Mortiferus' face. Then he said to a surprised animal handler, "Excuse me, but I need that," and snatched the bridle of the nearest racehorse still on shore. He was on the animal's back in a flash. The startled horse reared and screamed, but Skeeter had stayed with horses ornrier than this. He slammed heels into the animal's flanks and brought its head and forelegs down with a savage jerk on the reins. The horse got the message: *This ain't no novice rider on my back*.

Skeeter hauled the horse's head around and kicked the animal into a fast gallop. The racing handlers yelled and cursed him, but he put distance between himself and *all* his pursuers in nothing short of miraculous time. This horse could *run*.

Skeeter laughed in sheer delight and leaned low over the animal's neck. The whipping mane caught his face with a wiry sting. The muscles bunching under his thighs rippled in perfect rhythm. He missed the iron Mongol stirrups, shaped like the tips of Dutch wooden shoes, to which he'd grown accustomed, but he hadn't lost his sense of balance—and he'd learned to ride bareback, just to prove to Yesukai that he could, and hopefully to be permitted the chance at learning to ride proper ponies with proper saddles. Pedestrians scattered out of his way with curses and screams. He laughed again at the horse's astonishing speed. "Must've liberated me a champion!"

It was several years overdue, but Skeeter had finally completed his manhood ritual. *Wow! Finally! My first real horse-thieving raid!* Too bad no Yakka clansmen were around to witness it and celebrate the occasion. The Yakka khan had not permitted Skeeter to go along on such raids, fearing his funny little *bogda* might be injured, which would bring bad luck. Skeeter grinned. *Never thought I'd get a chance to do this. Not bad for a kid who fell through an unstable gate and ended up in a place nobody thought he'd survive!*

He hated to give the horse up.

But riding a stolen race horse through Rome while its handlers and several really pissed-off gladiators were chasing him was not a smart move. And neither his Mama nor—particularly—his foster Mama had raised a fool. In fact, Yesukai's stolen bride had not only accepted her marriage, but had begun to rule her husband's yurt like a queen born to the task—and, alone among strangers, she had adopted the funny little *bogda* who was in much the same predicament, teaching him a great deal and smiling on him with great favor.

So, having learned caution from *both* his adoptive parents, Skeeter pulled the animal to a walk, cooling him out, then halted as soon as he dared and patted the beast on the neck. Dried sweat clung to his hand.

"You did good by me, fella. Thanks. I owe you. Too bad I can't make it up to you."

The horse blew softly into his face and nudged his chest, friendly-like. "Yeah," Skeeter said with a smile, stroking the velvety-soft nose, "me, too. But I gotta run and you've gotta race."

He tied the reins to the nearest public fountain, so the horse could at least get a drink of water, then set out to find himself a good, deep hidey-hole until the Porta Romae cycled sometime near midnight. The jingling of gold in the pouch at his waist sounded like victory.

Skeeter grinned.

Not a bad day's work.

Not bad at all.

CHAPTER THREE

Lupus Mortiferus didn't like losing.

In his line of work, defeat meant death. And like most gladiators, losing a wager was an almost omenlike foreshadowing of trouble to come. The Wolf of Death, as the School had named him, was going to find that miserable street vermin and shake his money loose, or see him die in the arena for thievery.

All he had to do was find him.

He and his friends stood muttering in a group as the cheat escaped on Sun Runner, one of the greatest champions ever to run in the Circus. The handler was beside himself with fury. Already several other handlers had mounted to give chase, but the thief had a good lead on a fast horse. Lupus Mortiferus didn't hold out much hope that *anyone* would catch the rat.

"So," Quintus nudged him with an elbow, "you were gonna make a hundred-fifty *aurii*, just like that, huh?"

"Guess the Wolf isn't as smart as he thought," another friend laughed. "Getting a little long in the tooth and a little short on savvy?"

Lupus just ground his teeth and held silent. He'd *needed* that money to start a new life. Having just purchased his own freedom last year, he'd barely begun to save enough to leave the arena for good. Then, in one glorious moment, some country rube offers the

43

chance to get there three times faster . . . and he turns out to be a sneak thief.

"You go on back," Lupus growled. "My big matches aren't for hours, yet. Think I'll follow those racing handlers, see what I can find. The Wolf does not give up *this* easily."

He took another round of ribbing—he had, after all, walked right into the rat's smiling arms—then stalked in the direction the racing handlers had gone. *I will find that little puke and I will by Hercules break every bone in his cheating body to pieces and after that I'll break the pieces into pieces—*

He met the riders coming back, leading Sun Runner by the bridle. Sweat had dried on him, but he'd been properly cooled out or the handlers wouldn't have been smiling in such enormous relief.

"Found him tied to a public fountain," one of them explained when asked. "Three blocks farther on."

Lupus nodded and stalked on. He found the fountain, but no trace of the thief. So he started bribing shopkeepers for information. He hit paydirt on the third bribe.

"Yeah, he strolled off that way, whistling like he owned the Emperor's palace."

"Thanks." Lupus flipped him a second silver *sestertius* and headed that way. The streets here weren't quite as twisted and winding as they were across the river. Lupus spotted him within five minutes. Every impulse in him said, "Now!"

But he held back.

If he followed the little snake back to his lair, he might recover more than just the money he'd lost. Who knew how much this rat had swindled since coming to Rome? The thief led him a merry chase. Evidently, he was intent on touring the whole blasted city. He paused now and again to buy wine and sausages with money he'd swindled from other victims, then bought a few trinkets a woman might enjoy wearing.

By the time the little rat recrossed the Tiber and stopped to stare at the great temple complex atop the Capitoline hill, Lupus was out of time. Either he had to shake the rat down *now* and get back his money or he'd miss the fighting matches for which he was scheduled today. He was actually advancing, hand on the hilt of his gladius, when a third alternative occurred to him.

He had noticed a couple of wide-eyed beggar brats staring at him and paused to consider what use he might make of them.

"Are you really Lupus Mortiferus?" the bolder of the two asked, eyes round with wonder and a glint approaching fear.

"I am."

Wide eyes went rounder.

Lupus smiled coldly. "Want to earn some money?"

Mouths dropped open. "*How?*"

"See that man?" he pointed out the thief. "Follow him. Find out where he lives and tell me and I'll give you enough silver to buy slaves of your own."

The boys gasped. "We'll follow him! But how can we let you know where he's gone?"

Lupus sighed. Starvation left a man stupid and these boys looked like they hadn't eaten properly in years. "One of you stay wherever he's gone," Lupus said patiently. "The other of you, come find me. I'll be at the starting boxes, waiting."

He gave each boy a couple of copper *asses* as incentive, showing them the silver in his purse as greater incentive, then headed grimly back toward the Circus. He had some fights to win. Given his mood, Lupus Mortiferus pitied his opponents today. The crowd ought to be *very* pleased with his performance. And afterward . . .

Afterward, a certain foreign thief would learn the bite of Roman revenge.

Agnes Fairchild's voice rose on a half-scream of hurt rage. "You *used* me, Skeeter Jackson! How . . . how *dare* you—"

"Agnes—"

"Don't touch me! My God, to think I gave you a ticket, money, *slept* with you! I hate you! All you wanted was a chance to sneak away and make a bunch of illegal bets!"

"Now, Agnes—"

"I could lose my job!" Tears in her eyes sparkled in the lamp light, but they were angry tears more than fear. "I can't believe you would do this to me." She hugged both arms around herself and refused to look him in the eye.

"Look, kid, you're a nice girl. I happen to like you a lot. But business is business. Good God, Agnes, you take a bunch of bloodthirsty perverts to the arena to watch men butcher each other, you ferry around zipper jockeys so they can rape prostitutes in downtime brothels, and you don't bat an eyelash, but let a man make a little wager—"

"Get out of my sight! I wish I'd never laid eyes on you, Skeeter Jackson! If I thought I could get away with it, I'd . . . I'd maroon you here! That'd be rich, leave you stuck in Rome with all the people whose money you swindled!"

Skeeter gave up. He'd broken up with his share of women, although he rarely understood why, exactly, but he'd never had one react this violently. Well, there was the exception of Margo. She'd said a few choice things to him, after she'd found out he wasn't a time scout after all. And he hadn't even managed to get her into bed!

All of which was useless to pursue. He would miss Agnes' company, particularly in the sack, but the amount of gold in the pouches at his belt was more than incentive to dismiss her serious overreaction. It'd only been one little day's wagering, for God's sake. Yesukai would've been singing his praises to the entire clan around the cookpots.

Oh, well. Easy come, easy go. So much for this scheme. Guess I'll have to come up with something else that doesn't involve a downtime gate. Of course, with his winnings today, he could take all the time he wanted, deciding his next intrigue. He left Agnes sitting in her private room at the Time Tours Inn and rejoined the festivities in the dining room, aware that she was crying as he shut the door, aware of a pang of guilt down inside himself, but also aware that she'd brought most of her anguish on herself.

Sheesh. One little bet.

You'd have thought he'd stolen her heart or something. *Women. Can't figure 'em, any way you look at it.* When he got back to TT-86, he was going to march straight into the Down Time Bar & Grill and get roaring drunk. Hell, he'd buy drinks for everybody there and get well-and-truly Mongolian *drunk* with friends. After the fit she'd pitched, he deserved a little celebration.

Maybe he'd even find someone willing to console him in the privacy of his apartment afterwards. Some sweet, soft-skinned tourist willing to assuage the sense of loss and loneliness he couldn't quite dismiss as he entered the raucous main room of the Time Tours Inn. Yeah, that was the ticket. Wine and women. Age-old cure for what ailed the heart.

Skeeter put on his best smile and wondered how

many pockets he might have the chance to pick before the Porta Romae Gate cycled a few hours hence.

The thief had taken up lodgings at an inn situated pleasantly on the Aventine. It bustled with customers. Lupus paid both boys and watched them scamper off, then stepped into the crowded room. A few people gave him odd looks, but he was served with good food and better wine than he'd expected. The man he sought was in a far corner, all smiles and triumph, talking to a plain-looking slave girl who smiled at him the way a well-bedded woman smiles at a man who's tumbled her frequently. Lupus hid his own smile as they left for more private surroundings, then heard the beginnings of an argument through their closed door. It ended with the thief storming back into the main room, thunderclouds in his eyes, whereupon he struck up a lively discussion with the nearest girl.

All does not go well, then, between master and concubine. He chuckled, finished his meal, and left the inn to wait for darkness. All he needed to do was wait until the guests bedded down for the night and the thief was his.

He *could* have called for the city watch to arrest the man, but his reputation was already damaged. So far, only his closest friends knew of his foolish loss. Let the city watch discover it, and his name would become a laughingstock from the Janiculum to the Campus Martius. This was a score he intended to settle personally. To his great chagrin, however, a banquet or great party of some kind was being celebrated inside, with loud laughter and singing in some barbaric tongue he couldn't place. It went on until the night grew very late.

"Will these colonial clods never bed down and sleep?"

Carts and heavily laden wagons rumbled past in the darkness, casting lantern light on weary-faced drivers and dark, rutted paving stones. Another hour passed, then another, and still the party roared on. Hugging his impatience to his breast like a well-honed dagger, Lupus waited.

What happened next surprised him beyond all belief.

Every single one of the revellers left the inn in a packed group, led by lantern light and collared slaves through the wagon-jammed, dangerous streets. The man Lupus sought was there amongst them, grinning like a trained monkey. Lupus followed, one hand on the pommel of his sword. He trailed the group to a wine shop on the Via Appia. Judging from the positions of the stars, it must be nearly midnight, yet nearly forty people entered the dark, silent wineshop. Some were giggling, some reeling, while some looked like they might be ill at any moment.

Lupus' prey entered without so much as a backward glance over his shoulder. An open door at the rear of the shop spilled lantern light into the now-empty shop front with its counters, stone benches, and tight-lidded amphorae of wine. Beyond was clearly a small warehouse where the shopkeeper stored his stock. Lupus slipped across the street and cautiously entered the public area just as someone closed the warehouse door. Darkness smothered him in an instant. He swore under his breath and waited for his night vision to return. He listened at the edge of the door, but could hear nothing.

Then a strange buzzing began to vibrate the bones of his skull. There was no real *sound*, but he clapped hands over both ears, trying to shut out the unpleasant sensation. *What manner of wine shop is this?* Sweat started out on his brow. He wasn't afraid, exactly—

The warehouse door opened again, unexpectedly.

Lupus hurled himself into the shadows behind the counter.

Some fifty people emerged from the warehouse room—*but none of them were the ones who'd gone inside moments before*. The last person through closed the door to the warehouse, leaving Lupus hidden in shadows while lanterns swung in the night and giggles and whispers in that same foreign tongue reached his ears. Lupus stared at the departing group, while the bones of his skull ached. Gradually the sound that wasn't a sound faded away. The men and women who'd just left the warehouse disappeared around a street corner.

Lupus emerged slowly from behind the humble limestone countertop, glancing from the closed warehouse door to the street corner and back. Then he tried the door. It wasn't locked. Someone had left a lamp burning; the shop owner must mean to return shortly, else he'd have blown out the lamp. Lupus searched the room thoroughly, if somewhat hastily, but found absolutely no trace of the forty-odd people who had entered this room moments earlier. Nor could he find a doorway or hidden trap in the floor. The room was absolutely empty, save for racks of dusty amphorae. The nearest of those, shaken gently, proved to be full.

Standing in the center of the deserted room, Lupus Mortiferus felt an unaccustomed trickle of fear run up his spine. His quarry had vanished, apparently into thin air, taking Lupus' hard-won money with him. Lupus swore softly, then returned the amphora to its place in the rack, turned on his heel, and strode out again. He *would* discover the secret of that wine shop. The people who came and went from it had to come through *somehow*, as they were not spirits from the underworld, but flesh-and-blood men and women. And since Lupus—superstitious though he might be—did not believe in outright magic, he would find that way through. All he had to do was follow the next group more closely.

And once through . . .

Lupus Mortiferus, the "Wolf of Death" of Rome's great Circus, smiled cruelly in the starlight. "Soon," he promised the thief. "Soon, your belly will meet my blade. I think you will find little enough stomach for my revenge—but my steel will find more than enough of your stomach."

Laughing darkly at his own joke, Lupus Mortiferus strode away into the night.

Gate days always packed in the customers at the Down Time Bar & Grill. With the Porta Romae cycling, Marcus had all he could handle keeping up with drink tabs and calling sandwich orders to Molly. The clink of glassware and the smell of alcohol permeated the dim-lit interior as thickly as the roar of voices, some of them bragging about what they'd done/seen/heard downtime and others drowning whatever it was that had shaken them to the core and yet others denying that anything at all was bothering them.

All in all, it was a pretty normal gate day. Marcus delivered a tray full of drinks to a table where Kit Carson and Malcolm Moore were sharing tall tales with Rachel Eisenstein. The time terminal's physician wasn't taken in by either man, but she was clearly having a good time pretending to believe the world's most famous time scout and La-La Land's most experienced freelance time guide. Marcus smiled, warmed more by their welcoming smiles than their more-than-generous tips, then moved on to the back room, shimmying skillfully between pool players intent on their games, to a corner where Goldie Morran was deeply involved in a high-stakes poker match with Brian Hendrickson.

Marcus knew that look in Goldie's eyes. He held in a shiver. She must be losing—heavily. Brian Hendrickson's face gave away nothing, but the pile of money on his side of the table was a good bit larger than the pile on Goldie's. Several interested onlookers watched silently. Goldie (who somehow reminded Marcus unpleasantly of a certain haughty patrician lady a former master had visited on carefully arranged assignations), glanced from her hand to meet Brian's steady regard. Her lip curled slightly, sure of him. "Call."

Hendrickson showed his cards.

Goldie Morran swore in a manner Marcus still found shocking. More money travelled to the librarian's side of the table.

"Your drinks," Marcus said quietly, placing them carefully to one side of cards, money, and outthrust elbows.

Out in the main room, a familiar voice sang out, "Hey, Marcus! Where are you?"

Skeeter Jackson was back in town. He hid a pleased grin.

Marcus quietly collected empty glasses from the poker table, noted the lack of a tip from Goldie and the modest tip from the librarian, then hurried out and found his friend beaming at the entire roomful of patrons.

"Drinks," he announced elaborately, "are on the house. A round for everyone on me!"

Marcus gaped. "Skeeter? That is . . . that will be very expensive!" His friend never had that kind of money. And the Down Time was *crowded* tonight.

"Yep! I scored big for a change. Really big!" His

grin all but lit up the dark room. Then he produced a wallet *full* of money. "For the drinks!"

"You won the bets?"

Skeeter laughed. "Did I ever! Serve 'em up, Marcus." He winked and handed Marcus a heavy pouch, whispering, "Thanks. That's for your help." Then he sauntered over to a table, where he found himself the center of much attention, most of it from tourists. The pouch Skeeter had given him was very heavy. Marcus began to tremble. When he opened the drawstrings, the number—and *color*—of the coins inside made his head swim. There must be . . . He couldn't see properly to count the money. But if it wasn't enough to pay off his debt, it was close. Very, very close. His vision wavered.

Skeeter had remembered.

Marcus knew that in this world of uptimers and 'eighty-sixers, grown men did not weep, as Roman men did with such free abandon. So he blinked desperately, but his throat was so thick he couldn't have spoken to save his own life. Skeeter had *remembered*. And actually followed through on the promise. *I won't forget*, Marcus made a silent vow. *I won't forget this, my true friend*.

He stuffed the money into a front jeans pocket, deep enough to keep it safe from pick pockets, then blinked fiercely again. He wished desperately he could leave the Down Time and share his news with Ianira *now*, but he had several hours left on his shift and she would be in the middle of a session with an uptime graduate student, one of many who consulted—and paid—her as a singular, primary source. She had told him once that some uptime schools did not allow students to use such recordings or notes, considering them faulty, if not downright fraudulent, sources. Anger had sparked like flint against pyrite in her eyes, that anyone would dare to question her honesty, her integrity.

But a lot of other schools *did* accept such research as valid. Marcus discovered a deep, abiding joy that Ianira would no longer have to reduce herself to selling off little pieces of her life just to save money for Marcus' debt. He could tell her later of his good fortune, of their good friend and ally. Already he anticipated the joy in her dark eyes.

Perhaps I can even support another child. A son, if the gods smile on us. Thus preoccupied with dreams, Marcus started taking the drink orders Skeeter's generosity had prompted. Skeeter plopped down enough cash to buy the drinks he'd promised and then some.

Goldie Morran and Brian Hendrickson emerged from the back just then, evidently because Goldie had run out of either money or patience. Their admiring entourage followed like schooling fish.

"What's this about drinks being on Skeeter?" Goldie demanded.

Skeeter rose lazily from the seat he'd taken and gave her a mock bow. "You heard me right. And you know I've got the money." He winked at *her* this time.

Ahh . . . Goldie had done the money changing for Skeeter's winnings. Goldie's expression deepened into lines of bitterness. "You call a couple of thousand *money*? Good God, Skeeter, I just dropped that much in one poker game. When are you ever going to graduate from the penny-ante stuff?"

Skeeter froze, eyes going first wide then savagely narrow. He was the focal point of the entire room, tourists and 'eighty-sixers alike. A flush crept up his face, either of embarrassment or anger—with Skeeter, it was never easy to tell.

"Penny-ante?" he repeated, with a dangerous glint in his eyes. "Yes, I suppose from your point of view, that's what I am, Goldie. Just Skeeter's penny-ante bullshit, same as always. Now, if I had your juicy situation, maybe I'd hit it big a little more often, too. You're no better than I am, Goldie, under all that fancy crap you hand your customers."

A sewing needle dropped to the wooden floor would have sounded like an alarm klaxon in the silence that followed.

"And just what do you mean by that?" Goldie was breathing just a touch too hard, nostrils pinched one moment, flaring the next, lips ash white.

"Oh, come off it, Goldie. You can't con *me*, we're too much alike, you and I. Everyone in La-La Land knows you scam any customer you can." Several tourists in the room started visibly and stared at Goldie with dawning suspicion. Skeeter shrugged. "If I had a fancy shop and the chance to snatch rare coins at a fraction of their worth, or had the kind of bankroll you've conned over the years, hell, I could drop a few thousand in a poker game, too, and not miss it.

"Like I said, you're no better than I am. You scam, I scam, and everybody here calls us backstabbing cheats. If you didn't use all that fancy crap in your head about coins and gems, you couldn't scam half of what I do in a week. Frankly, coins and gems is *all* you know. Hell, I could probably top you two or three to one, if you had to make a living the way I do."

Goldie's cheeks went slowly purple, nearly matching her hair.

"Are you issuing a challenge to *me*?"

Skeeter's jaw muscles clenched. Something in his eyes, a glint of steel harsh as the Mongolian desert skies, caused Marcus to shiver. Then Skeeter grinned, slowly, without a trace of mirth in those steely eyes.

"Yeah. I think I am. A challenge. That's a good idea. What about it, Goldie? Shall we give it a week?

Anything you make using knowledge of rare coins, gems, antiques and the like doesn't count. At the end of the week, the person with the most cash takes the whole pot. How about it? Do we have a bet?"

The reek of tension and sweat filled the crowded room as every eye swivelled to Goldie Morran, the dowager con artist of La-La Land. She merely curled a lip. "That hardly seems like a stake worth bothering myself over, considering how little you manage to rake in during an average week." Her eyes narrowed and a smile came to thin lips. Marcus shivered. *Walk carefully, my friend, she means to have blood.* "I don't make fools' bets."

Skeeter took a dangerous step forward, eyes flashing angrily in the dim light. "All right, how about we up the stakes a little, then? We'll make it a *real* bet. Let the wager run for *three* weeks—hell, let's make it one month, even. That'll take us right through the holidays. At the end, loser leaves TT-86, bag and baggage, and never comes back."

Goldie's eyes widened for just a moment, causing Marcus to bite his lips to hold back his protest—never mind a dire warning to take care. Then she actually laughed. "Leave TT-86? Are you mad?"

"Are you chicken?"

For an instant, Marcus thought she might actually strike him.

"Done!" She spat out the word like a snake spitting venom. Then she whirled on poor Brian Hendrickson, a man who wouldn't have cheated a stray flea. He was watching the whole affair round-eyed. Goldie stabbed a long-nailed finger at him. "You. I want you to officiate. This is a for-goddamn-real bet. I win and we're rid of that two-bit little rat for good."

Skeeter's cheeks darkened. But that was the only

sign of emotion. He smiled. "I win and we're finally rid of the Duchess of Dross."

Goldie whirled on him, lips open to snap back something scathing, but Brian Hendrickson stepped between them.

"All right, we have a wager challenged and accepted." The librarian glanced from one to the other. "You two have no idea how much I would give to get out of this, not to get stuck in the middle, but with a wager this serious, somebody's got to keep you two as honest as possible."

He sighed, then reluctantly admitted, "I guess I'm the man to do it, since I know as much about rare coins and gems as you do, Goldie. All right, every day each of you reports to me. I hold all winnings and track all losses. I judge whether a winning counts. Goldie, you are forbidden to use your expertise to scam tourists. You'll have to find some other way to cheat your way to victory."

Brian's eyes revealed clearly how little pleasure he was taking in this, but he went doggedly on. "Money earned legally doesn't count. And one more thing. If either of you gets *caught*, you automatically lose. Understood?"

Goldie sniffed autocratically. "Understood."

Skeeter glared at her for a moment, naked desire for revenge burning in his eyes. Marcus remembered what Skeeter had said, that night he'd been so drunk he'd started confiding secrets Marcus had never dreamed existed. He'd known already that his friend carried with him a monstrous capacity for cold, calculating vengeance. That icy-cold desire now left Marcus terrified for Skeeter's safety. He wanted to shout, "You don't need to prove yourself!" but it was far too late, now. The money in his jeans pocket felt heavier than ever, nearly as heavy as his heart.

His friend would spend the next few weeks doing exactly the kinds of things Marcus was trying to make him *stop* doing, or he would risk having to leave the station forever. Marcus didn't want to lose a friend, any more than the Downtimer Council would want to lose a "Lost One" located and identified by one of their members. Marcus prayed to any Roman *or* Gaulish gods and goddesses that might be listening that Skeeter would win this bet, not Goldie.

She could afford to start over somewhere else.

Skeeter Jackson couldn't.

In that moment, Marcus felt a loathing of Goldie Morran he couldn't begin to put into words. He turned away, busying himself behind the bar, as Brian Hendrickson finished laying down the rules. He didn't notice when Goldie left. But when he glanced around the room and failed to find her, the relief that flooded through him left him weak-kneed. Conversation roared to a crescendo and he was so busy serving drinks, he didn't see Skeeter leaving either. He swallowed hard, sorry for the lost opportunity to speak with his friend, but he still had work to do.

So, very quietly, Marcus served drinks, collected bar tabs, and stuffed tips into his jeans, all the while worrying about the fate of his one good friend in all the world—or time.

CHAPTER FOUR

Lupus Mortiferus had not survived a hundred combats in the Roman arena by giving up easily. He waited from the Kalends of the month until a single day remained before the Ides, either he or his slave following the strangers who had emerged from that wine shop on the Via Appia in the middle of the night. Lupus watched men, women, quarrelsome children, and puckish teens gawk at marble temples, enter brothels with erect-phallus signs poking out of the sides of dingy brick buildings, or file excitedly into the circus to watch the racing and the combats.

For all that time, nearly half the lunar month, Lupus bided his time and whetted the edge on his gladius as sharp as he whetted his desire for revenge. He endured stoically the jokes and jibes that still continued. A few of the jokesters took their jests to the grave, blood and entrails spilling on the sands of the arena while the crowd roared like a thousand summer thunderstorms in his ears.

And then, the waiting was done.

They left in the middle of the night, as before, slaves showing the way with lanterns. Following them was ridiculously easy. Lupus ordered his slave home and slipped from one shadowed shopfront to another, booted feet soundless on the stone paving of the sidewalk. Several of the young men had clearly drunk too much; they reeled, clutching at slaves or at one another, and tried to keep up. As the group approached the wine shop on the Via Appia, Lupus quietly insinuated himself into the group, hanging near the back.

A slave near the front called out something in a barbarous tongue. The group entered the wineshop by twos and threes. Lupus noted uneasily that the slaves assigned to guard the group were carefully taking count of those who passed into the shop's warehouse. Just when he feared discovery, one of the young men near him began to void the contents of his alcohol-saturated stomach. Lupus hid a grin. *Perfect!* Slaves converged on the boy, holding his head and trying to urge him forward. The sight and smell of the boy's vomit triggered a chain reaction amongst the drunken youths. Another boy spewed as he stumbled into the warehouse. Lupus took his arm solicitously, earning a smile of gratitude from a harried woman wearing a slave's collar.

Elated, Lupus dragged the sick youngster into a corner and let him throw up the wine and sweetmeats he'd obviously gorged on during the day. Yet another boy in the group began to throw up. Women in stylish gowns moved away, holding their breath. Frowns of disgust wrinkled painted lips and manicured brows. A little girl said very distinctly, "Yuck." Lupus wasn't certain just exactly what the word meant, but the look on her face was clear enough. Even the older men were giving the sick boys a wide berth. Lupus was pressed into the corner with the sick youngsters, ignored by everyone except the boy who clung to his arm and groaned.

Then the air began to groan.

It wasn't an audible sound, but it was *exactly* like the painful buzzing in his skull the last time he'd been close to this warehouse. Lupus swallowed a few times and tried to find the source of the noise that wasn't exactly a noise. A hush fell over the crowd, punctuated messily by the sounds of wretchedly ill boys and a few murmured words of encouragement from their slaves. Lupus glanced at a blank stretch of wall, wondering yet again why everyone had crowded into this particular warehouse—

The wall began to shimmer. Colors scintillated wildly through the entire rainbow. Lupus gasped aloud, then controlled his involuntary reaction. A quick glance showed him that no one had noticed the sweat that had started on his brow. That was a relief, but it still took all his courage to continue looking at the pulsing spot on the wall. Captivated by the sight, he couldn't look away, not even when a dark hole appeared in the scintillating, circular rainbows, his hindbrain whispering to *run*! The hole widened rapidly until it had swallowed half the warehouse wall. Lupus fought back once more the instinct to run, then swallowed instead and whispered softly, "Great war-god Mars, lend me a bit of your confidence, please."

People started stepping into it.

They flew away so fast, it was as though they'd been catapulted by a great war machine. Someone took the other arm of the boy Lupus was "helping" and pulled him toward the gaping hole in the wall. Lupus wanted to stand rock-still, terrified of that black maw that swallowed people whole down its gullet. Then, thinking of vengeance and his carefully sharpened gladius, he drew a deep breath for courage and moved forward in the midst of the half-dozen boys who were manfully struggling to overcome their illness. Lupus hesitated on the brink, sweating and terrified—

Then squeezed shut both eyes and stepped forward. He was falling . . .

Mithras! Mars! Save me—

He went to his knees against something rough and metallic. Lupus opened his eyes and found himself kneeling on a metal gridwork. The boy who had gone through with him was vomiting again. Men hauling baggage stumbled past them, struggling to get around. Lupus hauled the kid to his feet and dragged him in the direction the others had taken, down a broad, gridwork ramp. Chaos reigned at the bottom, where several other of the boys were still holding up the line, vomiting piteously all over a young woman in the most outlandish clothing Lupus had ever seen. Everyone in line was trying to slide some sort of flat, stiff vellum chip into a boxlike device, but the boys were making a mess of the entire procedure. The young woman said something that sounded exasperated and disgusted and glanced the other way—

Lupus, who had no flat, stiff vellum chip to insert into the device, slipped quietly past and fled for the nearest concealment: a curtain of hanging vines and flowering shrubs that screened a private portico. Panting slightly and cursing the fear-borne adrenalin that poured through his veins the way it did just before a fight, Lupus Mortiferus took his first look at the place where the thief who'd stolen his money had taken refuge.

He swallowed once, very hard.

Where am I? Olympus?

He couldn't quite accept that explanation, despite the terrifying magic of a hole through a wall that sometimes existed and sometimes didn't. Atlantis, perhaps? No, that had been destroyed when the gods were young. If it had ever existed at all. Where, then? Rome *was* civilization in this world, although traders spoke of the wonders of the far, far east, from whence expensive silk came.

Lupus didn't know the name of the cities where silk was spun into cloth, but he didn't think this was one of them. It wasn't a proper "city" at all. There was no open sky, no ground, no distant horizon or wind to rustle through treetops and evaporate sweat from his skin. The place was more like an enormous . . . room. One large enough to hold the towering Egyptian obelisk on the spine of the Circus Maximus—with room to spare between its golden tip and the distant ceiling. The room was large enough that he could have laid out a half-length chariot-race course down its length, had there not been shops, ornamental fountains and ponds, decorative seats, and odd pillars with glowing spheres at the top scattered throughout its length, along with a riot of colorful Saturnalia and other, unfathomable, decorations from floor to ceiling. The delighted shrieking of young children brought home just how lost he was: a mere child of five clearly knew more about this place than he did.

Staircases of metal *everywhere* climbed up to nothing, or to platforms which served no sane purpose Lupus could divine. Signs he could not read scattered strange letters colorfully across the walls. A few areas were fenced off, leaving them inaccessible despite the seeming innocuous blankness of the walls behind them. The image of the wine shop's wall opening up into a hole through nothingness was so powerfully and recently embedded in his soul, Lupus shuddered, wondering what lay behind those innocent-seeming stretches of wall. People dressed as Romans mingled with others in costumes so barbaric and foreign, Lupus could only stare.

Where am I?

And where, in all this confusion of shops, staircases, and people, was the thief he sought? For one terrible moment, he shut his eyes and fought the urge to charge straight up the ramp and back through the hole in the wall. He managed to bring shuddering breaths under control only with difficulty, but he did control himself. He was the Death Wolf of the Circus Maximus, after all, not a milk-fed brat to fear the first strangeness life hurled his way. Lupus forced his eyes open again.

The hole in the wall had closed.

He was trapped here, for evil or good.

For just a second, terror overrode all other concerns. Then, slowly, Lupus gripped the pommel of his gladius. The gods he worshipped had answered his hourly prayers in their own mysterious fashion. He was trapped, yes.

But so was the thief.

All Lupus had to do was find a way to pass himself off as a member of this sunless, closed-in world long enough to track the man down, then he would wait for the next inexplicable opening of the wall and fight his way back home, if necessary.

The corners of his lips twisted into a mirthless smile.

The thief would rue the hour he had cheated Lupus Mortiferus, the champion Death Wolf of Rome. That decision holding hard-fought fear at bay, Lupus clutched the pommel of his sword and set out on his hunt.

Wherever populations of illegal refugees spring up without legal status inside an existing, "native" population, certain networks are formed almost as automatically as baby whales swim straight for the surface to gulp that first, essential breath of air. Almost by unconscious accord, mutual aid systems will emerge to help illegal aliens survive, perhaps in time even thrive, in a world they do not understand, much less control.

In the time terminals that had grown around those

areas where gates formed in close-enough profusion to warrant building a station, this unwritten rule held as true as it did in the squalid streets of L.A. or New York, in the streets of every major coastal city, in fact, where refugees of The Flood which had followed The Accident, crowded together for safety, almost without hope of finding any, each and every pitiful one of them without papers to prove their identity or country of origin. Those uptime refugees struggled to survive under even worse conditions, sometimes, than refugees trapped forever on the time terminals. It didn't bear mentioning the living conditions of the tidal waves of refugees fleeing endless, senseless wars raging throughout the Middle East and the Balkans. Whole armies of them fled illegally across national borders, fleeing genocide at the hands of enemies, many of them dying in the attempt.

Men and women, children and strays, those who wandered into the terminals through open gates and found themselves trapped without uptime legal rights, without social standing, protected by the thinnest of "station policies"—because the uptime governments couldn't decide what to *do* about them—set up social systems of their own in courageous attempts to cope. A few went hopelessly mad and wandered back through open gates, usually unstable ones, never to be seen again. But most, desperate to survive, banded together in sometimes loosely, sometimes tightly knit confederations. Often speaking only the common language of gestures, they shared news and resources as best they could, sometimes even going so far as to hide from official notice any newcomers who might be exploited or injured by regulations and officialdom's sometimes harsh notice.

On TT-86, management under Bull Morgan made such extreme efforts necessary only rarely, but all downtimers shared a common bond few uptimers could really understand. It was the experience of being lost together. Like the Christian sects of Rome which had once met in the catacombs beneath the city or the cells of Colonial American patriots hiding out from British armies and meeting in any root cellar or thicket they could find, La-La Land's downtimer Council met underground. Literally underground, beneath the station proper, in the bowels of the terminal where machinery (which filled the air with chaos and noise) kept the lights running, the sewage flowing, and the heated or chilled air pumping; down where massive steel-and-concrete support beams plunged into native, Himalayan rock, the refugees created their culture of survival.

Amidst the noise and whine of machines they barely understood, they met in the cramped caverns of La-La Land's physical plant to bolster one another's courage, pass along news of critical importance to their standing, and share fear, grief, loss, and triumph with one another. A few had taken it upon themselves to hold special classes in uptime languages, while those most able to understand the world in which they were trapped did their best to explain it to those least able.

Uptimers knew about it, but most didn't pay much attention to the "underground society's" activities. On TT-86, management cared enough to provide an official psychologist on the payroll, whose sole duty was to help them adjust, but "Buddy" didn't really understand what it meant—emotionally, in the depth of one's belly—to be torn away from one's home time and become trapped in a place like the bustling time terminal that La-La Land had become over the years.

So downtimers turned to their own unofficial leaders in times of need or crisis. One of those unofficial leaders was Ianira Cassondra. Sitting waiting for Marcus to return to home to her, she spent a quiet moment bemused with the thought that her own history was, in many ways, more unlikely than the odd world in which she now led others through an unlikely existence. Ianira, born in Ephesus, the holy city of the Great Artemis Herself, had learned the secrets of rituals no man would ever understand from priestesses who followed the old, old ways. Ianira, secluded from the world as only a priestess of Artemis could be, was then, at sixteen, ripped from that world and sold into virtual slavery through the marriage bed—tearing her away from beloved Ephesus to the high citadel of Athens, across the Aegean Sea. Ianira, abandoned by her kinsmen, was left in the shadow of the dusty Agora where Athenian men met under blazing clear light to stroll amidst vendors of figs, olive oil, and straw baskets while they discussed and invented political systems that would change the world for the next twenty-six hundred years. Secluded from all that she knew, Ianira had tried to learn the mysteries of the patron goddess of her new home, only to be kept a virtual prisoner in her new husband's gyneceum.

Ianira the "Enchantress," who had once danced beneath the moon in Artemis' sacred glade, bow in hand, hair loose and wild, had prayed to her mother's ancient Goddesses to deliver her—and, finally, *They* had heard. One night, Ianira had fled the gyneceum and its imprisoning "respectability," driven by grief and terror into the night-dark streets of Athens.

Half bent on seeking asylum in Athene's great temple at the crowning height of the city—and half intent on throwing herself from the Acropolis rather than endure another night in her husband's home—Ianira had run on bare feet, lungs sobbing for air, her body weak and shaking still from the birthing chair in which she had so recently been confined.

And there, in those silent, dusty streets where men changed history and women were held in bondage, her prayers to Athene, to Hera, to Demeter and her daughter Proserpina, Queen of the Underworld, to Artemis and Aphrodite and even to Circe the Enchantress of Old, were finally answered. Pursued by an enraged husband, she ran as fast as she could force her flagging body, knowing all too well what fate awaited her if her husband caught her. Ianira's bare toes raised puffs of dust in the empty, moonlit Agora, where the columns of the gleaming white Hephestion rose on a hillock to one side and the painted Stoa where philosophers met to discourse with their disciples rose ghostlike before her in the haunted night.

Still bent on trying to reach the shining Parthenon above her, Ianira darted into an alleyway leading up toward the Acropolis and heard a beggar man seated on the ground call out sharply, "Hey! Don't go through there!"

A glance back showed her the figure of her husband, gaining ground. Terror sent her, sobbing, up toward Athene's great temple. She literally ran into the solid wall of a small cobbler's shop hugging the cliff face, staggered back—

—and saw it happen.

Inside the open doorway of the cobbler's shop, the dark air had torn asunder before her disbelieving eyes. Her gown fluttered like moth's wings as she faltered to a halt, staring at the pinpoint of light and movement through it. Dimly, she was aware of people crowding around her, her husband's curses at the back of the crowd. She hesitated only a moment. At the embittered, battered age of seventeen, Ianira Cassondra lifted her hands in thanks to whichever Goddess had listened—and shoved past startled men and women who tried to stop her. She stepped straight into the wavering hole in reality, not caring what she found on the other side, half-expecting to see the grand halls of Olympus itself, with shining Artemis waiting to avenge her defiled priestess.

She found, instead, La-La Land and a new life. Free of many of her old terrors, she learned to trust and love again, at least one man who had learned caution from harsher masters than she had yet found. And even more precious, something she had not thought possible, she had found the miracle of a young man with brown hair and a laughing heart and dark, haunted eyes who could make her forget the brutality and terror of a man's touch. He would not marry her yet. Not because she had left a living husband, but because—in his *own* mind—he was not honorably free of debt. Ianira had never met this man who owned Marcus' debt, but sometimes when she went into deep trance, she could *almost* see his face, amidst the most unlikely surroundings she had ever witnessed.

Whoever and wherever he was, waiting for Marcus to finish his days' labors, Ianira hated the hidden man with such a passion as Medea had known when she'd snatched up the dagger to slay her own sons, rather than let a replacement queen raise them like slaves. When—if—he returned, Ianira mused, she herself would find no barriers to taking up her own dagger and punishing the man who had treated her beloved so callously. It would not be the first time she'd offered the pieces of a sacrificial human male to ancient Artemis, she who was called by the Spartans Artamis the Butcher. She had thought herself long past the need for such bloody work; but when her family was threatened, Ianira Cassondra knew herself capable of *anything*. Quite a change from that time in her life when the thought of sleeping with a one-time slave would have been revolting to her—but the contrast between a year of "honorable" marriage and Marcus' tender concern for a stranger lost in a world the gods themselves would have found bewildering, had worked a magic Ianira could recognize. Sharing Marcus' bed, his fears and dreams, Ianira gave him children to ease the pain in his heart—and her own.

To her surprise, Ianira found she not only enjoyed the humble, mundane chores she had never before been forced to do, but also she enjoyed the surprising status and acclaim her abilities and personality had earned her. Odd to be so suddenly sought after—not only by other lonely downtimer men, but by tourists, uptimer students, even professors of antiquities. In this strange land, Ianira had discovered she could make many things, beautiful things: gowns, baubles and ornaments, herbal mixes to help those in suffering. After a few of these items had sold, demand was suddenly so great, she'd asked Connie Logan if she would please teach her to use one of the new machines for sewing, to make her gowns faster.

Connie had grinned. "Sure. Just let my computer copy down any embroidery or dress patterns you use and you've got a deal!"

Connie was a shrewd businesswoman. So was she, Ianira remembered with a smile. "The embroidery? No. The dress patterns? Yes, and welcome."

Connie shook her head and sighed. "You're robbing me blind, Ianira, but I like you. And if that Ionian chiton you're wearing is any example of what you can do . . . you've got a deal."

So Ianira used Connie Logan's workshop to create the chitons she was stockpiling toward a future business of her own. She'd spent her entire pregnancy with Gelasia sewing, making up little bags to hold dried herbs, learning to make the simple but beautiful kinds of jewelry she recalled so clearly from her home—

and her now-dead husband's. And finally it paid off, when she got the permit from Bull Morgan to open a booth, which Marcus made for her in his free time. They painted it prettily and set up for business.

Which was good, if not as phenomenal as she'd once or twice hoped. But good, still, more than enough to pay for itself and leave extra for family expenses, including Marcus' debt-free fund. Theirs was an odd marriage—Ianira categorically refused to acknowledge the year of rape and abuse in Athens as a legitimate marriage, as she had *not* consented—but the odd marriage was filled with everything she could have wanted. Love, security, children, happiness with the kindest man she'd ever known . . . sometimes her very happiness frightened her, should the gods become jealous and strike them all down.

Marcus reeled in from work the night the Porta Romae cycled, far gone in wine he rarely took in such quantities, and shook his head at the supper she'd kept warm for him. Ianira put it away efficiently in the miraculous refrigerator machine, then noticed silent tears sliding down his cheeks.

"Marcus!" she gasped, rushing to him. "What is it, love?"

He shook his head and steered her into the bedroom, not even bothering to undress either of them, then held her close, nose buried in her hair, and trembled until he could finally speak.

"It—it is Skeeter, Ianira. Skeeter Jackson. Do you remember me laughing when he left for Romae, promising to give me a share of his bet winnings?"

"Yes, love, of course, but—"

He shifted a little, pressed something heavy inside a leather pouch into her hand. "He kept his promise," Marcus whispered.

Ianira held the heavy money pouch and just listened, holding him, while he wept for the kindness of an *up*timer friend who had given him the means at long last to discharge his heavy debt and finally marry her.

"Why?" she whispered, not understanding the impulse which had driven a man universally regarded as a scoundrel to such generosity.

Marcus looked at her through eyes still flooded with tears. "He knows, I think, a little of what we have known. If he could only find what we have found. . . ." Marcus sighed, then kissed his wife. "Let me tell you." Ianira listened, and as Marcus' tale proceeded, vowed to store in her heart the story of Skeeter Jackson, who had, in his boyhood, stumbled through an open gate into an alien land.

"He was drunk that night," Marcus whispered to her in the darkness, so as not to waken their young daughters in the crib beside their shared bed. "Drunk and so lonely he started to talk, thinking I might understand. What he told me . . . Some of it I still do not understand completely, but I will try to tell it to you in his own words. He said it began as a game, because of his father . . ."

The game, Skeeter had recalled through a haze of alcohol and pain, had begun in deadly earnest. "It was my father's fault, or maybe my mother's. But you know, even when you're only eight, you can figure the score, figure it 'bout as accurately as any bookie making odds in New York. Dad, he bought the whole Pee-Wee League basketball team matching uniforms. Made sure our games got local TV coverage. Did the same for my Junior League baseball team. Spent a lot of money on us, he did. And you know what, Marcus? He never came to a game. Not one. Not a single, stinking, stupid game. Hell, it wasn't hard at all to figure the score.

Dad didn't give a damn about *me*. Just cared 'bout how much prestige he could buy. How many customers his publicity would bring in, God *damn* him. He wassa good businessman, too. So rich it hurt your teeth just thinkin' about it."

Marcus, only vaguely comprehending much of what Skeeter said, knew that the young man was hurting nonetheless, worse than any resident he'd ever listened to on a late, slow night at the Down Time Bar & Grill. Skeeter stared into his whiskey glass. "Fill 'er up again, would you, Marcus? That's good." He drained half the glass in a gulp. "Yeah, that's good . . . So, it's like this, I started stealing things. You know, things at the mall. Little stuff at first, not because I was poor, but because I wanted something I got by myself. I guess I just got too goddamn sick of having Dad throw some expensive toy at me like a bone to some flea-bitten dog that had wandered in, just to keep it quiet."

He blinked slowly and gulped the rest of the whiskey, then just reached for the bottle and poured again. His eyes were a little unfocussed as he spoke, his voice a little less steady. "In fac', I was at th' mall the day *it* happened. After The Accident, you know, that caused the time strings, ever'body knew a gate could open up anywhere, but, hell, they usually cluster together, you know, like the TV said all my life, in one little area small enough to build a time station around 'em and let the big new time tour companies operate through 'em. But, my friend," he tipped more whiskey into his glass, "sometimes gates just open up, no warning, no nothing, in the middle of some place ain't no gate ever been seen before."

He drank, his hand a little unsteady, and entirely without his volition, the story came pouring out. He'd been careless, that time, they'd caught him shoplifting the big Swiss Army Knife. But he was little and blubbered convincingly and was slippery enough to dodge away the minute their guard was down. He'd considered, for a few moments after the guard grabbed him, *letting* the scandal hit the papers and television news programs, just to get even with his father. But Skeeter didn't want the game to end that way. He wanted to perfect it—*then* present his Dad with a scandal big enough to wreck his life as thoroughly as he'd wrecked Skeeter's, game after missed baseball and basketball and football game, lonely night after lonely night.

So away he dodged, into the crowded mall, with the angry guard hot on his heels and Skeeter whipping around startled shoppers, dodging into department stores and out again through different exits on upper levels, and skidding through the food court while the guard giving chase radioed for backup.

It was all great fun—until the hole opened up in the air right in front of him. The only warning he had was an odd buzzing in the bones of his head. Then the air shimmered through a whole dazzling array of colors and Skeeter plunged through with a wild yell, face flushed, hair standing on end, T-shirt glued to his back with sweat and his sneakers skidding on nothing.

He landed on stony ground, with a sky big as an ocean howling all around him. A man dressed in furs, face greased against a bitter wind, stared down at him. The man's expression wavered somewhere between shock, terror, and triumph, all three shining at once in his dark eyes. Skeeter, winded by the chase and badly dazed by the plunge through nothingness, just stood there panting up at him for endless moments, eye locked to eye. When the man drew a sword, Skeeter knew he had two choices: run or fight. He was used to running. Skeeter usually found it easier to run than to confront an enemy directly, particularly when running allowed him to lay neat traps in his wake.

But he was out of breath, suddenly and shockingly frozen by the bitter wind, and confronted with something a few thieving raids at the mall had not prepared him to deal with: a man ready to actually *kill* him.

So he attacked first.

One eight-year-old boy with a stolen Swiss Army knife was no match for Yesukai the Valiant, but he did some slight damage before the grown man put him on the ground, sword at his throat.

"Aw, hell, go on and kill me, then," Skeeter snarled. "Couldn't be worse'n being ignored."

To his very great shock, Yesukai—Skeeter learned later just exactly who and what he was—snatched him up by his shirt, slapped his face, and threw him across the front of a high-pommelled Yakka saddle, then galloped down a precipitous mountainside that left Skeeter convinced they were all going to die: Skeeter, the horse, *and* the madman holding the reins. Instead, they joined a group of mounted men waiting below.

"The gods have sent a *bogda*," Yesukai said (as Skeeter later learned, once he could understand Yesukai's language. He had heard the story recounted many times over the cook fires of Yesukai's yurt.) He thumped Skeeter's back with a heavy hand, knocking the breath from him. "He attacked brave as any Yakka Mongol warrior, drawing the blood of courage." The man who'd slung him over his saddle bared an arm where Skeeter had cut him slightly. "It is a sign from the spirits of the upper air, who have sent us the beginnings of a man to follow us on earth."

A few younger warriors smiled at the ancient Mongol religious tenet; grizzled old veterans merely watched

Skeeter through slatted eyes, faces so perfectly still they might have been carved of wood.

Then Yesukai the Valiant jerked his horse's fretting head around to the north. "We ride, as I have commanded."

Without another word of explanation, Skeeter found himself bundled onto another man's saddle, thrust into a fur jacket too big for him, a felt hat with ear flaps tied under his chin—also too big for him—and carried across the wildest, most desolate plain he had ever seen. The ride went on for hours. He fell asleep in pain, woke in pain to be offered raw meat softened by being stored between the saddle and the horse's sweating skin (he managed to choke it down, half-starved as he was), then continued for hours more until a group of black-felt tents he later learned to call yurts rose from the horizon like bumps of mold growing up from the flat, bleak ground.

They galloped into the middle of what even Skeeter could tell was some kind of formal processional, scattering women and children as they smashed into the festive parade. Screams rose from every side. Yesukai leaned down from his saddle and snatched a terror-stricken young girl from her own pony, threw her across his pommel and shouted something. The men of the camp were running toward them, bows drawn. Arrows whizzed from Yesukai's mounted warriors. Men went down, screaming and clutching at throats, chests, perforated bellies. Deep in shock, Skeeter rode the long way back to the tall mountain where he'd fallen through the hole in the air, wondering every galloping step of the way what was to become of him, never mind the poor girl, who had finally quit screaming and struggling and had settled into murderous glares belied by occasional whimpers of terror.

It was only much later that Skeeter learned of Yesukai's instructions to his warriors. "If the *bogda* brings us success, I command that he be raised in our tents as a gift from the gods, to become Yakka as best he can or die as any man would of cold, starvation, or battle. If he brings the raid bad luck and I fail to steal my bride from that flat-faced fool she is to marry, then he is no true *bogda*. We will leave his cut-up body for the vultures."

There was no compassion in Yesukai for any living thing outside his immediate clan. He couldn't afford it. No Mongol could. Keeping the Yakka clan's grazing lands, herds, and yurts safe from the raids of neighbors was a full-time job which left no room in his heart for anything but cold practicality.

Skeeter had come to live in terror of him—and to love him in a way he could never explain. Skeeter was used to having to fend for himself, so learning to fight for scraps of food like the other boys after the adults had finished eating from the communal stew pot wasn't as great a shock as it might have been. But Skeeter's father would never have troubled himself to say things like, "A Yakka Mongol does not steal from a Yakka Mongol. I rule forty-thousand yurts. We are a small tribe, weak in the sight of our neighbors, so we do not steal from the tents of our own. But the best in life, *bogda*, is to steal from one's enemy's and make what was his your own—and to leave his yurts burning in the night while his women scream. Never forget that, *bogda*. The property of the clan is sacred. The property of the enemy is honorable gain to be taken in battle."

Boys, Skeeter learned, stole from one another anyway, sometimes starting blood feuds that Yesukai either ended cruelly or—on occasion—allowed to end in their own fashion, if he thought the wiser course would be to drive home a harsh lesson. Hardship Skeeter could endure. Fights with boys twice his age (although often half his size), nursing broken bones that healed slowly through the bitter, dust-filled storms every winter, learning to ride like the other boys his age, first on the backs of sheep they were set to guard, then later on yaks and even horses, *these* Skeeter could endure. He even learned to pay back those boys who stole from him, stealing whatever his enemies treasured most and planting the items adroitly amongst the belongings of his victim's most bitter enemies.

If Yesukai guessed at his little *bogda*'s game, he never spoke of it and Skeeter was never reprimanded. He desperately missed nearly everything about the uptime home he'd lost. He missed television, radio, portable CD players, roller blades, skate boards, bicycles, video games—home versions *and* arcade games—movies, popcorn, chocolate, colas, ice cream, and pepperoni pizza.

But he did not miss his parents.

To be accepted into the Yakka clan, with its banner of nine white yak tails, as though he actually were *important* to someone, was enough, more than enough, to make up for a father who had abdicated all pretense of caring about his family. Not even the mother who—after her son had been missing for five years only God knew where, more than likely dead, the son who had been rescued by a time scout who'd given his life rescuing Skeeter—had welcomed him home with a cursory peck on the cheek, obligatory for the multiple media cameras. She had then, in her chilly, methodical way, calmly set about making lists of the school classes he'd need to make up, the medical appointments he'd need, and the new wardrobe that would have to be obtained, all without once saying, "Honey, I missed you," or even, "How did you ever survive your adventure?" never mind, "Skeeter, I love you with all my heart and I'm so glad you're home I could cry."

Skeeter's mother was too busy making lists and making certain he was antiseptically clean again to notice his long, still silences. His *father's* sole response was a long stare of appraisal and a quiet, "Wonder what we can make of this, hmm? TV talk shows? Hollywood? At least a made-for-TV movie, I should think. Ought to pay handsomely, boy."

And so, after two weeks of bitterly hating both of them and wishing them gutted on the end of Yesukai's sword, when Skeeter's father—in the midst of signing all the contracts he'd mentioned that first day—decided to send him to some University school to have his brain picked on the subject of twelfth-century Mongolian life and the early years of Temujin, first-born son of Yesukai—merely for the *fee* it would bring, Skeeter had done exactly what Yesukai had taught him to do.

He had quietly left home in the middle of the night and made his way to New York by way of a stolen car to continue his real education: raiding the enemy. The man and woman who'd given him life had become members of that enemy. He was proud—deeply proud—of the fact that he'd managed to electronically empty his parents' substantial bank account before leaving.

Yesukai the Yakka Mongol Khan, father of the one-day Genghis Khan, had begun Skeeter's formal training. New York street toughs furthered it. His return to La-La Land, a time terminal he recalled as a half-finished shell of concrete with few shops and only one active gate open for business, run by a company called *Time Ho!* was the journeyman's equivalent of completing his unique education.

So, when Skeeter said, "My father made me everything I am today," he was telling the bald-faced, unvarnished truth. The trouble was, he was never sure which father he meant. He possessed no such uncertainty about which man's values he'd chosen to emulate. Skeeter Jackson was a twenty-first century, middle-class, miserable delinquent who had discovered happiness and purpose in the heart and soul of the Yakka Mongol.

And so he smiled when he worked his schemes against the enemy—and that smile was, as others had sometimes speculated, absolutely genuine, perhaps the only "genuine" thing about him. 'Eighty-sixers had become the closest thing Skeeter now had to a family, a tribe to which he belonged, only on the fringes, true; but he never forgot Yesukai's lesson. The property of Clan was sacrosanct. And there *was* no greater pleasure than burning the enemy's yurts in the night—or, metaphorically, scamming the last, living cent out of any tourist or government bureaucrat who richly and most royally deserved it.

If others called him scoundrel because of it . . .

So be it.

Yesukai the Valiant would have applauded, given him a string of ponies for his success, and maybe even a good bow—all things that Skeeter had coveted. La-La Land was the only place where a latter-day Mongol *bogda* could practice his art without serious threat of jail. It was also the only place on earth where—if life grew too unendurable or the scholars caught up with him—he could step back through the Mongolian Gate, find young Temujin, and join up again.

"Y'know," Skeeter slurred, downing yet another glass of whiskey, "nights when m' luck's down and I got no one, sometimes I swear I'm gonna do just that. Walk through, next time th' Monglian—Mongolian—Gate opens. Haven't done it yet, Marcus. So far," he rapped his knuckles against the wet surface of the wooden bar, "m' luck always takes a turn for the better, jus' in time. But my Khan, he always said luck alone don't carry a man through life. Tha's why I work so damn hard. It's pride, don' you see, not jus' survival. Gotta live up t' Yesukai's standards. And genr'ally—" he hiccuped and almost dropped his glass, "—genr'ally it's fun, 'cause a' bureaucrats anna' damn arrogant tourists are a bunch a' idiots. Incomp'tent, careless idiots, don' even know wha's around 'em." He laughed a short, bitter laugh. "Let'm stay blind 'n deaf 'n stupid. Keeps the money coming, don't it?"

He met Marcus' gaze with one that was almost steady, despite the appalling amount of whiskey he'd consumed.

"If no one else unnerstan's, so be it. 'S not their life t' live. 'S mine." He thumped his chest, staining a Greek chiton of exquisite cut and embroidery when the remaining whiskey in his glass sloshed across the garment and puddled in his lap. "Mine, y'unnerstand. My life. And I ain't disappointed, Marcus. Not by much, I ain't."

When Skeeter began to cry as though his heart were breaking, Marcus had very gently taken the whiskey glass from his hand and guided him home, making sure he was safely in bed in his own apartment that night. Whether or not Skeeter recalled anything he'd said, Marcus had no idea. But Marcus remembered every word—even those he didn't quite understand.

When Marcus shared the precious story of Skeeter Jackson with Ianira, she held her beloved close in the darkness and made sacred promises to her Goddesses. They had given her this precious man, this Marcus who cherished not only Ianira herself, but also their beautiful, sloe-eyed daughters. They had given Ianira a man who actually *loved* little Artemisia and tiny little Gelasia, loved their cooing laugher and loved dandling them by turns on his knee and even soothing their tears, rather than ordering either beautiful child left on the street to die of exposure and starvation simply because she was *female*.

There in the sacred privacy of their shared bed, Ianira vowed to her Goddesses that she would do whatever lay in her power to guard the interests of the man who had given her beloved the means to discharge his debt of honor. When Marcus joined with her in the darkness, skin pressed to trembling skin, she prayed that his seed would plant a son in her womb, a son who would be born into a world where his father was finally a free man in his own soul. She called blessings on the name of Skeeter Jackson and swore a vow that *others* in the downtimer community would soon know the truth about the smiling, strange young man who made such a point to steal from the tourists yet never touched anything belonging to residents— and always treated downtimers with more courtesy than any 'eighty-sixer on the station, with the possible exceptions of Kit Carson and Malcolm Moore.

Ianira understood now many things that had been mysterious to her. All those cash donations, with no one taking responsibility for them . . . Downtimers had a champion they had not dreamed existed. Marcus, not understanding why she wept in the darkness, kissed her tears and assured her in ragged words that he would prove himself worthy of the love she gave so freely. She held him fiercely and stilled his mouth with her own, vowing he had proven his worthiness a thousand times over already. His response brought tears to *her* eyes.

In the aftermath of their love, she held him while he slept and made plans that Marcus would neither understand nor approve. She didn't care. They owed a debt which was beyond profound; Ianira would repay it as best she could. And the only way she could think to do that was to further the fortunes of the man who had given Marcus the means to purchase back his sacred honor.

Ianira kissed Marcus' damp hair while he slept and made silent, almost savage, decisions.

CHAPTER FIVE

Wagers in La-La Land were big news. Essentially a closed environment for full-time residents, gossip and betting took the place of live television and radio programs, except for a couple of new on-terminal news programs run more like "gossip hour" than a real news broadcast. The Shangri-La Radio and Television Broadcasting system, an experimental outfit, to say the least, ran taped movies and canned music when down-and-out newsies weren't conducting official gossip sessions.

And like all other newsies, who were snoops at heart, if someone bet on something, everyone in La-La Land would eventually hear about it, the process just speeded up a little now thanks to S.L.R.T.B.'s inquisitive, intrusive staff. Even minor bets, like how long it would take a new batch of tourists to react to pterodactyl splatters on their luggage, became juicy tidbits to pass along over a beer, across the dinner table, or over the new cable system.

When two of Shangri-La Station's most notorious hustlers made a wager like the one Goldie Morran and Skeeter Jackson had made, not only did it spread like wildfire through the whole station, it captured the top news slot of the hour for twenty-four hours running and made banner headlines in the *Shangri-La Gazette*: POCKETS—PICK 'EM OR PACK 'EM! The banner headline was followed immediately, of course, by intimate details, including the full set of rules laid down by librarian Brian Hendrickson.

Skeeter read that article with a sense of gloom he couldn't shake. Everyone who *lived* on TT-86 knew he never went after residents, but now the *tourists* would be warned, too, drat it. He crumpled up the newspaper and glared across Commons, wondering how much Goldie had scammed so far. Goldie had no such principles where cheating and theft were concerned, which meant residents were watching their wallets and possessions with extra care. It hurt Skeeter that many now included *him* in that distrust, but that was part of the game.

He glanced up at the nearest chronometer board to see which gate departures were scheduled and pursed his lips. Hmm . . . The Britannia Gate to London tomorrow, Conquistadores this afternoon, medieval Japan through Edo Castletown's Nippon Gate in three days, and the Wild West gate to Denver in four, on a clockwork routine of exactly one week. He didn't like the idea of going after tourists headed for the ancient capital of the Japanese shogunate. Some were just gullible businessmen, but lots of them were gangland thugs—and all too often the businessmen travelled under the protection of the gangs.

Skeeter had no desire to end up minus a few fingers or other parts of his anatomy. If he were desperate enough, he'd risk it, but the other gates were better bets. For now, anyway. The nearest gate opening would be the South American "Conquistadores" Gate. That would present plenty of opportunity for quick cash. He could set up more elaborate schemes for the later gates, given the time to work them out. And, of course, he kept one eye eternally peeled for Mike Benson or his security men. He did *not* want to get caught and

Benson would have security crawling around all the gates, now that word of the wager was out.

Skeeter cursed reporters everywhere and went to his room to get into costume. If he had to dodge security, he'd better do something to disguise himself. Otherwise, he'd be looking for a new home next time Primary cycled. The fear that he would be forced to do just that put the extra finishing touches on his disguise.

When Skeeter finally finished, he grinned into the mirror. His own birth mother—God curse her— wouldn't have recognized him. He rubbed his hands in anticipation—then swore aloud when the telephone rang. Who could possibly be calling, other than Security or some damnable snoop of a reporter who'd somehow dug up the truth about Skeeter from some dusty newspaper morgue?

He snatched the phone from the hook, considering leaving it to dangle down the wall, then muttered, "Yeah?"

"Mr. Jackson?" a hesitant voice asked. "Skeeter Jackson?"

"Who wants to know?" he growled.

"Oh, ah, Dr. Mundy. Nally Mundy."

Skeeter bit his tongue to keep from cursing aloud.

That goddamned historical scholar who interviewed downtimer after downtimer had been here so long he was practically considered a legitimate 'eighty-sixer. Well, Skeeter wasn't a legitimate downtimer and he wasn't about to talk to Nally Mundy or any *other* historical scholars about *anything*, much less his years in Mongolia. In some ways, scholars were *worse* than newsies for nosing around in a guy's private life.

Mundy must've seen the news broadcasts or read the *Gazette*, which had reminded him to make The Monthly Call. Sometimes Skeeter genuinely hated

Nally Mundy for having come across that years-old scrap of newspaper clipping. Some thoughtless fool must've put it into a computer database somewhere, one that had survived The Accident, and Mundy—thorough old coot that he was—had run across it on a search for anything that survived relating to Temujin.

He actually groaned aloud while leaning his brow against the cold wall. The sound prompted a hesitant, "Have I called at an inconvenient time?"

Skeeter nearly laughed aloud, imagining all too clearly what the good historian must be thinking. Skeeter's reputation with women being what it was . . . "No," he heard his voice say, while the rest of him screamed, *Yes, you idiot! Tell him you're screwing some tourist through the bed so you can get out of here and steal anything you can get from all those Conquistadores! They're even stupider than you are!* But he couldn't very well *say* that. Fortunately, Dr. Mundy rescued him from saying anything at all.

"Ah, well, good, then." The good doctor—like all 'eighty-sixers—knew better than to ask Skeeter anything about his current affairs (business or otherwise), but some men were stone-hard persistent about Skeeter's *past* affairs. "Yes, then, well, to business." Skeeter reined in considerable impatience. He'd heard all this before from the fussy little man. "I'm starting a new series of interviews, you see, with generous compensation, of course, and there is so much you could reveal about Temujin's early years, the father and mother who molded him into what he eventually became. Please say you'll come, Skeeter."

Skeeter actually hesitated a moment. Generous compensation, huh? The old fiddler in other people's lives must've received a beaut of a grant from somewhere. And Skeeter *did* need money badly, for the bet. But Brian Hendrickson would *never* allow

money earned from an interview with Nally Mundy
to count toward his bet.

"Sorry, Doc. Answer's still no. Don't want my name
and photo scattered all over the goddamned world.
I've made a few enemies, you know, over the years.
Professional hazard. I'd be pretty goddamned stupid
if I let you put my name and photo all over your next
little research paper. Hell, it wouldn't be stupid, it'd
be *suicidal*. Forget it, Doc."

A nasal sigh gusted through the receiver. "Very well,
then. You do have my number?" (Skeeter had thrown
it into the trash a *long* time ago.) "Good." Mundy took
his silence for assent, a trick Yesukai had taught him:
when to speak and when to hold silent as a lizard on
the sun-warmed rocks. "If you change your mind
Skeeter, whatever the reason, whatever the hour, *please*
call me. We know so very little, really about Temujin,
his early childhood, his relatives—anything that could
shed light on the boy who grew up to be Genghis
Khan."

Skeeter did realize enough to know that sending
researchers down the gate would be tantamount to
murder. The scout who'd brought him back had died
in the attempt. Either Temujin's band of hunted
brothers and followers would kill them, or Temujin's
enemies would. He really *was* the only source. And
since Yesukai had taught him the knack of remaining
silent, he did so. The Dreaded Call would come every
month of every year, anyway, regardless of what Skeeter
did. Maybe one of these days he'd even be desperate
enough to accept Mundy's terms. But not yet. Not
by a long shot.

"Well, then, that's it, I suppose. I always hate letting
you go, young man. One of these days I'm going to
read in the *Gazette* that you've ended up dead through
one of your endless schemes and that would be a great

loss to scholarship. A very great loss, indeed. Do, please call, then, Skeeter. You know I'll be waiting."

Skeeter ignored the nearly overt sexual overtone to that last remark and thought, *Yeah, you'll be waiting in a pine box before I tell you a single syllable about Yesukai and his wife and their son* . . . The moon would turn blue, hell would freeze over, and Skeeter would settle down to a nice, *honest* way to make a living before he talked to Nally Mundy.

Yakka Mongols did not betray their own.

He snorted, checked his disguise in the mirror, smoothed out the smudge on his forehead where he'd leaned against the wall, then put Nally Mundy and his grandiose dreams of a Pulitzer or Nobel—or whatever the hell he'd win for Skeeter's interview—all firmly out of mind. He was actually whistling a jaunty little war tune when he locked his door and headed for the Conquistadores Gate with its truncated pyramid, colorful wall paintings, fabulous Spanish restaurants, "peasant" dancers whirling to holiday music played on guitar and castanet, their full skirts and rich, black hair flying on a wind of their own making—and, of course, dozens of piñatas in wild colors and shapes, hanging just out of reach, due to be smashed open at the appointed hour by as many kids as wanted to join in the fun.

Skeeter was whistling to himself again as he pilfered the equipment he'd need, then headed off to the Conquistadores Gate to see what profits might be drummed up.

Goldie Morran tapped slim, age-spotted fingers against the glass top of her counter and narrowed her eyes. Publish their bet, would they? She'd find a way to get even with that idiotic reporter, make no mistake about that. And the editor, too—another score to settle.

Goldie smiled, an expression that signalled to those who knew her well that someone's back was about to be stabbed with something akin to a steel icicle.

Goldie did not like to be crossed.

That ridiculous little worm, Skeeter Jackson, wasn't the only upstart on this time terminal who would pay for crossing her. The *nerve* of him, challenging *her* to such a bet. Her smile chilled even further. She'd already made arrangements for his eviction and uptime deportation, through a little side deal she'd made with Montgomery Wilkes. "I'll rid you of that little rat," she'd purred over a glass of his favorite wine.

Montgomery, nostrils pinched as though speaking to her were akin to smelling a skunk dead on the road for five days, said, "I know the kind of games you play, Goldie Morran. One day I'll catch you at them and send *you* packing." He smiled—and Goldie was smart enough to know that the head ATF agent on TT-86 had the power and the authority to do just that, if he caught her. Light glinted in his cold, cold eyes, always shocking with their contrast to his bright red hair. His smile altered subtly. "But for now, I'm more interested in Skeeter Jackson. He's a pest. Technically, he never enters my jurisdiction, so long as he doesn't try to take anything uptime, but he's bad for business. And that's bad for tax collection."

He leaned back in his chair, black uniform creaking where the creases bent, and held her gaze with a glacial smile.

Goldie, maintaining a smile that hurt her face, nodded solemnly. "Yes. I understand your job very well, Montgomery." Better than he understood it himself, the autocratic . . . "Believe me, I know just how bad for business the Skeeters of this world are. So . . . it's in our mutual interest to be rid of him. I win a harmless little wager, you say goodbye to a thorn in your side forever."

"If you win."

Goldie laughed. "*If?* Come, now, Monty, I was in this business before that boy was *born*. He doesn't have a chance and he's the only one in Shangri-La Station who doesn't know it. Draw up the papers. Date 'em. Then toss him through Primary and good riddance."

Montgomery Wilkes actually chuckled, a laugh Goldie got on tape—thereby providing the necessary proof she needed to win that little private wager on the side with Robert Li about the outcome of her conversation with the head ATF agent. Montgomery Wilkes had then drained his glass, nodded as pleasantly as she'd ever seen him nod, and had taken his leave, plowing through a crowd of tourists like a wooly rhinoceros charging through a scattered herd of impala.

Back in her shop, Goldie once again tapped her fingertips against the cool glass of her counter, then swept away the latest copy of the *Shangri-La Gazette* in one disgusted movement. The newspaper fluttered into the trash can at the end of the counter, settling like dead butterflies. *Skeeter win? Ha! That little amateur is about to eat his boast, raw.* The shop door opened, admitting half-a-dozen customers due to depart in a few hours through the South American Conquistadores Gate. They needed to exchange currency. Goldie smiled and set to work.

Marcus' shift ended shortly after the cycling of the Porta Romae, which left him rubbing shoulders with crowds of men and women dressed as wealthy Romans. Although he knew them to be impostors, he could not overcome the ingrained need, beaten into him over years, to scurry deferentially out of their way, to the extreme of hugging the wall with his back flat against the concrete when necessary to avoid offending any single one of them. Most were decent enough and a few even smiled at him—mostly women or young girls, or swaggering little boys full of themselves and willing to share their excitement with any passerby.

Several young men, however, had been seriously ill—a common enough occurrence for returning tourists. Downtimers like himself, hired as cleaning staff for the time terminal, were busy mopping up the mess. Marcus nodded to one he knew passingly well, a Welshman from Britannia who had pledged some sort of lifelong oath to Kit Carson—a time scout Marcus held in awe, almost more because of the kindness he showed Marcus than because he had once survived the Roman arena.

When Marcus nodded to Kynan Rhys Gower, he received a return grimace and half-hearted smile. "Stupid boys," Kynan Rhys Gower said carefully in the English everyone here used—or tried to. "They drink much, yes? Make stink and mess."

Marcus nodded Roman fashion, tipping his head back slightly. "Yes. Many tourists come back sick from Rome. Especially boys who think they are men."

Kynan's sun-lined face twisted expressively as he rolled his eyes toward the ceiling. "Yes. And Kynan Rhys Gower washes it."

Marcus clapped his shoulder. "I have done worse work, my friend."

The stranded Welshman—who had no hope at all of ever returning home, having stumbled into La-La Land through an unstable gate that had not opened again—met his gaze squarely. "Yes. Worse work. In Rome?"

Marcus didn't bother to hold in the shiver that caught his back. He couldn't have, had he tried. "Yes, in Rome." He was just about to speak again when a man dressed in an expensive tunic, wearing a gladius belted to his waist, stepped out from behind a vined portico and shot a tentative glance both ways before heading past them. Marcus blinked. He knew that face. Didn't he? He stared at the man's retreating back. Surely he was wrong. The face in his memory, the face *that* man wore, didn't belong to a tourist—it was someone he'd seen in Rome long ago, before his latest master had brought him to Time Terminal Eighty-Six then vanished uptime on his ever-mysterious business.

"Marcus?" Kynan asked quietly. "Something is wrong?"

"I—I'm not sure. I—" He shook his head. "No. It could not be. It is only a man who looked like someone I once saw. But that is impossible. All tourists look alike, anyway," he added with a feeble attempt at a grin.

Kynan laughed dourly. "Aye. Ugly and rude. I finish, yes? Then maybe you come to my room, we eat together?"

Marcus smiled. "I would like that. Yes. Call me on the telephone."

Kynan just groaned. Marcus laughed. Kynan Rhys Gower still called the telephone "Satan's trumpet"— but he'd learned to use it and was beginning to enjoy its convenience. Marcus had no idea who "Satan" was supposed to be. He cared very little for the religious beliefs of others in La-La Land, figuring it was a man's own business what gods he worshipped.

Whoever this "Satan" was, Kynan feared him mightily. Marcus admired the courage it took the Welshman to use the telephone. He was hoping time would cement the tentative friendship growing between them. Marcus had many who called him "friend" but very few he could truly call on *as* friend when trouble struck.

"I will call," Kynan agreed, "when I wash this. And myself." His grimace was all too expressive. Kynan's disgust of tourists ran far deeper than Marcus', who found most of their baffling antics amusing more than maddening.

"Good." Marcus gave him a cheery smile, then headed in the direction of his own rooms in Residential to shower and change clothing and see what he might contribute to the joint meal out of the family's meager supplies—riches, compared to what Kynan Rhys Gower would have at *his* place, though. He wondered if Ianira might have left one of her famous cheesecakes in the refrigerator. He grinned, recalling the sign Arley Eisenstein had posted in the Delight's menu-holder the last time Ianira had sold him a recipe: "A Bite of History . . . A Taste of Heaven." If she'd left any of their last one, he could raid a slice or two to contribute. Marcus' grin deepened as he recalled Ianira's astonishment over the *serious* discussions even important politicians and philosophers of Athens had held routinely on the merits of this or that type of cheesecake. He hadn't known the delicacy was so ancient.

Arley had paid her enough money that she'd been able to open that little stall he'd made for her in the Little Agora section of Commons, near the Philosophers' Gate, which was owned by the uptime government. Even Time Tours, the biggest company in the business, had to pay to send its tour groups through Philosophers' Gate. Tickets to ancient Athens were *expensive*. Several touring companies had even approached Ianira about guiding, for a fabulous salary and benefits. She'd turned them down in language they'd found shocking—but which Marcus understood in his bones.

He would not have set foot through the Porta Romae again for anything less than rescuing his family.

He was strolling toward her booth, to ask if she might like to join him at Kynan's place for dinner, when he spotted the man with the gladius again. Whoever the fellow was, he ducked furtively through a door which led to the storage rooms of Connie Logan's Clothes and Stuff shop.

Finding that peculiar, Marcus paused. Was the man on Connie's payroll? He knew the eccentric young outfitter constantly hired agents to travel downtime researching costumes, fabrics, utensils, and other assorted items used in daily life on the other side of La-La Land's many gates, but Marcus didn't know this man.

And there was still that odd tingle of near-recognition chilling his spine. It couldn't be . . . could it? He decided to wait, settling down beside a shallow pond stocked with colorful fish, and watched the door. Brian Hendrickson strolled by, deep in conversation with a guide. They were speaking Latin. From the sound of it, Brian was in the middle of a language lesson, stressing the finer points of conversational Latin to the relatively new guide. Across the way, Connie's storeroom door opened again. The man Marcus was following stepped out into the open. A woman nearby started to giggle. Even Marcus gaped. Cowboy chaps over jeans, topped by a Victorian gentleman's evening jacket, finished off by a properly wrapped but ludicrous toga and stovepipe hat . . .

For an instant, his gaze locked with the other man's. A dark flush stained weathered cheeks. The man Marcus was positive he'd seen before ducked back into Connie's warehouse. The giggling tourist caught a friend's attention and hurried over to tell her what she'd just seen. The door opened again moments later; this time, his quarry emerged wearing only the jeans and chaps and a western-style shirt. Marcus noted that he still wore the gladius, however, hidden carefully beneath the leather chaps. That worried him. *Should I report this?*

Concealed weapons were against station rules. Openly carried weapons were fine. But only when stepping through a gate was one permitted to conceal one's personal weapons. Those were the rules and Marcus was careful to live by them. But he also knew it wasn't always a good idea to mix one's affairs with those of a stranger. Well, he could always report the fellow anonymously to Mike Benson or one of his security men through a message on one of the library computers.

Or he could simply ignore the whole thing and go take that shower. He had just about decided on the latter course of action when the stranger turned to glance back at him. Something in the movement, the set of the mouth and the dark light in those eyes, clicked in Marcus' memory. Shock washed through him like icy water. He gripped his seat until his hands ached. It wasn't possible . . . yet he was *certain*. As certain as he had ever been about anything in his life. Sweat started under his shirt and dripped down his armpits.

Rome's Death Wolf, Lupus Mortiferus, had come to Shangri-La.

What purpose could the Circus's deadliest gladiator possibly have in coming here? Marcus the former slave didn't know—but he intended to find out. He owed the men and women who'd befriended him here that much. Heart in his throat, blood pounding in his ears, Marcus waited until the Wolf of Death turned his attention elsewhere, then cautiously eased from his seat and began to follow.

Skeeter Jackson, in heavy disguise, wheeled his cart toward a tourist near the Conquistadores Gate. The man was in the middle of a nasty harangue directed at a harried tour guide. Her face was flushed with anger, but her job prevented her from venting it. Skeeter stepped in with a smile.

"Sir, baggage check for leave-behind luggage?"

The man turned to note the other tagged suitcases on Skeeter's cart, each tag with the owner's name and hotel scrawled across it, with the tear-off stub missing. The tour guide's eyes met Skeeter's and widened in recognition. For a second, he thought he'd been blown for good. Then her eyes flashed briefly with unholy joy. She winked and fled, leaving Skeeter's quarry to his just deserts.

"Why, yes, that would be convenient. That idiotic guide—"

It was the same old story. Stupid tourist doesn't read the rules, then takes out his mad on the guides. Skeeter smiled as charmingly as he could—which was *very*— and tagged the man's expensive leather bags, tearing off numbered receipts which he handed over. "Thank you, sir. All you need to do to reclaim your luggage on return is present those claim stubs to your hotel. Have a good trip, sir."

The man actually tipped him. Skeeter hid a grin, then maneuvered his now-full cart toward the edge of the growing crowd. And there, just as he was passing a woman whose cases were also on his cart, it happened. He came eye-to-eye with Goldie Morran.

"Is that the man?" Goldie asked the tourist whose cases Skeeter had "checked."

"Yes!"

Goldie smiled directly into Skeeter's eyes. That was when he noticed security ringing the area.

"All's fair in love and bets, Skeeter, darling." Goldie's eyes glinted far back in their depths with murderous amusement.

It was either ditch hard-won gains or lose the bet—

and his home. Skeeter did neither. Goldie's own mouth
had uttered his one chance for salvation.

"Mike!" he yelled, "Hey, Mike Benson! Over here!"

Goldie's eyes went round and her pinched mouth
fell slack.

Benson lost no time approaching. "As I live and
breathe . . ."

Before he could finish, Skeeter said indignantly,
"Here I am saving these poor folks from Goldie's
clutches, making sure she doesn't make a grab for their
luggage, and *she* has the nerve to accuse *me*—well,
Mr. Benson, I want you to take a good look at these
tags, here. I was on my way to all these hotels to turn
over these cases, when Goldie, here, furious I'd got
in her way, started making nasty accusations."

Every tourist within earshot was goggle-eyed,
listening to nothing else.

Mike's forehead creased with vertical *and* horizontal
lines. "And you just expect me to swallow that pack
of—"

"Not only do I insist you believe it, I *demand* an
escort to every one of these hotels so I can make sure
every bag is locked safely away. Don't trust Goldie,
Mr. Benson. She might have me waylaid by some of
those paid thugs of hers."

Mike Benson stared from one to the other, then
started—astonishingly—to laugh. "Look at the pair
of you. Priceless! Okay, Skeeter my boy, let's go put
these cases in the hotels' lock-up rooms. I'll go along
just to be *certain* nobody waylays you on the trip."

Skeeter seethed inwardly, having hoped Mike would
let him just trundle his cart away for some time to
rifle the contents of watches, cameras, jewelry, etc.
Instead, he smiled and said, "Sure thing."

"Just a minute!" Goldie snapped. "If you're so
altruistic, why the disguise?"

Skeeter smiled into her eyes, noting the fury in them. "Why, Goldie, so your agents wouldn't recognize me and drop a sap across the back of my head to get these." He waved expansively at the suitcases. "There's gotta be a fortune in uptime jewelry in 'em, and who better than you to break up the pieces and fence the stones?"

Without waiting for a smarter and potentially deadlier protest from Goldie, Skeeter shoved his cart forward through the gaping crowd and sang out, "Coming, Mr. Benson? Gotta lot of work waiting, getting these good people's cases back safe."

Benson did as he'd promised, following Skeeter to each and every hotel on Skeeter's list. He verified each case as it was put into storage, then checked his list against Skeeter's supposed-to-be-fake manifest of names, hotels, uptime addresses, the works, not to mention the claim-ticket numbers. He grunted when the work was finally done. "Huh. Kept you clean this time, at least."

"But—Mr. Benson, you wound me. Honest."

"Don't 'Mr. Benson' me, punk. I was a damned fine cop before you were even born, so give it a rest. You came close, buddy, but you slithered out of it. Just be sure I'll be watching you double-close from now on."

"Well, sure. Hey, thanks for the escort!"

Benson just gave him a dour look. Skeeter lost no time vanishing into the thick holiday crowds, heading for the hotel he had "borrowed" the cart and claim tickets from. He didn't want to leave any loose strings if Benson should question the hotel manager or bellhops. Not that Benson could prove anything. He just didn't want to go through what Benson benignly referred to as his "lean-on-'em-a-little-and-they'll-sing" speech.

Although as the head of ATF's presence on TT-86,

meaning that technically, Montgomery Wilkes was the highest-ranking officer of the law on the station, Monty's actual jurisdiction was limited to the Customs area near Primary (much to Monty's everlasting, abiding rage, since he guessed how often he got hoodwinked outside that jurisdiction).

In all else, Benson reigned supreme. And if he wanted to keep Skeeter locked up for a month on bread and water, just for questioning, there was nothing in the station's charter that prevented him from doing just that. It was one of the reasons Skeeter was always so careful—and it was also the impulse behind his effort to try a little scamming downtime, away from Benson's watchful eye.

Of course, that'd nearly gone sour, *would have* if not for that gorgeous racehorse. The Lupus Mortiferus incident had prompted Skeeter to give up any further thoughts of downtime scamming until he knew a *whole* lot more about the culture he was planning to rip off. He understood far better, now, why guides and scouts spent all their free time—most of it, anyway—studying.

That Skeeter's target would be Rome again was a foregone conclusion, despite his somewhat desperate, drowning promise. He intended to hit rich Romans often and hard, because the arrogant bastards *deserved* it so much. But not just yet. He needed a lot of hours in the library and its soundproof language booths. And before he could do so much as that, he needed to win a little bet, first. Goldie had already proven ruthless enough to *arrange* for him to get caught.

Goldie'd get what she had coming, of *that* Skeeter was certain.

He could hardly wait to wave bye-bye as she hauled as much as she could afford to pay taxes on when she was forced uptime and use the rest of her assets to make bail. Skeeter chuckled. If things *really* went his way, he might even have enough at the end of the bet to buy out what Goldie couldn't take with her, including that breeding pair of Carolina parakeets some visitor had brought back from Colonial Williamsburg. Extinct birds, and she had a breeding pair of 'em. Could get more any time she wanted, too, by pulling the right strings—the ones attached to her downtime agents. Skeeter made a little wager with himself that Sue Fritchey didn't even know they were on station.

Well, if it came down to those birds (rumor had it Goldie was actually attached to them, emotionally) or Skeeter's continued life on TT-86, he'd know exactly what to do. Call up Sue Fritchey and make her famous all over again. Undoing Goldie in the process.

The klaxon and announcement came over the Commons' big speakers, warning of the impending cycling of the Conquistadores Gate. Skeeter grinned, wondering what had happened to Goldie after he'd left. Hopefully, at least a *third* of what she deserved, interfering like that in one of his scams. At least now he'd been warned about the way she intended to play this out, which *might* give him the edge he needed to win. Disconsolately, thinking of the *thousands* of bucks' worth of easily sold items in those lost suitcases, Skeeter headed for the library to have Brian value his "tips" into the official betting ledger.

Skeeter hunted him out behind the front desk, where the librarian was busy updating the computer's research index, actually deleting the lurid red "stamp" across the face of an entry page that read: ALL KNOWN COPIES DESTROYED IN AFTERMATH OF THE ACCIDENT. LIBRARIAN WILL UPDATE THIS LISTING SHOULD THIS STATUS CHANGE.

Brian didn't get a chance to remove very many of those stamps from the system.

"Hey, Brian. What turned up somewhere?"

Hendrickson swung around to face him. "Oh, it's

you." His accent was wildly at odds with his appearance, which was that of an ex-military, scholarly gentleman. His dark face curved into a genuine smile. Despite the words, he kept smiling. "Somebody found a copy of Pliny the Younger's collection of histories hidden in their grandparents' attic. Asked the nearest university were they interested or should they just toss it out? The university *paid* 'em for it—a hundred-thousand, I believe it was—and had an armored car with armed guards pick it up for safe transportation. *After* they sealed it in a nitrogen atmosphere.

"Anyway, the university scanned the whole bloody thing and started selling copies on CD to every time terminal library, every other university or public library that wanted one. Library of Congress asked for *five*."

Skeeter, who had no idea who Pliny the Younger was, managed to pull off a sufficiently impressed whistle of appreciation. "Weren't taking any chances, were they?"

"No. It's the last known copy in the world. A translation, as it happens, which is too bad, but still a copy, nonetheless. To scholars and scouts, it's absolutely priceless."

"Huh. I know you're not supposed to try and steal artwork from downtime unless you can prove it would've been destroyed anyway. Same goes for books and such, huh?"

"Oh, absolutely." Brian's eyes twinkled. "And Skeeter— don't even *think* of trying it. Stolen antiquities are out of both Mike's *and* Monty's jurisdiction. *That's* a federal matter and the bully boys uptime don't look too kindly on somebody breaking—at least, getting *caught* breaking—the First Law of Time Travel."

"So that's why Robert Li's our official representative of—" he had to stop a moment to recall the actual *name*, not just the acronym "—the *International Federation of Art Temporally Stolen*? So he can copy the stuff for everybody's use, then send an I.F.A.R.T.S. agent downtime to put it back where it came from?"

"Precisely. There's an enormous uptime market for such things." Brian looked at him. "And if you decide to join ranks with the breakers and smashers raping our past of its treasures, I'll testify at your trial and urge the death penalty."

Brian Hendrickson's intensity scared him a little. Skeeter held both hands up, palms toward the librarian. "Hey, I was just curious. I've got a lot of catching up to do myself, you know, since I never really finished grade school—never mind high school."

Homesick longing struck him silent before he could go any further.

Brian looked at him in an odd fashion for a moment, then—in a much gentler voice—asked, "Skeeter? Just why *did* you come here?"

"Huh? Oh." He dug into his pocket, pulled out the coins and bills he'd received as "tips" on the almost-successful suitcase pilfering he'd attempted, and explained what had gone down.

Brian glanced at the money, repeated Skeeter's story *word-for-word* (not scary—*terrifying*) then shook his head.

"What do you mean, the tips don't count?"

Brian Hendrickson, his dark face set now with lines of distaste, all trace of his earlier joy wiped away by deep unhappiness, said coolly, "You earned those tips for fair labor. If you'd succeed in stealing the luggage, the contents would've counted, but the tips still *wouldn't* have. So I can't count them now, even though they're all you managed to hang onto."

"But—but the damned tourists are *warned* they're supposed to check leave-behind luggage at the hotels, not with 'curbside' guys like me. The tips *are* stealing, same as the luggage would be."

Brian just shook his head. "Sorry, Skeeter. A tip is, by definition, something earned as part of a service accorded someone else. The cases are safely locked away, the tips are income—pure and simple—so your twenty-oh-seventy-five doesn't count."

Skeeter stuffed the bills and coins back into his pockets and stalked out of the library.

Who'd ever heard of such a thing, not counting scammed tips?

CHAPTER SIX

"Please have your timecards ready so the scanner can update them as you approach the gate . . ."

Goldie had, fortunately, managed to escape the angered, hot-blooded Spaniards who were the most frequent customers through the Conquistadores Gate. One lady about ten years Goldie's junior shoved through the crowd to follow.

"Wait! Wait, please, I wanted to thank you!"

Goldie stopped and turned, allowing a puzzled smile to drift into place. "Thank me? Whatever for?"

"For . . . for saving my luggage." The woman was still out of breath slightly. "You see, my husband and I were going downtime to research some of our ancestors. We'd planned to attend the hotel's Christmas ball as a kind of celebration after we got back and, I know I'm silly, but I packed away my gown and great-grandmother's diamond tiara, necklace, and a few other matching pieces *in* that suitcase. You've saved me so much grief! I never *did* believe the ridiculous story that young man told the security chief and neither did Rodrigo. Please, let me say thank you."

She was holding out a slightly used bill with a one and an undetermined number of zeroes after it.

"I couldn't possibly," Goldie protested weakly, having deciphered the number of zeroes. *A thousand dollars?*

105

"Oh, please, Rodrigo and I have more money than we know how to spend, but those jewels are absolutely irreplaceable. Please. Take it."

Goldie faked reluctance beautifully, allowing the other woman to push it into her slack hand. She closed careful fingers around the bill, and while she maintained an outward mask of surprise and lingering reluctance, inwardly she was gloating. *A thousand bucks! A thousand! Wait until Skeeter hears about this! Maybe he'll choke on envy and we'll be rid of him even sooner!*

Goldie thanked her generosity, pocketed the bill, reassured her that she hadn't missed the gate departure yet, then watched her disappear into the crowd milling around the waiting area. Then, exulting in her good fortune, Goldie headed toward the library, grinning fit to crack her skull. *Strike one, you little fool. Two more and you're out for the count!* Nobody loved a wager more than Goldie Morran—and nobody else in La-La Land came remotely *close* to Goldie's orgasmic pleasure at cheating to win. It was *not* how the game was played that counted with Goldie. It was about how much she could rook out of the opposition's wallet, downtime coinage, or bank account.

Just a few more days and Skeeter Jackson would be gone.

For good.

She passed Kit Carson, who was sitting at a cafe table sharing a beer with his pal the freelance guide, Malcolm Moore. She grinned and waved, leaving them to stare after her.

Let 'em wonder.

After what Skeeter had tried to do to Kit's grandkid, those two would surely be more appreciative than most when Goldie's plans came to full fruition. Goldie very carefully did *not* think about what *she* had very nearly done to Kit's granddaughter. Even Kit had eventually admitted the whole disaster had been entirely Margo's doing, accepting the challenge to go after those diamonds through an unstable gate.

Too bad about losing that scheme, though. Goldie sighed. Win some, lose some. At least Margo was uptime at school, toiling to repay her grandfather the money Kit had paid Goldie for that worthless hunk of African swampland. Goldie patted her pocket and regained her smile, then headed for the library so Brian Hendrickson could record her "take" in his official bet ledger. He might even laugh when she recounted her tale of that cretinous woman giving her a *reward*. La-La Land's librarian had so far found very little humor in Goldie and Skeeter's bet. This ought to change his tune.

Goldie didn't exactly *need* to stay in Brian's good graces to continue her own profitable business, but burning bridges unnecessarily was just plain-and-simple foolishness. There were certainly times when Brian's encyclopedic memory had proven useful to her. And there would doubtless be other times in the future she'd want to call on his knowledge. So, scheming and dreaming to her heart's content, Goldie Morran smiled at startled scouts on their way into or out of the vast library and found Brian Hendrickson on his usual throne.

The expression in his eyes was anything but welcoming.

"Hello, Goldie. What are you doing here?"

She laughed easily. "What do you think, silly?"

Brian just grimaced and turned back toward the master computer file he was updating.

"Here." She set out the thousand dollar bill that idiotic but *wonderful* woman had given her. "Put this on my ledger, would you, dearie?"

He eyed the money. "And how, exactly, did you come by it?"

She told him.

Then stormed out of the library, money stuffed back into her pockets. How *dare* he not count it?

"Reward for good deeds doesn't count, my eye! That overstuffed, self-important—"

Goldie *seethed* all the way back to her shop.

Once there, among her shining things, Goldie comforted herself with the knowledge that Skeeter's "tips" hadn't been counted, either. Then she got to work. Part of her mind was busy figuring out how to scam the next batch of tourists unfortunate enough to enter her shop, while another part was preoccupied with how to foil Skeeter's next attempt. That—plus a swig from a bottle she kept in reserve under her counter and fifteen minutes' solitude with her beloved, deeply affectionate Carolina parakeets—got her through a long, dead-flat afternoon. Not a single tourist entered to exchange uptime money for down or downtime coinage for uptime credit.

By the time Goldie closed her shop for the day, she was ready to do murder. And Skeeter Jackson's grinning face floated in the center of every lethal fantasy she could dredge up. She was going to win this bet, if it was the last thing she ever did.

And Skeeter would pay in spades for daring to challenge *her*!

Goldie entered the Down Time Bar & Grill, ordered her favorite drink from Molly, the downtime whore who'd stumbled through the Britannia Gate into TT-86, and settled in the billiards room to wait for some drunken tourist who *thought* he knew how to play the game to wander in and become her next victim.

Lupus Mortiferus was afraid—almost as afraid as he'd been his first time on the glittering sands of the Circus. He struggled not to show it. Nothing about this insane world made sense. The languages bombarding his ears were very nearly painful, they were so incomprehensible. Every now and again he would hear a word that sounded almost familiar, making the wrenching dislocation even worse. Some of the lettering on the walls reminded him of words he knew, but he couldn't quite make out their sense. And everywhere he turned were mysteries— terrifying mysteries—that beeped, glowed, hummed, screeched, and twittered in alien metals and colors and energies he would have called lightning or the ominous glow of the evil-omened lights in the northern night skies, had they not been imprisoned by some god's hand in pear-shaped bulbs, long tubes and spiralling ones, plus all manner of twisted shapes and disturbing colors of glass.

And the sounds . . .

Voices that erupted from midair, coming from nowhere that he could see, blaring messages he couldn't begin to understand.

Have I fallen into a playground of gods?

Then, unbelievably, he caught a snatch of Latin. Real, honest Latin.

" . . . no, that isn't at all what I meant, what you have to do is . . ."

With a relief that left him almost in tears, Lupus found the speakers, a dark man who was certainly of African origin: Carthaginian, perhaps, or Nubian— although his skin was too light for Nubia. He was speaking with a shorter, nondescript man in shades of brown at whom no one in Rome would have given a second glance.

Lupus followed them eagerly, desperate for someone he could actually communicate with in this mad place. He followed them to a room—a vast, echoing chamber of a room—filled with shelves of squarish objects made from thin vellum and rows of . . . what? Boxes men and women sat before and *talked* to—and the boxes talked back, their glowing faces flashing up pictures or streams of alien words.

Lupus held in a shiver of terror and wondered how to approach the dark man who clearly knew Latin better than the brownish one. He was about to approach when two *other* men entered and collared the dark-skinned man first. Lupus melted into the shadows behind a bank of tall shelves and hugged his impatience to his breast, biding his time until the dark man who could speak Lupus' tongue would be alone and approachable.

"So," Kit Carson asked, relaxing back into his chair, "what do you have planned for Margo's visit?"

Malcolm Moore flushed slightly. The light in Kit's eyes told him exactly what Kit expected them to do. Fortunately, Kit approved—provided Malcolm's intentions were honorable and he took reasonable precautions against pregnancy.

"Well," Malcolm said, running a fingertip through the condensate on the tabletop, "I was thinking of a little visit to Denver. I've checked my log entries— there shouldn't be any risk of Shadowing myself. I wasn't in London during the week the Denver party will be downtime."

Kit nodded. "I think that's a good idea. Margo should like it, too—and it'll complement her American History studies very nicely."

Malcolm grinned. "Sure you won't come along?"

Kit just grimaced. "I *was* in London that week. That whole month, in fact. You two lovebirds go along and have a good, careful time." Kit sighed. "It's strange. I didn't think it would happen, but . . . her letters are changing, Malcolm. Their tone, the intelligence behind her observations and comments."

Malcolm glanced up, noting the furrow on Kit's brow. "So you did notice? Figured you wouldn't miss it. She's growing up, Kit." That brought a flinch to his friend's eyes. He'd just barely begun to know her when she'd vanished: once, almost for good, the second time off to college. Trying to help his friend get used to the idea, Malcolm said, "Hell, Kit, she *grew up* in that filthy little Portuguese gaol. But now she's growing in ways it's hard to put into words."

Kit nodded. "Yeah."

Malcolm punched Kit's shoulder. "Don't take it so hard, Grandpa. Her mind's coming alive. I can hardly wait to see what directions her thoughts take her next."

Kit laughed sourly. "Just so long as it isn't toward a South African diamond field." Then Kit blinked and stared past Malcolm's shoulder. "Speak of the devil . . ."

Goldie Morran passed, smiling so sweetly at them Malcolm wondered who'd just died.

"What can *she* be up to?"

Kit laughed sourly. "Given that wager between her and Skeeter, God knows. Want to play tag-the-nanny goat and follow along?"

Malcolm grinned. "If that sour old goat has ever had kids, I'll eat this table. Goat I'll allow. Nanny? Not even in the British sense, Kit." His grin deepened, however. "Sure sounds like fun, though. Quick, before we lose her!"

Kit's eyes glinted as they scurried for the door, dropping more than enough money on the front counter to pay for consumables plus tip. Each of them knew the consequences should Goldie ever discover the double scam they'd pulled on her with Margo's help—not that she could really *do* anything, not legally, anyway. Their uptime diamond strike was one of La-La

Land's best-kept secrets. And *that* was a monumental achievement in its own right.

Malcolm and Kit quickly determined that Goldie Morran's goal was the library. They took up places at computer terminals near the counter, ostensibly doing research, but more than close enough to overhear Goldie's screech when her "take" was disallowed.

She stalked out of the library in a towering rage.

Kit stepped over to Brian's counter. Malcolm abandoned his computer, too, and leaned on his elbows beside Kit.

"So what's new?" Kit asked casually.

His long-time friend gave him an evil stare, then shrugged. In his wonderful, outlandish accent, he muttered, "Oh, why not. You're not involved, after all." Brian Hendrickson grimaced expressively, the skin around his eyes tightening down so much Malcolm grew alarmed. Then, curtly: "They have begun a war of attrition. A *serious* one. Goldie just spoiled one of Skeeter's schemes in a way that could have been fatal—for Skeeter, anyway. I suppose spoiling each other's schemes is better than letting them rip off unsuspecting tourists, but this . . . I didn't think their idiotic wager would turn this deadly. I suppose I should've seen it coming from the very start."

He wiped his brow with a handkerchief plucked from a pocket, then neatly folded and replaced it with such style, Malcolm found himself seriously envious of the librarian's unconscious panache. Malcolm clearly needed to do a covert study of Brian's movements and work until he'd copied them motion-perfect. On London tours, those elegant movements would serve him well. Particularly with the hopeful plans he'd been developing in the back of his mind. Then Brian sighed mournfully. "I still can't believe I allowed myself to be drawn into this."

Malcolm, who was about to comment that Brian had voluntarily put himself exactly where he was, abruptly spotted a man in Western getup watching them ferally from the shadows across the room. He blinked. *Not a scout, not a freelance guide, not even a Time Tours, Inc. guide.* Malcolm made it his business to keep close watch on the competition—particularly since Time Tours, Inc. was indirectly responsible for the death of his previous employer and close friend.

The mystery-man's face arrested his attention for a moment. *But I've seen that face before, I know I have. But where?* Maybe a tourist Malcolm had approached at some point, looking for a job? God alone knew, he'd begged work from thousands of transient tourists over the past several years, before he and Kit and Margo had become repugnantly wealthy. (They didn't flaunt it—didn't need to—but it certainly was a great deal of fun, just *looking* at his bank account's balance, which had hovered near negative numbers for so long.)

Maybe one of the tourists had remembered him and was looking for a good guide?

No . . . whoever he was, his attention was focused directly on Brian. For some reason he couldn't explain, that very fact sent a chill racing up Malcolm's spine. He wondered if he should speak, then thought better of it. If Brian Hendrickson had a profitable side deal going with someone, it was none of his business. But he did use it as an excuse to leave, now they'd discovered what they'd wanted.

Malcolm nudged Kit with an elbow. "I think there's someone waiting to talk to Brian. Why don't we grab a bite of lunch. I'll fill you in on my plans for Margo's visit."

Brian's expression cheered immensely. "Miss Margo

is returning? Capital! Have her come by and say hello, would you?"

Kit laughed. "Count on it. Malcolm's taking her to Denver. Even *with* her studies at school, she'll have timescout-type research to do before they step through the Wild West Gate."

Brian chuckled. "It's a date, then."

Malcolm cast a last, uneasy glance at the man in cowboy getup standing in the shadows, then shrugged the whole thing off. He had better things to look forward to: like Margo's kisses. He grinned in anticipation. The ring he'd had made from the sample diamond she'd sent was ready and waiting. All she had to do was say yes. Counting the hours and minutes until Primary cycled and brought her back into his life again, Malcolm strolled out of the library with his hopefully future grandfather-in-law and suggested the Epicurean Delight for lunch.

"We haven't been in a while. And I understand Ianira Cassondra's been selling Arley some ancient Greek cheesecake recipes—long lost delicacies and confections."

Kit nodded. "The Greeks were so fond of cheesecake, we have written complaints from a Greek, a married man who asked for cheesecake for his dinner and was, um, to put it delicately, irate when he didn't get it. Weren't there supposed to be dozens of different flavors?

Malcolm nodded. "Yeah. And from what I've heard, just one slice of whatever type of cheesecake he's made for the day is enough to make a California billionaire pay a thousand or more just to get the whole thing!"

Kit laughed, an easy, relaxed sound that reassured his friend. "Sounds great," Kit agreed—vehemently. "I've been hearing those same rumors and *I*, my friend, am a cheesecake-a-holic. Let's test it out, eh?"

Malcolm chuckled and thumped his friend's wiry, granite-hard gut and said, "At least you work it off somewhere."

Kit grimaced. "Sven Bailey is a fiend from Hell. He even *looks* like one."

"So I'd noticed. And so Margo complained— bitterly—those first few lessons with him. And then, would you believe it, our little imp started to *love* having Sven kick her around the mat like a sack of squashed potatoes."

"Ah, yes; but she learned, didn't she? C'mon Malcolm, let's eat! Skimpy lunch and all the cheesecake we can hold!"

They set out, laughing like kids. The "cowboy" they'd left lurking behind in the library was so far from his thoughts, it was almost as though the man had never existed.

Ianira Cassondra was attempting to sell an amber-and-silver bracelet and necklace set to a genuine tourist through the howling idiocy of her self-proclaimed acolytes. Did uptimers have nothing better to *do* with their lives than hound and harass her, day and night, month after tedious, temper-provoking month? The Little Agora was seething with gossiping 'eighty-sixers when Chenzira Umi—a grey-haired, stately Egyptian merchant who'd fallen, a drunken accident, through the Philosophers' Gate not too many months after Ianira had stumbled through—elbowed and shoved his way to the side of her little booth.

In Greek, which he spoke only well enough to dicker—*nobody* else on station (except the Seven) spoke his ancient Egyptian (although Ianira knew well enough that Chenzira earned much of his meager living by teaching his long-dead language's proper pronunciation, including some odd inflections, to uptime scholars), Chenzira reported. "Goldie badly done. She broke attempt by Skeeter."

"*What?*"

Ianira paled so disastrously the tourist dickering over the jewelry actually noticed—and frowned in genuine concern.

"My dear," he said in the drawling tones of an American Texan, "what in thunderation's wrong? You're whiter'n the underbelly of a rattler what's just shed his skin. Here, honey, sit down."

"Thank you, no, please, I am fine." She fought off shock and worry and mastered both, *plus* her voice. "I apologize profoundly for causing you distress. Did you want the bracelet and necklace for your wife?"

He glanced from Ianira to the jewelry, the calmly waiting Chenzira, bringer of bad tidings (noticeable in *any* language), then up at the surrounding vultures. He scowled impartially, evidently not liking his face and voice recorded without his permission any more than she did.

"How long these nosy bastards—uh—vultures been after you, honey?"

"Too long," Ianira said, half under her breath.

His pop-up grin startled her. "Hell, yeah, I'll take 'em, and throw in some of those funny-lookin' scarves there. Marty, my wife, she's nuts about stuff like that— yeah, those, right there—and what's this little doohicky here for? *Love* charm? Well, hell, gal, gimme a dozen of *those!*"

His friendly grin—despite Ianira's inner turmoil— was infectious. She rang up the bill, bagged everything into velvet bags she'd sewn herself—ending with one large easy-to-carry parcel with a secure drawstring, and handed him the itemized bill she'd written out in a somewhat shaky hand.

He handed back double the price listed on every

item, gave her a jaunty wink and an, "It'll be fine, honey, don't you fret, now, hear?" and vanished into the crowd before she could protest or give back the extra money. She stood trembling for a moment, the sounds and bright sights of the Commons washing over her like a dim, color-puddled dream, while she stared at money she and the father of her children so desperately needed, while on all sides, six to seven deep, her maddening acolytes Minicammed, voice-recorded, and jotted notes on every single second of that interchange. She wanted to scream at them all, but knew from experience any action other than business as usual would bring twice as many watchers who'd stay another week hoping a revelation would be near.

Chenzira leaned closer, his disgusted tone of voice helping bring her whirling mind back on track. "If I your beauty and charms had, Ianira, I, too, such deals make would. You demon are—under soft skin!" Gentle, deep laughter took any possible accusation from Chenzira's words. Along with the other downtimers in The Found Ones community—not to mention being elected to The Council of Seven almost from his first few weeks here—Chenzira was a born haggler, as many an unfortunate downtimer had discovered to his or her woe.

And since Chenzira Umi was as shrewd a man as Ianira had ever met, she, too, merely smiled. "And had I your canny wits," she countered calmly, "I would not be a huckster of this junk."

Chenzira smiled; but said nothing, in that mysterious Egyptian way of his. Ianira received the impression—a strong one—he still deferred to her as Head of the Seven. Then he leaned close again and said very quietly in his own language, which *all* of The Seven now had to learn, "You must convene the Council. The Seven must decide what is best and summon a general

Council immediately afterwards to vote on it. This atrocity, this interference *must stop*."

"Yes," she agreed, already somewhat proficient in Chenzira's native language. A smile tugged at her lips as she imagined the idiotic, eavesdropping throng trying to translate *this* conversation!

She asked—also in Egyptian—"Could you watch my shop a little?"

He nodded.

Ianira bolted from the booth, outrunning her merciless followers by a few staggering strides to a nearby hotel lobby. "Private in-house phone?" she gasped, damning the fact that women's clothing from her own time was *not* designed for an all-out, freedom-winning dash.

The desk clerk, who knew Ianira's reputation—and pitied her for the never-ending madness of her enthralled seekers—stepped back and all but shoved her into the hotel office, muttering, "Lock the door and I'll hold 'em at bay."

She gave him a startled glance of thanks, then banged shut the door and snapped the lock. It was cool and quiet inside the hotel office. She lifted the receiver and dialed a trustworthy in-house line. One phone call, she knew, would lead to others. Many others.

Having set things in motion, she returned to her stand, having to push her way through angry Seekers, all of whom were taller than she was, and forced on a bright smile for a couple of genuine customers who'd stopped to "window-shop."

"Thank you, Chenzira Umi," she said formally. "You have been of great help."

Chenzira's unexpected grin (as the Seekers took up their disgruntled positions, furious they'd missed even those few, short moments of The Great One's words) startled Ianira.

"What?" she asked.

Chenzira nodded at the man and woman peering at her stock. "Your previous customer knows them. They lost no time seeking out this 'find of the year' if I remember the words. I am not yet so good at English."

"Thank you, Chenzira Umi," she breathed as she turned toward her customers with a bright smile.

Chenzira Umi was long gone, faded into the crowd as nondescript as any other bald tourist, before Ianira noticed the new price markers. Her eyes widened ever so slightly: in her absence, he had doubled the price on *everything* she sold. And the customers were buying: jewelry, Greek-style clothing for both men and women (in a matching pattern she'd sewn lovingly), scarves, and charms of all sorts.

Even all the copies she had in stock of a little, hand-done booklet Dr. Mundy had helped her write, print, and bind, which they'd titled, *There I Lived: Athens in Its Golden Age and Ephesus, 5th Century B.C. Trading Center and Home to The Great Temple of Artemis, Seventh Wonder of the Ancient World*. The booklet was nothing, of course, to the scholarly work he was building from the sessions she spent with him, but it was a decently scripted, informal "chatty" little booklet full of odd little facts and anecdotes, some previously unknown until Ianira's arrival. It was a popular item, even outside the sales to maddening Seekers.

One of her long-term plans as First of the Seven was to assist other downtimers in writing similar booklets, which she would then sell and pass along the money to the authors, taking no commission, for this would be Found Ones' business, not her own.

By the time La-La Land's first-shift "business day" was over, that single phone call made from the cool, quiet hotel office—she must remember to reward that wonderful, understanding clerk with some little trinket of thanks—had borne its intended fruit. Ianira made her way to the madhouse of La-La Land's School and Day-Care Center where her daughters played with the other children. She picked them up, then took back-station staircases down into the bowels of Time Terminal Eighty-Six for a secret meeting of The Found Ones.

Since this was an informal meeting, no ceremonial garb was needed nor were her daughters a nuisance to anyone. Others of the Seven who had arrived ahead of her were already discussing the news. The day after Skeeter Jackson's gift to Marcus, Ianira had passed word of his true standing to other women in the downtimer community and they, in turn, had passed it to their men. Word had traveled through the entire community before bedtime. For the first time since their arrival, the downtimers of La-La Land knew that, alone of the uptimers, they had found someone who *understood*.

Many who had looked on him with disgust as a simple thief had immediately begun to cheer on his exploits. *Anything* to punish the uptimers who used them for grunt labor, without a single thought for their welfare, was worth a cheer or ten. Astoundingly, in a few short days Skeeter had rapidly taken on the status—thanks to Ianira's judicious meddling—of their champion and hero for causing uptimers to suffer monetary losses and public humiliations.

Also thanks to Ianira, it became unwritten law that Skeeter's past was a private secret to be kept from all uptimers on the station. Parents warned children— and those children held their tongues.

Word of the wager between Skeeter and Goldie Morran, at first simply an affair between uptimers, had abruptly taken on new significance. Fear like the shock-waves of an earthquake travelled through their community. If Skeeter Jackson lost his bet, they would lose their spirit-champion. So when Ianira placed that phone call and word spread that Goldie Morran had deliberately spoiled one of Skeeter's attempts, and that a general session would follow a meeting of the Seven, narrow-eyed men and women gathered in the depths of Shangri-La Station to discuss what should be done about it, while wide-eyed children listened in silence to the anger in their elders' voices.

"We could slide a knife between her ribs," one grey-haired man muttered.

"Poison would be better," a younger man countered. "She would suffer longer."

"No, we don't need to kill her," Ianira said over the babble of voices as she joined the other Six on the low dais. Silence fell as abruptly as night fog rolled over the wharves of Ephesus. The Seven had previously decided the only course they *could* safely take. Now it was up to the Seven to convince the others.

She held her daughters close, partly from protective love she could scarcely give coherent tongue to, and partly because she was—as a former high-ranking Priestess of Artemis—aware of the symbolism their stance of togetherness roused. Those who stood nearest to her saw not only a mother and her children, but looked at her little girls and understood in their viscera that the children's father owed more than anyone on this station to Skeeter Jackson.

Which was precisely what she *wanted* them to think.

Had she been born uptime rather than down, she'd have been running the government inside two years.

Although most of the gathered Found Ones came from times and places where women were expected to remain silent on pain of beating, even men who had grown to grey-beard stature had learned to respect Ianira—and in this matter, she had the right of a mother whose children were threatened. That right was so universal, even those men who had found the adjustment to TT-86 and—in particular—the status of women in TT-86, held their tongues and listened in respectful silence.

She looked from face to silent face and nodded slowly, understanding their message without the need for words. "We don't need to kill her," Ianira repeated. "All we need to do is ensure she loses her bet."

The smiles that lit multiple eyes—dark eyes and light ones, black and grey and brown and blue ones, and the occasional clear amber or green ones—all were smiling, cold as Siberian ice.

"Yes," someone on the edge of the crowd murmured, "the gems dealer must lose that bet. Which would be the better strategy, Council? Help Skeeter with his work? Or plot to destroy the money-changer's schemes?"

Ianira laughed, tossing thick, black hair across one pale shoulder. "Destroy the money-changer's schemes, of course. Skeeter can hold his own when it comes to stealing from the uptimers who kick and rob so many of us. All we have to do is make sure the money changer steals less. *Much* less. It ought to be fun, don't you think?"

Laughter rippled through a group which moments before had been grim enough to contemplate violent murder, consequences be damned—just the thing the Seven had feared. Agreements were made to watch the money-changer's every move. Assignments were given to those best suited to the task of foiling Goldie Morran's schemes—or, if necessary—stealing her winnings before she could "log" them with Brian, as the rules of the wager demanded.

Ianira kissed her daughters' hair and smiled softly.

Goldie Morran would rue the day she had dared interfere with Marcus' patron and champion. Rue it as bitter as wormwood and never once guess why she failed in her every effort. Ianira pledged silent sacrifices to her patron Goddess Artemis of moon-pale hunting dogs and silver arrows notched through eternity to her moon-wrought bow, as well as pledges to her adopted Goddess, Pallas Athena of spear and shield, Athenian war helmet and above all *Justice*, should they secure victory for Skeeter Jackson.

She left the meeting with her own assignment and returned home to put supper into Artemisia and Gelasia, then put both girls into their little beds. She worked on Council business, while waiting with great anticipation for Marcus to finish his shift at the Down Time Bar & Grill.

She hummed an *old* tune as she worked, one her grandmother had taught her as a child, all the while quietly hugging to herself the secret of the astonishing money she'd made at the booth today—thanks to wise, old, mercenary Chenzira's meddling with her prices. In the all-but-silent backdrop of their apartment, the dinner she'd prepared for her love bubbled and simmered its way toward perfection in the endlessly miraculous oven.

Goldie was cashing out money for tourists returning uptime from a tour when she spotted them: three small, innocent-looking coins that were worth several thousand dollars each, they were so rare. Avarice warred with caution. She wasn't supposed to make use of her knowledge to obtain them. She couldn't buy them at a fraction of their value and claim the collector's price or Brian would disallow them completely. So she smiled in her cold heart and simply short-changed the tourists. Stealing the coins should certainly count. She waited until the batch of tourists had gone before putting up her "Out to Tea" sign and locking up the shop.

She could hardly wait to gloat to Skeeter about the day's success. Goldie headed for the library at full tilt, a battleship plowing through seas of disgruntled tourists, and cornered Brian behind his counter.

"Brian! Just take a look at these! Stole 'em fair and square!"

Brian examined the coins with care. "Very nice. Mmm . . . Yes, very nice, indeed. Let's see, now." He glanced up, a frosty look in his dark eyes. "Valuing these is really quite simple. This one, that'll give you a bet credit of twenty-five cents, this one's face value is what, thirty-five cents? Hmm . . . The silver content of this one's a little thin. I'd say about a buck thirty for the three."

Goldie stared, mouth agape and not caring who saw it. She honestly couldn't find her voice for whole seconds. When she finally *did* find it, heads turned the length of the library.

"*What?* Brian Hendrickson, you know perfectly well what those three—"

"Yes," the librarian said repressively, interrupting her before the tirade could build momentum. "Their *collector's* value is probably in excess of five thousand dollars. But I can't give you that kind of credit for them and you know it. Rules of the bet. You stole a couple of coins. Face value—or metals value, whichever is higher. That's it. Feel free to sell them for what they're really worth, but you won't get credit for that on the bet."

He pulled out a little ledger book and made an entry. Goldie couldn't believe it. A dollar and thirty stinking cents. Then she caught sight of Skeeter's last entry in a column next to hers: zero.

That was something. Not much, but something.

Goldie stormed out of the library, determined to eat Skeeter Jackson's liver for breakfast. Chuckles behind her only rubbed salt in a raw wound. She'd pay Brian back, too, she would. Just wait and see if she didn't. A buck-thirty. Of all the humiliating, backstabbing—

A feathered *Ichthyornis* screamed past on a power-dive into a nearby fishpond. The splash drenched Goldie from waist to knees. She screeched at the toothed bird and cursed it in language that caused mouths to drop in a fifty-foot radius. Then, catching herself, Goldie compressed her lips, glared at the people staring at her, and sniffed autocratically.

Skeeter might be behind, but a dollar and thirty cents wasn't a lead, it was an insult. She'd show that upstart little pipsqueak what an amateur he really was or her name was not Goldie Morran. She smiled tightly. The expression hurt the skin of her face and started a nearby toddler whimpering against its mother's skirts.

Goldie Morran had not yet *begun* to scam.

Skeeter, having successfully picked several pockets in a crowded cafe, returned to the library to hand over his take for Brian to hold, per the rules of the bet. When he caught sight of Goldie's last entry, he laughed out loud.

"A buck thirty?" His laughter deepened, the primal joy of a half-wild Mongol who has pulled one over on the enemy.

Brian shrugged. "You're taking the news more cheerfully that she did."

"I'll bet!"

Brian said repressively, "You already have, Jackson. Now beat it. I have *real* work to do."

Skeeter laughed again, refusing to be insulted, and

let his imagination linger on what Goldie's face must have looked like as she received the unpalatable news. Bet her face had gone nearly as purple as her hair! He strolled out of the library, hands in pockets and whistling cheerfully. The Commons certainly was a pretty place this time of year . . .

A heavy hand grabbed his shoulder, spinning him roughly around. His back connected with a concrete wall, driving the breath momentarily from his lungs. Skeeter blinked and focused on the face of a man he'd last seen standing on the banks of the River Tiber, cursing him for all he was worth.

Oh, shit—

Lupus Mortiferus.

In modern clothes and a towering rage. "Your entrails aren't really worth a hundred-fifty gold *aurii*—but they'll do!"

"Uh . . ." Skeeter said, trying to buy time before the gladiator choked and/or stabbed the life out of him. *How the hell did he get onto the station?* Not that it mattered. He was *here*—and one look into those dark, murderous eyes told Skeeter he was about to die.

Or worse.

So Skeeter did the only thing that might possibly save him. He dropped to the floor like a limp rag doll. His opponent paused just an instant too long. Skeeter rolled, kicked Lupus Mortiferus' feet out from under him, scrambled up, and *ran*. A bull's bellow of fury followed him. One quick glance showed the enraged gladiator in close pursuit. *No river to jump into this time. No horse to steal, either. How the hell did he get into TT-86?*

He wove and dodged through the dense holiday crowds, ducked past a cluster of blinking, six-foot-five decorations, and shouldered someone aside when they blocked his way. An autocratic screech and a splash were followed by Goldie Morran's voice cursing him in language almost as colorful as Yesukai at his best. He took a brief second to wish he'd had the time to enjoy the sight of Goldie dripping wet from purple hair to spike-heeled toes—but that gladiator was right on his heels. He rounded the fish pond and pounded through Edo Castletown. In his wake, men dressed like samurai shouted obscenities at his pursuer, who shoved several of them bodily to the floor in his charge.

Ooh, Yakuza, Skeeter thought with a wince as he glanced back to see tattooed men swearing at the gladiator's back. Too bad they hadn't managed to lay hands on him.

He pounded out of Edo Castletown into Frontier Town, with its Wild West Gate, bars, saloons, and show-girl halls. Frontier Town's saloons offered a confusing maze of darkened rooms where bar girls served whiskey, poker games lasted until all hours, and rinky-tink piano players hammed it up on artificially battered upright pianos. Skeeter ducked into the nearest, sliding *under* a series of tables in the dim-lit bar, scattering card players and whiskey glasses in his wake as men jumped back in startled surprise. Then whole tables crashed to the floor behind him. The gladiator had waded in, snarling something in Latin. A fist fight broke out somewhere to his rear. Skeeter didn't care. He dove across the bar, catching a glimpse of the barkeeper's shocked expression in the mirror, then hauled butt back for the door while Lupus Mortiferus battled his way through a mob of really pissed-off "cowboys"— including at least one wrathful time scout who knew martial arts.

Having bought himself a couple of minutes' lead, Skeeter blasted through the saloon doors into the

bright Commons again and pelted back through Edo
Castletown, where the first Shinto observances had
begun at the new shrine. A deep bell-tone shimmered
through the air as the first worshipper pulled the
bell-rope to sound the gong that would catch the
attention of the resident, sacred *kami*. A glance over
his shoulder revealed the irate gladiator battling his
way past a dozen *really* irate Yakuza thugs. Lupus
Mortiferus had knocked them down on their first
dash through Castletown, causing them to lose serious
face in public. They were out for vengeance. He
grinned, leaped the low fence marking off the new
shrine, gaining traction in the expanse of white gravel,
ducked *under* the shrine, and vaulted the fence on
the other side while outraged Japanese curses poured
after him in waves. One swift glance showed Lupus
Mortiferus in even greater trouble as the worshippers
vented righteous ire upon the gladiator.

Sorry about that, really, Skeeter told the certain-
to-be-offended *kami*. *I'll, uh, come ask your pardon
later. Honest.*

Skeeter cut hard into a side corridor leading toward
the maze of corridors that made up Residential. A
bellow in the distance told him the chase, although
badly slowed for Lupus Mortiferus, was still on.

Skeeter pelted up a staircase and rounded a wicked
bend at a full run, grabbing a heavy rope garland and
swinging around the *outside* of the girder that
supported a balcony platform above, using it like
Tarzan's vines to whip around at maximum speed.
Below him, gasps of shock and fear arose from the
packed Commons floor. *Great. All I need's an audience.*
Three changes of corridors, two more staircases, and
another turn brought Skeeter out onto a wide balcony
of shops and restaurants overlooking Commons.

Far back, but rounding the corner after him, Lupus

Mortiferus was still coming. *Cripes, doesn't anything stop that guy?* Skeeter tipped over clothing racks, cafe tables, and fully-lighted Christmas trees. He kept running, providing any and all barriers he could that the gladiator would have to jump or pick up first, then skidded down a gridwork staircase, mostly sliding down the banister. A flock of roosting pterosaurs screeched and took wing in protest. They swooped and dove, knocking wreathes, plastic candy canes, and all sorts of other decorations off girders and balconies—which created panic amongst the tourists gaping in his wake.

Skeeter heard curses—but they were farther and farther behind. He hit the next balcony level still running flat out, slammed a seven-foot plastic Santa to the balcony floor behind him, and spotted an open elevator. Skeeter grinned and dove into it. He punched 5 and the doors closed. The elevator shot upward, carrying him to the upper floor of a hotel's graceful balcony. Skeeter stepped out onto lush carpet, rather than bare gridwork, hearing the very distant sounds of pursuit below, then slipped into the hotel's hallway, covered with a different color carpet, but just as luxurious as the balcony's. Skeeter jogged easily down the line of gilt-numbered doors and found an interior elevator which took him to the basement.

Under the hotel were weapons ranges and a gym. Skeeter ducked through the gym, found another elevator tucked back in the men's shower area, which had been placed there for the convenience of residents who wanted to head straight up after a workout. He rode it up to the third level of Residential.

When he finally stepped out into a silent corridor, there was no sign of the gladiator. Skeeter leaned against the wall and drew several deep breaths, then slowly relaxed. He couldn't help grinning. What a chase! Then reality settled over him like a blast of Mongolian snow. With

Lupus Mortiferus on the station, Skeeter was in real trouble. What to do about it? Skeeter narrowed his eyes. He could always go to Bull Morgan and report the downtimer, but that would mean having to confess his downtime scam to the station manager. And that would get him into serious legal trouble with Management—with a probable eviction from TT-86 as the result. He wouldn't need to lose the wager to lose his home.

If the gladiator were reported—and questioned—the result would be the same. The damned gladiator would be given refuge, but Skeeter would be kicked uptime to fend for himself in a world he had grown to hate. And if that gladiator caught up with him, he was a dead man.

"Great," Skeeter muttered to the listening walls. "Not only do I gotta win this bet, now I gotta stay alive while doing it."

He straightened his shoulders and lifted his chin. The boy who'd survived life in Yesukai's camp wasn't a quitter. He was no professional fighter—certainly no match for someone like Lupus Mortiferus—but he knew a few tricks. He wasn't happy, but he'd cope.

He always had, no matter what life handed him.

Tired, hungry, and thirsty, Skeeter headed for his little apartment, hoping Lupus Mortiferus didn't tumble to the fact that any computer in La-La Land listed his address bold as a Mongolian sky, on an entry screen Skeeter couldn't hack into and purge—not without drawing serious attention to himself from Mike Benson's sharp-eyed gang. He thumbed open his door and retreated into his private little refuge to fret over the problem, knowing as he opened the fridge for a beer and turned on the shower that wishing would *not* make this particular problem vanish.

He took a long pull from his beer and made the wish anyway.

From his viewpoint, Skeeter figured the gods owed him a break or two. For once, maybe they'd listen?

Lupus Mortiferus stood panting in the middle of an empty corridor, hand on the pommel of his gladius, eyes narrowed in a rage that filled his veins until his ears roared with it. *Where* had that little bastard slipped away to? So close . . . and the rat had vanished into thin air.

Again.

"I will find you, *odds maker*," Lupus swore under his breath. "And when I do . . ."

Meanwhile, he had to find someone to communicate with. That dark-skinned man had answers Lupus needed. It took him nearly an hour of confused wandering through the mad place before he found it again, but find it he did. And the man was still there, perched comfortably behind a wooden counter. Girding on courage as though it were armor, Lupus strode up to the counter and greeted him in Latin.

The man glanced up, surprise showing in deep brown eyes. "Hello. Guide? Or scout? Don't think I've seen you before. Just in from another station? Brian Hendrickson, Station Librarian."

The man stuck out a hand.

Lupus stared at it, wondering what in the world the man was babbling about. The words were Latin, but their meaning . . . He might as well have been speaking some obscure desert tongue like Palmyrene or the incomprehensible babble of a Scythian horseman.

"Well," the man was saying, staring at him with rising curiosity, "the computers are at your full access, of course. With that getup, I'd thought you were headed down the Wild West Gate. Planning on a freelance trip to Rome? It's a lucrative gate, certainly, and thanks to Kit's leaning a little on Bax, Time Tours is giving freelancers a freer hand with the customers. You shouldn't have any problem at all making a good living if you decide to stay."

The man made no sense at all. With a rising sense of panic he couldn't control, Lupus tried to marshall a single question, but found his tongue glued to the roof of a mouth gone dry with fear. *The gods make sport of me for fun. . . .*

Whatever the man said next, it wasn't in Latin. His brow furrowed in open puzzlement. That was more than Lupus could take. He couldn't afford to be found out as an imposter in this place of divine madness. He bolted for the door. *Mithras, help me*, he prayed in growing misery. *I don't know where to go or what to do*. Lupus didn't quite run down the bewildering confusion of staircases, ramps, shops, ponds, and imitation streets that made up the main room of this world, but he moved fast enough to put distance between himself and the man who was most certainly coming to the conclusion that Lupus did *not* belong here.

He was halfway down the long, long stretch of room when he realized he was being followed. The man was younger than he, brown-haired and slender enough that Lupus could easily break him in half with bare hands. Lupus knew a jolt of fear that stabbed from heart to groin, anyway. The gods who ran this mad playground had found him out.

Then anger, pure and simple, scalded him to his bones.

I have been swindled, cheated, and dragged out of my very world. I will not submit meekly to this!

He took a side corridor that led into a quiet, private part of this world and hid in a shadowed niche. Sure enough, the young man following him took the same turn. Lupus gripped his sword and slid it sweetly out of its scabbard. *Someone* would give him answers or pay the consequences of their refusal.

He waited patiently for the quarry to come close enough to strike.

One moment, Marcus was completely alone in the Residential corridor, having lost sight of his quarry. The next, he was crushed painfully against the wall, sword at his throat. He gasped. Lupus Mortiferus . . .

Shock detonated in the other man's eyes. Marcus only realized he'd gasped the man's name aloud when the gladiator demanded, "You know who I am?"

"I—" Marcus thought he might well faint from terror. How many men had the Wolf of Death killed during his bloody career? The thought of leaving Ianira and little Artemisia and Gelasia alone, trying to survive without him, drove him nearly to gibber. "I know—I know you, yes. I saw you, once. Many years ago. Before a fight. At—at one of the gladiator feasts—"

The sword blade stayed pressed against his throat. "Where am I? What place is this? And why have the masters of it sent you trailing my steps?"

Marcus blinked in surprise. "Nobody sent me. I saw you earlier and thought I recognized you. I—I just wanted to ask what you were doing here. You shouldn't be here at all. Please, I beg of you, Lupus Mortiferus, don't kill me, I have children, a family—"

The blade remained at his throat, but the pressure eased up just a bit. "Kill you?" the gladiator snorted. "The only man in this mad place who speaks Latin that makes sense? Do you think the Wolf of Death a complete fool?"

Marcus began to hope he might survive. "How *did* you come here? The Roman gate is very well guarded—" His eyes widened. "Those boys who got sick, when the gate cycled. You must have come through during the confusion."

Lupus Mortiferus narrowed dark eyes. "Gates? Talk sense. And answer my question! *Where am I?*"

Marcus knew he'd once been a slave, but it had been years since anyone had used that tone with him. "The last time I saw you," he dared flare back, "you were still a slave. Where is your collar? Or have you run from the school?"

Lupus' dark eyes widened. For an instant, Marcus saw his own death reflected there. Then—shocking him beyond all reason—the Wolf of Death lowered his sword. "I bought my freedom," he said quietly. "Then the money I earned with this sword, the money I was saving to start a new life, was stolen by a black-hearted street-rat of a foreigner. I followed him here." The threat returned to his eyes. "Now tell me, *where is 'here'?*"

Marcus blinked several times, struggling with emotions that ran the gamut from pity to terror and back again. "If you will put away the gladius, I will tell you. In fact, if you put away the gladius, I will take you to my own rooms and try to help you as best I can. What I have to say will not be easy for you to understand. I know you are a proud man, Lupus Mortiferus—you have a right to be—but you will need help to survive here." Some glint in Lupus' dark eyes told Marcus he'd hit a raw nerve. "I have a woman and daughters to support, but I will do my best to help. From what I remember, you didn't begin your life in Rome either. In that, we have something in common. You have asked for answers. I offer them and more. Will you come with me?"

The gladiator paused for several heart-shattering moments, then sheathed his sword under the ridiculous cowboy chaps. The gladius snicked softly into place under the concealing leather. "I will come. I think," he said softly, "the gods have left me no choice."

The admission shocked Marcus speechless.

But he recalled all too vividly his own first days in La-La Land, with their wrenching, sick dislocation and the terror every sight and sound brought. This man had been badly wronged by someone from TT-86. Marcus would do what he could to make amends.

The Wolf of Death followed silently behind as Marcus led the way toward his small apartment. He wondered with a sinking terror in his gut what Lupus Mortiferus would do when he saw Ianira's delicate beauty. He was strong enough—and ruthless enough— to take her while Marcus watched helplessly from the floor, bloodied and dazed, perhaps even bound and gagged. Surely Lupus would adhere to guest/host laws? But Lupus was neither Roman nor predictable. Marcus had no idea what he would or wouldn't do.

But he had given his word and Lupus Mortiferus had been wronged.

And the laws here, he recalled with effort, were not those of Rome. If Lupus Mortiferus tried to hurt his beloved, he *could* call for help—or send her and his daughters to live with others who could and would protect them.

Afraid and torn between honor and multiple duties, Marcus led the gladiator to his little home deep in the recesses of Residential.

Ianira had just taken a cooling cheesecake out of the oven, placing it on a rack on the counter beside simmering pots and sizzling pans filled with their dinner, when the apartment door opened. She glanced up, a smile on her lips . . . and let the smile die, unborn, at the look in Marcus' eyes. His face was ash pale.

He held the door for a stranger dressed for the Denver Wild West Gate. Eyes downcast, Marcus' posture screamed his feelings of fear and inferiority. The stranger's dark gaze darted about the room, paused briefly on her, then returned to a scrutiny of the room as though expecting it to contain lethal traps.

With her eyes alone, Ianira sought Marcus' gaze and begged the question: *Is this the man? Your former master?* She realized she'd begun to tremble only after the slight movement of Marcus' head indicated, *No, this is not the one.*

The relief that flooded her whole being was shortlived. If this were not Marcus' mysterious uptime previous master, who, then, that he inspired such terror and deference in her beloved? When Marcus spoke, he spoke in Latin and kept his voice soft—the voice of a slave addressing a social superior from his own world.

"Please, you are welcome to my home. This is Ianira, the mother of my children. A high-born woman of Ephesus," he added with just a touch of defiant pride in his eyes and voice. The dark-eyed stranger gave Ianira a long, clear-eyed stare which left her trembling again—from anger, this time. She knew the look of a man hungry for a woman's body. That look was a ravening fire in this man's eyes when he stared at her.

"Ianira, Lupus Mortiferus has stumbled through the Porta Romae in pursuit of a man who stole his money. He needs shelter and our help."

Ianira relaxed marginally, but remained alert for trouble. Why was Marcus so visibly shaken, so subservient, if all he offered was asylum to a fellow downtimer in need? By rights, he should be playing the role of social superior, not struggling to hide obvious terror.

Taking the plunge, Ianira recalled her duties as

hostess in Marcus' home. "You are welcome as our guest," she said in her careful Latin. Marcus spoke Greek better than she spoke Latin. Their common household tongue was English. Living as they did, it was a survival ritual they practiced as much for the sake of their children as for the practice speaking the dominant language of the time terminal. Most of the languages Ianira heard spoken on the station—particularly Japanese—were utterly beyond her. But English she learned from necessity and Latin she learned from love. She could even understand a little of Marcus' native Gaulish, although he rarely used it except to swear at or by gods neither Athens nor Ephesus had ever known.

Marcus gazed worriedly at the man who continued to stare at Ianira as though the jeans and T-shirt she wore didn't exist. The look sent chills down her back and made her long to close her hands around a weapon to defend herself.

"Ianira," Marcus added with a touch more courage in his eyes, "is highly placed on the Council of Downtimers in this world. She owns her own business and is well respected even by those from uptime, who control the fate of all downtimers who stumble into the station. She is important in this world." The warning in his voice was unmistakable—and it had effect. Lupus Mortiferus' look changed from that of a man who is considering taking what he desires by force to that of speculative curiosity.

Marcus ended the introductions by saying quietly, "Ianira, Lupus Mortiferus is the most famous gladiator to fight in the Circus Maximus at Rome. He has won the Emperor's favor many times and has killed his way to victory in more than a hundred fights by now, I should guess. He will need our help adjusting to La-La Land and to find the thief he seeks. It is his desire to find that thief, recover his stolen money, and return home."

That was against the law. They both knew it.

But a man like Lupus Mortiferus, who had survived combat in the arena, wasn't likely to abide by any such rule. Clearly, Marcus wanted only to help him regain his money as quickly as possible so the man *would* leave again. Ianira found herself agreeing with that silent desire which burned so brightly in Marcus' frightened eyes. She did not want Lupus Mortiferus to stay on Time Terminal 86. The shorter his visit, the greater her peace of mind. But until he left, he was an invited guest in the home of the father of her children.

She gestured gracefully, playing the role she had learned so well under the lash in her husband's home. "Please, come in. Sit down. The evening meal is nearly ready. It is very simple fare, but nourishing, and there is Greek cheesecake for afterward."

Lupus Mortiferus' eyes came back to hers. "Greek? I thought you were from Ephesus?"

"I was born in Ephesus, yes, but came to live in Athens for a year before stumbling through the Philosophers' Gate, as it is called here. You came here by way of the Porta Romae."

Lupus treated them to a mirthless laugh. "Gate of Rome. How incredible. So you really did live in Athens? The cheesecake is genuine?"

She held back a proud, haughty smile by main force of will. Romans felt a humble respect for anything Greek, believing—as well they ought!—that Greek culture *was* culture.

"I have heard much of Greek cheesecakes from wealthy patrons."

Ianira forced a light laugh. "Indeed, my recipes are genuine. I knew them by heart—and I *was* born about six hundred years before you were."

Shock detonated in the man's dark eyes.

Ianira laughed again, knowing she played a deadly game, but knowing also that she could more easily risk it than a man. "Welcome, Lupus Mortiferus, to La-La Land, where men and women from many different places and times come together under one roof. You have much to learn. Please. Sit down and rest. I will bring refreshments for you and serve the dinner. Then we will talk of things you must know in order to survive here."

The piercing look he gave her was difficult to interpret, but he took a seat on their plain brown couch. The vinyl squeaked as the leather of his chaps rubbed it. Ianira noticed the sword half concealed beneath them, but said nothing. Guest laws notwithstanding, Lupus Mortiferus was a man lost in a world he could not possibly comprehend—one that Ianira herself, after three years, took mostly on faith, translating "technology" into "magic" for anything she didn't understand.

For what it was worth, she knew there were *up*timers who did the same when confronted by the power of the gates through time.

As for the weapon, keeping it would reassure him, more than any words of welcome they could offer. Ianira served fresh fruit juice to the men, deciding against the wine she'd previously planned for their dinner—she had no intention of serving alcohol to a potentially explosive guest—then returned to the kitchen. Marcus would normally have joined her to help, but the presence of their guest held him against his will in the room that served double duty as living and dining area.

Artemisia, strapped into her toddler's high chair beside the device that kept foods and drinks wonderfully chilled, even frozen, cooed and giggled at her mother's reappearance. Ianira stooped to kiss her child's hair, then filled a bottle with apple juice and gave it to the little girl. While Gelasia slept peacefully in the crib in their one bedroom, Artemisia sucked on the rubber nipple contentedly, gurgling occasionally as her wide, dark eyes followed her mother's movements around the kitchen.

Low male voices, intense and frightening, crept like ghosts into the warm kitchen. Irrationally, Ianira wanted to stand between her children and their new guest with the gun Ann Vinh Mulhaney had taught her to shoot. She *knew* her reaction was irrational and overprotective, but the Goddess' warnings of impending danger were not to be lightly ignored.

Why hast thou sent this man, Lady? she asked silently, addressing her frightened prayer to the great patroness of Athens itself, wise and fierce guardian of all that was civilization. *I fear this guest, Lady. His glance causes me to tremble with terror. What warning is this and how should I listen for Thy answer? Is he the danger? Or merely the messenger? The portent of a greater danger to follow?*

In the closed environment of La-La Land, there were no sacred owls to give her omens by the timing of their cries or the direction of their flight. But there was in-house television. And there were birds—strange, savage, toothed birds so ancient that Athene herself must have been young when their kind flew the darkling skies of Earth. Artemisia, her attention caught by the moving colors of the television screen, dropped her bottle of juice against the high chair's tray with a bang. A chubby finger pointed.

"Mama! Fish-bird! Fish-bird!"

Ianira looked—and felt all blood drain from her face. She had to clutch the countertop to keep from sliding to the floor. An *Ichthyornis* had struck a brown fish and was devouring it while it struggled. Blood flowed in all-too-lifelike color. Ianira lunged across the narrow kitchen, driven by terror, and snapped off the machine with shaking hands. The screen went dark and silent. Fear for Marcus rose like sour bile in her throat.

No, she pled silently, *keep this death away from our threshold, Lady. He has done nothing to merit it. Please . . .*

Ianira's hands were still trembling when she carried the dishes out to their small dining table and offered the food she had prepared for their evening meal. It took all her courage to smile at their guest, who tore into the food like a ravening wolf. Lupus Mortiferus . . . Wolf of Death . . . Ianira did not yet know precisely *how* danger would come to Marcus through this man, but she was as certain of it as she was certain that her shaky breaths were barely holding terror at bay.

Ianira Cassondra had lost one family already.

She would do murder, if necessary, to keep from losing another.

CHAPTER SEVEN

The Britannia Gate was rich with possibility.

Skeeter chose a likely looking mark dressed in expensive, Victorian-style garments and followed him discreetly until the "gentleman" entered a public restroom. Skeeter entered behind him, took care of business, then—while they both washed their hands at the automatic sinks—he dared break the cardinal rule of silence in the men's washroom.

"Travelling to London, too?" he asked, buttoning the fly of his own Victorian-era togs.

The man shot him a startled glance. "Er, yes."

Skeeter smiled. "Take some friendly advice. That place is *crawling* with pickpockets. Worse than you'll ever read in Dickens." That, at least, was God's own truth. "Don't carry all your money in some predictable place, like a pocket wallet. Some nine-year-old kid'll snatch it and be gone before you even know it's missing."

"I—yes, we were warned about pickpockets," the man stammered, "but I wasn't quite sure what I should *do* about it. Someone suggested maybe I should ask an outfitter, you know, for a moneybelt or something—"

"I'll show you a trick I learned the hard way." Skeeter winked. "Wrap your money in a handkerchief and tuck it inside your shirt, so it sits inside the waistband of your trousers."

The mark looked doubtful.

"Here, let me show you what I mean." He pulled out a standard white handkerchief stuffed with his own money and demonstrated. "Here, I have a spare hanky. You try it."

The man looked doubtful for a moment longer, then relaxed. "Thank you. I will." He pulled a *huge* bankroll out of an expensive leather wallet and tucked the money into the center of the hanky, tying it clumsily.

"I'm afraid I'm not very good at this."

"Here, let me help."

Skeeter tied the corners expertly and tucked it into place, showing the mark exactly how the handkerchief was supposed to fit. Then he retrieved it and said, "Try it again" as he tucked his own money-filled hanky back into his own waistband.

The mark—having no idea that Skeeter had deftly switched handkerchiefs on him—tucked Skeeter's much smaller "bankroll" into his slacks. "Yes, that works wonderfully! Thank you, young man. Here, let me give you a tip or something . . ."

"No, I wouldn't dream of it," Skeeter reassured him. "Hope you have a good visit in London. Some really spectacular sights. Can hardly wait to get back, myself."

He grinned at the other man, then strolled out of the washroom gloating over his success. With any luck, the tourist wouldn't discover the switch until he was *through* the Britannia Gate. Time Tours would bail him out for the duration of the tour—although they'd charge him double price as refund for their trouble—and he'd learn a valuable lesson he clearly needed about hanging onto what was his.

Meanwhile, this haul ought to put Skeeter several hundred ahead of Goldie. He headed directly for the library to have his winnings logged, whistling cheerfully. A group of half-grown boys in Frontier Town—*aw*, *nuts, looks like the uptime abandonees just cut class again*—dashed out of a restaurant directly in his path, yelling and whooping in an excess of energy. Crashes and yells inevitably followed their retreat. Skeeter snorted. Bunch of mannerless hooligans, smashing up anything they could lay hands on just for jollies.

Time Tours, Inc. and the smaller touring outfits tried every trick they could to keep parents from taking kids downtime. After that kid in Rome had gotten himself killed and Time Tours had ended up settling for a huge sum of money (despite the fact it was entirely the fault of the stupid kid and his too-bored-to-be-bothered parents), the outward ripple was as simple as it was inevitable: *no* touring outfit wanted *any* kid running wild downtime.

So the new policy to cope was simple: parents either signed a waiver and paid an enormous extra fee for kids' downtime tickets, or they "abandoned" the kids on the station. Theoretically, Harriet Banks, the Station's school teacher, was assigned to watch them. In practice, Harriet had to watch—and teach—Residents' kids, keep tourists' kids from leaving, and make certain that none of the toddlers or infants in the Day Care Center were injured, sick, or just plain obnoxious with the other kids. Skeeter thought Bull should've done something ages ago or one of these days he was going to find himself with a full School and Day Care Center and *no one* to mind the store.

Bored, usually spoiled, tourists' kids got out of hand constantly, running wild through the station like feral dogs through a butcher's shop. Skeeter found himself caught up in their midst while they darted in mad circles, shouting, "Bang, I got you!" and "No, you didn't, you louse, you missed me clean!"

Several caromed off his shins in their antics.

"Hey! Watch the toes!"

"Sorry, mister!"

They darted away, still shouting and playing their idiotic game. Those boys were too old to be playing cowboys and Indians. They were at that uncertain age when their games should've been more like "who can look up the prettiest girl's skirt first?" He muttered under his breath—then halted mid-mutter.

The next words out of him were so foul, an *Ichthyornis* took offense, shook out its oil-free, sodden feathers, and flopped over to another bush to finish drying its wings.

There was no mistake. Skeeter felt nothing but emptiness inside the waistband of his pants. Disbelieving, he actually jerked his shirt out of his slacks and stared. The handkerchief was gone. So was his own wallet, from his back pocket.

Those murderous, conniving little—

The boys had run in the general direction of Goldie Morran's shop.

That she'd stoop to bribing *tourists*—tourists' *kids*—to roll him, right there in public . . . The humiliation was unendurable. Bet or no bet, Goldie was gonna pay for this one. Skeeter stormed toward her shop in a towering rage, not even certain what he meant to do. A dark-haired girl stepped into his path, barring his way. Skeeter tried unsuccessfully to step around, felt his mind go strangely grey and distant, then blinked and found himself staring into Ianira Cassondra's bottomless eyes. The exotically beautiful girl who lived with Marcus took hold of his arm, her grip urgent.

Skeeter saw the self-styled acolytes who followed her *everywhere* closing in through the holiday crowds.

"There is no time to explain properly, Skeeter. Just let it go," she murmured softly. "Goldie Morran is not the only one on this station with supporters. She will not win her bet. This I swear by all I hold sacred."

She was gone so fast, he wasn't certain for several moments she'd actually been there. He stared after her, wondering what in the world she had meant, and confirmed that his senses hadn't lied, because there went her entire retinue of acolytes clutching cameras, notepads, vidcams, and sound recorders in eager hands, trailing after her like boy dogs after a svelte little bitch in heat. Skeeter really didn't know what to think. Sure, he'd given Marcus that money, which meant he and Ianira must be grateful to him, and he'd been donating money to The Found Ones for months and months, but even if they were serious, what could Marcus and Ianira do against Goldie Morran? The Duchess of Dross had powerful allies and agents *everywhere*.

Still, Ianira's impassioned words disturbed him. They could get themselves thrown off the station, interfering with an uptimer's business which Skeeter profoundly did *not* want to happen: the only place they *could* be sent would be an uptime prison. Without their kids. Skeeter gulped. Things were getting too far out of hand, much too fast, all because that purple-haired *harpy* couldn't content herself with putting into motion her *own* scams.

No, she had to do everything possible to destroy *Skeeter's.*

Another part of him, the scared-kid part of him hidden down inside, desperate to stay on TT-86 at any cost, actually prayed Ianira *had* cooked up some scheme that would cause all sorts of hell for Goldie Morran—just one that wouldn't put Marcus and his little family in danger. Whatever she'd meant, she'd diverted Skeeter's dangerous rage long enough to cool into sensibility. If he'd actually gone into Goldie's shop, there was no telling what he might have done.

Standing for murder charges would *certainly* get him kicked off the station.

Rubbing his chin speculatively, Skeeter decided to kiss goodbye the lost bankroll and wallet. He could always get the station ID cards replaced, even the Residents-Only ATM cards, allowing access to on-station bank accounts. Not that his had much in it, currently. Most of his winnings from Rome were already gone. He grimaced, realizing he'd have to eat his pride to go into Bull Morgan's office and admit a vividly edited version of what had happened so he could get replacement cards. As for the lost bankroll he'd stolen, he'd just try again somewhere else, with some other scheme or maybe just some other restroom and mark. He didn't have much choice. Even if he *did* face Goldie down, he couldn't prove anything. And she'd make him a laughingstock for falling prey to one of his own tricks. Ianira was a smart girl. Skeeter owed her more than he'd realized.

He sighed philosophically and changed course, heading for Bull Morgan's office before trying the Prince Albert Pub to see what action he might pick up there. If he didn't score something big soon, he was a lost man. As he took the lift to the station manager's capacious office on the second floor, Skeeter realized Ianira's comments had shocked him in another way: he *did* have people rooting for him, friends among the downtimers he hadn't realized would back him so staunchly.

Very well, he would try harder. For their sake as well as his. It was comforting to know he wasn't entirely alone.

Kynan Rhys Gower had no love for Skeeter Jackson. It was said by those who knew that Skeeter had attempted to seduce the grandchild of Kynan's liege lord, Kit Carson, by passing himself off as something he was not. Kynan had not been a resident of Time

Terminal Eighty-Six when Skeeter Jackson had lied about being a time scout. But during the period when Kynan was struggling hardest to adjust to his new life, he had very nearly been killed protecting the lady Margo. Therefore, any man who would stoop so low as to besmirch her honor was—and had to be—a sworn enemy.

However, life in this place he had been forced to call home was never as simple and straightforward as it had been in his own time. He began to realize the depth of that truth when Ianira, a Greek beauty some called the Enchantress, but who seemed to Kynan a very devoted wife and mother, called for a Downtimers' Council meeting in the bowels of the time terminal. There, she revealed word of the latest development in the bet between the Scoundrel and Goldie Morran—and what he heard made Kynan Rhys Gower's blood sing.

Goldie Morran was stealing from the Scoundrel. But Ianira wasn't pleased. Instead, she was asking their help. Ianira Cassondra was actually asking them either to steal back from Goldie, or to ruin as many of her schemes as possible, to pay a debt she and Marcus—unbelievably—owed the Scoundrel, along with all other Found Ones. He'd missed the last meeting due to his work schedule and hadn't had a chance to catch up on Council business since. Everything he heard amazed him.

A thief had actually given money to a downtimer, to the whole community of downtimers, keeping his word. Kynan despised the philandering Scoundrel. But the chance to act against Goldie Morran, with the Found Ones' full Council blessings . . .

Kynan Rhys Gower, too, had a score to settle, one it would give him great pleasure to set right. The scars on his back and chest were mute testament to what

Goldie Morran's greed and persuasive, silver tongue had wrought—mute testament to the near loss of his life in the fetid, steaming heat of an African twilight, with witch hunters hard on his heels and a crossbow bolt aimed dead at the lady Margo's breast.

Goldie Morran had lied to him about the conditions under which he was to work for her, had lied to him about the extensive, potentially fatal dangers, then had arrogantly refused to pay him because their "adventure" had failed. It was his liege lord, Kit Carson, who had risked death in more ways than even Kynan could understand, Kit Carson who had rescued Kynan from the clutches of the Portuguese witch hunters, Kit Carson who had made certain that the wounds Kynan had sustained were mended by the great magic available to healers here. And it was Kit Carson who had paid him solid coin for his part in the work Goldie Morran had hired him to do. And paid him, moreover, twice the amount Goldie had named.

Kit Carson was Kynan's liege lord, Goldie Morran a proven enemy. Kynan might not love Skeeter Jackson, but if helping that scoundrel's cause brought disgrace and banishment for Goldie Morran, well, there were worse ways a man could spend his time and effort. He needn't actually help Skeeter *make* money, all he needed to do was prevent Goldie from earning any. The stranded Welshman chuckled to himself and began laying careful plans.

Goldie was sipping wine at an "outdoor" cafe table in Victoria Station, listening to the tourists preparing for departure down the Britannia Gate. One of them, seated nearby, was a florid-faced man who kept wiping his brow with a handkerchief and patting his coat pocket.

"I tell you, Sally has been after me so long I finally

agreed to bring her on this tour, but I had no idea it would all be so *expensive*! The ticket into Shangri-La, the ticket through the Britannia Gate, the hotel bills here and downtime, the *costumes*. Good God, do you know how much money I just dropped in that Clothes & Stuff place? I tell you, I'm down to my last five thousand and Sally will pitch a fit beyond belief if I don't buy her expensive presents in London, and then there's the ATF tax to pay on whatever we bring back. . . ."

His companion, looking bored, just nodded. "Yes, it's expensive. If you can't afford it, don't go."

The disgruntled man with the florid face huffed. "That's easy for you to say. You don't live with my wife."

The other man at the table glanced at a pocket watch. "I'm due on the weapons ranges. See you later, Sam."

He paid his bill and departed, leaving the florid Sam to mop his brow all by himself. Goldie smiled and moved in. She picked up her wine glass and approached his table.

"Mind if I join you?"

He glanced up, surprise widening his eyes, then belatedly mumbled, "Sure, sure, sit down."

Goldie took her seat with the dignity of a dowager empress settling into the ancestral throne. "I'm sorry, but I couldn't help overhearing your conversation. I hope you don't think it forward of me, but there are ways to cut the cost of a time tour. Considerably. You can even turn a tidy profit on occasion. If," she smiled, "you're . . . mmm . . . willing to bend the rules a little? Nothing genuinely illegal, mind you, just a tad . . . exciting. I've tried it dozens of times, myself, or I wouldn't recommend it."

She sipped her wine and waited, smiling politely.

Her mark blinked a few times, taking in Goldie's expensive Victorian-era tea-gown and glittering jewelry.

He blinked a few times more, swallowed loudly enough to be heard two tables away, then went for it. "What ways?"

Goldie leaned forward slightly, just touching Sam's hand with well-manicured fingertips. Diamonds winked from one ring, sapphires from another. "Well, as you know, we uptimers are legally forbidden to bet on sporting events downtime—boxing, horse races, that sort of thing—because we might be able to find out the results in advance. ATF considers that an unfair advantage."

She allowed a tinge of aristocratic disdain to creep into her voice and glanced derisively in the direction of Primary, with its Bureau of Access Time Functions tax collectors, luggage-searching busybodies, and officious bureaucrats.

Sam grunted once. "So I've been told. Our guide said we'll be watched to keep us from doing any betting while we're in London. Interfering, high-handed . . ."

Goldie let him rant at length, then brought the conversation around toward her intended direction again. "Yes, I know all that, dearie." She patted his hand. "As I said, I've done this dozens of times. It's very simple, really. You find out the winners of whatever race you want to bet on, then give that information and your money to one of the downtimers hanging around the station. Many of them pick up odd jobs at the last minute for Time Tours as baggage handlers, so it's really a very simple matter to arrange. The downtimer places your bet and collects your winnings. You give him a small cut, and *voila!* You've helped defray expenses, at the very least. And best of all, you split the earnings *downtime*, so you can either convert it to uptime money the ATF can't touch or buy a few trinkets to bring home as souvenirs."

Goldie lifted her wineglass, tilting it so that the endless

light in the Commons glittered on the jewels adorning her fingers. *Come on, Sammie boy. Go for it. Not that any downtimer'll come near your lovely bankroll.* She smiled politely and sipped wine as though the outcome of his decision meant nothing whatsoever to her. *Hook him, then tell him the idiot downtimer wandered through a gate and Shadowed himself, went "Poof!" money and all. Complain to management if you like, but of course, it's your word against mine and there's that matter of admitting an attempt to place an illegal bet. . . .*

Sam wiped his brow one last time with a wilted handkerchief, then said decisively, "I'll do it! I will. Tell me how."

Goldie set her wineglass down. "As it happens, I've already made arrangements with a gentleman to place a bet for *me* this trip. He can place a bet for you, as well, on the same race. The wagering stands at ten-to-one. I'm placing ten grand on it. This time next week, I'll have a cool hundred thousand more in my retirement fund."

Sam, his face flushed now with excitement rather than nerves, reached for his coat pocket and pulled out a fat wallet. Goldie salivated and swallowed while toying idly with her wineglass to keep her fingers from trembling in anticipation of all that lovely money.

"How much . . ." Sam was muttering. "How much to risk? Oh, hell, here. Have him bet it all."

The man handed her British pound notes which added up to five thousand dollars, American. Goldie smiled again, her predatory heart singing. Then a shadow fell across the table. They both glanced up. Goldie widened her eyes in astonishment.

"Kynan Rhys Gower!"

"I come, lady, as I promise. The bet, lady. Do I hear right? I make bet for this man, too?"

Goldie blinked once, owl-like, aware that her lips

had fallen into a round O of surprise. Then she forcibly recovered her composure. "Why, yes, that's right, Kynan. I just didn't realize you'd come early to collect my stake."

"I prompt, lady. Place bet good. All bets." He winked.

Then he plucked the money from nerveless fingers before she could part lips to protest. Kynan bowed and kissed her hand gallantly, then bowed to Sam, who was beaming, clearly impressed by the charade. Goldie didn't know what to do.

But if Kynan Rhys Gower thought she'd let him out of her sight, he was a greater fool than she thought.

The Welshman bowed again and started to leave.

"If you'll excuse me," Goldie said hastily, "Kynan and I have business of our own to finish."

"But—"

"Don't worry, we'll be on the tour together. I'll catch up to you at the Britannia Gate, Sam."

Goldie fled after the Welshman, who had already vanished around a corner of Victoria Station's cobbled, twisted "streets" of shop fronts, cafes, and pubs. She spotted him ahead and picked up speed.

"Kynan!"

The Welshman ducked into a pub and vanished in a wooden-floored room with air so thick from cigar smoke and alcohol fumes, it was as though a marshland miasma rose from dozens of beer mugs, brandy snifters, whisky glasses, and stinking black stogies. Goldie stood glaring from the threshold until her eyesight adjusted, but there was no sign of Kynan Rhys Gower.

"Has anybody seen Kynan Rhys Gower?" she demanded of the crowded room at large.

"Headed toward the loo, love," someone sang out.

Grim-faced, Goldie stormed into the men's room, not caring a fiddle for the shocked men who grabbed at open flies and cursed her in scalding terms when she started searching stalls.

Kynan was *not* in the "loo."

She emerged, color rising high in her cheeks from sheer *ire*.

Then someone came past, saying, " . . . won't believe it! Biggest domestic screaming fight I've ever seen! Yelling cat and dog, they are, her waving a fist full of money at him, and the poor schmuck trying to explain it was for her he'd got himself swindled. . . ."

Goldie cursed once aloud, explosively, earning curious stares from several 'eighty-sixers hanging on this gossip.

"Something wrong, Goldie?" Rachel Eisenstein asked, her brow furrowing slightly.

"Not a thing!"

Rachel shrugged and turned back to the storyteller. "Think it'll require stitches before they're done?"

Goldie stormed away from the terminal's head physician and the rest of the gossipers yammering about *her* money.

That . . . that honor-bound, incompetent, downtime *rat*!

He'd given the blasted money back to Sam's *wife*!

She beat a dignified, hasty retreat toward her money-changing shop, seething inside as she tried to come up with some other scheme that would net her a big gain over that mongrel cur, Skeeter Jackson.

Goldie slammed shut the shop door so hard, the bell jangled wildly against the glass. She stalked behind her counter and indulged in at least five minutes of unrestrained, sulky *cursing* where nothing but her glittering coins and jewels could hear.

Then, drawing several savage breaths, she added Kynan Rhys Gower to the list of names she owed serious paybacks. And then—caution overcoming wrath—she carefully struck his name off her list again. For reasons personally painful to recall, Kynan Rhys Gower was under Kit Carson's personal—and far-reaching—protection. After what Goldie Morran had suffered as a result of Kit's wrath, she did *not* want to find herself on the losing end of another deal with Kenneth "Kit" Carson, world-famous time scout and land-shark businessman.

Goldie muttered under her breath. "Damn meddling scouts, guides, *and* downtimers, one and all." She turned her savage anger toward a more productive target: Skeeter Jackson. She had to know what he was up to. After that blitzkrieg attack by those boys she'd hired, he'd gone virtually underground. Goldie tapped long, manicured nails against the glass countertop, noticed the rings she'd borrowed from her inventory. She replaced them in the glass case with a snort of disgust, then reached thoughtfully for the telephone. She might not have won this battle, but the war was far from over.

All communities, no matter their size, have rituals by which they measure the passage of time and gauge the meaning of life. These rituals serve purposes beyond seemingly superficial appearances; they provide necessary cohesion and order within the primate group to which humanity belongs, they sustain continuity in the endless chaos of life, they ensure proper passage from one phase of life into the next as the individual grows from childhood into adulthood responsibility and from there into old age, all within the context of the social group to which that individual belongs. This need for ritual is so profound, it is locked within the genetic code, transmitted over the generations from the vast distance of time when Lucy and her predecessors roamed the steaming plains of Africa, learning to use tools and language in a hostile, alien world—a world whose harsh beauty struck awe into the soul, a world where the terror of instant death could not be fully comprehended.

And so humans learned to survive via the evolution of rituals, changing not so much their physical bodies as their cultural, social patterns of behavior. In a world without rituals, humans will create their own, as in the gangs of lawless children who had before and still did, after The Accident, terrorized the streets of major cities.

The more chaotic the world, the greater the need for ritual.

La-La Land was an utter morass of conflicting cultures, religious beliefs, and behavior patterns. Its very nickname reflected the insane nature of the small community of shopkeepers, professionals, law-enforcers, medical personnel, scholars, con artists, time-tour-company employees, stranded downtimers, freelance time guides, and the most insane of all the residents, the time scouts who explored new gates, risking their lives with each new journey alone into the unknown past.

In order to keep the peace, Station Management and representatives of the uptime government both had laid down sets of rituals—codified into law—by which residents and tourists alike were required to abide. Others sprung up naturally, as such things will any time human beings come together into more or less permanent groupings of more than one. (And, in fact, even hermits have their own rituals, whether or not they care to admit it.)

In La-La Land, there were two rituals of paramount importance to every resident: Bureau of Access Time Function's incessant attempts to enforce the cardinal rule of time touring, "Thou Shalt Not Profiteer from

Temporal Travel" and the residents' unceasing attempts to thumb their collective noses at said cardinal rule.

The High Priests of the two opposing factions were Bull Morgan, Station Manager, whose sole purpose in life was to maintain an orderly, profitable station where a body could do pretty much as he or she pleased, so long as the peace was kept—and the other was Montgomery Wilkes, head ATF agent, a man dedicated to enforcing the cardinal rule of time touring at all cost.

Inevitably, when Bull and Montgomery locked horns, sparks flew. This, in turn, had given rise to a third universal ritual in La-La Land. Known affectionately as Bull Watching, it involved the placement of bets both large and small on the outcome of any given encounter between the two men. In its classic form, Bull Watching provided hours of entertainment to those men and women who had chosen to live in a place where light blazed from the ceiling of the Commons twenty-four hours a day, but where the only real sunlight came from the occasional trickle through an open gate.

In this sunless, brightly lit world, it was inevitable that Montgomery Wilkes would grow ever more bitter as residents flouted his authority at every possible moment and made bets that infuriated him about every word he did or did not utter. When Goldie Morran came to him with her plan to rid the station of Skeeter Jackson, he saw a golden opportunity to rid it of Goldie Morran, as well—a woman he knew in his bones broke the cardinal rule of time touring with every gate that opened, but was slick enough not to get caught.

In taking that wager with Skeeter—and then coming to him—she had sealed her own doom.

Montgomery Wilkes intended to deport *both* of the scoundrels before this business was done. That decision made, he indulged in a little ritual of his own. He called it "inspecting the troops." The ATF agents assigned to TT-86 called it words impossible to repeat in polite company.

Dressed in black uniforms that crackled when they walked, their hair cut to regulation length (Montgomery had been known to use a ruler to measure hair length to the last millimeter), every ATF agent in the ready room snapped to attention when he stalked in, six feet, one hundred-eighty pounds of muscle, close-cropped red hair, crackling green eyes, and set lips that underscored the lines of discontent in his face.

As he faced his agents, eyes alight with a martial glow that struck terror into their collective hearts, he said, "The time has come for you to start living up to those uniforms you wear. This station has hemmed us in, crowded us into a corner, prevented us from doing much more than searching luggage and levying taxes on the few items that actually get transported uptime. Meanwhile, we sit by and watch while out-and-out crooks scam fortunes under our very noses."

Shoe leather creaked in the silence as he paced the front of the room. He turned to glare at the nearest agents. *"Enough!"*

With brisk movements, he switched on a slide projector and clicked controls. Goldie Morran's pinched countenance filled a ten-foot wall.

"This is Goldie Morran. Gems and rare coin dealer, money changer, currency expert, and con artist." Slides clicked in the silence. "This is smiling Skeeter Jackson. I don't think I have to tell you what kind of rapscallion this two-bit thief is." He cleared his throat deliberately, pinning the nearest agent with a baleful green stare. "I also know that every one of you has heard by now about their little bet."

Not a single agent in the room dared crack a smile;

not with the boss pacing three feet away. A few began to sweat profusely into their stiff black uniforms, wondering if their side bets on the outcome of "the wager" had been discovered.

"Ladies and gentlemen," he folded his hands behind his back and stood in the center of the projected image of Skeeter Jackson, so that the colors from the slide wavered across his uniform and face like stained glass taken from a madhouse, "we are going to let these two have enough rope to hang themselves. I have had a *bellyful* of watching these 'eighty-sixers hoodwink their way through life, as though the sacred laws which we have been hired to uphold didn't even exist. We may not be able to deport them all and close down this station, but by God, we can catch these two! And I intend to do just that. By the end of the week, I want Goldie Morran and Skeeter Jackson in custody for fraud, theft, and anything else we can think up and make stick. I want them deported uptime to jail where they belong, or I'll have the reasons why a crack troop of ATF agents is incompetent to catch two smalltime crooks in a closed environment. Is that understood?"

Nobody said a word. Hardly anybody breathed. Many kissed pensions goodbye. Without exception, they cursed the fate that had landed them in this career, on this station, under this boss.

"Very good. Consider yourselves warriors in a timeless battle of good against evil. I want undercover teams combing this station, looking for anyone who might testify against either of those two. I want other undercover teams to set up sting operations. If we can't catch them in a fair scam, we'll by God entrap them in one of our own making. And if I hear of *anyone* betting on the outcome of this wager, I'll have pensions, so help me! Now move it! We have work to do!"

Agents in black fled the room to receive assignments from their captains and lieutenants and sergeants. Montgomery Wilkes remained behind in the empty ready room and gazed cold-eyed at the projected visage of smiling Skeeter Jackson. "I'll get you," he said softly to the colored light on the blank, ten-foot wall. "I will by God get you. And it's about time Bull Morgan understood just who the law around here really is."

He stalked out onto the Commons on course for the station manager's office.

CHAPTER EIGHT

Like most time terminals, TT-86 attracted gifted scholars from around the world, many of them the very best at what they did. Robert Li was no exception. As an antiquarian, he was sought out by private collectors and museums alike as a consultant and had been instrumental in identifying numerous quality forgeries.

There was good reason for this: no one excelled Robert Li at *producing* forgeries of the genuine article. His work was—usually—strictly legal. Tourists and museum reps often brought items uptime to his studio to be reproduced in exquisite detail, which were then exported to museums around the world as legal replicas bearing the Li trademark. Occasionally, however, like most other 'eighty-sixers, Robert Li would get a bellyful of ATF's high-handed tactics.

He had an exceptionally strong—if unique—sense of right and wrong. The closer Montgomery Wilkes' people watched his operation, the more ire he swallowed until, inevitably, it broke out in such indignant expressions as assisting thieves smuggle out their wares! (Of course, only *after* he'd charged them a substantial amount of cash to reproduce the item.)

Even so, far more frequent were the times when scouts had returned "stolen" items to their original times when he felt an item *shouldn't* go missing—

although, again, he usually reproduced it, first. And occasionally, an item crossed his counter that was so breathtaking, so unique that he simply couldn't resist. He could wax rhapsodic about Ming porcelain, but Greek bronzes threw him into utter fits. Unknown to ATF—or anyone else, for that matter—Robert Li kept a private safe the size of his bedroom, where he stored his most precious belongings. His collection of ancient bronzes rivalled that of the Louvre and surpassed that of uptime collectors with far more money than he had.

Some things, one simply did not sell.

Greek bronzes were one; friends were another.

Goldie Morran was, at heart, a cheating scoundrel who would've sold her own teeth, if they'd been worth enough, but she was also a friend and one of the few people in the world whose knowledge of rare coins and gems approached his own. Goldie had done him a favor or two over the years, obtaining items here and there which his heart had coveted, and he harbored a secret admiration for her skills.

Unlike Kit Carson, he never tried to best her at billiards or pool, knowing his own limitations as fully as his strengths. Normally Goldie would've respected his lack of desire to wager against her. He was equally aware, however, that with Goldie's livelihood on the line, she would consider nothing sacred. So when she entered his studio, Robert Li buttoned his pockets, locked the cases and cabinets he could reach, and put on his best smile.

"Why, Goldie, what a surprise to see you."

She nodded and placed a carbuncle with ornate carving across its upper surface on a velvet pad left lying on the countertop.

"What do you think of it?"

He eyed her speculatively, then picked up the gem

and a jeweler's loupe. "Mmm . . . very nice. The depiction of the statuary on the spine of the Circus Maximus is excellent and I've never seen a better representation of the turning posts. Who forged it for you?"

Goldie sniffed, eyes flashing irritation and disappointment. "Bastard. How'd you know?"

He just gave her a sorrowful look from under his brows.

Goldie sniffed again. "All right, but would it fool most people? Even a discerning collector?"

"Oh, without a doubt. Unless," he smiled, "they hired someone like me to authenticate it."

"Double what I said before. Triple it. How much?"

Robert laughed quietly. "To keep quiet? Or provide authentication papers?"

"Both, you conniving—"

"Goldie." The reproach in his voice was that of a lover wounded by his lady's mistrust.

"Robert, you owe me a few. I'm desperate."

"ATF's watching me like a hawk. Word's out: Monty's planning to nail you *and* Skeeter, send you both packing to an uptime jail."

Goldie could swear more creatively than anyone Robert Li knew—and he knew *all* the time scouts operating out of TT-86.

Robert knew better than to pat her hand, but sympathy seemed called for. "Well, I suppose you could always poison Wilkes, but I think it would be easier to steer clear of anyone you don't know for the next few days. This place is *crawling* with undercover agents."

Goldie's eyes, sharper than ever, flashed dangerously. "Bull know about that? If ATF's undercover, they're way outside their jurisdiction and Montgomery Wilkes for damn sure knows it."

Before Robert could answer, Kit Carson entered the shop, sauntering over in a gait calculated to appear lazy, but which covered ground with astonishing speed. "Hi. Heard the news?"

"*Which* news?" Goldie demanded, exasperation coloring her voice.

Kit chuckled and winked at Robert. "Reliable eyewitnesses said the shouting could be heard *through* the soundproofing."

"Bull and Monty?" Robert asked eagerly. "Ten says Monty stepped over the line just a tad too far this time."

"No bet," Kit laughed. "You'll never guess what Bull's done now."

Goldie, carefully covering the carved carbuncle with her hand, asked, "Bull 'fishpond him'?"—referring to the time Margo had taken offense at being mauled by a multibillionaire with a thing for nubile redheads. Margo had thrown him into the fishpond.

Kit laughed heartily. Robert Li was sure Goldie had *intended*, with careful calculation, to remind Kit of that particular incident. And such a ruckus the dripping-wet old goat had raised, too, threatening to sue everything and everyone he could.

Fortunately, Bull Morgan had pointed out that said goat would have to file suit in the jurisdiction where the assault had taken place, then explained that no lawyers *at all* were permitted to hang their shingles anywhere inside TT-86. Better that way for *everyone*.

Of course, the way Margo looked and moved . . .

A man could hardly be blamed for trying. Malcolm Moore was one lucky son if she said yes.

Kit leaned forward conspiratorially. "Good guess, but nope, you're *way* off the mark."

Kit's little audience leaned forward, unaware they did so. Kit grinned. "Bull Morgan had Mike Benson place dear old Monty *under arrest*. Threw him into the brig with seventeen boozers, half-a-dozen brawlers, and three flea-bitten thieves clumsy enough to get caught."

"*WHAT?*"

The demand came out in stereo, Goldie's screech hitting soprano.

Kit's grin lit his thin, mustachioed face like an evil jack-o-lantern. "Yep. Seems like during their, er, meeting over jurisdiction up in Bull's office, Monty's sense of outrage and diligence to the letter of the law prompted him to, um, an assault."

Robert Li gasped. "Monty *hit Bull*? And he's still alive?"

"Oh, no," Kit laughed, eyes twinkling. "Much better than that. Monty *assaulted* Bull's prize porcelain of the Everlasting Elvis. You know the one, sat on his desk like some serene Buddha for years after he, er, borrowed it from that cathouse in New Orleans."

Goldie's eyes went as round as the carbuncle she'd tried to hide from Kit's sharp-eyed gaze. "He broke Bull's *Elvis*?"

"They're still digging pieces out of the wall. And ceiling. And carpet."

"Oh, dear God," Robert said hoarsely, covering his eyes. "You know what this means?"

"Oh, do I ever. Open season on ATF agents *and* station security alike. The fights—and they're getting dirty, fast—have already started. Just thought I'd warn you. Things are likely to get hot around here for a while. Oh, one last thing."

He winked at Robert. "That carbuncle you're trying to hide, Goldie? Forget selling it to that sweet young thing who asked if you could find her one. She's the newest narc on Monty's payroll."

Goldie's mouth dropped open. Robert grinned. Kit

rarely had the pleasure of catching her so completely off guard. Goldie very primly closed her mouth. Then, with as much dignity as she could muster, she said, "I am not even going to ask. Good day, gentlemen."

She took her carbuncle and left.

Robert glanced curiously at Kit. "This girl you're talking about. Is she really Monty's?"

Kit chuckled. "Hell if I know. But she walks and talks like ATF, for all the lace and perfume and goo-goo eyes she's been making at Skeeter Jackson. He hides every time she comes near. And I've *never* known that boy's instincts about undercover cops to fail."

"She sounds guilty to me," Robert chuckled. "Poor Skeeter. Poor Goldie. What terrible, tangled webs."

Kit grinned. "Yeah, well, hey, they wove 'em all by themselves, didn't they? I just don't like the idea of ATF throwing its weight around where it's got no real jurisdiction. They mind their checkpoints, we mind our business. Problems like Goldie and Skeeter, we handle internally."

Robert Li laughed aloud, recalling just how Kit had "handled" his own family "problem" with Skeeter. The youngster was still gun-shy whenever Kit was around.

"When's Margo due in?" he couldn't resist asking.

Kit's world-famous grin flickered into existence. "Next time Primary cycles. Malcolm's taking her to Denver."

"So I heard."

"Is nothing secret around here?"

Robert Li chuckled. "In La-La Land? Get real. Whoops, here comes a customer."

Kit wandered out past a young woman who wandered in. Kit paused in the doorway, giving Robert the high sign that *this* girl was trouble, then left whistling jauntily. Robert Li watched the tourist narrowly as she paused to look at antique furniture brought uptime from

London, then glanced appreciatively at a cabinet filled with jade jaguar gods.

"Is there anything in particular I could help you with?" Robert asked politely.

"Hi. I was wondering if you could help me out? I'm interested in buying something for my Dad's birthday and he's crazy about Roman antiquities. And he's a sports nut, too. So when this gems dealer showed me a gorgeous stone with a carving of the Circus Maximus on it . . ." She batted eyelashes a half-inch long and let the sentence trail off. She *was* all lace and perfume and goo-goo eyes. And her voice would've liquefied thousand-year-old honey. But Kit was right: this kid walked like a trained agent and despite the melt-in-your-mouth patter, her voice held a burr that told Robert, *Monty's riding 'em hard, all right. This kid's out for blood.* Robert Li folded his hands into the sleeves of the Chinese-style Mandarin's robe he affected while in his studio and waited for her to continue. Having a Chinese maternal grandfather gave him certain physical attributes that came through despite his mother's Scandinavian heritage; it also gave him an excuse to go inscrutable on demand. The tactic, so effective with other customers, even threw *her* off-stride. She floundered visibly for a moment, then recovered.

"I was hoping you could give me an appraisal, you know, so I'd be sure I was paying a fair price for it."

"I am an antiquities dealer," Robert said humbly, "with some small knowledge of furniture and a slight interest in South American jades, but I do not presume to claim expertise in valuing gemstones."

"There's an IFARTS sign in your window," she challenged, as perfectly well aware as he what was required to become an IFARTS official representative.

"Dear lady, I fear my consultation fee would be a complete waste of your money."

"Consultation fee?"

"A trifling charge for my time and services. It is not against IFARTS rules and one *does* have to make a living." He smiled politely. "I fear a thousand dollars to tell you, 'I don't know' would be a great strain on the budget of someone as sensible as I perceive you to be. Surely you could go to one of the gems dealers on the station for such an appraisal?"

Her eyes narrowed in dawning suspicion. "Everyone recommended you."

"I would, of course, be happy to do my best, but there is also my reputation to consider. Think what damage I would do if I valued such a thing wrongly. You would be cheated, the current owner of the gem would be cheated and possibly greatly offended, and no one would trust my judgment again. I know my limits, dear lady, and my reputation will not stand such a strain as you ask."

She compressed her lips. He could all but see the thoughts seething behind her eyes: *You're in on it, you bastard, you're all in on it and I'll never prove a thing on her....*

"Thank you," she said curtly. All trace of sweetness and goo-goo eyes had vanished. "I hope you have a pleasant day."

The hell you do, girlie. Robert smiled anyway. "And a pleasant day to you. And your father. May his day of birth be blessed with the freedom in life he so earnestly desires."

Robert thought for a moment she would actually break cover and scream at him that Montgomery Wilkes wouldn't be in jail long, by God!—but she didn't. She just marched out of his studio as though she were on parade ground. *She's young,* Robert sighed, *and that idiot Wilkes is ruining her already. What a tight-fisted, anal-retentive fool.* Then Robert reminded himself that the ATF—no matter how attractively packaged—was the enemy and busied himself placing a few phone calls. There were friends who deserved fair warning before that little number came to call.

Clearly, she was out for Goldie's blood.

Robert Li sold many things, for many prices.

But he had never sold a friend. Not even a snake of a friend like Goldie Morran. Just because she'd sell *him* out at a moment's notice didn't mean *he* needed to reciprocate her lack of morals, never mind plain bad manners. And that was something ATF agents just didn't seem to comprehend. Not the ones trained by Montgomery Wilkes, anyway. Sometimes Robert wondered what drove the man so. Whatever it was, it boded ill for many an 'eighty-sixer before this business with The Wager was finished.

He dialed a number from memory.

A voice on the other end of the phone said, "Hello?"

"There's a sweet young thing on Monty Wilkes' staff making the rounds, trying to sting Goldie, and maybe you in the process. She just left here and she's goddamned good. All honey and goo-goo eyes until she realizes she can't have what she wants. Can't miss her. Just thought you ought to know."

"Huh. Thanks. I'll start passing around word, myself. You wanna take A to M or N to Z?"

"I'll finish in the group where I started. A to M."

"N to Z it is. Thanks for the tip-off."

The line went dead.

Robert grinned. Then punched another set of numbers.

"Your attention, please. Gate One is due to open in five minutes. All departures, be advised that if you have not cleared Station Medical, you will not be permitted to pass Primary. Please have your baggage ready for customs inspection by agents of the Bureau of Access Time Functions, who will assess your taxes due on downtime acquisitions . . ."

Malcolm Moore leaned over to Kit and said, "I wouldn't want to be in that line today. Those agents look bloody angry."

Kit chuckled. "You'd think with their boss in jail, they'd be more relaxed, not edgier than ever. Of course, after the fights some of 'em have been in . . ."

Half the male agents in sight sported blackened eyes and bruised knuckles. A few of the women bore scratches down their cheeks. Mike Benson had been forced to discipline half his own staff—then, he'd had to order the ATF agents into temporary quarters in one of the hotels nearest Primary, just to separate them from Station Security until the worst blew over.

"I rather expect most of them wish Skeeter Jackson and Goldie Morran had never been born, never mind made that idiotic wager," Malcolm noted wryly.

Kit glanced up at the chronometer board again.

Malcolm laughed. "The clock won't move any faster just because you keep staring at the numbers."

Kit actually flushed, then rubbed the back of his neck. "Yeah, well, I guess I've missed the brat."

Malcolm cleared his throat. "Well, since you mention it, I am rather anxious to see her again."

Kit gave him an appraising glance. "Yes. She might say no, you realize."

"I know." The quiet anguish in his voice betrayed him. He couldn't shake the fear that his notorious luck might still be holding steadily on "bad."

"She might say no to what?" a voice boomed behind them.

Malcolm winced. He and Kit turned to find Sven Bailey, hands on hips, watching them like a bemused bulldog.

"What in bloody hell are you doing here?" Malcolm muttered.

Sven grinned, a sight that made most men's blood run cold. "Waiting for my pupil, of course. Gotta see if she remembers anything I taught her."

Kit chuckled. "If she doesn't, we'll *both* wipe up the mat with her."

"Oh, goodie." Sven Bailey, widely acclaimed the most deadly man on TT-86, rubbed thick-fingered hands gleefully. "I can hardly wait. I never get to have that much fun with the tourists."

Malcolm rubbed one finger along his nose. "That's because the tourists would sue."

The terminal's martial arts and bladed-weapons instructor grunted. "No lawyers allowed in La-La Land and you know it."

A new voice said, "Good thing for you, too, isn't it, Sven?"

They glanced around to find Ann Vinh Mulhaney grinning up at him. Very nearly the only person on TT-86 who dared laugh *at* Sven Bailey, the petite shooting instructor's eyes sparkled with delight. Their matched heights produced a comical appearance: squat fireplug, stolid beside a sleek bird of prey.

"What is this," Malcolm muttered, "a welcoming committee?"

"Well, she *is* my student," Ann pointed out. "I'd like to say hello and see if she remembers anything." Her eyes flashed with unspoken humor, whether at Malcolm's discomfiture or in remembrance of Margo's early lessons, Malcolm wasn't sure.

Sven just snorted. When Ann glanced curiously at her counterpart, Kit chuckled. "That was Sven's excuse, too. You two are complete fakes. Why you should even like that brat after what she put us all through is beyond me."

"*Like* her?" Sven protested. He managed to look hurt—an astonishing feat, considering that his eternal expression was that of a rabid bulldog about to charge. "Ha! Like her. That's good, Kit. I just want another look at that Musashi sword guard of yours. You know, the one you said I could peek at if I trained her."

"And I," Ann said sweetly, pulling off the wheedling tone far more effectively than Sven, "covet another week in the honeymoon suite at the Neo Edo." She batted her eyelashes prettily.

Kit just groaned. Malcolm grinned. "You're as bad as they are, Kit, if you expect me to buy that theatrical groan any more than I buy their excuses."

Kit just crossed his arms and compressed his lips in a pained expression, as though he'd crunched down on a poisoned seed pod and didn't know whether to spit or curse. "*Friends*." Disgust dripped like ice from his voice.

"Kit," Ann laughed, touching his shoulder in a friendly fashion, "you are the biggest fake of any 'eighty-sixer walking this terminal. It's why we love you."

Kit just snorted rudely. "You sound like Connie Logan. Do all the women on this station get together and compare notes?"

Ann winked. "Of course. You're famous. Half the tourists who come here are dying for a glimpse of *the* Kit Carson."

Kit shuddered. His loathing of tourists was La-La Land legend. "I would remind you, I'm not the only famous 'Kit Carson' by a long shot."

Sven nodded sagely. "But you're both scouts, eh?"

Kit grinned unexpectedly. "Actually, I'm not named for Kit Carson, Western scout, at all."

All three of them stared. Malcolm scraped his jaw off the floor before the others. "You're not?"

Kit's eyes twinkled wickedly. "Nope. I used to build

balsa airplanes and launch 'em when I was a kid, then shoot 'em down with a slingshot off the side of some cliff. Dahlonega, Georgia," he added drily, "might not have much left but a checkered history, but cliffs we had in plenty. So when I started hitting every little balsa plane I'd made with a nice, fat rock, he took to calling me 'Kit' for his favorite WWII Ace Pilot, L. K. 'Kit' Carson. Came darn near to matching Chuck Yeager's record."

"A fighter pilot," Sven said, eyes round with lingering astonishment. "Well, hell, Kit, I guess that's not too bad a thing, being named after a flying ace. Ever have a chance to do any real flying?"

Kit's expression went distant. Malcolm knew the look. "Yeah," he said very softly.

Before anyone could pry, the station announcer interrupted.

"Your attention, please. Gate One is due to open in one minute . . ."

The four watched in companionable silence as the circus of a Primary departure wound up to a crescendo of baggage searches, purple faces, outraged protests, and the exchange of shocking sums of money collected by agents in no mood to put up with anyone's lip on this particular departure. By the time the gate began to cycle, causing the bones behind Malcolm's ears to buzz, tempers were ragged on both sides of the tables.

"Good thing the gate's about to open or we'd have a fight or two, I think," Malcolm muttered to no one in particular.

"Yep," Sven said with characteristic loquacity.

The sound that was not a sound, heralding the opening of a major gate, intensified. Beyond the imposing array of barriers, armed guards, ramps, fences, metal detectors, X-ray equipment, and dual medical stations stood a broad ramp which rose fifteen feet into the air, then simply ended. Light near the top dopplered through the entire visible spectrum. Then Shangri-La Station's main gate—and sole link with the rest of the uptime world—dilated open.

Uptimers streamed into the station, hauling baggage down that long ramp toward the Medical station barring the way. One by one, station medical personnel scanned and logged medical records. Malcolm waited in a cold sweat for the one slight figure in all that crowd he'd waited months to see—and dreaded meeting again. Then, before he was ready for it, she was there, hair back to its natural flaming red, all trace of brown dye banished until she was ready to take up time scouting as a professional.

Margo . . .

Malcolm's belly did a rapid drawing in. How could he have forgotten what that little slip of a girl could do to a man's body chemistry, just by walking down an ordinary ramp? Margo was dressed—to Malcolm's astonishment—in a chaste little floral-print dress that came nearly to her ankles. The swing of its long skirt and the way it clung to skin he vividly recalled the taste and touch of did bad things to Malcolm's breath control. Her hair was longer, too, and—if possible—sexier than ever as it curled around her ears. *Oh, God, what if she says no? Please, Margo, don't walk down that ramp and tell me you've met some boy at school. . . .*

She caught sight of him and her face lit up like Christmas on Picadilly. She shifted a heavy duffle bag to wave and blow a kiss right at him. His belly did another rapid drawing in that made breathing impossible. He waved back. His knees actually felt weak.

"Buck up, man," Kit muttered in his ear. "You're white as a sheet."

The ring in his pocket all but burned him through

the cloth. He'd thought to give it to her here, but with all these well-intentioned onlookers . . . Then, again before he was ready, she'd cleared station medical and dropped the duffle bag to run straight into his arms.

Margo Smith had not forgotten how to kiss.

By the time they disentangled, spontaneous applause had broken out even amongst tourists Malcolm had never laid eyes on. Margo flushed, grinned, then flung her arms around Kit.

"I missed you!"

"Humph!" Kit said, crushing her close despite the attempt at pretense. "The way you greeted Malcolm, I thought you'd forgotten your grandfather existed!"

Margo shocked them all by bursting into tears. "Forget you?" She hugged him more tightly than ever. "Don't you count on it!"

Malcolm cleared his throat while Kit shut his eyes and just held her. After the losses Kit had suffered, Margo's impromptu demonstration meant more than she could possibly know. And after the terrible fights they'd had, it was good to see that look on Kit's face.

Eventually she dried her eyes and sniffed sheepishly. "Sorry. I really did miss you. Sven! And Ann! You came to see me!"

Ann hugged her former pupil tightly. "Welcome home, Margo."

Sven Bailey, true to his nature, demonstrated his affection by launching a snap kick right at her midriff. Margo wasn't there when it should have connected. Despite the hampering cloth of her long dress, she danced aside and managed to land a stinging punch before grabbing Sven and hugging him tightly. He made a single sound of outrage, turned as red as Margo's hair, and extricated himself with slightly-less-than-excessive force.

"Huh. Good to see you remembered some of what I drilled into you, girl."

Margo grinned. "Just a little. Care to spar later? I've been practicing."

Sven Bailey's eyes lit up like an evil gnome's. "You're on!"

Then, shocking everyone, he picked up Margo's luggage and set out with it, calling over one shoulder, "Neo Edo? Kit's apartment? Or Malcolm's place?"

Margo flushed bright pink, glanced guiltily at Kit, bit one lip, and said, "Uh, Malcolm's?"

Kit's face fell until Margo hugged him again and whispered, "Just for tonight, okay? I mean, well, you know."

Kit turned brighter red than Sven had.

Ann laughed aloud. "That's twenty you owe me, Kit."

Kit just produced the money and said repressively, "You had *better* be safe about it, Margo."

Margo put out a pink tongue. "I promised *that* before I went off to school. And I don't break my promises." At his look, she added, "Not anymore. I *learned* that lesson! But I want dinner with you at the Delight, so you'd better not have any dates lined up for tonight!"

Kit relaxed into smiles again. "Arley's already reserved our table."

"Good! College food sucks!"

"Watch your mouth," Kit said mildly.

"Well, it does." But she smiled as she said it.

Her gaze caught sight of the brave decorations strangling Commons and her mouth and eyes turned into little O's of wonder. "Oh, Malcolm, look! When did *that* happen?"

Kit laughed. "Another new 'eighty-sixer tradition you haven't been introduced to yet. Winter Holiday Decorations Contest. The vendors around each gate try to outdo one another. *Last* year, a three-story, arm-waving plastic Santa caught fire."

"Oooh, bet the stink of that took a while to clear."

Malcolm chuckled. "Yes. *Whichever* way you choose to interpret that."

Margo sighed. The gaudy spectacle was clearly, in her eyes, utterly enchanting. Then she shook herself and glanced at Kit. "Oh, uh, by the way? I've decided going back uptime to that school you got me into is a complete waste of time. Brian's got a much better library and, well, it's just *awful*!"

Before Kit could erupt into a violent temper, Margo held out one hand. "Just think about it. We'll, uh, talk more later. Okay?"

Kit hrumphed and said, "All right, my girl, but you're gonna have to talk pretty fast and damn convincingly to change my mind."

Margo laughed, a grown-up burble more than a childlike giggle. "Oh, I will. Don't you fret about that."

When she grabbed Malcolm's hand, Malcolm felt like the air around his brain was fizzing and sparkling. He wondered if Margo could actually feel how hard his heart was thumping through the contact of her fingers against his.

"Any interesting prospects in that group?" Ann, who'd taken in the entire by-play with wide, fascinated eyes, asked. She nodded toward the other uptimers as they headed down the brightly lit, gloriously garish Commons.

"Hmm . . . actually, yeah. There's this group of paleontologists headed downtime through the Wild West Gate. Couple of Ph.Ds, three grad students. They're all set—they think," she chuckled, "to study the Bone Wars."

"Bone Wars?" Ann echoed, sounding astonished.

Margo glanced up at Kit, looking smug as a cat that's sneaked a choice morsel off someone's plate. "Yeah, the Bone Wars. There were these two paleontologists, see, Cope and Marsh, who got into a war with one another collecting fossils from the American West. It was kind of an undeclared wager to see who could name the most new specimens and mount them in museums back east. Heck of a wager, too, let me add. Their agents would actually sneak into one another's camps and smash up specimens, shoot at one another, real exciting stuff. But they brought out a king's ransom in dinosaur bones, between them, because of the competition. Named tons of new species and genera and stuff. So, anyway, these guys—well, one of the grad students is a woman—they want to study it first-hand. Said they've already got their own weapons, rifles and pistols, but they were all cased up for the trip through Primary. I made 'em promise to show me their rifles and stuff before they left and made 'em swear to God and all the angels they'd see you for lessons first. I think one of 'em would rather touch a live rattlesnake than the guns he brought along."

Ann grinned. "Good girl!"

Margo chuckled. "It was easy. The four of 'em who were guys were drooling all over themselves for an excuse to talk to me." She rolled her eyes. "*Men*."

The stab of white-hot jealousy that shot through him stunned Malcolm. Margo glanced up quickly. She must have felt his hand twitch, because she said, "You all right, Malcolm?"

"Fine," he lied. *Just what do these so-called paleontologists look like?* He studied the incoming uptimers, but there were so many, he wasn't sure which group they might belong to.

Margo squeezed his hand. "Hey. Malcolm. They were boring."

The way her eyes sparkled when she smiled made his insides go hot and cold. "Really?" *There, that had come out reasonably steady. Buck up, man, as Kit says. She hasn't said no yet.*

Margo flounced as only Margo could. Malcolm followed the movement with a tortured gaze. She added, "Hah! Their fossils would've been more interesting! I just wanted a peek at their rifles."

Kit laughed. "Malcolm, I'd say you just won *your* standing bet, eh?"

Margo colored delicately. "I wouldn't say that. The time limit on *that* bet ran out ages ago."

Malcolm sighed. "Well, there are other ways of getting your life's story, I suppose."

"Hmm. We'll just have to see how creative you are, Mr. Moore." But she squeezed his fingers.

"At least," Kit said, eying them askance, "you seem to be picking up your American history nicely. Maybe Malcolm's idea wasn't such a bad one, after all."

"Malcolm's idea," Malcolm growled, "was supposed to be Malcolm's surprise."

Margo just looked up at him, wide-eyed. "You planned a surprise for me?"

Heat rose into his face. "Yeah. And Grandpa's doing his damndest to spoil it."

"Got a bet on?" Margo asked suspiciously.

"Not me," Malcolm sighed. "But I wouldn't be surprised if Kit does."

"Kit and everyone else in La-La Land," Ann laughed. "Mind if you have company for dinner, or is this a family affair?"

Margo blushed. "Uh, would you mind if we had lunch tomorrow, instead?"

"Not at all." Ann had to reach up slightly to ruffle Margo's hair. "Imp. It's good to have you home."

She strolled off with a backward wave.

Kit rubbed the back of his neck. "I, uh, have some things I have to take care of . . ."

"So soon?" Margo wailed.

He glanced at Malcolm. "I think Malcolm wants you to himself for a while. Grandpa can wait. But not long," he added with a fierceness in his voice that his playful smile could not quite disguise.

She hugged him tightly. "Promise."

Kit kissed the top of her head, then gently disentangled himself. "Dress up pretty for dinner, okay?"

"I will."

He ruffled her hair much the way Ann had, then left Malcolm alone with her. Malcolm swallowed hard, finding his throat suddenly dry. "Did you, uh, want to catch a bite to eat first?"

Margo's green eyes smoldered. "I'm starving. But not for food. C'mon, Malcolm. It's me. Margo."

He ventured a tentative smile. "That therapy of yours seems to have helped."

She grinned. "Yeah, the rape counsellor I've been seeing is good. She's helped unkink me a whole lot. But I like being in your arms better." Without warning, those smoldering eyes filled with tears and she threw her arms around him. "God, I've missed you! My head *aches* with everything that horrid school stuffs into it! I want you to hold me and tell me I'll get through this."

"Hey, what happened to my little fire eater?"

Wetness soaked through his shirt. "She got lonely."

Had any uptime boys comforted her during that loneliness? Malcolm hoped not. "My place is this way," he murmured, wrapping an arm around her. "We, uh, have a lot to talk about."

"Yeah?" She brightened and sniffed back tears. "Like what?"

"Oh, lots of stuff." They caught an elevator for Malcolm's floor. "Goldie and Skeeter are in the middle of a *wager*, for one. Whichever of them scams the most in a month—and Goldie can't use her knowledge of rare coins and gems—gets to stay in La-La Land. The other one has to leave."

Margo's eyes widened. "You're kidding? That's a serious wager!" Then she grinned, evilly. "Any way we can help Skeeter?"

"I thought you hated him!"

Margo laughed, green eyes wicked as any imp newly-arrived from Hell's own furnace. "I do. But Goldie deserves worse than what we gave her. *Lots* worse." The steel in her voice reminded Malcolm of his favorite poet:

But when hunter meets with husband,
  each confirms the other's tale:
The female of the species
  is more deadly than the male. . . .

"Huh. Remind me never to get on your wrong side, young lady." The memory of those terrible days in Rome, searching for her, were almost more than he could bear. Margo's squeeze on his hand said a great deal more than her eyes, and *they* spoke of a pain and longing that hurt Malcolm like a physical blow. His faltering hopes began to regain their feet.

Sven Bailey had left Margo's luggage in the "lock-me-tight" mail bin outside each Resident's apartment. Malcolm unlocked the bin, rescuing Margo's cases, then opened his door and ushered her inside.

"You've redecorated! Wow! You actually have *furniture*!"

Malcolm shrugged. "A little money never hurts."

Margo laughed. "Don't be upset with me, Malcolm. I know it's my fault I nearly got us killed, but see. Something good *did* come of it." She swept a grand gesture at the room, nearly knocking over a lamp. "Whoops! Sorry."

That was his Margo, all right. But would she be *his* Margo?

"I, uh, had a little something, I, uh, that is . . ."

"Malcolm," she took both his hands in her own, "what *is* it? It's *me*. The addle-brained brat you had to rescue off a Portuguese witch-burning pyre. You're actually shaking! What's wrong?"

He stared into those bottomless green eyes, filled now with worry and even the beginnings of fear. When she reached up and brushed her lips across his, he felt something inside his soul melt. If she said no . . .

"It's okay, Malcolm. Whatever it is. Just tell me."

No more stalling, he thought grimly. Then he fumbled in a pocket for the little velvet box. "I, uh, went uptime for a little vacation, had this made for you."

She opened the box curiously, then went absolutely white.

"Malcolm?" Her voice wavered. So did those luminous green eyes.

"Will you?" he whispered.

An agony of indecision passed across her heart-shaped face, causing Malcolm's heart to cease beating.

"Malcolm, you know my heart—my whole *soul's* set on scouting," she whispered. "You—you wouldn't object?"

He cleared his throat. "Only unless you objected to my coming along."

Her eyes widened. "But—"

"I thought it was high time I got over being a coward."

Margo was suddenly in his arms, crying and kissing him at the same time. *"Don't ever say that! Do you hear me, Malcolm Moore? Never, ever say that!"*

Then she handed back the ring and held out her hand. Her fingers were trembling. It took Malcolm three tries to fumble the ring onto the engagement finger. A golden band to circle the heart line and hold it fast to his heart . . . Margo closed her fingers around the shank of the heavy ring and gazed silently at it for long moments. A diamond she'd nearly died locating in Southern Africa glittered in soft lamplight. "Yes," she whispered. "Oh, yes, Malcolm. I will."

Then, before Malcolm could do more than start breathing again, a look of stricken dismay widened her eyes. "Oh, Lordy, what's Kit going to say?"

Malcolm managed a wan chuckle. "Grandpa approves."

An Irish alley-cat glare he knew so well transformed her adorable, heart-shaped face as the eyebrows dove together and green eyes smoldered. "He does, does he? Am I the only one on this station who didn't know I was getting married?"

Malcolm rubbed his nose in embarrassment. "Well, uh, you know La-La Land."

"Do I ever." But the look in her eyes softened. "Margo Moore. I like the sound of that."

The sound of his name linked with hers did strange things to Malcolm's blood chemistry. The light in the room dimmed. "So . . . How's Denver sound for the honeymoon? I've got tickets. . . ."

Margo's kisses were enough to drive a sane man over the brink. When they came up for air, Margo breathed against his lips, "Sounds perfect. Now stop stalling, Malcolm Moore, and take me to bed!"

He carried her there, long dress trailing, without another word spoken. He was afraid the brutal violations she had suffered at the hands of those damnable Portuguese traders would somehow raise a barrier between them that neither could overcome. But the softness and passion he remembered so well from Rome redoubled in the silence of his bedroom, sending Malcolm nearly out of his mind with the need to touch and cuddle and bring joy where she had suffered so much pain. After their loving came to a shuddering, reluctant end, Margo cried again, nearly as hard as she had that terrible day in Rome. But this time instead of running, she clung to him and let him comfort her with silly, nonsensical words meant to reassure. Evidently they did, because she fell asleep cradled against the hollow of his shoulder, tear trails streaking her cheeks and his bare skin. Malcolm kissed her hair and marvelled, wondering if she would ever trust enough to share her mind as she had come to trust sharing her body.

The ring glittering softly on her left hand gave him hope. It was a start, anyway. Just as this joining had been. Malcolm lay awake, languorous and wondering, for hours, just holding her while she slept. When she finally woke, their second coming together was even sweeter than the first. And this time, as she drifted off once more against his chest, the words he had longed to hear came like a sigh in the darkness.

"I love you, Malcolm Moore. Hold me . . ."

And so he did.

CHAPTER NINE

"His name is Chuck," the voice on the other end of the phone said. "Chuck Farley."

Skeeter had no idea who the caller was, but they had his undivided attention. "Yes? What about him?"

"He came through Primary alone. Without a tour group. He's wearing a money belt he didn't declare through ATF. Right now, he's asking around at the hotels for the best time periods to visit."

The line went dead before Skeeter could ask who the caller was, why they'd called him, or how they'd obtained this juicy tidbit of information. Was Goldie setting him up? Or the ATF? Or was this legit? He hadn't forgotten Ianira's strange intensity on the subject of who was going to win this bet.

Maybe he possessed more allies than he'd realized.

Skeeter decided to hunt up Mr. Farley and see for himself what this lone uptimer might be up to. And if that money belt were for real . . . then Skeeter might just win his wager in one fell swoop. All it would take was a little finesse on his part. The question was, which scheme to use in the initial approach? Rubbing his hands in anticipation, Skeeter set out to do a little snooping of his own.

Scouting the territory in advance, Yesukai had taught him, was key to any victory. He'd find out what Chuck Farley was up to and use that to craft his plans to deprive the gentleman of that well-filled, undeclared money belt. Skeeter grinned and headed toward the Commons with a jaunty whistle.

"Undeclared? You're sure?" Goldie's voice came out sharp, excited.

"Positive. I saw it under his shirt when he went to the can. And it's *fat*. Could be thousands tucked into that thing."

Golden dreams floated before Goldie's eyes, like sugar plums and gallant Nutcracker princes, along with visions of Skeeter in handcuffs, hauled kicking and protesting through Primary by Montgomery Wilkes while she waved bye-bye like a sweet little grandmother.

"What's his name and where is he now?"

The voice on the other end chuckled. "Calls himself Chuck Farley. He's hotel hopping, asking questions. Like what gates are the best to visit. Doesn't seem to have any particular destination in mind. Thought that was a might odd, so I started asking around. Time Tours says he doesn't have a ticket through any of their gates and none of the little companies have him booked through the state-owned gates, either."

"Well, well. Thank you very much, indeed."

Goldie hung up the phone thoughtfully. Either they had a speculator on their hands, intent on making an illegal fortune, or they'd stumbled across a rich fool looking for a thrill. No telling, until she had the chance to chit-chat him personally. Whichever the case, she intended for that money belt and its delightfully undeclared contents to end up in *her* possession. Idiot. Chuck Farley had no idea that he'd just stepped into Goldie Morran's parlor. And like the nice, gentle spider she was, she set about weaving her silken webs of deceit to pull in this fat little fly all for herself.

❖   ❖   ❖

Skeeter stood in the shadows of a fake marble column across from the Epicurean Delight, watching a slim, nondescript fellow with dark hair and unremarkable eyes read the posted menu. Chuck Farley wasn't much to look at, but the trained eye revealed the unmistakable presence of that money belt the anonymous tipster had telephoned about. Skeeter was about to step out into the open to join him in "perusing" the menu when Kit Carson, Malcolm Moore, and—of all people—Margo Smith showed up, chatting animatedly. Skeeter swore under his breath and kept to the shadows. Margo sported an enormous diamond on her left ring finger. *Huh. What she sees in that guide is beyond me*. Malcolm Moore was even more nondescript than Chuck Farley, with a notorious string of bad luck dogging him, to boot.

Of course, he'd been a little more prosperous lately. Some scheme he and Kit had going—and the fact that Skeeter couldn't get the real dope on it was driving him crazy. Nonetheless, he kept a tight rein on his curiosity—Skeeter was even more curious than the next 'eighty-sixer, but he steered far clear of *anything* connected with Kit Carson. Yesukai had taught him well—Skeeter knew when he was outgunned. The clever warrior chose his prey with care. Glory was one thing; stupidity quite another. Five years in Yesukai's yurt had more than taught Skeeter the difference.

The group paused outside the Delight, exchanging polite words with Farley as they glanced over the menu. *Come on, go inside, already, before he decides to take a seat*.

Farley nodded courteously in return and joined the long line of uptime patrons waiting for a table. Unless one were a Resident, tables at the Delight were difficult to come by. Reservations were booked weeks in advance and long waits were the norm. But Residents always found a spot at one of the "reserved" tables

Arley Eisenstein held for 'eighty-sixers. Skeeter's mouth watered. The scents wafting out of the world-famous restaurant tantalized the senses, but Skeeter didn't have the kind of money to foot the bill for a meal at the Delight, not even when he *wasn't* saving every scrap of cash he owned to win a wager like this one.

Of course, he *had* conned his way in a time or two, getting some trusting uptimer with more money than sense to buy him a gourmet meal. But that didn't happen often, and the fact that Skeeter was ravenously hungry only made matters worse. Voices from waiting patrons floated across the Commons, making it impossible to hear what Kit Carson and his party were saying. Skeeter hugged his impatience to himself. If they would just go in, he could wander over and find a reason to strike up a conversation with Chuck Farley.

A downtimer Skeeter recognized as the Welsh bowman who'd come through that unstable gate from the Battle of Orleans a few months back pushed a wheeled dustbin past, then paused and exclaimed aloud. Margo hugged him, laughing and asking questions Skeeter couldn't quite hear. When she showed off the ring on her hand, the Welshman made deep, deferential bows to both Kit and Malcolm.

Kynan Rhys Gower was one of the very few downtimers Skeeter didn't feel comfortable around. For one thing, the man had pledged some sort of medieval oath of fealty to Kit, which made his business very much Kit's business—and therefore very much *not* Skeeter's. For another, the Welshman looked murderous every time he glanced in Skeeter's direction. Skeeter had no idea what he'd done to antagonize the man, having never recalled even speaking directly with him, but then, the Welshman's temper *had* manifested itself in decidedly odd ways since his arrival. He was unpredictable, at the least.

At times, he'd bordered on certifiable—like the time he'd attacked Kit with nothing but a croquet mallet, bent on murder.

Skeeter crossed both arms over his chest and slumped against the column. *Great. An impromptu welcome home party right in front of my rich little mark. Talk about luck* . . . Maybe Malcolm Moore's was contagious? Skeeter certainly hadn't had much luck bringing any of his schemes to fruition since challenging Goldie to this stupid bet. *What was I thinking, anyway? Everyone knows it's impossible to beat Goldie at anything. If anyone's certifiable, it's me.* Still, the challenge she'd thrown down had stung his pride. He hadn't really had a choice and he knew it. Probably she'd known, too, blast her for the backstabbing harpy she was. At least Brian Hendrickson's records proved Goldie's lead a small one. A couple of good scams and he'd be ahead. Well ahead.

Skeeter leaned around the column to see where his "mark" was—and heard a solid *thunk* next to his ear. Startled, he turned his head. A knife haft quivered in the air, the metal blade still singing where it had buried itself in the plastic sheathing of the fake column. Skeeter widened his eyes. If he hadn't leaned around just when he had . . .

He jerked around, looking through the crowd—

Oh, God.

Lupus Mortiferus.

The gladiator charged.

Skeeter bolted, yanking the knife out of the column as he went, so he wouldn't be completely weaponless if the enraged Roman actually *did* catch up with him this time. Diners waiting patiently in line stared as he dashed past, knife in hand, with a gladiator in cowboy chaps in hot pursuit. A sting made itself felt along the side of Skeeter's neck. He swore and swiped

at it, then gulped. Blood on his fingertips told him
just how close he'd come. A swift glance down showed
a thin line of drying blood on the edge of the knife
he'd snatched.

Holy . . . if that was poisoned . . . then he'd be in
big trouble, and soon. His legs went shaky for a couple
of strides, then he dodged up a staircase and pounded
down a balcony crowded with shoppers. Weaving in
and out between them, Skeeter made it to an elevator.
The door opened with a soft ding. He dove inside and
punched the top floor. The elevator doors slid closed
just as the enraged gladiator stormed past an outraged
knot of shoppers.

The car surged smoothly upward. Skeeter collapsed
against the wall, pressing a hand to his neck. *Damn,
damn, damn!* He needed to go to the Infirmary and
have Rachel Eisenstein look at this. But pride—and
fear—sent him plunging into the heart of Residential,
instead. If he reported the injury to Rachel, he'd have
to explain how he'd managed to sustain a long slice
across the side of his neck. And that would lead to
unpleasant confessions about profiteering from time
travel . . .

Nope, a trip to the infirmary was out.

And that blasted downtimer might have learned
enough about La-La Land by now to anticipate him
going to the clinic, anyway. Skeeter cursed under his
breath and headed for home. By the time he made it
to his apartment, Skeeter was trembling with shock
and blood loss despite the hand he kept tightly pressed
to the wound. Blood seeped between his fingers to
drip down his shirt. He was tempted to call Bull
Morgan and report the attack, consequences be
damned. That gladiator *scared* him. Winning the wager
with Goldie was one thing. Dying for it was quite
another. Hand shaking, he locked the door and

stumbled into the bathroom, swearing softly at the ashen cast of his face when he switched on the light.

He dabbed gingerly at the long, shallow slice, hissing between his teeth. "Sorry, Yesukai, but that *stings*." Antiseptic, antibiotic cream, and bandages made him look like the victim of a wide-jawed vampire. "Turtle-neck sweaters for a while," Skeeter muttered. "Just great. I really, genuinely hope that goddamned knife wasn't poisoned."

If it had been, he'd know soon enough.

He still wavered between calling Bull Morgan and keeping silent as he switched off the bathroom light and stumbled into his living room. He switched on the in-house TV news channel and flopped into his favorite chair, exhausted and scared and still trembling slightly. He needed food and sleep and painkillers. Food and sleep could be had without leaving the apartment. Painkillers . . . well, aspirin thinned the blood, which was no good. He'd have to settle for something like ibuprofen, if he had any.

The evening newscast's theme music swelled through the darkened little apartment. La-La Land's news program was, like the *Shangri-La Gazette*, more a gossip forum than a real news show. Most of the so-called journalists who drifted into and out of the anchor job were muckrakers who couldn't get work uptime for one good reason or another. They tended to shift from time terminal to time terminal in the hope that some juicy tidbit worthy of a real network job would relaunch their uptime careers. They also complained perennially about the lack of budget, equipment, and studio room. Skeeter shrugged—and winced. After his return uptime as a child, he'd grown utterly disgusted with them, camping out on the lawn for a chance at a photo session and maybe even an exclusive with the kid who'd lived with Genghis Khan's father and the toddler who would become Genghis Khan, himself.

Journalists had been a large factor in his decision to simply leave during the night and head for New York.

In the Big Apple, rotten to its scheming, seamy core, stories like his could easily be buried under the sensationalism of exposé after exposé on corrupt politicians, waving crime, and the spreading violence and sin that made the City *the* place for one little half-wild adopted Mongol to practice hard-won skills. Skeeter sighed. Those had been rough years, rougher in many ways than living in Yesukai's camp. But he'd survived them. The thought of going back . . .

I could always walk through the Mongolian Gate again, he told himself. *Temujin's out there somewhere fighting for his life against Hargoutai and his clan right about now. Temujin would take me in, might even remember the boy who used to do tricks to amuse him at night while the men were busy eating and telling stories and drinking themselves so sick they'd have to go outside and vomit. Living with Temujin'd certainly be better than going back to New York.* Just about anything would be better than going back to New York. He wasn't sure he'd live long, if he went back, and Skeeter Jackson had become terribly fond of creature comforts, but there were fates worse than dying young in battle.

Speaking of which . . . should he call Bull Morgan or not?

The news program he'd been waiting for had come on, flashing the familiar, sickly-sweet face of "Judy, Judy Janes!" onto the screen. She smiled at the camera, looking (as always) every eyelash-batting bit as idiotic as she *sounded*. But her opening statement caught Skeeter's attention *fast*.

"A disturbance this evening on the Commons just outside the Epicurean Delight has left 'eighty-sixers mystified and Security baffled. An eyewitness to the event, well-known station resident Goldie Morran, was willing to share her impressions with our viewing audience."

The camera treated Skeeter to a close-up of The Enemy.

Skeeter swore creatively. In Mongolian.

"Well, I couldn't be sure, everything happened so fast, but it looked to me like Skeeter Jackson bolted from behind that column over there and ran from a man I've never laid eyes on."

"Are you positive about that identification, Ms. Morran?"

Skeeter's official station identification photo appeared briefly on screen, grinning at the audience. The caption read "Unemployed Confidence Artist." Skeeter saw red—several seething shades of it.

The camera cut back to the Commons and Goldie's moment of triumph. Her eyes glittered like evil jewels. "Well, no, I couldn't swear to it, but as you know, Skeeter and I have made a rather substantial wager, so I've been at some pains to keep track of his movements. I'm afraid I wouldn't do Station Security much good as a prosecution witness, but it certainly did *look* like him. Of course," she laughed lightly, "we get so many scoundrels through, and so many of them look alike . . ."

The rest of the report was nothing more than innuendo and slander, none of it provable and every word of it calculated to wreck any chance he had at conning a single tourist watching that broadcast out of so much as a wooden nickel. Skeeter closed his fists in the semidarkness of his apartment. Report his injury? Hell would freeze first. He'd win this wager and kick that purple-haired harpy from here to—

Skeeter punched savagely at the channel changer. His apartment flooded with soothing music and slowly-shifting vistas taped both downtime as well as uptime. He'd deal with that pissed-off gladiator as best he could, on his own. *Nothing* was going to sour this wager. Not even Lupus Mortiferus and his fifty goddamned golden *aurii*.

He found the nearly fatal knife and closed his hand around the hilt. Skeeter Jackson wasn't a trained fighter—he hadn't been old enough when "rescued" by an astonished time scout—but he knew a trick or two. Lupus Mortiferus might just be in for as big a surprise as Goldie Morran. He flipped the knife angrily across the room, so that it landed point-first in the soft wallboard. *Nice throwing blade.* Bastard. That knife was *not* an ancient design. Either he'd stolen it . . . or someone was helping him.

Skeeter meant to find out which. And, if someone were helping him, *who*. The sooner he found out, the better. Neutralizing that gladiator had become imperative.

Unlike most Mongols, who learned early to place a very low value indeed on human life, Skeeter Jackson valued his most highly. He did not plan to die at the hands of a disgruntled downtimer who went around cutting out the tongues of the poor wretches he owned and gutting people for sport and coin.

Stranded as he was between the two worlds that had molded him, Skeeter Jackson listened to music in his darkened apartment, endured the thumping pain in his neck, and wrestled with the decision over whether or not to kill the gladiator outright by some devious method, or scheme some way to send him back where he belonged—permanently.

It was a measure of how deeply those two worlds

tugged at him that he had not resolved the question by the time he nodded off to sleep in the early hours of the morning.

Malcolm joined Margo as she emerged from the shower, aglow in a healthy, sexy way that made his insides turn to gelatin. He managed to find his voice and keep it steady. "You always did look great in skin, Margo."

Margo just beamed and winked, then adjusted her towel invitingly to dry her back.

Malcolm groaned and seized the towel, but managed to dry her back as gently as he might a frightened fawn. "Been doing your homework, then?" He couldn't believe how husky his voice sounded.

Margo started to laugh. "You bet! Every free moment I get outside of classes. You wouldn't believe the nickname some of my friends have given me."

"Oh?" Malcolm asked, raising one brow to hide the knot of fear that some of those friends might be young and masculine enough to capture her attention.

"Yes. Mad Margo. That's what they call me. I don't go to parties or overnighters or field trips—unless they're related to something important I'm studying—and I positively *never* go out on a date."

"Sure about that?" Malcolm half-teased.

Green eyes that a man could get lost in turned upward and met his, quite suddenly serious and dark. "Never." She squeezed his hand. "Do you honestly think all those little boys who swill beer and brag about their conquests could possibly interest me? After what we've been through, Malcolm? It'd take an act of God—maybe more—to pry us apart."

Malcolm dropped the towel and kissed her tenderly. It didn't stay tender long. When they finally broke apart, panting and on fire, Malcolm managed, "Well. I see."

Margo's eyes laughed again, the green sparkle back where it belonged. "Just wanted to convince you, is all."

Malcolm ran the tip of his tongue over swollen lips, then grinned. "Good!" But when he bent for another go-round, Margo laughingly danced away, causing his mind and gut actual pain.

"Oh, no. I'm squeaky clean. I'd like to stay that way for at least another hour, Mr. Moore!" Then she darted into the bedroom they shared and emerged less than two minutes later, clad in very chic black jeans, a sweater that would've made an old man's eyes pop, and dark, soft boots. Malcolm realized with a jolt that her clothing had Paris stamped all over it. She didn't flaunt herself in trendy, gaudy colors but stuck by well-made items that would be in style forever. "All right," she said, fluffing her hair as it dried—hair that looked like a Parisian salon had styled it—"you mentioned something about lunch?"

"Mmmm. Yes. I did, at that. Very well, Margo, gentleman it shall be—for now!"

He wriggled his brows wickedly. Margo laughed, secure of him. They left the apartment and found the corridor to the nearest elevator shaft. They moved easily, hands locked. The air between them sizzled with unseen but palpable heat. When they stepped into the elevator, Margo said huskily, "Your place or mine? After lunch?"

Malcolm couldn't hold back the jolt of need that went though him, but he retained enough presence of mind to recall that Margo, while nominally on vacation, needed to spend some educational time *outside* Malcolm's bed. Or couch. Or dining room floor. Or . . .

He sighed. "Neither just yet. There's someone I think you ought to meet."

Green, expressive eyes went suddenly suspicious. "Who?"

Malcolm chuckled and tickled her chin. "Margo Smith, are you turning jealous on me? Anyway, you'll like her. Just trust me on this one. She lived here already, but hadn't set up her shop yet when you first came to La-La Land. But she's well worth meeting. Trust me."

"Okay, I'm game. So after lunch, show me!"

For a moment Margo sounded *exactly* as she had just a few short months ago. Nice to know not *everything* had grown up quite yet. He didn't *ever* want that part of her to change. "I'll show you, all right," he chuckled. "But *before* lunch. I insist."

Margo pouted while Malcolm punched the button for Commons. The elevator whirred obediently upward. Malcolm steered her into the Little Agora District, vastly different from the genuine Agora's golden era. For one thing, there were no tethered or caged animals waiting to be purchased and ridden or eaten. For another, neither Socrates nor his pupils were anywhere to be seen. Instead, there was one particular booth positively jammed with customers. Other booth vendors looked at the crowded one with expressions that ran the gamut from rage to deep sorrow. Malcolm drew Margo straight toward the jam-packed booth.

Of course.

"Are you sure whoever this is won't mind interrupting her sales? She's got a ton of business there."

Malcolm grinned. "She'll thank *us*. Trust me."

He shoved and elbowed his way through the crowd with shocking rudeness, until Margo found herself staring at the most exotically beautiful woman she had ever seen. Her eyes, black as velvet, were far older than the early twenties she seemed to be. Even as Margo stared, wondering what it was that was so compelling about her, the woman broke into an exquisite, somehow ancient smile. "Malcolm! Welcome!"

Margo felt herself shrink in stature and confidence. While she'd been off at college, alone, Malcolm had been free to . . .

"Ianira, this is Margo. She is Kit Carson's grand-daughter and the woman I plan to marry."

Another dazzling smile appeared, this time directed disconcertingly toward Margo. "I am honored to meet you, Margo," she said softly. "Malcolm is a twice-lucky man." The dark eyes seemed to pierce her very soul. "And he will take away the pain in your heart, as well, I think," she said in an even softer voice. "He will make you forget your childhood and bring you much happiness." Margo stared, unable to figure out how she could *know*, unless someone of the few who *did* know had gossiped. Which in La-La Land would be entirely in character, except the only people who *knew* were her father, her grandfather, and Malcolm Moore.

When she glanced around for Malcolm, she realized with a jolt that every "customer" at the booth was busy either writing furiously, holding out a tape recorder, or fiddling with the focus on a handheld vidcam. Sudden fury swept her; she made a grab at and barely hung onto her temper at the intrusion into her privacy. Margo took a deep breath, then deliberately turned back to Ianira. Margo found a smile far back in those dark eyes, a smile which understood her anger and the reasons for it. "Thank you," she said slowly, still rather confused, because she was *certain* neither Kit Carson nor Malcolm Moore would have told *anyone*. And she was utterly certain her *father* had never set the first toe on TT-86's floor. Ianira's return smile this time was every bit as enigmatic as the Mona Lisa's, yet reminded her of graceful white statuary recovered from lost millennia to stand, naked or artfully draped, in vast, marble museums.

Malcolm said quietly, "Ianira Cassondra came to TT-86 a few years ago. Through the Philosophers' Gate."

"You're a downtimer, then? I hadn't guessed," she added, as Ianira nodded slightly. "Your English is fabulous."

A brief smile like sunlight on cloud tops passed over Ianira's face. "You are too kind."

Nervous, Margo focused her attention on the actual booth and its contents. Exquisitely embroidered cotton and linen gowns similar to the one Ianira wore were neatly folded up amidst dress pins, hair decorations, lovely scarves, tiny bottles of God only knew what, piles of various kinds of stones and crystals—with a select few hanging on cords to catch the light—charms of some kind which looked extremely ancient, carved carefully from stone, wood, or precious gems, even little sewn velvet bags closed by drawstrings, with tiny cards on them which read, "Happiness," "Wealth," "Love," "Health," "Children" in fake "Greek-looking" letters. There were even incense sticks, expensive little burners for them, and peeking out here and there, CDs with titles like *Aphrodite's Secret: The Sacred Music of Olympus*.

And, topping it all off, extraordinary jewelry of an extremely ancient design, all of which looked real, and from the prices could've been.

"You have quite a booth," Margo said, hearing the hesitation in her own voice.

Ianira laughed softly, a sound like trickling, dancing water. "Yes, it is a bit . . . different."

Malcolm, ignoring the crowd around them with their scribbling pens, tape recorders, and vidcams, said, "Margo, you remember young Marcus, don't you?"

"The bartender from the Down Time? Yes, very well." She could feel the heat in her cheeks as she recalled that first, humiliating meeting with Kit. The blush was innocent, as it happened, but Ianira might wonder. "Why?"

Malcolm smiled and nodded toward Ianira. "They're married. Have two beautiful little girls."

"Oh, how marvelous!" Margo cried, completely forgetting her earlier doubts. "Congratulations to you! Marcus is so . . . so gentle. Always so anxious to put a person at ease and treat them like royalty. You must be very happy."

Something in those fathomless dark eyes softened. "Yes," she whispered. "But it is not wise to speak of one's good fortune. The gods may be listening."

While Margo pondered that statement, Malcolm asked, "Have you had lunch, Ianira? Margo and I were just on our way. My treat, and don't give me any lame excuses. Arley Eisenstein's made enough money over the cheesecake recipes you've already given him, you might as well share the taste, if not the wealth."

Unexpectedly, Ianira laughed. "Very well, Malcolm. I will join you and your lady for lunch."

She lowered prettily painted plywood sides and locked the booth up tight with bolts shot home from the *inside*, then finished off with a padlock. They smiled when Ianira finally joined them. Ianira held a curious, largish package in brown paper tied up with string, which reminded Margo of a favorite musical with nuns and Nazis and narrow escapes.

"Special delivery after lunch?" Malcolm asked.

Ianira just smiled. "Something like, yes."

Margo, oblivious to that exchange, found herself envying the way Ianira walked and the way that dress moved with every step she took. She tried, with some fair success, to copy Ianira's way of moving, but something was missing. Margo vowed silently to buy one of those gowns—whatever it cost—and try out the effect on staid, British Malcolm Moore, who melted in her arms and kissed her skin with trembling lips as it was, every time they made love.

Unhappily, the entire mass of curious scribblers, tapers, and vidcammers followed close on their heels all the way down the Commons.

"Who *are* those people?" Margo whispered, knowing that whisper would be picked up and recorded anyway.

Ianira's lip curled as though she'd just stepped in excrement. "They are self-appointed acolytes."

"*Acolytes?*"

"Yes. You see, I was a high-ranking priestess in the Temple of the Holy Artemis at Ephesus before my father sold me in marriage. I was only part of the price to close a substantial business transaction with a merchant of ivory and amber. The man he gave me to was . . . not kind."

Margo thought of those horrid Portuguese in South Africa—and her father—and shivered. "Yes. I understand."

Ianira glanced sharply at her, then relaxed. "Yes. You do. I am sorry for it, Margo."

Margo shrugged. "What's past is past."

The statement rewarded her with another brilliant smile. "Exactly. Here, it is easier to forget unhappiness." Then she laughed aloud. "The day the ancient ones"— she pointed to the rafters, where fish-eating, crow-sized pterodactyls and a small flock of toothed birds sat—"came through the big unstable gate, I hid under the nearest booth and prayed *someone* would rescue me. When I dared peek out, I found the huge one covered in nets and the small ones flying about like vengeful harpies!"

Both Margo and Malcolm laughed softly.

Malcolm rubbed the back of his neck, while his cheeks flushed delightfully pink. "You should've seen *me*, that day, trying to hold that monster down and getting buffeted around like a leaf in a tornado. I finally just fell off and landed about ten feet away!"

They were still laughing when they reached the Urbs Romae section of the time terminal. Malcolm steered them into the Epicurean Delight's warm, crowded interior, toward one of the tables eternally reserved for 'eighty-sixers. Frustrated acolytes seethed outside, unable to get in without the requisite reservations or status as 'eighty-sixers. Tourists, most of whom had made reservations months in advance, stared at them with disconcerting intensity. Margo heard a woman nearby whisper, "My God! They're 'eighty-sixers! *Real* 'eighty-sixers! I wonder who?"

Her lunch companion gasped. "Could he be Kit Carson? Oh, I'm just dying to catch a glimpse of Kit Carson!"

"No, no, didn't you see the newsies? That's Malcolm Moore, the mysteriously wealthy time guide, and that's Margo Smith, Kit Carson's granddaughter. I remember it because it was a granddaughter he didn't even know existed. Made headline news on every network for an entire half an hour! I taped the stations I wasn't watching, just to compare versions. I can't *think* how you missed it. And that other woman seated with 'em? Just you take a guess as to who *she* is?"

"I—I'm afraid I don't recognize her—"

"You know all those Churches of the Holy Artemis that've been springing up all over the place? Well, that's Ianira Cassondra, the *Living Goddess*, an enchantress who knows the *ancient* ways. Lives here, now, to escape persecution."

The other woman's eyes had widened so far, just about all that remained of her face was eyes. "*Really?*"

It came out a kind of repressed squeal. "Oh, oh, where's my camera—?"

She fumbled a small, sleek camera and pointed it toward them.

Margo flushed red. Ianira looked merely annoyed. Malcolm just grinned, first at Margo, then at the ladies who'd been whispering so loudly; then he rose from his chair and bowed at the waist, tipping an imaginary tophat. The flash momentarily blinded Margo, catching Malcolm mid-hat-tip. Both women went white, beet-red, and hungry-eyed all in the space of two seconds. Then they beamed what they thought were seductive—or at least winning—smiles back at him.

"Hey," Margo said, wrapping her fingers around his, "you're took. An' don't you go 'round forgettin' it, now, or I'll hafta take a skillet to you!"

He chuckled. "Just part of the show, dear. Never know when it'll get you a rich customer. Besides, you're not allowed to hit me until *after* we're married." He lifted one brow, then. And just *when* did you start learning Wild West lingo?"

"Oh, a while back, I reckon."

He wrapped gentle fingers around her wrist and scowled his blackest, enraged scowl. "You two-timin' me, woman, with some no 'count cow-punchin' range rat?"

"Oh, God, that's depressing. And I thought I was actually making progress with it." She batted his hand away from her wrist. "You're terrible. Love you anyway." Then, "I didn't notice tourists doing that sort of thing last time."

"Oh, they were. You just didn't notice because you were too busy turning that alley-cat glare on everything and everyone who stood in your way—even those poor, abused books you used to read and fling across Kit's apartment whenever you got frustrated. Or attempting to toss Sven on his backside, if it killed you."

Margo went beet-red again. "Didn't know Kit'd told you about the books," she mumbled, noticeably not apologetic about trying to mop up the gym with the instructor who'd given her multiple bruises every single night.

His eyes softened. "Hey, Margo. It's okay. We all got out in time and you're doing wonderfully well, now that you're into your studies so deeply."

Margo just nodded, afraid to try her voice.

Ianira, who had taken in the entire exchange silently, began to chuckle. "You will do well, the pair of you." Two heads whipped around guiltily. Ianira laughed aloud. "Oh, yes. Fire of Youth and Caution of Experience— with streaks of childlike play and frightened love in you both. Yes," she smiled, "you will do well together." Before either of them could speak, Ianira stretched slightly. "Oh, what a relief to get away from those hounds." She pointed silently with her glance toward the window where her acolytes stood with despairing expressions, then said something low in ancient Greek, something that sounded holy and apologetic.

When she'd finished, and Margo was *sure* she'd finished, she asked curiously, "Don't they drive you crazy? Do they follow you around like that all the time?"

"Very nearly, and yes." Expressive eyes went suddenly tired. "It does get a bit wearing at times. Still, a few of them are actually teachable. I am told, for I will never be allowed uptime, that I have sparked an entire revival of Artemis worship. You heard those women. Simply by being here and occasionally speaking directly to a few of them," again, she nodded very slightly to the window, "I have accidentally begun something that even I do not know where the ending will lie."

"Yeah, you have. Believe me, have you ever. There are no less than *three* Artemis temples just on campus, because response was so high they had to build another and then a third one to hold all the students attending the ceremonies. How many are in town, I don't think anyone knows."

Ianira pondered that in silence—and judging by her eyes—sorrow.

"Hey, Ianira, don't feel so terrible. I mean everything we do or don't do, say or don't say has an impact on something or someone else. And none of us know even half, never mind *most* of the endings. I mean, look at the Church of Elvis The Everlasting."

"El-vis?" Ianira asked uncertainly. "I do not know this god."

Margo giggled. A genuinely delighted, little-girl giggle. "Yeah. Elvis Presley, singing star. Here's an aging rock 'n' roll legend found dead on the *toilet*, for God's sake, with a whole bunch of chemicals in his blood. That was back in 1976. Wasn't too long before folks started writing songs about him, or claiming they'd seen The Everlasting Elvis at some grocery store or in their living rooms, or maybe hitchhiking some interstate and a trucker lets him in, talks to him for a while, then he'd say something like, 'Gotta go, now friend. Good talkin' to you. See you at Graceland some day.' Then he just vanishes."

Ianira was laughing so hard, there were tears in her eyes. "Please, Margo, what is a 'rock 'n' roll' singer? Why was this El-vis so popular?"

Surprising them both speechless, Malcolm shoved back his chair, ran impromptu fingers through his hair so it looked more or less appropriate, then in an astonishingly good imitation of Elvis' voice, sang a stirring, blood-pounding rendition of "Heartbreak Hotel." Complete with world-famous hip thrusts. He grabbed up the vase from their table and sang into the pink carnation as though it were a microphone and crooned the chorus to applause, whistles, and feminine shrieks. Then with a single movement, he whipped the dripping carnation and tossed it—straight at Margo. She let out a sound somewhere between scream and fainting ecstasy while the transformed Malcolm bowed to the thunderous applause all through the Delight. He bowed to every corner in turn, saying, "I wanna thank you for comin' and sharin' my show. I love you all, baby. Gotta go, now. My 'nanner sandwich is waitin'."

He sat down to another thunderous round of applause, shrieks for "MORE!" and an entire hailstorm of carnations. All three ducked, finding themselves covered in no time with dripping wet flowers.

"See," Malcolm grinned, coming up for air—with a red carnation stuck sideways in his hair—"no sequined suit, no fancy guitar—in fact, no guitar at all, and I'm not nearly as good an imitator as lots of guys are. But you saw the response from the people in here." They were still brushing off carnations. Malcolm signalled for a waiter. "They went completely nuts. *That's* the definition of the ultimate rock 'n' roll star: being so good at what they do, their audiences go crazy. Happened with the Beatles, too; but they called Elvis 'The King of Rock' *long* before he died and got himself apotheosized."

Margo took up the rest of the explanation as best she could. "Pretty soon, there was a single 'Church of Elvis the Everlasting.' The main temple was—is—his estate at Graceland, Elvis' mansion near Nashville, Tennessee. Trouble was, while lots of folks made the pilgrimage, lots more couldn't afford it. So before you know what's happening, there are *thousands* of Churches of Elvis the Everlasting, all over the country.

And all of 'em mail their cash tithes overnight express to the High Temple at Graceland."

Margo grinned. "Man, you should *see* that place! There was a documentary on it one Friday night a few weeks back, and since I didn't have much to do, I watched it." She rolled her eyes. "A *real* king would be jealous. There's an altarpiece, must be twenty-four feet of black velvet, with another piece coming down the pulpit to the floor. Believers who can sew are still working on it. The Everlasting Elvis on the pulpit is finished—gold and silver threads, diamonds, rubies, emeralds, you name it, they used it to decorate that drop of cloth.

"And no cheap, synthetic velvet, either, but the real stuff that would cost me, let's see, at *least* seven weeks of saving up every bit of my allowance, just to buy a piece of real velvet as big as the altar piece, never mind the twenty-four-foot runner. *That* is supposed to illustrate the entire *life* of the Everlasting Elvis."

Margo giggled. "I can't help wondering if they're going to show him ascending as the Elvis Everlasting, rising into grace from that toilet seat he died on? Oh, that whole *place* is crazy. The whole *fad* is crazy. Worshipping a dead rock 'n' roll singer? Puh-leeze."

Ianira was still wiping tears of hilarity from the corners of her eyes. "Your whole uptime world, I think, is just as crazy as worshipping a dead man. You have a gift, Margo, for telling a story." Ianira's smile was brilliant. "You could go into training, fire-haired one. So few see so clearly at your age."

Margo flounced in place. "Humph. It ain't the age, it's the mileage," she muttered, paying tribute to one of her favorite last-century classics.

"You see what I mean?" Ianira said softly. "You just did it again. You *should* get training before you go scouting on your own. You may well have need of it someday."

Margo couldn't say anything. Once again, Malcolm came to her rescue. He passed menus around and said lightly, "Ianira, who has accumulated quite a bit of 'mileage' for *her* age, has become something of a celebrity uptime, as you mentioned with all those temples on your campus. Right after The Accident, there was a group of kooks, I forget what they called themselves—"

Margo supplied the answer: "The Endtime Saviors."

"Yes," Malcolm said with a "thank you" and a kiss both pantomimed, "these Endtime Saviors decided right after The Accident that the End was upon us. They kept looking for a sign. A prophet who would usher in the next age of mankind. Or should I say 'womankind'? Unfortunately, they've decided Ianira *is* that sign. She's regarded as a prophetess, the Voice of the Goddess on Earth."

Margo rubbed the tip of her nose. "Well, if she can say to everyone what she said about me and my poor, checkered past, I can understand why."

"No," Ianira laughed softly. "It is just that you and I resonate so closely. Our experiences, different as they are, have enough similarity to feel the resonance and understand clearly its source."

Margo shook her head. "I dunno. I guess if that's how you do it . . ."

Ianira smiled slightly. "It is part of my training in the Mysteries of Artemis, you see, in the great Temple at Ephesus, where I was born. Oh, how I miss Ephesus!" Her exotic eyes misted for just a moment and it came to Margo with a jolt just how terribly homesick most downtimers must be, torn away from everything they knew and loved, never allowed to go home, wandering at best from menial job to menial job, maybe even switching stations in the hopes of improving their situation—

Margo thereby swore a sacred oath to treat *all* downtimers, not just Kynan Rhys Gower, a great deal more courteously.

Ianira was still speaking. "After marriage, when my *husband* carried me across the Aegean Sea to Athens, pride of Greece, I vowed to study as best I could the Mysteries of the majestic Athene who guarded his city. Not even *he* could deny me that, not with my stature from Ephesus. So I learned— and learned to hate my life outside the Temple, inside *his* gyneceum."

Margo, round-eyed, could only reply, "Oh. I—I'm sorry."

Malcolm chuckled. "Hits most people that way. Ianira's name means the Enchantress, you know. She's what you might call an international, temporal treasure, locked away safe and sound inside TT-86's concrete walls."

Ianira flushed and made a small sound of disagreement.

"Say what you will," Malcolm said mildly, "an international, temporal treasure is exactly what you are. Dr. Mundy—a professor of history who interviews the downtimers," he added for Margo's benefit, "—says it constantly. Best information he's found in all his life, he says, and he's getting it all in glorious detail from *you*, Ianira. Besides," he winked, "being an international, temporal treasure does pays the bills, doesn't it?"

Ianira laughed aloud. "You are impossible, Malcolm Moore, but yes. It does, handsomely. It was a good idea Marcus had, to put up such a booth when crassly miseducated, uptimer fools began to seek me out. We're almost out of debt to the Infirmary, now."

"That's great, Ianira. I've very happy for you. I know how close it was with your little girl."

Ianira gave him a sad, sweet smile. "Thank you. It was in the hands of the gods—and Rachel Eisenstein, may the Lady bless her eternally—but she is now healthy enough to return to the Station Babysitting Service and School. I would dearly *love* to get my hands on the tourist who brought that fever back to the Station with him! Malcolm, after lunch, perhaps you would care to join me? I always go there after lunch to check on my babies. And I have an idea which may help relieve a bit of the strain on poor Harriet Banks. She tries so hard and it is just not fair."

Malcolm just said, "Yeah. I know. I'll be happy to come along. Got a few ideas of my own, I do. We'll compare notes after lunch. Margo?"

She shook her head, eyes apologizing to Ianira as best she could. "I have to get in some weapons practice before we go to Denver. I'm a little rusty and even if I weren't, I'd still practice because my scores just weren't all that good before my, uh, adventure. So I thought I'd try out a couple of period rifles, a few handguns, see how I do with them."

"You are wise," Ianira smiled that archaic, mysterious smile. "A woman who thinks herself without limits is a dangerous fool—and I have seen so very many of them." The acolytes were still outside, filming and scribbling notes. Ianira glanced their way with the merest flick of her gaze, but managed to convey utter contempt for the lot of them. Margo blinked, having no earthly idea how she'd just done that, but wanting to learn the secret of it for herself.

Ianira reached out and covered Margo's shocked hand. "You have begun to understand that you have limits, Margo, even as all humanity has limits. What I find even more astonishing—and delightful—for a girl your age, you have already discovered what many of them," she nodded toward the window, "will never discover." Then once more, the offer came, causing even Malcolm to stare.

"It would be my great joy to train you, Margo, for there is such a fire in your soul as I have not seen since my childhood, when my own dear instructor, the sister of my mother, was chosen as High Priestess. Light would dance from her hair, her fingertips, there was so much fire inside her. She did many great things and was everywhere honored as a great and shrewd leader during times when leadership was desperately needed.

"You look nothing like her, Margo, yet you could *be* her. And, youthful as you are, you have already taken the first steps on your own journey to wisdom." Then, letting go Margo's hand, which tingled as though live electricity had poured through it, Ianira fished under the table and slid the brown-paper packet over toward Margo. When Margo gave her a puzzled look, Ianira said softly, "Your Malcolm is a man with a beautiful soul. He is dear to us, to the Council of Seven, to the whole community of downtimers, The Found Ones. Consider the contents of the package a wedding gift from all of us, so that you might please Malcolm even more than you do now, and so that Malcolm will not just love you, but worship you, for that is what you both need and deserve. Nothing less will do. I can only hope this offering of silly trinkets will help."

"Uhm," Margo cleared her throat. "Do I open it now? Or save it for the wedding night?"

Ianira laughed. "That is your decision. But the way Malcolm is staring from you to that package and back, with such speculation in his eyes, I would suggest you open it now."

Margo glanced over and saw the intense hunger in Malcolm's face, which turned bright red when he realized he'd been caught out. Hastily he cleared his throat and said, "I was only curious, after all."

Both women laughed. Margo dipped into an across-the-shoulder purse no bigger than a diskette box and pulled out a small but useful Swiss Army knife. She made quick work of the string, then turned the carefully tucked package onto its back, took a deep breath, and opened it.

Inside lay the most exquisite gown from Ianira's rack and jewelry nestled in its fold: not the cheap stuff, but the stuff that had the look and feel of genuine antiquity.

"Oh!—My God! Oh, my *God*! Ianira, you shouldn't have—I can't possibly accept—"

Ianira stopped her attempted refusal by leaning forward and placing soft fingertips across Margo's lips. "Just accept. As a friend."

Margo's eyes filled. "Why are you doing this? I just met you—"

"Oh, no, child. We have known each other through many lifetimes. Wear it and please each other, that you also may be together for many lifetimes."

Margo didn't hear much through the next few seconds. She kept staring at the lines of sparkling embroidery, the heavy silver necklace, bracelets, earrings, with all the stones in them prepared in the ancient way: simple, round-topped cabochons, even the diamonds. It was beyond beautiful. Margo could find no words to say how beautiful it was.

Ianira and Malcolm were speaking again, forcibly yanking Margo out of uncustomarily deep thoughts. "—firearms practice schedule on her own, same with the martial arts. And she studies, my God, the girl studies!"

Ianira laughed softly. "Would you have her any other way?

Malcolm said without hesitation, "No."

Ianira glanced over to Margo. "I will ask the Lady's blessing on your practice."

"Hear, hear," Malcolm agreed. "After lunch, you go play with guns. I'll come down later and see how you're doing, get in a little practice, myself. Then we'll get clean, eat in, and try on that," he nudged the half-opened package, "before bedtime. *Well* before bedtime."

Margo smiled her best, heart-stopping smile. One elderly gentleman—well, he was hardly a gentleman— at finding himself the focus of that smile, had literally collapsed on the street, leaving strangers to hunt his pockets for the nitroglycerin and to call the ambulance. After that experience, Margo was careful just how far she turned on that particular smile—and then realized with a jolt that she and Ianira weren't so different, after all. It startled her into meeting the other woman's gaze.

Ianira knew. Somehow, she knew exactly what Margo had just discovered. Moreover, she approved, eyes twinkling merrily. Margo swallowed hard as the silent invitation passed over Malcolm's bent head. *Someday*, Margo attempted to convey with eyes and tiny gestures. *Someday I will seek you out for training. I have the funniest feeling I'm supposed to study with you, that I am going to need to learn what you teach me.*

Ianira merely nodded and smiled again, a mysterious little smile full of knowledge and agreement. Margo smiled back her acceptance.

Malcolm the Ever-Vigilant (missing the exchange entirely) glanced up from his menu and smiled at them both. "Well, then, what shall we order for lunch?"

CHAPTER TEN

One look at the firing line and Margo's gut muscles tightened in dismay.

Please, anyone *but that bunch!*

Maybe they were just finishing up their session?

Margo's nostrils pinched tight, causing her upper lip to curl in a completely unconscious expression of disgust. The group of five intent paleontologists she'd met at the uptime station in New York, where Shangri-La's Primary opened, were just beginning to unpack a luggage cart, laying out their sundry gun cases for a private lesson.

Aw, rats. Some of Ann's lessons took *hours* to complete.

She didn't dislike the paleontologists, exactly. Well, not the woman, anyway. But three of the four men had spent their entire time in Primary's uptime waiting lounge all but drooling while they stared directly at her. Or, rather, at her chest. It was a reaction she was more than accustomed to, but she still didn't like it.

Chalk up another change, Margo. You don't like being stared at anymore.

Already, the group had noticed her and the renewed stares made her feel like a sleazy 42nd Street hooker. Margo began to consider—seriously—buying some of the uglier but more fully concealing peasant clothing in Connie Logan's Clothes & Stuff.

Paleontologists, hah!

The only truly interesting thing Margo had discovered about them was where and when, exactly, they were heading. Cope and Marsh had fought over a *huge* chunk of territory. She shook her head slightly.

The damned fools were deliberately walking right into the middle of the fight, hoping to rescue one of the new-species fossil skeletons that one side or the other had smashed up into tiny, useless fragments, so that it had been lost to science forever. The girl, one of three graduate students selected for this trip, had explained; at least, she'd mentioned something about a diary one of their professors had stumbled on in a used bookstore, written by one of the actual field agents charged with bringing back as many intact new specimens as possible.

Using that diary as a guide, they'd plotted out this madcap adventure and actually expected not only to find and rescue one or more of the smashed skeletons, but to get the bones back through the Wild West Gate and uptime to the museum affiliated with their university.

Margo was glad they'd had enough sense to take her advice and get some good instruction on how to use whatever they'd brought along, but that did *not* mean she wanted to practice with them.

Come on, Margo, bear up! Maybe if I take that farthest lane? If it's not reserved already, it ought to do. The lanes were sometimes reserved in advance for a scout who was planning to push an unexplored gate and wanted to learn to use a nice, little hideout gun. It was a practice Kit disapproved of—and a habit he had very carefully made certain she *never* picked up, but scouts were independent agents, so to speak, so each made his own decisions on what to take downtime. Kit had warned her there were a few really marginal scouts who routinely broke what he considered to be *the* sacred rules of scouting.

Carrying a gun downtime into an unknown time and place, where any gun might be an anachronism, wasn't stupid. It was suicidal.

She didn't spot anyone else on the range, though, which bolstered her hopes. The paleontologists were talking excitedly while dumping gun cases onto Ann's benches. *Lots* of gun cases. Margo winced at the way they just casually bounced the stuff around, allowing them to slide to the floor, banging them together, using the muzzle end of a thin leather case to shove a larger, much heavier case farther down the bench to make room for the rifle with its now-possibly-ruined front sight. They'd be learning about sighting in and zeroing rifles, or Margo didn't know Ann Vinh Mulhaney.

When Ann noticed that only one of her five students was opening the gun cases for inspection, while four of the group had their attention directed elsewhere, she glanced around. Then smiled so brightly Margo's eyes misted a little.

"Oh, it's you," Ann laughed. "I thought maybe Marilyn Monroe's ghost had jiggled in or something."

That statement caused several reddened faces and sudden diligence with as-yet-unloaded gear. Margo's face had gone terribly hot. Marilyn Monroe, the twentieth-century sex goddess? *That*, Margo would never be, but she enjoyed the compliment just the same. Ann nodded her over. Margo would have *loved* a long heart-to-heart with Ann—but now was not the time.

Oh, well, she thought as she headed resolutely toward them, *at least I'll finally get to see what firearms these "learned" idiots brought along*. Making the best of it, Margo covered the intervening space with a cheery, "Hi, Ann! Hope things have been fantastic."

Ann laughed and gave her a swift—hard—hug, then stepped back. She had to look up a fair ways to find Margo's eyes—and Margo was not even remotely tall. Ann was just *tiny*.

"Yes, they have been. Utterly and completely fantastic. I'm going to have another kid in about seven months." She patted her belly gently. "So no wrestling," she chuckled. "Anyway, that's Sven's forte, not mine." Her eyes crinkled in a fond smile as she studied Margo. "Just look at you, girl. You're still growing! I thought so, earlier, but the way Malcolm was mauling you, it was hard to tell."

Margo's cheeks flushed again, hotter than before. The ring on her finger tugged downward, it was so heavy. She knew Ann had noticed it the moment she'd walked into the range.

"Good!" Ann decided, hands planted on hips in her usual stance. "You look better with some meat on those bones and some color in your cheeks, you scrawny little Irish alley cat. One thing's for sure, that baleful green glare hasn't changed. Not a bit."

Margo grinned. "How're the wagers going?"

Ann blinked. "Wagers?"

"About how soon I'll be in your condition."

"Oh, *that* wager." Ann's eyes crinkled again. "Hot and heavy betting, both for and against. Everyone knows how determined you are about your profession, but everyone also knows that Malcolm Moore is a very, um, how to put it—intense individual when it comes to getting what he wants."

They grinned at one another. Then Margo noticed the paleontologists, who stood listening in silence, several of them round-eyed with shock. *Aw, rats. Here I am doing just what I said I wouldn't do*.

Ann, perhaps guessing some of what was happening inside her head, just touched the back of Margo's hand with her fingertips, bringing her back to the reality outside Margo's thoughts. Margo blinked. Ann asked gently, "Have you come to brush up with a lesson? If you did, you'll have to wait a while. Or do you just want to brush up with a stack of targets and whatever you care to shoot?"

Margo nodded. "Thought I'd try a Winchester model 73 first. Malcolm's taking us to Denver, so I thought I might as well tackle period rifles. I'll try a model 76 Centennial later."

"Just those two?"

Margo let go a genuine, healthy laugh. "And who taught me to carry only the right weapon for the job? This is just this *morning's* practice session. Tomorrow morning I have a date with handguns of every imaginable design and manufacture, just so long as they were invented *before* 1885; then Sven gets a crack at me before lunch."

Anne's eyes brightened. "Oooh, can I come watch? I don't have a class scheduled . . ."

Margo just rolled her eyes. "I can't stop you. Besides, I might need help crawling out of the gym."

Ann laughed heartily. "Okay, imp. It's a deal." Ann's eyes sparkled with anticipation. "You're head's on straight, kid, even if you *were* stuck in an uptime college for six months. A college I'm *certain* does *not* have a shooting range."

"Are you kidding?" It came out sour as early Minnesota apples, still green and hard as walnuts on the tree. "A *shooting* range? No way real." That new bit of uptime slang hadn't filtered down to La-La Land yet, given the startlement in Ann's eyes.

"They just outlawed metallic emery boards, for God's sake."

Ann shook her head, eyes dark with sorrow. "It's been lousy uptime for a *long* time. Why do you think we moved our family to Shangri-La Station?" She shivered at some memory she was unwilling to share, then sighed. "Well, you might as well get started. Use lane four, if you don't mind. I'm going to start the class on basic safety before we move to pistol and rifle types. You know where the keys are, right?"

Five sets of jaws dropped—again.

Margo grinned back. "Yep. I even"—she dropped a wicked wink—"know where you hide the pole guns and laser-guided dart guns, never mind the *really* cool stuff. Hey, is that Browning Automatic Rifle working again? I really liked shooting it before it malfunctioned." She considered pride versus humility in front of this bunch of geeks, and decided on humility—hoping it would be a lesson to *them*. "And I'm still utterly mortified that I, uh, caused it to malfunction last time I used it, then couldn't figure out how to machine a new part. Is it fixed yet? I did send the money to repair it." She batted pretty lashes and sounded wistful as a half-drowned kitten.

Ann just laughed. "Oh, you're impossible as ever, imp. Weepy one second, hellbound-for-leather the next. Go on and get whatever you need and let me get back to *paying* customers." Her smile took any possible sting out of the words. But she had not answered Margo's question about the B.A.R. *Rats!*

Before she left, Margo glanced at the rifles and pistols that had been quietly laid out on the benches while they spoke. *Uh-oh. Thought so. Smart—but stupid. Typical academicians. You'd think they'd eventually change.*

Margo found the keys right off, then unlocked a largish room built inside the range itself. Made entirely of steel four inches thick in every dimension, with a heavy door whose hingepins were on the *inside*, it contained firearms of literally every time period from their invention in the 1300s onward. Door still open, she half heard Ann say lightly to her new students, "Why did I . . . Margo . . . keys? Oh, that's only because . . . time scout. Still in . . . already very good at her job. Her first scouting adventure . . . very dangerous . . . unstable gate. But she got everybody out but one . . . malaria."

Margo squirmed—*all* 'eighty-sixers knew who'd pulled her bacon out of the fire (literally) on that trip; but she was still young and vain enough to wish she could've seen the expressions on those stuffy academic faces as it registered: a *woman* time scout. She grinned—then suddenly sucked in air as a horrifying thought sent her belly plummeting groundward.

Oh, damn! She figured she had about three months before those five idiots out there blabbed to every uptime newsie in the business that a *woman* time scout by the name of Margo Smith was working out of TT-86. She'd be *swarmed* over by reporters, particularly the tabloid kind. And they were nearly *impossible* to shake off once they got interested in you.

Now she'd *never* get any studying done. She abruptly understood her grandfather's uncompromising, lifelong hatred of news reporters. *Well, Margo, my girl, just make the best of it and maybe you'll build up a reputation big enough to satisfy even your ego.*

She grinned at herself, having learned quite a few things about Margo Smith this day she'd never even guessed existed, and plucked a beautiful Winchester Model 73 .44-40 from the rifle rack, automatically checking to be certain it wasn't loaded. She laid it carefully aside, muzzle pointed away from the open door. She found ammo for a Model 76 Centennial in .45-75 Winchester, remembering vaguely that Ann carried a couple of the rifles in stock. She discovered a beauty of a lever-action Winchester Model 76

Centennial—clearly *original*—which was very similar to the 73, but beefier and in a more powerful caliber. It, too, was safely unloaded. The Centennial was for *serious* shooting. She'd have to remember to ask Ann to reserve them for the Denver trip.

The size of the 76 caused Margo to remember Koot van Beek's rifle and that great, horrid Cape Buffalo. That was a barely scabbed over memory, too. She hastily snagged the Centennial, along with a modern cleaning kit with brushes for both rifles. Never, ever again would Margo travel down a gate without the right weapons close at hand.

Putting aside the memory, Margo carted all the items to an empty shooting bench on lane four. Ann glanced up and nodded approvingly, her goggles in one hand, her ear muffs slid down around her neck, in "lecture mode."

"Let me know when you're ready to go 'hot,' Margo," she called down the line.

Margo nodded and curiously studied the beginning of the lesson as she prepared to practice. It looked from here like the paleontologists were giving Ann a *very* difficult time.

One of them—Margo's electronic earmuffs picked up conversations from an astonishing distance—demanded in a voice that would have frozen lava, "We are *not* renting and wearing this crap! Why would we possibly need eye and hearing protection? This is *supposed*"—the word dripped venom—"to be a trial run for our field work. We'll have none of this junk downtime! Will we?"

Margo continued shamelessly eavesdropping—how else did one survive in a cruel world, particularly when one was studying to become a real scout whose *job* was to overhear and remember just such conversations? Ann was clearly working hard not to shout obscenities in Vietnamese *and* Gaelic at her recalcitrant pupils.

As Margo's first, lamentable lessons had shown, while Ann could instruct willing students to a high degree of skill, she couldn't instill intelligence. Result? Some customers refused to listen, went downtime improperly armed and/or trained, and usually came back needing a hospital—or staying downtime in a long pine box.

Time Tours, Inc., of course, liked to keep that kind of publicity to a strict minimum, but the company executives—looking for ever more gate profit—did nothing about *requiring* weapons or self-defense training before allowing a tourist to go downtime. Lessons with the terminal's pro's were strictly on a voluntary basis.

Maybe she ought to suggest required classes to Bull Morgan. She snorted. He'd no doubt tell her it was a tourist's business to get training, not his, and if they were stupid enough to go downtime without it, they deserved whatever they got. Besides, Bull Morgan would *never* pass such a rule, because La-La Land was a place where folks fought, ignored, and thumbed noses at rules, rather than making new ones.

At any rate, it looked like Ann could use some help corralling this bunch of jerks into *listening* instead of tossing their academic credentials around like spiked morning stars. She sighed and left everything on her chosen bench, muzzles pointed downrange, then plunged in.

"Hi, guys!" Margo called, friendly-like, baiting her hook with a honeyed voice. Margo smiled sweetly, a dire warning to every person who knew her well— Ann actually winced—then she swept off shooting glasses and protective earmuffs and shook out vibrant hair.

"See these?" She held out the earmuffs, determined to give this her best effort. "These are hearing protectors. On a firing range, you wear them. Period. You can lose most of your hearing mighty fast unless you put hearing protection on *before* somebody starts target practice."

"How would you know?"

One man she couldn't quite see shot the question in her general direction.

She shrugged. "Because I lost part of my hearing in this ear on a deadly little street in Whitechapel one bitter cold morning in 1888."

Silence reigned.

She didn't add that Malcolm had done the shooting. But the hearing loss, slight as it was, was genuine. She added, "I lost more when an unstable gate opened up and I fell through it right into *The* Battle of Orleans. Joan of Arc and some really pissed off English knights and archers and some even *angrier* French nobles were taking a beating and hating it. Orleans was a really *intense* battle. Damn near got myself killed—twice— before I was back safe in the station's infirmary.

"Then some more of my hearing went bye-bye in South Africa, running from sixteenth-century Portuguese traders. I got caught in the middle of a firefight. Some friends of mine who'd figured out I was in trouble had come to help and I got caught between them and a whole, unwashed *mass* of murderous traders who were *really* riled up. They'd already decided to burn my assistant and me at the stake."

Margo managed to hold back the near-instinctive shudders such memories brought—and in suppressing them, Margo understood her grandfather more than she'd ever believed possible. It was little wonder he'd turned her down so rudely in the Down Time Bar & Grill that first day.

"Believe me, black powder guns are *loud*. You *do*

want to be able to hear when you get downtime?"
Margo questioned sweetly.

"As for these," she wiggled the clear, wrap-around
shooting glasses between two fingers, "even a novice
should be able to figure out what they're for. I do take
it that nobody *wants* to go blind?"

Nobody answered, despite an angry stirring near
the back of the group. Margo shrugged. "They're your
eyes and ears. You got replacements lined up for 'em,
go right ahead without the safety equipment. But
then," she smiled sweetly again, "I'm wagering you're
just the teeniest bit brighter than that. By the time
you've earned a master's, never mind a Ph.D, you've
supposedly learned what's irrelevant and beneath
notice from what's not only correct, but essential.
Right?"

Behind the paleontologists, Ann had covered her
lips with both hands to hold in laughter. Tears appeared
in her eyes when five heads nodded like marionettes
in sync.

"Thanks, Margo, for taking your time to help out.
I'm sure these folks will save their ears from the noise
you're about to generate!" Ann added pointedly. The
group sheepishly picked up its safety equipment and
began donning it.

Margo retrieved her Winchester Model 73—the
most popular rifle in the Old West—from her own
shooting bench. She loaded the Model 73 and called
out, "Ann, I'm going hot!" She then lined up her first
shot.

BOOM!

To her right, all five paleontologists jumped, despite
the dampening qualities of their hearing gear.

BOOM! *A little high and right*, she muttered to
herself, correcting her aiming point rather than
adjusting the sights, using a method called "Kentucky

windage," where you simply moved the sight picture to the other side of the target the same distance you missed or until you simply "felt right." The third BOOM! put the bullet exactly where she wanted it: inside the ten ring. She finished the magazine, pleased that the only shots outside the nine ring were those two initial placement shots. *Didn't throw a single round!* And that, despite months without even picking up a gun. She continued with her practice, nonetheless.

After a while, Margo smiled at her latest target and put the rifle down. She was tempted to return to the group, if only to see what sort of firearms they had, but was reluctant to disturb Ann's class any more than she already had. As if divining her interest, Ann looked up and waved Margo over.

Upon her arrival, Ann motioned almost imperceptibly for Margo to hold her own inspection. Margo realized this inspection—and everything that went with it—was, in fact, a lesson Ann was using to judge *her* improvements, her judgment. She took a good, long look at the neatly arranged firearms. She confirmed at a glance what she'd suspected earlier.

"Mmmm . . . they do have some nice Winchester Model 94's here, don't they, Ann? It really is too bad." She glanced over toward the paleontologists. "You're gonna have to ditch 'em, every last one. Anachronistic as he-heck. For one thing, the whole feed system on a 94's different from the Model 73 and 76."

A deep, angry voice behind the knot of grad students demanded, "What does that have to do with anything? Standing right here they look just alike!"

Hooo, boy. Ivy League and pissed. Not good.

She shook her head. "Sorry, but no, they don't look alike."

"Not at all," Ann chimed in, startling Margo at first

until she saw the tiniest bit of a dip from Ann's left eyelid. She felt better immediately.

"Now," Ann was saying, "where you're going, some folks are going to see those Model 94's up-close enough to notice."

"Can't be avoided," Margo added, enjoying the see-saw rhythm as they took turns. *Maybe if I'm desperate for something to do on weekends, I could try my hand at teaching. I've got pretty good credentials, after all*.

Modest, Margo was not. And finally she could revel in it to her heart's content, the way cats simply fold their bodies into pretzel-twists around *anything* loaded with catnip.

"Young woman," one of the men began, voice surprisingly deep for the acceptably trendy cadaver he called a body, "are you questioning *my* judgment? *I*," he went on, arrogant as a New York cabbie, "either suggested or chose each and every one of these firearms myself." He cleared an Ichabod Crane throat delicately, feigning (and not very well) humility. "NCAA Rifle Team four years running. Harvard."

Harvard? Aw, nuts! I'm losing my touch. She'd have bet for sure he was a Yalie.

She caught and held his gaze squarely, long enough to let him know she wasn't impressed, then replied politely, "Well, sir, I'm sure you were wonderful with a perfectly balanced match rifle—Anscheutz Model 54? Thought so," as he nodded stiffly.

Someone behind the tall professor said, "Wow! A real classic!" to which someone else whispered, "And a college rifle team! Do you have any idea how scarce those are now?"

Margo hid a smile as the man's face went red—though humiliating him would be so easy and so fun, the point was to get the folks to learn. Before the man could turn and chastise the speakers, Margo said forcefully, "An Anscheutz Model 54's a great match rifle—but choosing a gun to bet your *life* on is a little bit different.

"No," she revised, "a *whole lot* different."

The professor, his pride clearly damaged, opened his mouth to reply. In the pause, Ann stepped in, a savvy businesswoman smoothing ruffled feathers.

"You'll have to forgive Margo's abrupt manner, Dr. Reginald-Harding. I do assure you, all time scouts are usually a bit . . . direct."

The professor's scowl lightened. Ann Vinh Mulhaney gave him her most winning smile, a sure sign that she personally detested him, all the while coveting as much of his grant money as she could shake loose. "But scouts *do* know what they're talking about—if they didn't, they wouldn't survive long. And this one," she nodded toward Margo, "has had the best possible training available. I taught her firearms and other projectile weapons, Sven Bailey taught her martial arts and bladed weapons. 'Kit' Carson set up her whole training schedule and did a good bit of the teaching. Then, of course, the best freelance time guide in the business, taught her what the rest of us didn't. Like how to really survive downtime in the East End of London, 1888."

Sounding as if he were sucking lemons, the professor said, "Well then, would you please explain why our firearms are either anachronistic or unsuitable?"

Ooh, bet it hurt your platinum tongue to say that.

"All right." She could be civil if he could, although it cost her considerable effort. But she *was* learning. It was a skill that would doubtless stand her in *very* good stead as a scout. It was also, she realized abruptly, a skill her grandfather had perfected long ago to stay alive and had retained as a life-long habit, just to protect himself from crowds of awestruck uptimers gawking and asking him stupid questions. He'd shouted and fumed at her because he *knew* what she had yet to learn for herself: controlling pride and anger were utterly critical for a scout, something she hadn't realized before.

Good grief! These idiots were actually *teaching* her something!

"All right. First, open the actions—Ann will assist you, if necessary—and check to be sure your rifle is unloaded."

They went through the drill, she and Ann moving back and forth along the line, correcting here, demonstrating there. Clearly, La-La Land's expert firearms instructor was having the time of her life, taking Margo's orders—for this, too, was a test of everything Margo had learned from her. *Good thing I kept studying at college with those books Kit sent.*

Margo nodded. "Okay, work the action and look down into the top of the loading mechanism while you do it."

They obeyed, opening and closing the actions slowly.

"Notice anything?"

One of the younger men spoke up first. "The loading ramp flips up, like a toggle. And there is not so much room in the loading ramp and chamber as with many rifles."

"Very good."

The young man started, looking up in brief astonishment; then grinned belatedly. "Thanks."

"Okay, class," Ann took her turn in an astonishingly commanding voice, "anybody guess why the Model 94's feed system is constructed that way?" It was clear that only the younger man had much knowledge about guns in general. He glanced at all the others, finding only blank faces, before clearing his throat. "It would be a fairly smooth way to bring a cartridge into the chamber. Not so many moving parts, I think."

Ann nodded. "Very good." She glanced at Margo, silently saying, "Over to you."

Margo drew a deep breath for courage and plunged in feet first, her limited experiences gripped in both hands like daggers.

"Yes, you've noticed something very important about the Winchester 94. The 94's feed system *does* flip like a toggle, or to use an easier analogy, it tips like a teeter-totter every time you shoot, to bring a new cartridge up into the chamber. Okay, everybody lay down their rifles and gather 'round me."

In a moment, she was loosely surrounded by the group. "Now look," she picked up the Model 73 and proceeded to tip it up so everyone could watch, "at the difference here." She worked the lever slowly, so they could *see* the difference. "On a Model 73 or 76, the feed system just moves straight up and down. Like an elevator. That's important to all of you for your downtime research. Anybody care to guess why?"

Several chewed their lips. The young woman spoke up. "Because somebody'd notice the difference while we're getting our gear together in Denver?"

"Too right. No Old Westerner's going to miss *that* difference. They pay attention to guns. All guns. For one thing, guns keep 'em alive, and I haven't met a man yet who didn't just *love* tinkering with the toys—or tools—of his choice."

Both male grad students went red at the unintended double entendre. She ignored them as she ignored most *boys*. "Now, go get your Model 94s and keep the muzzles pointed toward the ceiling."

Eventually, they all returned to her side, Model 94s held carefully, muzzles rigidly pointed toward the ceiling.

"Okay. Look at the outside of each rifle. This side plate on my Model 73, for instance, doesn't exist at all on your Model 94s. Again, every Old Westerner who notices that *your* rifles don't have a side plate— and believe me, someone, maybe *several* someones, will notice! So the second they spot that little detail, they'll know it's something they've never seen before. And they'll get mighty curious about it. Curiosity about your group or your gear is the very *last* thing you want."

She smiled coldly and drove home the point like hammering in a wooden stake.

"Any Old Westerner seeing these 94s is going to wonder just what in heck they are and where in heck you got 'em. I think the only other Model 94s in existence in 1885 were in a workshop in Ogden, Utah, where the Browning Brothers were just finishing up inventing it. Winchester bought up the rights like a fish snapping up a fly, because the improvements the Browning Brothers had made over the Model 73 and the Model 76 were so good.

"But the Model 94 didn't come out for a while, because Winchester had to buy manufacturing rights from the Browning Brothers, and they had to play with the design a little until it was as good as *they* could make it, then Winchester had to tool up their factory to accommodate the changes the 94 would require, that sort of thing—all the normal delays between prototype and commercial release."

Before she could say anything else—or any of the paleontologists could draw upon their courage to ask a question—the weapons-range door opened, admitting a cool draft, Malcolm, and closely following him, Kit Carson.

CHAPTER ELEVEN

Gasps went up from those who'd seen photographs. Malcolm just grinned, ignoring the sound, which set her heart beating so fast that cute young grad students might have never existed. Malcolm had a breathtaking smile that turned her insides—and occasionally her very bones—to melted marshmallow.

"So *there* you are!" Malcolm exclaimed, relief on his long, craggy, sun-and-wind scoured face. "I thought maybe you'd come down here to spar with Sven. We looked. He's miffed."

Margo said smugly, "I'm saving up for that. If he throws me twice, I'll fast for a whole day."

Kit grinned. "I'll make sure you honor that one, my girl."

She put her tongue out, then kissed Malcolm, just thoroughly enough to set him on fire, but not quite thoroughly enough to push him over the edge and *carry* her out of here. She finally broke the kiss, smiling up into his eyes with a promise of more to come later, then all but crushed Kit's ribcage. It startled him, but he didn't let go before she did. He did lower his head to kiss her hair several times, as though he couldn't believe this was happening.

When she looked up into his eyes, she saw joy and tremendous pain there. "I'll make it up," she whispered, "all of it. I'll even tell you my whole life's story. I should have a long time ago, but I was scared. After class, okay?"

Kit just closed his eyes.

"I'll—yes, please." Then he opened his eyes again, cleared his throat. "I believe you have a class to teach?"

She sighed, then commented wryly, "Yeah. Like everything else I do, it appears to be part of my training."

Kit and Malcolm nodded approvingly, Kit adding, "A fine lesson for you to learn—and all on your own, too." Margo wrinkled her nose at him, then turned back to the class of goggle-eyed scientists.

Margo took Malcolm's arm, wrapping it possessively around her waist so he all but surrounded her. Determined to do this right if her tongue shattered from all the gilding one was supposed to learn to master gracefully, she said, "This gentleman with his arm around me is Dr. Moore, Freelance Temporal Guide, sought out by members of the very oldest names and fortunes in the world, men and women who bear European titles of nobility, Americans of the greatest industrial and computer families in the nation, prestigious members of the press and the glittering stars of New Hollywood.

"They seek Dr. Moore for assistance with private tours away from the main Time Tours itineraries so they won't have to endure the endless chatter of the riff-raff who take the same tours. Dr. Moore is also a successful gemstone speculator," Malcolm squeezed warningly, "a doctor of philosophy in both anthropology and classics, and, to my greatest happiness, my fiancé."

A few faint groans reached them, bringing laughter to Malcolm's eyes when she glanced up.

Kit, however, was staring at her oddly.

"And this renowned hero," she said, slipping loose of Malcolm's grip just long enough to take her grandfather's calloused hand, "is the most famous recluse on Earth. You are deeply privileged to meet one of *the* original time scouts who pushed the major gates the first time they began popping open and closed on a regular, stable schedule. Knowing the danger that he might shadow himself, he continued pushing gates until the odds were simply too great, then settled down as owner of one of the world's most prestigious hotels, the New Edo, right here in TT-86, where he pushed most of the tourist gates Shangri-La Station possesses. It is, indeed, my intense pleasure to introduce the legendary Time Scout of Shangri-La Station, Kit Carson." She deliberately left out the fact that he was her grandfather.

Round eyes stared back at Kit, with *all* the grad students looking as though they might faint in the presence of a living god.

Kit, moving very close to her, muttered, "Where the hell did you learn to speak all that flowery bullshit?"

Margo, eyes flashing, answered in an equally soft whisper, "At that moronic college you sent me to. Make me take *etiquette*, will you!"

Etiquette was another class she'd been forced to take, in place of the math class she'd needed—badly. Margo had desperately wanted to master her log and ATLS—Absolute Time Locator System—with greater skill, and that meant plowing through mathematics. So, when she could not argue, wheedle, or tempt her way into the class she really needed, above all others, she'd left the registrar's office in a storming rage— and made other plans, which included buying all the requisite books for the class she'd been denied and studying them until slow comprehension dawned for each and every formula or proof the books contained.

With her greater understanding, she performed the same ritual each night: she'd finish supper and rush from the cafeteria back to her room, where she studied until it was nice and dark. If the night sky was clear—as it often was in winter—she'd grab her ATLS and log and jog down to the courtyard which four dormitories completely enclosed. Margo then shot one star fix after another, recording her findings by whispering into her computer log.

She would then return to her room, ignoring the odd looks from other students who'd seen her in the courtyard, talking to herself and pointing a little box at the sky over and over, and the lustful looks of those who didn't care how crazy she was, just so long as they could get their hands on what was beneath her designer jeans that fit her derriere like they'd been sewn on. Margo, completely aware of both types of stare, ignored each equally, regained her room and checked her calculations very carefully, for each star fix she'd shot.

She still wanted that class, but she was getting much better at the mathematic formulae needed to calculate exactly where you were by shooting a star fix. And she *had* learned her accursed "etty-ket." Got a stinking A+ for it. *Some use modern etiquette and oratory is going to be downtime through an unknown gate.*

Then she realized there was something wrong with her grandfather's expression. Kit's eyes actually blazed with anger and his sandy eyebrows dove until his entire forehead was a mass of wrinkles—a few of which she, herself, had regretfully put there.

"We'll talk about this later, in private," he muttered. "I want to know everything there is to know about that place. *Everything.*"

At least he's not mad at me, Margo thought cheerfully. Nobody, not even Margo, wanted to be on the downside of Kit Carson's temper. She'd been there all too often to want to find herself there again.

"And Margo," Kit added, without a trace of a smile, "do Grandpa a favor, huh? Cut the etiquette crap and sound like yourself, or I'll drag you over to the gym and slam the living daylights out of you until you start sounding like my grandkid again."

Margo, a little angry, a little relieved, a whole lot aware of how much he loved her—and the only way he knew to express it most of the time—met his gaze with a wicked twinkle in her eyes and a dangerous smile on her lips. "Tsk-tsk, child-beating? Shame on you." Her smile deepened. "As for slamming the living daylights out of me, you could try."

Kit's black scowl was part of the way she always remembered him. Before he could speak, she whispered, "Oh, don't worry, I hate that stuff, too. I'll be good."

Kit relaxed visibly, then grinned and ruffled her hair affectionately. "Okay, fire-eater. Go show 'em your stuff. *After* you finish introductions." As Margo did not know the names of any of the scientists, she turned to Ann to help. Surely Ann would know the names of her clients.

As the introductions progressed, Margo found that Kit could still surprise her. She told herself she shouldn't have been so startled when Kit greeted each politely—in whatever language they might happen to speak besides English: Yiddish with Dr. Rubenstein, honest-to-God Ukrainian with Vasylko, whose eyes widened until just about all you could see was a vast double pool of blue under a shock of ice-blond hair. Vasylko stammered out his reply in Ukrainian, saying something that caused Kit to smile. A greeting in Arabic brought a flush to Katy's cheeks. Clearly, she remembered enough Arabic to understand what Kit had just said.

Then he turned to assess the other Ph.D. paleontologist. "I've admired your work, Dr. Reginald-Harding.

I saw the American Museum of Natural History after The Accident. What you've done to raise money to restore the building, never mind repair and remount the fossil skeletons and other priceless displays approaches the miraculous. It's a pleasure to meet you at last."

Both men shook hands, Dr. Reginald-Harding just a little bit awestruck, if Margo were judging accurately his body language and the stunned look in his eyes. Kit, evidently noticing the same thing, gave out his world-famous smile.

Then Kit turned his attention to the remaining graduate student. Adair MacKinnon just stared at him, whole face slack and increasingly red when Kit addressed him in Gaelic.

"No?" Kit sighed. "Ah, well, your education isn't complete, then, anyway, is it? You'll have plenty of time to learn it before earning your Ph.D."

Adair flushed even more and stammered, "Always . . . always meant to learn it, 'cause I've got to, you know, before I become The MacKinnon. Sometimes . . . never mind."

Kit nodded understanding of what Adair had left unspoken.

Introductions completed, Dr. Rubenstein stepped forward immediately, shaking Kit's hand, then Malcolm's. "Gentlemen, it's an honor, believe me. You, sir, are known *everywhere*," this to Kit, "and you, Dr. Moore are a lucky man. Damned lucky. You both trained this young lady? She's a bit blunt," he said with a smile, rubbing his chin, "but she knows what she's talking about. Very, very well. And her, mmm, 'forceful' suggestions have all been to the point and excellently stated." This time, Samuel Rubenstein smiled at her. "I can see, now, where your excellent education comes from."

Perversely, she was peeved. *Not good enough on my own, but the minute Kit Carson strolls in, I'm a sensation. Buddy, you ain't seen nuthin' yet.* Outwardly, she said a bit breezily, "Oh, well, there certainly is that, and believe me, their tutoring is *profoundly* educational"—she could *feel* the snort Kit held in— "but there's a lot of bookwork, too. A *whole* lot. So much, you *never* stop learning. Do you, Grandpa?"

It was the first time she'd ever called him that. He stiffened momentarily, speechless, while he stared down at her.

"That's right," he managed. "Even though I'm retired, I'm still learning, just in case. I've recently tackled an ancient Chinese dialect and Croatian stripped of all Serbian influences, vocabulary, and so on, to add to my other languages, and I've been reading and taking notes from a complete history of the Croatian people, both of which I'll have to transfer to memory sufficiently for instant recall if I ever decide to risk going down that new gate at TT-16. Not a tourist gate, not at all; but the research potential is said to be fabulous." His eyes actually glittered with intense interest.

The paleontologists were clearly impressed.

Kit just ruffled his granddaughter's hair, saying everything he wanted to say with that touch and the look in his eyes.

Margo cleared her throat, wishing desperately for once that they were alone and someplace private where they could just *talk*. She *needed* to tell him what had really happened to her mother, Kit's lost daughter— the one he hadn't known he possessed until Margo told him about her, the little she'd been *able* to tell him, except her name and that she was dead. Margo cringed at the memory of that talk by the fishpond on Commons. She'd been so inexperienced, so uneasy, so afraid of him, she literally *hadn't* been able to tell him what his eyes had begged to know.

This time, she wouldn't be such a coward. And she'd hold him while he cried over her mother's brutal murder, robbing him of a child he'd never met.

Whoops, getting too maudlin, Margo. You have a job to do and you can't do it snuffling goddamned tears, of all things.

So she said to her somewhat abashed students, "Oh, by the way, all of you should stop by Connie Logan's Clothes and Stuff, not just for period-appropriate clothing—she's got the best and you can rent it for much less than buying it—but also be sure to buy a good Old West dictionary, so you won't sound quite so green. Old Western speech is nearly unintelligible to anybody else from *anywhere* else. To Old Westerners, anybody who *can't* speak it is a greenhorn. Learn the language you'll need to know."

She'd picked up a little at school, but she'd have to study it like mad before she and Malcolm went to Denver.

"But," Adair MacKinnon asked, swallowing hard and sweating, "isn't it just a dialect of English?"

"No," Malcolm said quietly. "Unless you can tell me the *exact* Old West meanings and pronunciations—without having to think about them—of churn-twister, cienaga, a Jerusalem undertaker, the word 'jewelry' or the phrase 'jewelry chest,' then you'd better hit the library and find yourself a good Old West-English/English-Old West dictionary and start memorizing it. You're going to *need* it for three months in rough country, away from the more 'civilized' vicinity around Denver."

Adair stuck to his guns. "I can understand the need to speak like a native, but why so adamant about it? So-called dudes from the East wouldn't have spoken it, after all. And just exactly what do 'Jerusalem undertaker' or a perfectly normal word like 'jewelry' really *mean*?"

"Yes," Malcolm replied, "dudes don't speak Old West when they arrive. They're lost in an alien culture, trying to survive and blend in gradually with what they find. In short, they're intrusive greenhorns, and greenhorns are considered fair game."

"Very fair game," Kit added solemnly. "The range wars weren't quite as bad as depicted in the movies, although they were bad enough, and Dodge City had a lower per capita murder rate than, say, New York or Washington, D.C. during, oh, the mid 1990s. But attacks on dudes by a single, experienced man, or a gang of them, were very common. Even swindlers could make a killing, saying one thing that meant another altogether, which the dude would find out too late, once his money or land or horse or whatever he'd risked was long out of his possession. And having made a legal contract, there was absolutely nothing the poor sop could *do* about it. Except maybe hire himself a gun-hand—if he had enough money left— to hunt down the rat and kill him."

Margo took Kit's hand again, more carefully this time, realizing she was squeezing it so tightly, his fingernails were turning purple. "Grandpa pushed the Wild West Gate," she put in, eyes aglow as she gazed up at Kit.

He harrumphed and muttered, "Lots of time scouts pushed lots of gates. Nothing heroic in walking through the Wild West Gate, of that I may assure you. There were other gates that were *much* harder to step through."

A subtle reminder of Margo's disastrous mission into Southern Africa. She flushed, but held tight to his hand.

Dr. Rubenstein nodded. "The Roman Gate, I expect, was an extremely difficult one."

Kit laughed. "Oh, it was easy to get *in*. Getting *out* again proved a rather interesting test of wit and skill."

And that was how he dismissed one of the most dangerous, nearly lethal adventures he'd ever encountered. His involuntary fight in the Circus Maximus was legend the world over.

"Well," Margo muttered, "I, uh, guess I'd better get on with my own practice and let you take over the class, Ann."

The diminutive firearms instructor nodded gracious thanks for helping break the class the way a horse-breaker might soften up and civilize a particularly unruly horse.

Kit said very softly, "We'll wait on the benches until you're finished."

She nodded, holding in another sigh. *Another bleeding test . . .*

But this time she put up no arguments, no protests, no childish tantrums. She simply put on her safety gear, called out, "Line's going hot!" so everyone else donned safety gear—including Kit and Malcolm—and got busy finishing the other two boxes of .44-40's, scoring well in toward the center of the black despite her nervousness; then she switched to the heavier Centennial and did herself proud with three boxes of almost perfect nines and tens. She did throw a couple of rounds here and there from sweating palms and aching arms and eyes that burned and wouldn't focus properly, but even though she was out of practice, her scores were good and she knew it.

"Well?" she asked as she handed over the targets.

The two most important people in her life put their heads together, poring over the targets, marking each shot outside the nine ring. Finally they looked up again.

"Well, frankly," Kit began, "you could use some more practice and work on your upper arm strength, but pretty damned good for a first try after several dry months."

Margo let go her tense fear and abruptly felt like she was floating on fizzy bubbles that tickled her all the way to the ceiling.

"Hey," Malcolm called, "come down out of the clouds, will you?"

She sighed inwardly and allowed the wonderful fizzing bubbles to waft her gently toward the floor. She blinked and found herself staring into Malcolm's eyes. "Yeah?" she asked softly.

He didn't say a word. He just kissed her until those dratted, wonderful fizzing bubbles came back. When she came up for breath, she was actually dizzy.

"Wow! Where'd you learn to do *that*?"

Malcolm touched her cheek. "From a certain red-headed imp I know. She's very, um, motivational."

Margo blushed to her toes. Malcolm only smiled.

"Shall I, um, put everything away so we can get the heck out of here?"

"Y-e-s," Kit drawled, devilment in his eyes, "I think that would be appropriate. We'll stuff down some dinner, then if it's possible, I think I'd like to pry you away from Malcolm for a while, so it's just you and me, okay?"

"Yeah," was all she could manage.

They helped her clean the rifles, just to speed up the process, then she put away all her gear and locked up the gun room, returning the keys carefully where they belonged. That done, Margo Smith hooked arms through both Malcolm's and Kit's. They left the range aware of the still-awestruck gazes that followed them.

Once outside, beyond the soundproof glass, they all started laughing like complete idiots. But it was a healing laughter, as well, washing away awkwardness and lonely pain and leaving only the new closeness and the utterly reaffirmed love Margo felt for both of these men. It was a love she felt she didn't deserve, but was by God going to *try* to deserve.

"Last one to the elevator's a goose's egg!" Margo called, sprinting off like a gazelle.

Not at all surprisingly, Kit arrived just behind her, his hand covering hers just as she punched the elevator button. Malcolm wheezed up a moment later.

"Out of shape," Kit chided.

"Hah! Blame that on your insatiable granddaughter."

Kit just laughed and winked at Margo, who flushed red as a beet. But she was still laughing. The elevator carried them and their hilarity upward in efficient silence, until the doors opened again and their laughter spilled out onto the Commons. They headed for the Epicurean Delight and a dinner that would certainly be a momentous occasion.

At least, it would if Kenneth "Kit" Carson had anything to say about it!

CHAPTER TWELVE

Marcus was on duty in the Down Time Bar & Grill when *he* strolled in, casual and cool as a general surveying newly levied troops on the Campus Martius. A glass slipped from nerveless fingers and shattered on the floor behind the bar. *He* glanced Marcus' way, noted him briefly with a flick of disinterested gaze, then took a seat near the back as though Marcus didn't exist.

Fear and anger both ripped through him, piercing as the shockwaves of an unstable gate. The years he'd spent on TT-86 had changed him more than he'd realized, had eased the harshness of certain memories with the fair treatment he'd received here, where men like Kit Carson and Skeeter Jackson saw him as a man, not a possession. He'd come to realize over the years that he was free, that no one had the right to call him slave, but in that single, blinding instant when his one-time master's eyes had slid dismissively away from his, the memory of his slavery had crashed down around him like a cage of steel bars.

Marcus stood rooted to the floor, unable to believe he had actually forgotten that terrifying, familiar, casual dismissal of his very humanity. What it felt like in his soul to be reminded—

"Hey, Marcus, clean up that mess!"

The manager, frowning at him.

Hands shaking uncontrollably, Marcus knelt and swept up broken shards of the bar glass. When the job was done and the pieces dumped into the trash bin, Marcus washed and dried hands that refused to hold steady. He drew a deep breath for courage. He didn't want to cross that short distance of space, but knew it had to be done. He still owed a terrible sum of money to this man whose name he'd never actually known, merely calling him *Domus*, same as any other slave would address a master. He recalled all too clearly the cold humor in the man's eyes when he'd first laid eyes on Marcus in that stinking slave pen.

He left the relative safety of the space behind the bar and approached the dim table near the back. *His* glance flicked up again, studied Marcus with brutal appraisal, a herdsman judging the health of prize stock. Marcus' insides flinched.

"Your order?" he whispered, all voice control gone.

His one-time master had not changed much during the intervening years. A little leaner, a little greyer. But the eyes were the same, dark and glittering and triumphant.

"Beer. Whiskey chaser."

Marcus brought the drinks as ordered, trying desperately to still the jittering of glassware on his small, round tray. Quick eyes noted the dance and smiled.

"Very good," he purred. "That will be all."

Marcus bowed and departed. He felt the dark touch of the man's gaze on him through the next hour, watching him work as he served drinks, collected bar tabs and tips, made up sandwiches and snacks for the ebb and flow of customers, and prayed to all the gods to get him through this ordeal. *Why has he come?* pounded behind his eyelids. *Why has he not spoken to me again? I have the gold to repay the debt of my purchase price. I have it . . .*

And above all other questions, again and again, *Why does he not speak? He just sits and watches.* The man finally finished his beer and left money on the table, departing without a backward glance. Marcus had to brace himself against the bar to keep his feet.

"Marcus?"

He jumped so badly he nearly went to the floor. The manager braced him with a hasty arm.

"You feeling okay? You look sick."

I am sick! Marcus wanted to cry out. "I—do not feel well, I am sorry . . ."

"Hey, you got plenty of sick time coming. Go on home and take some aspirin, get some rest. I'll call Molly—she could use some overtime pay. If you don't feel better by tomorrow, call Medical."

Marcus nodded, numb to his bones. "Thank you." Very carefully, he wiped his hands on a bar towel. He hung it up with great deliberation, then crept out of the Down Time Bar & Grill into the brilliance of the Commons. His former master was nowhere to be seen. What was he to do? The man had said nothing, left no instructions to meet him, made no arrangements to turn over the notes Marcus had so carefully compiled over the years. He didn't know what to do. He didn't even know the man's name, to check the hotel registries. Perhaps he meant to save the meeting for the privacy of Marcus' little apartment?

To return to the apartment, he would have to pass Ianira's booth in Little Agora. What could he tell her, when he knew nothing, himself? Marcus half hoped he could slip past her without being seen, but Ianira spotted him straight away. Her lovely eyes widened. The next instant she'd left a customer and a whole retinue of devotees gaping after her. She flew to his side like an arrow into his heart.

"What is it? You're ill . . ." She laid a hand against his cheek.

Marcus, aware that his former master might be anywhere, watching and assessing and planning, felt himself unbearably torn between the desire to crush Ianira to him and draw comfort from her strength versus the even fiercer desire to protect her and their children.

"*He* came into the Down Time today," Marcus said a little unsteadily. "The—my old master." Ianira's luminous dark eyes widened; her lips, exactly the shape of Artemis' divine silver bow fully drawn to strike, parted in shock. Before she could speak, Marcus added, "Can you—can we afford it if you close up the booth?"

Worry furrowed Ianira's brow. "Why?"

Marcus had to draw an unsteady breath before he could speak. "I want you to take Artemisia and Gelasia and go someplace safe until I know what he wants. He said *nothing*, Ianira, just came in, watched me for an hour, and left without a word. I was once his slave, Ianira! He still thinks . . . will act as though . . . if I cannot protect you and our children, what kind of man *can* I be?"

The look in her eyes wounded him. He forced himself to continue. "And no downtimer has real rights in this world. I am afraid for you. He could so easily do terrible harm, make trouble with the uptimers whose laws bind us, maybe even try to take you for his own—by force!"

His hand on hers trembled. He would die to protect her and their children. He was just afraid his one-time owner would move on Ianira before Marcus could take proper precautions.

Ianira's glance darted around the brightly lit Commons

as though searching for their unseen enemy. Tourists, oblivious of their terror, sauntered past, laughing and chatting about upcoming adventures downtime. Her retinue of idiotic followers had left the booth and half surrounded them. Ianira, glancing at that follow-her-come-what-may crowd, compressed soft, sensuous lips until nothing remained but a hard, white line.

"You are right to fear," she whispered, her voice so low even Marcus had a hard time catching the words. "I feel that someone watches, someone besides these people," she waved a negligent hand toward her awestruck devotees, "but I cannot find him. There are so many minds in this place, it confuses the senses. But he *is* here, I know it." Marcus knew she had innate gifts he could barely understand, plus training in ancient ways and rites no man could ever comprehend. Her glance into his eyes was frightened. "I will stay with friends in The Found Ones until we know. You are wise, beloved. Take great care." Then the look in her eyes shifted, hardened. "I *loathe* him," she whispered fiercely. "For putting that look in your eyes I hate him as much as I hate my pig of a husband!"

Her lips crushed his, all too fleetingly, then she whirled and left him. The "costume" she wore—no different from the ordinary chitons she'd worn on the other side of the Philosophers' Gate—swirled in a flutter of soft draperies and folds. Astonishingly, downtimers from all parts of the Commons, summoned only the gods knew how, appeared from nowhere and surrounded her, most forming an impenetrable barricade to keep her acolytes from following. Others formed a guard—and unless Marcus were greatly mistaken, theirs was an *armed* guard—to protect the Speaker of the Seven and her offspring. He knew they would be taking a swift, back-corridor route to the station's School and Day Care Center to pick up the girls. Then she vanished around a corner in Residential and was gone.

Marcus stayed where he was, making sure she was not followed. A few of the acolytes tried to, but that living wall managed to discourage them—forcefully for one or two insistent, insolent vidcam operators— then they, too, were gone around the same corner.

With The Found Ones, Ianira and their children ought to be safe from the monster who'd brought him here, who had then left him uptime with nothing but instructions that made no sense. That "master" had then blithely joined the line to depart TT-86, leaving Marcus—who was deep in shock from *everything* he heard and saw—to fend for himself. He recalled nearly every detail of that nightmare of a day. No one here had seemed to speak his native tongue.

Instead, he'd heard smatters of barbaric tongues, so many and spoken so fast he felt dizzy. He'd recognized none of them. Haphazard stairs that went nowhere had eventually led him into the arms of the "gods" who ruled this place. Eventually, he'd met the man named Buddy and after that, a group of men and women in more or less his same position, who took him in and helped him adjust through the worst of the transition.

Marcus was startled from his painful memories by a downtimer named Kynan Rhys Gower. Marcus knew this man to be a close friend of Kit Carson's. He was casually closing up Ianira's booth, setting items on the counter inside and locking the sides down, and fending off Ianira's followers with a helpless gesture and a convoluted sentence in Welsh that only the gods could probably decipher. He escaped the crowd, which settled itself around the booth as though they meant to wait forever. Kynan pushed his wheeled waste bin past Marcus' chosen place of vigil.

"Your woman and children are safe, friend," the Welshman murmured, pausing to pick up some bit of trash near Marcus' feet. He deposited the waste in his bin and moved on. Marcus closed his eyes, thanking all the gods for that miracle. Then, straightening his shoulders and drawing in a deep breath, Marcus headed resolutely for their apartment. His old master would doubtless seek him there and reveal his orders. What he would do when Marcus repaid him the price of his purchase and asked him to please take the records Marcus had compiled and never return . . .

A *Roman's* reaction, Marcus could have judged without giving the matter a second thought. But Marcus' one-time master was not Roman. He was an uptimer with unknown motives, unknown ways of thinking. He had set Marcus a very specific—if mystifying—task. Would he be willing to give up a source of information placed so well to gather the details he clearly wanted very badly? What would he do? What would he say? Marcus could always appeal to Bull Morgan for help—if it came to such desperate straits. The Station manager would protect him, if no one else would. The thought of his one-time master facing down Bull Morgan and a squad of Station Security helped soothe the tremors ripping through his insides.

But he was still deeply afraid.

"Mr. Farley?"

The man who'd emerged from the Down Time Bar & Grill glanced around, surprise evident in his dark eyes. "Yes?"

Skeeter Jackson gave him a brilliant smile and a fake business card. "Skeeter Jackson, freelance time guide. I heard you were looking for a downtime adventure, checking out the gates we have here at Shangri-La Station."

Farley glanced at his card, then studied him. "I'm gathering information," he allowed cautiously.

Skeeter, maintaining that smile at all cost, wondered if Chuck Farley had witnessed Skeeter's panic-stricken flight from that double-damned gladiator—or the newscast which had followed. "If you wouldn't mind a friendly piece of advice . . ."

Farley nodded for him to continue.

"Time Tours offers some nice packages, but frankly, they'll gouge you for every extra service they can conjure up. The small outfits that rent the government-owned gates are a better deal, although the gates don't lead to quite as interesting time periods. Your best bet is to hire a freelancer. Then, if you decide on a non-Time-Tours gate, all you do is pay the government's gate fee plus your guide's fees, plus downtime lodging, meals, that kind of thing. Much cheaper than a package tour. Of course, it depends on what you want, doesn't it?"

Farley's eyes were cool and unpleasantly alert. "Yes."

"If you do settle on a Time Tours package, you might still consider a private guide." Drawing on the patter he'd heard Malcolm Moore use so frequently, he added, "There are some extraordinary experiences the package deals simply skip over, because they can't herd that many people around and not be noticed. Hiring a freelancer to go along with you lets you break away from the main tour group whenever you want. You could," he dredged up an example he'd researched on the computers, "go down towards Ostia, for instance, and look at the big Claudian harbor under construction. Magnificent sight, that harbor, but it isn't on the package tour."

He smiled again, winningly.

Farley merely pocketed his card. "Thanks for the advice. I'll consider it."

Without another word, he simply turned and walked off.

Skeeter stood rooted, silly grin still pasted on his face. His insides seethed. *Goddammit, I'm losing my touch! Just when I need it most, too. What's with people this month?*

He *had* to get access to that guy's money belt.

Skeeter headed for the library and started checking hotel registries on one of the computer terminals. Farley had to be staying *somewhere*. He started with the less expensive hostelries and worked his way up to the luxury hotels before he found the entry he sought: Farley, Chuck. Room 3027 Neo Edo. Skeeter just groaned and leaned his brow against the cool monitor screen. The Neo Edo. It figured. Kit Carson's hotel.

Well, he hadn't run out of disguises yet.

If he could get into the hotel without being recognized, he could get into Farley's room. And if he could get into the man's room, he could steal anything in it. If he were lucky, he'd catch the guy during a shower and simply make off quietly with the money belt around his *own* waist. He still couldn't quite believe the guy had turned him down as a freelance guide.

Swearing softly under his breath, Skeeter headed home to try out one of his disguises on the employees of the Neo Edo Hotel.

Goldie Morran found Chuck Farley seated at a table in Wild Bill's, a saloon-style bar in Frontier Town. He was reading the latest copy of the *Shangri-La Gazette* with apparent interest.

"Mind if a lady joins you?" she purred.

He glanced up, blinked, then set the paper aside. "Suit yourself."

The measuring look he gave her and the coolness of his greeting didn't bode well, but he did signal for a waitress. The rinky-tink jingle of the upright piano at the back of the room, its player costumed with gartered shirtsleeves and a battered beaver hat, rose above the sound of laughter, conversation, and the clink of glasses. The waitress, a saucy downtimer who—if rumor were correct—had earned more gold flirting with miners than the miners themselves had earned over an average year's digging, winked at Goldie, one hustler to another, friendly-like. Goldie smiled.

"What'll it be?" She rested hands on well-curved hips, while her breasts all but spilled out of her tight-laced costume. If Chuck Farley were affected by the sight, it didn't show in any way Goldie could see. Maybe he preferred men? Goldie didn't care who he slept with, or why, so long as she obtained possession of his money.

"A drink for the lady. I presume," he added sardonically, "that she's buying, since I didn't invite her."

Goldie managed to keep smiling, although she'd vastly have preferred slapping him. "Whiskey, Rebecca. Thank you. And yes," she added smoothly, "I am buying. I did not come here to steal a drink or two off an unwary tourist."

Some hint of mirth stirred far back in his eyes. "Very well, what *did* you come here for?"

As Rebecca threaded her way back through the crowded bar to fill Goldie's order, Goldie leaned back in her chair. "I am given to understand you're looking for something besides the usual tours."

Farley's smile was thin. "News certainly moves around fast in this place."

Goldie laughed. "That is too true. Which is why I

wanted to talk to you before someone disreputable tried to swindle you." She handed over her card. "I have a shop on the Commons. Money-changing, rare coinage, gems, that sort of thing. My expertise is considerable."

Farley's thin smile came again, although it didn't touch his dark, watchful eyes. "I've heard of you, yes. Your reputation precedes you."

How he meant that, Goldie wasn't quite sure. Nor was she at all sure she liked the way he continued to watch her, like a waiting lizard.

"Not knowing what you had in mind, of course," she said, accepting the whiskey glass Rebecca brought and pointedly dropping money onto the table to pay for it, "I thought we might chat for a few minutes. Since you didn't seem interested in any specific tours, I thought perhaps you'd come to Shangri-La with something else in mind."

His eyes narrowed slightly. "Such as?"

"Oh, there are all sorts of reasons people come here," Goldie laughed. "Some people come just to eat at the Epicurean Delight. Then there's that Greek prophetess all those wacky uptime bimbos follow around like she was Christ on Earth." She smiled at the memory of Ianira's hordes. Goldie had made more than a little profit from them.

"But I didn't come here to talk about oracles and the fools who believe them. Occasionally we're visited by the shrewd individual or two who understands the investment potentials a place like Shangri-La has to offer."

The corners of Farley's lips twitched. "Really? What sort of investments?"

Goldie sipped her whiskey. Farley was cool, all right. Too cool by half. "Well, there are any number of lucrative ventures a man with wit and capital could turn to his advantage. There are, for instance, the shops that supply the tourists, restaurants—even the small ones turn a fabulous profit. Captive audience, you know." She laughed lightly. Chuck Farley allowed a small smile to touch his lips. "Then there are businesses like mine. Capital invested in rare coins obtained by downtime agents could increase nine, ten times the initial investment."

Again, that small, sardonic smile. "I thought the first law of time travel was, 'There will be no profiteering from time.' The ATF has copies of it posted everywhere, you know."

Somehow, Goldie received the impression from the mirth far back in those dark eyes that Chuck Farley didn't give a damn about the first law of time travel.

"True," she smiled. "But money exchanged from downtime purchases which is then invested right here in Shangri-La isn't covered by that law. You're only in violation if you try to take your profit uptime.

"So, the possibilities for shrewd investment are limitless for a man with capital and imagination." She sipped at her whiskey again, still watching him over the rim of the glass. "Best of all, the money you invest in, say, a business here on Shangri-La is taxed only at the rate it would be uptime. Frankly, you can make a killing without ever breaking a single law."

She smiled politely while he leaned back in his chair and studied her face. The corners of his lips moved slightly. "You interest me, Goldie Morran. I like your style. Gutsy, polished, sincere. I'll be in touch later, perhaps."

He tossed some coins onto the table to pay for his own drink, gathered up his copy of the *Gazette*, and left her sitting there, seething. She knocked back the remaining whiskey and followed him out, but he'd vanished into the mob milling around the Commons.

People gawking at the stores, the ramps, the chronometers, the gates, the waiting areas, the prehistoric beasts picked up from that absurd, unstable gate into the age of the dinosaurs—that was all she could see every direction she turned. She compressed her lips, furious that he'd turned her down and then simply vanished.

Just what the devil was Farley after, anyway?

Disgruntled in the extreme, Goldie set out for her shop. She'd gone only a few strides when she noticed Skeeter Jackson deep in conversation with a tourist. Drat the man! She was seriously of a mind to march over and tell that luckless tourist what a cheating fake he was, to spoil whatever profit he expected to pick up. Why she had ever agreed to this idiotic bet—

Goldie blinked. Someone was stalking Skeeter. A reddish-haired man in Western-style clothing that somehow didn't match the way he moved . . . Her eyes widened as recognition hit home: the downtimer who'd chased Skeeter before. Then she noticed the truly wicked blade he was silently drawing from beneath a set of leather chaps. Goldie drew in her breath sharply.

For an instant, spite and malice held her silent. Spite, malice, and greed. If Skeeter were dead, all bets were off and she could stay in La-La Land with no one to fault her. The man crept closer. Goldie's stomach churned at the look of hatred in the stranger's eyes, etched into his attentive, absorbed face. Skeeter was Goldie's rival and a scoundrel and probably deserved what he was about to get more than anyone she knew. But in that instant, she realized she didn't want to watch him die.

Not particularly because she cared what happened to Skeeter, but murder was messy. And bad—very bad—for business. And for a fleeting instant, she also realized victory by default over a dead man would be about as sweet as vinegar on her tongue. So she found herself moving across the Commons faster than she'd moved in years.

Skeeter and his target were deeply engrossed in conversation near the waiting area for the Wild West Gate. The man creeping up on him sidestepped around an ornamental horse trough filled with colorful fish and tensed, ready for the final lunge. Goldie glanced around, wondering if she could find a weapon, or someone from Security, even something to use as a diversion.

Overhead, ten leathery, crow-sized pterodactyls perched in the girders, eying the fish in the horse trough. Skeeter talked on, oblivious to the closeness of impending death. *Ah-ha!* Goldie darted over to a vending cart which sold hats, T-shirts, and other trinkets, and said, "Sorry, gotta borrow this," to the startled cart owner.

She snatched up a toy bow and arrow set and nocked the arrow, pulled back expertly, then let fly. The arrow whizzed true to its mark: the rubber tip smacked right into the flock of startled pterodactyls. The whole lot of them took wing with ear-bending screeches and dove straight down. Goldie ducked under the cart. Skeeter jerked his gaze up and around—and saw the man with the long knife. His eyes widened.

Then he took off faster than Goldie had *ever* seen him run.

The man with the knife swore in what had to be Latin and bolted after him. Angry pterodactyls swarmed in his way, screaming like maddened crows mobbing a jaybird. Leathery wings buffeted the man's face. Claws raked his hair. He yelled something furious and tried to cut at them with his long knife. Skeeter's tourist, a pretty redhead, screamed and took refuge behind the horse trough. Other tourists scattered while those at a safer distance started to point.

Someone shouted for Security. Someone else yelled for Pest Control. The man fighting off the pterodactyls abruptly realized he was attracting attention to himself. He swore again and took off in the opposite direction Skeeter had taken—none too soon, as Security arrived hard on his heels.

"What's going on?"

The shaken tourist Skeeter had been trying to swindle crawled out from behind the trough. "A man with a huge knife! He tried to attack the guy I was talking to—then those things—" she pointed at the pterodactyls still flitting angrily above their heads "—started diving everywhere and—and I don't know where he went. I just hid behind this."

Security officers took the man's description from the shaken tourist while Goldie slipped quietly away in the confusion. The vendor she'd borrowed the bow and arrow from just gaped after her. Goldie returned cautiously to her shop, making sure no one from Security had followed, then locked the door and sat down to do some very serious thinking. Skeeter Jackson had picked up a lethal enemy somewhere. Or somewhen. He *had* changed an enormous sum of money after that last trip of his through the Porta Romae. Goldie would've bet the very gold in her teeth that Skeeter's attacker had been swindled downtime and had somehow come through the gate looking for revenge.

She shivered slightly behind her glass cases filled with coins, gems, and other precious items brought uptime by various gullible tourists. Wager or not, she was glad she'd acted. But there was one thing she intended to find out, or her name was not Goldie Morran, and that was the identity of the man who'd come so close to killing Skeeter.

Yes, finding out who he was and why he was after that wretched little con artist might just come in very handy. She might not want to see Skeeter murdered, but she had no qualms at all about seeing him arrested. Tapping her fingers thoughtfully against the cool glass countertop, Goldie wondered who to contact about the mystery man's identity. She had all sorts of agents spotted about the station, willing to do a little spying for her as well as the odd downtime courier job. Goldie sniffed autocratically and picked up the phone.

Time was running, but she *would* find out.

There were, after all, only so many places in La-La Land a man could hide. Someone would know. And once *she* knew, the man chasing him would know. And when *he* knew, Skeeter Jackson's days on Shangri-La would be over for good. She started calling her paid agents all over the station.

CHAPTER THIRTEEN

Marcus made his way home and entered the cramped apartment. It was echoingly empty. Ianira had packed in haste, leaving most of her own things in favor of taking the children's necessities. He touched one of her Greek gowns, breathing in its scent, almost smiled at the sight of prosaic jeans hung neatly on hangers in her half of their closet. He crushed the heavy fabric beneath his hands.

Marcus had known this day would eventually come.

He just hadn't known it would tear his vitals so mercilessly.

Marcus swore savagely in a language no other man, woman, or child on TT-86 ever used—with the rare exception of his beloved Ianira, to whom he had taught a little of it—then found the aspirin in the medicine cabinet. He downed five tablets to relieve the fierce throbbing in his head and wished bitterly he could afford strong alcoholic beverages like Kit's special bourbon, brought to TT-86 from some secret, downtime escapade. But he didn't have the money for such luxuries.

He didn't have money for *anything*.

Marcus swore again, hating himself for the tremors he couldn't quite suppress. He'd come to believe in himself as a free man. But the man who had purchased and brought him here would—sooner or later—

demand an accounting. Marcus brought out the notes he had laboriously compiled over years of bartending and listening to the talk of men and women far gone in their boasting. He brought out the money he had so carefully stockpiled from the little metal box at the top of the bedroom closet. He changed out of his working clothes into a clean pair of blue jeans and a respectable shirt, one Ianira had surprised him with from a shop in Frontier Town on his last birthday. He smoothed down the fringe with unsteady fingers and swallowed down a throat gone dry. His face in the mirror was ashen despite the stubble of beard along his chin.

If he tried shaving now, he'd cut himself to ribbons.

Able to think of nothing else to do to prepare himself, he sank into a chair facing the door to wait. When the telephone shrilled, Marcus actually knocked the chair over. He disentangled himself, and made it to the phone before the answering machine switched on.

"Hello?"

"Marcus," that familiar voice said—notably in English, not Latin. "We have business to discuss. Come to the Neo Edo, Room 3027. Bring your records."

The line clicked in his ear.

Marcus swallowed once in the silence. He still didn't even know the man's name. He swallowed again, against unreasoning fear. Nothing could really happen to him. And it was Kit's hotel he'd be going to, not some out-of-the-way corner of the terminal. Kit Carson was a friend. A powerful friend. Marcus clung to that thought.

Then he gathered up moneybox, records, and his courage and headed resolutely toward Kit Carson's world-famous hotel.

Getting into the Neo Edo was simple.
There were *lots* of ways into the luxury hotel besides

the main lobby. Probably more, in fact, than Kit Carson knew existed, unless the previous owner, the legendary Homako Tani, had left blueprints behind when he'd deeded the enormous hotel to his long-ago time-scouting partner. The Neo Edo's architect, working under Tani's direct supervision, had put in more melodramatic secret passageways, hidden entrances, and blind rooms built into the rocky foundations of the Himalayas themselves than even the gods of the mountaintops knew.

Skeeter had tried to pick locks on those doors more than once, slipping in through one of at least fifteen secret entrances he'd discovered thus far (and he hadn't even attempted the top three floors of the five-storey hotel yet, for fear of opening a hinged panel and emerging straight into Kit Carson's palatial office on the fifth floor. A gilt-and-wood dragon-shaped balcony, whose "scales" were Imperial Chrysanthemums, snaked completely around the open, atrium-style upper floor, which boasted bedrooms larger than his biological parents' entire home floorplan.

Rumor had it (and Skeeter's sources were pretty reliable) that Kit had discovered he owned the Neo Edo when a bunch of lawyers he didn't know had been allowed into La-La Land just long enough to hand-deliver a copy of Homako Tani's will, a brief letter, and the deed to the hotel.

Lawyers, however, were barred from conducting *any* official legal business (never mind set up a law firm!) in La-La Land by edict of none other than Bull Morgan. The squat, fire-plug of a station manager, who chewed cigars the way eight-year-olds chewed bubble gum, had put into place iron-clad rules he bent only when the "official lawyering" dealt with wills and inheritances.

In its way, so long as you obeyed the rules (or didn't

get caught breaking them), La-La Land was a sanctuary beyond compare. He grinned. No one—probably not even Kit—knew whether or not the Neo Edo's builder was really dead. Rumor (and here, even Skeeter's sources were of wildly mixed opinions) ran the gamut from Homako Tani dying at the hand of Japan's greatest warrior-artist-poet-swordsmith ever to live, Miyamoto Musashi, to walking up into the ceiling of the world and ending his last years as Dalai Lama in Tibet (not so far, actually, from the geographical, if not temporal, site of TT-86).

The world-famous temple at the roof of the world had finally been refurbished after tidal waves, earthquakes, famine, disease, and war with their hated northern neighbors had caused the great, sprawling bastion of communist socialism to crumble and finally leave Tibet to its prayer wheels, its solitary temples, its bamboo-munching pandas, and its mountains, where new snow falling on the great Himalayan peaks blew harshly.

Whatever the true story, Skeeter simply strolled into the lobby in his disguise, passed the huge mural of *Sunrise over Edo Castle*, which was supposed to be a copy of one that the same Musashi (who *might* have killed Homako Tani, for *any* possible reason, given Musashi's temper) had painted. Skeeter reached the elevator and pinged the little lighted circle.

Moments later, he was on the third floor, stealing toward Charles Farley's expensive room on a carpet thick and fine as any the kings of Persia might have ordered woven for their winter pavilions. The subtle pattern of black and white reminded him of snow leopards, or those elusive creatures of the Mongolian steppes, the silent white tiger glimpsed through blasts of snow and wind. Skeeter shivered, recalling his terror when ordered by Yesukai to join a winter hunt in the sacred mountains of the Yakka clan's homeland. He still didn't know whether it had been skill or luck that his arrow had brought down the snow leopard before the huge cat could claw him to death, but he would take to his grave the scream of his pony, knocked from under him and mortally wounded before he knew anything was near.

Skeeter shook off those memories with some irritation and concentrated on the matter at hand: breaking into Room 3027. First, he listened, ear bent to the door with a stethoscope to hear what might be taking place beyond the closed door. He caught the sound of the shower and a man's voice singing Gilbert and Sullivan off key. Skeeter smiled, carefully slipped the lock while disabling the alarm with a little tool he'd invented all on his own, and entered the darkened hotel room.

Farley sang on, as Skeeter began a methodical hunt of the well-appointed bedroom. He rifled through the discarded clothing on the bed, searched every drawer, under the mattresses, in the closet, under every piece of furniture, even managed to open the room safe, only to find it empty.

Where? Skeeter fumed.

He eased the bathroom door open and risked a peek inside.

Steam hit his face, along with an unpleasant bellow about mausers and javelins, but there was no sign of a moneybelt draped over the toilet, sink, or towel rack. Had he worn the damned thing *into* the shower?

The song—and the spray of water—came to an abrupt end. Farley's shower was over. Skeeter cursed under his breath and ran for the hall. He slipped outside, locked Farley's hotel room door behind him, and leaned against it, breathing heavily as his heart raced.

"What are you doing here?" a familiar voice demanded.

Skeeter yelped and came at least three inches clear of the floor. Belatedly he recognized Marcus. "Oh, it's only you," he gasped, sagging again into the door for support. "For a second, I thought Goldie'd set Security on me again."

Marcus was frowning intensely. "You were attempting to steal from the room."

Skeeter planted hands on hips and studied his friend. "I do have a wager to win," he said quietly, "or had you forgotten that? If I lose, I get tossed off station."

"Yes, you and your stupid bet! Why must you cheat and steal from everyone, Skeeter Jackson?"

Marcus' anger surprised him. "I don't. I never steal from 'eighty-sixers. They're family. And I never steal from family."

Marcus' cheeks had flushed in the soft lighting of the hall. His breathing went fast and shallow. "Family! When will you learn, Skeeter? You are not a Mongol! You are an uptimer American, not some unwashed, stinking hordesman!"

Shock detonated through him. How had Marcus known about that?

" 'A Mongol doesn't steal from his own kind,' " Marcus ranted on, evidently quoting some conversation Skeeter didn't remember at all. "Pretty morals for a pretty thief, yes? That is all you are. A thief. I am sick of hearing how the tourists deserve it. They aren't your enemies! They are only people trying to enjoy life, then you come and smash it up by thieving and lying and—" His eyes suddenly widened, then went savagely narrow. "The money you gave to me. The bet you made in Rome. You did not win it honestly."

Skeeter wet his lips, trying to get in a word edgewise.

"He came to me for *help*, damn you, because you'd

stolen the money for his new life! Curse you to your Mongolian hell, Skeeter Jackson!"

Without another word, Marcus turned and strode toward the distant elevators, passing them and opting for the staircase, instead. The door banged against the wall in an excess of rage. Skeeter stood rooted to the snowy carpet, swallowing. Why did he feel like bursting into tears for the first time since his eighth birthday? Marcus was only a downtimer, after all.

Yeah, a voice inside him whispered. *A downtimer you called friend and were drunk—or stupid—enough to confide the truth to.* Skeeter could lie to any number of tourists, but he couldn't lie to that voice. He had just watched his only real friendship shatter and die. When the door to Room 3027 opened and Farley stuck his head into the corridor, Skeeter barely noticed.

"Hey, you. Have you seen a guy named Marcus, about your size, brown hair?"

Skeeter stared Farley in the eyes and snarled out yet another lie. "No. Never heard of him."

Then he headed for the elevators and the nearest joint that served alcohol. He wanted to feel numb. And he didn't care how much money it took. He closed his eyes as the elevator whirred silently toward the Neo Edo's lobby.

How he was going to regain the friendship he'd managed to shatter into pieces, Skeeter Jackson had no idea. But he had to try. What was the point of staying on at TT-86, if he couldn't enjoy himself? And with the memory of Marcus' cold, angry eyes and that wintery voice sinking into his bones, he knew he would never enjoy another moment in La-La Land unless he could somehow restore good faith with Marcus.

He stumbled out of the elevator, completely alone in a lobby crowded with tourists, and realized that Marcus' anger was infinitely worse than all those long-ago baseball games where he'd played his heart out, alone, while a father too busy to bother stayed home and stole money from customers who didn't need the expensive junk he sold to any sucker he could pin down longer than five seconds.

The comparison hurt.

Skeeter found that nearest bar, ignoring tattooed Yakuza and wide-eyed Japanese businessmen, and got roaring, nastily drunk. Had his luck gone sour? Was all this a punishment for screwing over—and thus guaranteeing the loss of—his only friend? He sat there amongst the curious Japanese businessmen and thugs who stared at the gaijin in "their" bar, and wondered bitterly who he hated worse: His father? Marcus, for pointing out how much Skeeter had turned out like him? Or himself, for everything he'd done to end up just like the man he'd grown up despising?

He found no answers in the Japanese whiskey or the steaming hot *sake*, which he consumed in such enormous amounts even the Japanese businessmen were impressed, eventually crowding around to compliment and encourage him. A girl dressed as a geisha—hell, she might have *been* one, since time terminals could afford to pay the outrageous salaries their careers demanded—refilled his cup again and again, attempted vainly to flirt and draw him out with conversation and silly games the others played with enthusiasm. Skeeter ignored all of it, utterly. All he wanted was the numbing effect of the booze.

So he let them talk, the words washing over him like the cutting winds of the wide, empty Gobi. There might not be any answers in the whiskey, but alcohol made the emptiness a little easier to bear.

Three sheets to the wind (a sailing term, Skeeter had discovered years earlier when his father had taken them on a short cruise so everyone of any importance would see his new sloop), Skeeter was just about to give into to drunken stupor when the phone rang. He snagged the receiver, tripping and knocking over a chair on the way. "Yeah?"

"Mr. Jackson? Chuck Farley, here."

Surprise rooted him to the carpet. "Yes?" he asked cautiously.

"I've been thinking about your offer the other day. About time guiding. You had a good point. If you're not engaged, I'd like to hire you."

Skeeter recovered from his surprise gracefully. "Of course. What gate did you have in mind?"

"Denver."

"Denver. Hmm . . ." He pretended to consult a nonexistent guiding calendar while pulling himself together. "The best time for Denver's just a tad over two weeks from now, after the Porta Romae makes a complete tour cycle. Yes, I'm free for that Denver trip."

"Wonderful! Meet me in half an hour in Frontier Town. We'll discuss details. There's a little bar called Happy Jack's . . ."

"Yes, I know it. Half an hour? No problem. I'll be there."

"Good."

The line clicked dead. Happy Jack's was a wild place, where anything could happen. Especially to one particular fat money-belt. Skeeter grinned as he emerged from his apartment.

Profit, here I come!

Happy Jack's bore an enormous wooden sign over the entrance, of dancing, dueling cowboys shooting at one another's feet. A large glass window was painted in bright Frontier Town colors, as well, proclaiming the bar's name in red, blue, and garish gold. Skeeter pushed open the Hollywood-style saloon doors and entered the raucous establishment, where a piano player was already busy pounding out tunes popular in Denver—the lyrics of which would've given the NAACP a collective fit of apoplexy. Many of those popular old tunes, heard and bellowed in dance halls and saloons from New York to San Francisco during the 1880s, were *not* flattering to the darker races.

There was a running war between uptime delegations and Frontier Town bar owners over the playing of those songs, but no resolution was in sight. So the pianists played on, accustoming patrons to what they'd actually hear downtime—shocking, crude, racist, and all. Skeeter figured it beat having some uptime type throw a fit in the *real* downtime Denver, where more modern attitudes publicly and forcefully expressed would get a tourist into hot water fast.

Skeeter shook his head. Some folks just didn't get it. Human beings weren't nice, given half a chance not to be. If crusaders with legitimate gripes wanted to fix things, getting into legal wrangles with station bar owners wasn't the way to do it. Couldn't change the past, no matter what you did, and the bar keepers were just doing their part to acclimatize customers, after all. Crusaders needed to stay uptime and pour their resources into causes that might actually do some good: like raising the level of education for uptimers of *all* colors and breeds of human being. Same went for those enviro-nuts who wanted to go downtime and save the environment. Besides, it was plain wrong to murder a bunch of downtime commercial hunters and loggers for doing what their time thought perfectly normal.

For a half-wild, adopted Yakka Mongol, Skeeter just couldn't figure out what was so horrible about taking a good, long, clear-eyed look at one's past and facing whatever one found in it. Making up the past to fit whatever idea some politically correct group wanted to pass off as reality this week seemed a lot more dangerous to him than facing brutal facts, but then, he *was* just a half-wild, adopted Yakka Mongol in his innermost heart. What did he know from social theory and uptime politics?

Chuck Farley was there ahead of him, sitting at a table near the front and sipping whiskey. Skeeter smiled his best and slid into a chair. Above the roar of piano and human voices, he said, "Evenin' pardner."

Chuck smiled slowly. "Evenin'. Have a drink with me?"

"Don't mind if I do."

Farley signalled the waiter. A moment later, Skeeter was sipping some fine whiskey. *Ahh* . . . "Now. You wanted to plan a trip to Denver?"

Farley nodded. "What I really need is an experienced time guide to set up my trip and show me the ropes before I go through the gate."

"Well sir, then I'm your man. But my fee is high."

Farley reached into a coat pocket and extracted a bulging envelope. "Half of this is yours before we leave, half when we get back."

"You realize, sir, that tickets to the Denver Gate go quickly; we'll need to purchase them right away." Skeeter half hoped that Farley would hand over the money right then.

Instead, Farley put the envelope back and said, with the air of a man relieved not to have to bother with petty details, "I'll leave it to you, who knows the ropes, to make arrangements, then."

Skeeter grinned philosophically. "Sure thing. Where and when shall we meet next?" If this envelope was only a fraction of what Farley carried in that undeclared money belt, Skeeter would soon be a rich man.

Farley named a spot off the Commons in a quiet corridor near the Epicurean Delight. "We'll meet there in, say, an hour?" Farley added.

"I'll be there." Skeeter smiled.

"I'll be lookin' for you, pardner." Farley lifted his glass. "To adventure."

Skeeter clinked glasses and drained his whiskey. "To adventure. See you in an hour." *Perfect*, he gloated. *Just where I want him. Goldie's gone for good.*

He strolled out of the saloon and headed straight to the nearest money machine. He regretted having to front the ticket money himself, but he figured he needed to bait his hook with high-class worms to catch a rich fish. He then made his way to the Wild West Gate Time Tours ticket booth. "Hi, I'd like two spots on the Denver trip two weeks from now."

"Sure, plenty of tickets left." The woman behind the glass—who knew Skeeter as well as any long-time 'eighty-sixer—frowned and said, "But let's see the cash, Jackson."

He grinned, producing it with a flourish. The woman groaned. "Poor sucker. I pity him—or her. All right, here are your tickets."

She stamped generic tickets for the correct departure date and handed them over. "Don't forget to tell your rube he'll need his time card with him," she added sarcastically.

Clearly, she didn't expect Skeeter's supposed victim to make it anywhere near the Wild West Gate. Skeeter cheerfully blew her a kiss, then headed for the assignation with Farley behind the Delight. He whistled as he walked, tickets in his pockets, along with a little remaining cash of his own to buy supper with. He chuckled midwhistle. After he got possession of that money-belt, the little bit of his own money he carried would be insignificant by comparison.

Dinner at the Delight would be a welcome change from frozen soy patties with "seared-in" so-called grill patterns to look like beef. After the diet he'd grown accustomed to as a boy, they made him want to gag, but they kept body and soul together and just now, with the wager on, he couldn't afford luxuries like real beef in his freezer.

The corridor behind the Delight was long and deserted at the moment. Bins and chutes leading to composting rooms and incinerators in the bowels of the station lined the walls. Skeeter propped his back and the sole of one foot against the wall, whistling still, and waited. A sound off to his left distracted him. He glanced down that way—

Pain exploded through the back of his skull. He went down, knowing he was hurt, and felt his face connect with a monstrously hard floor. Then a cloth soaked in foul-smelling liquid covered his nose and mouth. He struggled briefly, cursing his stupidity and carelessness, but slid inexorably into a black fog even as hands searched his pockets.

Then the darkness closed over him and left him inert against the floor.

When he regained his senses, slowly, with a taste like the Gobi on his tongue and a sandstorm pounding the insides of his head, Skeeter groaned softly, then wished he hadn't. *Drugged* . . . He struggled to sit up and nearly retched, but made it to a sitting position propped more or less against the wall. Fumbling hands searched, but the tickets and all of his money were missing. Had Farley rolled him? Or some opportunist amateur new to the station? Or—just as likely—one of Goldie's agents?

He cursed under his breath, winced, and gingerly touched his throbbing head. He couldn't exactly report this mugging to Bull Morgan, now could he? "Hi, I was about to scam this uptimer when somebody jumped me with a sap and a chloroformed rag. . . ."

No, he wouldn't be talking to the Station Manager or anyone else about this one. Skeeter managed to gain his feet, then slid dizzily back to the floor and spent several miserable minutes bringing up the contents of his stomach. He was still coughing and wishing for a glass of water to rinse his mouth when hasty footsteps ran lightly his way.

"Skeeter?" a female voice said anxiously.

He looked up, wondering who she was. He didn't remember seeing her before.

"Skeeter, you are ill! Oh, Ianira will be so upset! Here, let me help you."

Her accent pegged her as a downtimer, probably Greek. Legs so wobbly he could barely stand unaided, he let her guide him through the back corridors to his own apartment, where she levered him expertly into the shower, stripped him down, and sluiced lukewarm water over his shivering body to clean up the mess. He leaned against the tiles, groaning, and pressed gingerly at the swelling on the back of his head.

Whoever she was, she reappeared with a towel and helped him out of the shower, dried him expertly, and got him into a comfortable robe, then assisted him across the short stretch of floor to his bed. He couldn't have made the walk unaided. She disappeared again, returning with a glass of liquid.

"Here. Sip this. It will settle your stomach and ease the pain in your head."

He sipped. It didn't taste as bad as he'd expected. Skeeter finished the glassful, then groaned softly and leaned back into the pillows. She pulled the covers up over him, switched off the lights, and settled into a nearby chair to watch over him.

"Hey," Skeeter mumbled, "thanks."

"Sleep," she urged. "You have been hurt. Sleep will heal."

Unable to argue with either her logic or the heaviness stealing across him, Skeeter closed his eyes and slept.

Marcus found Lupus Mortiferus in Urbs Romae, skulking near the entrance to the Epicurean Delight. The gladiator's eyes widened when Marcus charged right toward his place of concealment. He thrust his hand into the box of money he'd so carefully saved up and yanked out a fistful of coins from a bag that matched the amount Skeeter had given him.

"Here. This is yours."

Lupus took the wad of heavy pouch without comment, just staring at him. He glanced down at the money, then back at Marcus. "What has happened?"

Marcus laughed, a bitter sound that widened Lupus' eyes. "I have discovered an ugly truth, friend. I am a very great fool. The man who stole from you gave me that money. I thought he had won it fairly, betting at the Circus. Why I thought that, when he has never done an honest day's work in his life . . ."

Lupus caught him by the shirt. "*Who is he? Where is he?*"

For just an instant, Marcus almost answered. Then he jerked loose. "Where?" The laughter was even more bitter than before. "I don't know. And I don't care. Probably out trying to steal from someone else gullible enough to call him friend. As to who he is . . . I have given you hospitality. My woman and my children are in hiding and now I do not have enough money to repay the debt of my purchase price to the man who brought me here. And thief and scoundrel though he may be, I have called him friend. You mean to kill him. You will have to discover him yourself, Wolf."

❖   ❖   ❖

Goldie's network of contacts paid off. Specifically, a brilliant, impudent downtimer aged about fifteen, known to everyone in La-La Land as simply "Julius" had been the one to hit paydirt. Goldie sat down on a bench in Victoria Station, where the Britannia Gate would be cycling soon. According to Julius, all she had to do was *wait*. People strolled past three and four times as they explored the brilliantly decorated Holiday La-La Land—and Victoria Station had pulled out the stops in the annual competition, hoping to regain respect again after that enormous raptor of some sort had crashed through and fallen five stories, only to land with smashing force on cobblestones, wrought-iron benches, even smashing over a dainty street lamp with etched glass in its multiple panes. She hoped they took the prize money with a thousand points between them and their nearest competitor.

Goldie shook off too many memories and watched intently the tourists taking in the exuberant display, complete with a Victorian kid-sized railroad that began at Victoria Station and quickly picked up steam to circle the entire, lavishly decorated Commons. Many parents had vidcams with them to record junior or their darling little miss, eyes aglow and their laughter sparkling like Christmas bells.

Goldie snorted under her breath. Truth was, she hated children as much as she hated that tinkle-winkle noise of thinly silver-plated brass bells.

Goldie shrugged. She couldn't help being cynical. She'd seen it all before, year in and year out, as relatively poor uptimers with their big families took advantage of the special "one-cycle-pass" tickets to step through Primary and absorb as much of the holiday spirit as possible in the Wonderland of La-La Land before the Primary cycled again. But she'd put up a few requisite lights and bows around her shop and counted it time wasted. And speaking of time wasted . . .

Where was Skeeter's Nemesis?

Ordering herself to remain patient and seem the very picture of innocence, she sat regally on her bench in Victoria station, watching the crowds surge past, many pausing to take pictures of overhead decorations. Goldie noted they were tattered a bit in places by the prehistoric birds and pterosaurs that tended to roost in the girders.

One camera-bedecked geek got more than he had bargained for. An offering from one of the leather-winger screechers above splattered hideously across camera lens and body, the photographer's face, the eye not on the eyepiece, both cheeks, mouth and chin, never mind the mess running down into his hair. Laughter, most of it sympathetic, with the delighted, devilish kind coming from the kids in their mothers' tow, broke out across Victoria Station.

Goldie, chuckling along with everyone else, almost missed him. A pair of cow-chaps caught her attention. Her field of visual acuity narrowed as she looked this man over. Someone staying in the Wild West section, out to see the rest of the station's gilt offerings. Oddly enough, he wasn't laughing with the rest. Then he turned and Goldie looked straight into his face. *Ahh* . . . yes, that was him, all right. The dark scowl, the shock of short-cut reddish hair, the play of muscles as he moved, all confirmed the identity of the man with the knife. Just where he was sleeping was not immediately obvious; he looked tired, like a man who hasn't eaten enough in the past few days, and somehow frustrated. She didn't know his name—yet—but this very much the worse-for-wear gladiator was going to solve *all* of Goldie's problems and rid

Time Terminal 86 of that weasel Skeeter Jackson forever.

With a wave of her hand, Goldie signalled. Two *very* large, very muscular downtimers in her employ casually moved in, then grasped the astonished gladiator's arms—pinning them behind him (probably a career record for sudden, brutal defeat)—then steered him over to Goldie. A moment later, a young lad slid across the cobblestones on in-line skates, sending showers of sparks as he moved on the sides of his wheels rather than the bottoms. He did an impressive sliding stop on the bench rail, earning admiring looks from uptime kids on a tighter leash.

Born showman, Goldie thought. It was a very good thing that he'd ended up adopted by that downtimer couple Goldie'd run into. The pair had been running from taxes they couldn't pay and, in their terrified flight from slavers, accidentally ran straight through the Porta Romae into La-La Land. They'd had coins she'd been able to "help" them with.

"That him?" he asked.

"Yes," Goldie said, ginger-honey in her voice. "Would you please tell him that all I want is to talk to him about what he wants most. Tell him if he will make a promise not to run, I will deliver his enemy into his hands."

Young Julius spoke, his Latin pure and flawless, in a quiet, dignified manner that would have pleased even Claudius himself. (Goldie suspected Imperial Blood in him, because he hadn't been left on the city's heap of dung to be taken into adoption or—far more often—slavery, but had been exposed, instead, outside the gates of the Imperial palace, with a little placard around his neck that read, "So all shall know, this is Julius, son of a concubine who has died in childbirth. It is fit that her issue die also.") Goldie watched the gladiator's face as Julius translated her offer. His expression changed drastically in the space of five seconds. First, incredulity, closely followed by suspicious disbelief, then his glance darted this way and that, searching for nonexistent station security squads, from that to puzzlement, and finally very cautious acceptance of the truly odd situation in which fate had placed him.

"Please, Julius, ask our guest to sit beside me."

Julius didn't particularly get along well with the plebeian parents who'd raised him—he found them clinging and mindless—but he thanked all the gods for having landed them here. He absorbed more in one *day* in La-La Land than he'd ever learned from his adoptive parents. They didn't *want* to adjust (Jupiter forgive them if they attempted something new and radical, like flipping on a lightswitch rather than filling the apartment with smoke from candles and lanterns scattered here and there, too dim to see much of anything except shadows dancing on the wall).

Goldie Morran drew him out of deep thought. "Julius, would you be so kind as to explain to this man the location of the enemy he seeks?"

Julius grinned. Then turned to the big man beside him and started speaking rapidly in Latin.

CHAPTER FOURTEEN

Marcus turned on his heel and stalked away, leaving the gladiator to gape after him. He was aware that Lupus tried to follow, so he dodged through Victoria Station, only half aware when Julius' Lost and Found Gang hijacked Lupus Mortiferus' for Goldie Morran, of all people. By the time he returned to the Neo Edo, Skeeter had abandoned his attempt at theft and had long since gone. Marcus took the stairs, pounding angrily so the noise echoed up and down the stairwell, and emerged on the third floor, his meticulously kept records and depleted money box tucked under one arm.

"Curse him!" Marcus spat to the empty corridor.

He pounded on the door to room 3027 with a closed fist and wondered what he would say to the man whose debt he could not now pay. The door opened with alacrity. Marcus swallowed hard and faced down the man who'd bought him out of a filthy, stinking slave pen and brought him, fainting with terror, to La-La Land.

"Marcus," the man said with a tiny smile. "Come in."

He didn't want to go into that room.

But he stepped across the threshold, fingers white around the metal money box, and waited. The click of the door closing reached him, then a tinkle of ice against glass came in the silence. Liquid splashed.

Marcus recognized the label. His one-time master had a taste for expensive liquor. He did not, Marcus noted, offer a second glass to him. Cold and angry, Marcus waited while the man sipped and studied him.

"You've changed." The Latin rolled off his tongue as neatly as it had that day in Rome.

"That is your doing," Marcus replied in English.

One brow rose toward a greying hairline. "Oh?"

Marcus shrugged in that Gallic gesture which had survived the centuries. "You brought me here. I have listened and learned. I know the laws which forbid slavery and the laws which forbid you to bring men like me into this world."

Dark eyes narrowed.

"I owe you money," Marcus went on doggedly, "for repayment of the coin you spent for my purchase. But your slave I am not. This is La-La Land. Not Rome."

He dropped the record books on the bed. "There are the notes you sought. Men who travelled with the zipper jockeys to the brothels of Greece and Rome. Men who returned with the art you seek. Men who did business with Robert Li when they returned and men who did not."

He thrust out the money box. "Here is most of what I owe you. In another few seven-days, I will have earned the rest. If you would tell me your name," he allowed sarcasm to creep into his voice, "I will have it sent to you uptime."

His former master stood very still for a very long time, just watching him. Then, slowly, he accepted the money box and set it aside, unopened. "We'll discuss this later, Marcus. As for my name," a brief smile touched mobile lips without reaching dark, watchful eyes, "it's Chuck. Chuck Farley. At least," he chuckled hollowly, "it is today. Tomorrow . . ." He shrugged. "Let's see those records of yours, shall we?"

He held out a hand for them.

Marcus, torn between the desire to stand his ground and the hope that his one-time master understood and would be reasonable about the arrangements for the rest of the money, hesitated. Then slowly picked up the record books and handed them over.

"Ahh . . ." Chuck Farley settled into a chair and flipped on a light, sipping whiskey and poring over Marcus' notations, making occasional comments that meant nothing to Marcus. "Very interesting. Hmm, now I wonder—of course." And he laughed, darkly. Marcus fought a shiver. Farley read through each book before glancing up again. "You've done very well, Marcus. I am impressed by your eye for detail and the thoroughness of your notes." He gestured with the glass toward the ledger books. Ice cubes tinkled like bones against the glass. "Now, as for the other matter, let's just see how much you have left to pay off, shall we?"

He opened the money box at last and counted out everything Marcus owned—and almost every bit of what Ianira had earned. They'd kept back just enough to buy food for the children.

Farley whistled softly. "You managed to save all this while keeping a roof over your head on the terminal? I'm impressed again." His glance was full of smiles this time. Marcus repressed a shiver. "Here." He shoved the metal box aside and found another glass, poured whiskey for them both, this time. "We'll celebrate, shall we? Your emancipation. Yes, we'll drink to your emancipation. You should be able to earn the balance in no time."

Marcus accepted the glass automatically. In truth, he felt a little numb, unsure what to think or believe.

"In fact, you could discharge the rest of that debt in one little job, tonight."

Whiskey untouched, Marcus just waited.

Farley smiled. "Drink. This is a celebration."

He drank. The whiskey burned his throat. He managed—just barely—not to cough. Whiskey, of any kind, was not something his palate was accustomed to, despite the amount of it he dispensed to others in the course of a week.

Chuck Farley—or whoever he really was—was speaking. He tried to pay full attention, despite the heat and disconcerting dizziness spreading rapidly through him.

"Now. I'm heading through the Porta Romae tonight to do some art collecting. I have quite a bit of baggage with me and I don't want to leave it behind. Things always manage to get stolen from luggage left in the care of a hotel." His smile sent a shiver down Marcus' overheated back. "Hmm . . . I'll tell you what we'll do. Act as my porter tonight, help me get all that baggage to the inn, and we'll call the debt even. I know downtimers work as porters all the time. I'd save myself a good bit of money, if you agree, and you'd be out of debt." His eyes twinkled, but darkly, like black diamonds.

Farley was smiling, now, while the whiskey sank into Marcus' veins. Farley refilled his glass. "Drink up, Marcus! We're celebrating, remember?"

He drank, feeling the burning heat sink into his belly and spread like dizzy fire through his whole body. His head whirled. Return to Rome? The very thought terrified him so badly his hand, unsteady around the glass, sloshed expensive liquor onto even more expensive carpet. He drank just to empty the full glass and spare Kit Carson's cleaning bill.

Actually *return* to Rome? But it would be a quick, simple way to discharge the remainder of his debt.

Carry a few bags through the Porta Romae, then

return free of debt to the woman he loved and the children they had made together. It sounded so simple. Farley was smiling and chatting easily, now, refilling his glass, urging him to sit down, drawing him out about the men in his dry, factual notes. Marcus found himself talking about them, about the sexual art they had smuggled through for rich, uptime collectors greedy for rare, explicitly sexual items in pottery, stone, and ivory. Frankly, Marcus didn't understand the fuss. He'd grown up with so much of it around him, it was like walking past Connie Logan's and seeing the familiar figure in wildly mismatched clothes she was trying on for fit.

With Farley drawing him out, he talked and drank and through a haze of whiskey, heard himself agree to the bargain over his debt. Porter for a trip to Roma for complete freedom of debt. His honor was satisfied. But he couldn't help wondering if he'd made a bargain with the gods of the underworld themselves.

"Good! Very good." Farley glanced at his watch. "Just another hour, or so, and the gate will be cycling. We'd better get into costume, eh? I'll expect you back here in, say, fifteen minutes?"

Marcus found himself nodding dumbly, then stumbled into the hall and made his unsteady way down and down still farther to his empty apartment. He still had the tunic and sandals of his first days on the station, tucked away in a box at the back of the closet. They felt alien against his skin. He left the fringed shirt Ianira had given him sprawled across the bed, along with a note in an unsteady hand, leaving word of where he was going and why, then—garbed as a Roman of the poorest, most abused classes— returned resolutely to the Neo Edo.

In an hour, he would be free of all debt and obligation to the man calling himself Chuck Farley. He knocked on the door to Room 3027 and quietly collected the man's bags, following silently to the brightly lit Commons and the crowded waiting area surrounding the great Porta Romae.

"Wait here," Farley told him. "I have some money to exchange."

Marcus just nodded, standing guard over the bags as told. He wondered where Ianira was, wished he could tell her everything was turning out fine, after all, then noticed that Farley'd disappeared in the direction of Goldie Morran's shop. He considered warning the man against her, then shrugged. Farley clearly knew what he was doing. Exhausted, head still befuddled from the whiskey he'd swallowed, Marcus simply waited for Farley's return and the end of the coming ordeal.

Chuck Farley wasn't his real name, but it was admirably suited to his line of work—and sense of humor. Chuck was close enough.

He hid a smile, looking forward to the little scene about to unfold. Passing through the Urbs Romae section of the terminal, he paused to change clothing in a men's room, slipping into a custom-made harness arrangement under uptime clothes and stuffing his Roman disguise of tunic and toga into a shoulder satchel, then sought out the shop of that appalling, purple-haired gargoyle of a money changer. He entered as quietly as an owl on the hunt for a particularly delectable mouse.

The gargoyle glanced up from another customer. Goldie beamed at him. Chuck smiled politely back and waited, laughing inside already.

Ah, what joy it was, setting up someone who thought themselves a pro. . . . She finished hastily with the other customer, all but shoving him out the door in her greed.

"Mr. Farley, what a lovely surprise! Have you reconsidered?"

Chuck allowed himself a small smile. "Not precisely." He reached into the satchel holding his Roman garments and extracted from a side pocket the bait. "I wanted to discuss this with you." He rubbed the back of his neck as though self-conscious. "I was told you were the expert on such things." With well-practiced deference, he handed over a faded newspaper clipping.

Eyes glancing curiously from his face to the bit of paper, Goldie Morran scanned what he'd handed her. Avarice gleamed for a lovely instant. *Hook, line, and sinker.*

"Well, that is most interesting," Goldie Morran said with a slight clearing of her throat. "This is legitimate?"

"I assure you, it is. I'm something of an amateur historian and I was tracing some of my family's history. I came across this in my uptime researches into the Gold Rush in Colorado. Imagine my surprise." It came out droll enough to cause Goldie to laugh. He smiled and gestured to the newspaper clipping. "There I am, preserved for posterity, standing over the gold mine I discovered, while some primitive cameraman takes my photograph for the folks back home." He chuckled. "So, you see, I have this opportunity—destiny?—and all I require to fulfill it is a grubstake to purchase the blasted bit of ground."

"Ahh . . ." Goldie smiled and beckoned him to a comfortable seat on the customer side of her counter. "You'll be wanting to exchange uptime currency for American currency of the proper type for the Wild West Gate, then?"

"Exactly. I'll need a lot of money downtime to buy the camping gear, mining equipment, horses, and so on, to develop the mine quickly and make me seem legitimate. And you understand I don't want to exchange such a large sum of money officially—the ATF is suspicious, you know."

Goldie chuckled unexpectedly. "No wonder you weren't interested in any of my suggested investments. You had your own nicely arranged. Very clever, Mr. Farley." She wagged a talon at him. "How much did you have in mind to exchange?"

"A hundred thousand."

Goldie Morran's eyes widened.

"I did bring the cash," he added with a small smile.

"All right. A hundred thousand. I'll see what I have. There will, of course, be a small transaction fee included in the exchange rate."

"Oh yes, I quite understand," Farley reassured her.

She walked down the counter and opened up a locked drawer. She returned with a large wad of oversized bank notes and a handful of gold and silver coins.

He then dutifully unbuckled the money belt under his uptime clothing and counted out a hundred thousand-dollar bills. Goldie's eyes gleamed. She swiftly counted the money he handed to her, and pushed the unwieldy pile of downtimer money to him.

The exchange completed, Goldie smiled. "You realize sir, that you'll also need a good quantity of gold nuggets to take into the assayer's office as proof of your strike, in order to stake a proper claim."

Chuck looked taken aback. "I hadn't realized that. But I was told I'd need at least this much money to buy the new gear in 1885 because of the high prices during the gold rush. And this is all I have."

Goldie nodded, reminding Chuck of a cathedral downspout he'd once seen, come to full and hideous life. "Well, maybe I can help you. As it happens, I have a good bit of my own assets in the form of gold.

I'll give you the gold you need to substantiate your claim if you cut me in for a percentage of your strike. Say about fifty percent?"

Farley looked eager, then less so when she named the percentage. "Well, that seems a bit steep. How about twenty percent? After all, I did find it."

"Yes, but without my gold, you'll have to spend a lot of back-breaking, sweaty work just to rush into town to make your claim before the gate closes. Then you'll have to get back to your mine, wasting time that could be devoted to getting more gold out of the ground."

"True enough. Hmm, how about fifty percent and you agree to exchange my share of the gold dust I bring back without charging your usual fee?"

"Done, sir."

She dove into back room and after a short time came back with a rolling cart on which were piled small sacks with odd lumps sticking through the cloth. She pulled out a set of scales and calibrated weights from a shelf underneath the counter, and sat down.

"Now, mostly what I have is dust, but there are a few nuggets," she said with a smile. "This should be enough to convince the assayer about your strike." She set up the scales carefully, filling one side with brass weights designated in troy ounces. She opened a sack and tipped gold into the other pan until the scale read level. "At the current rates of exchange, that's a hundred dollars."

She was lying—it was actually more like thirty-five. Chuck said diffidently, "Er, isn't that a bit light?"

"Oops, sorry, these are the ones I reserve for the zipper jockeys. Let me get the real ones." She opened a drawer behind her, and pulled out another set of counterweights, and continued measuring out hundredweights until she'd finished with the pile. It was a big pile.

"You probably think it's odd that I happen to keep this much gold around. But I went through the big crash after the Accident, and I don't trust banks, not anymore."

Chuck rubbed the side of his nose and murmured sympathetically. "My dear lady, you are a life saver. A fortune saver," he added with a small laugh. "But I still have one problem." He gestured to the bags of dust and nuggets laid out across the top of the counter. "I can't very well go walking through the Wild West Gate with that in plain sight. I've got to look like someone who's been in the field for months, accumulating it. Do you have a period-style leather satchel, perhaps, that I could carry everything in?"

Goldie smiled in what she probably considered her most winsome manner. "I have just the thing. A set of saddlebags brought uptime by one of my agents— for you, no charge. I'll just go and get them."

She vanished into the back of her shop yet again.

Chuck was tempted to steal back his bills, just lying there on the counter, but he didn't want to risk being arrested when he came back. His fake ID was good, but why take unnecessary chances? Besides, getting caught by his boss for his little extracurricular activities on TT-86 would be bad for his health. Permanently.

He and Goldie concluded their business with a handshake, and Farley headed for the nearest public restroom to ditch his clothes, settle the heavy bags of gold into his carrying harness, and don his toga for the Roman gate. He rejoined Marcus, who waited quietly with his luggage. He smiled at the younger man, then headed up the ramp with the other tourists.

By the time Goldie discovered the scam and reported it, he'd be long gone. Chuck laughed aloud, softly, drawing a curious look from the slave he'd purchased all those years ago. Yes, he'd have given a great deal

to see the look on her face under all that purple hair.
Amateurs. Still chuckling, he slid his time card with
its fake identification into the reader, had his departure
time and date duly logged, and gestured to Marcus.
The young man hoisted the baggage and followed
silently through the gaping portal in the concrete wall
of Time Terminal Eighty-Six.

Unable to leave his apartment, he felt so ill,
Skeeter—in looking for ways to make some illegal profit
during his convalescence, hit quite suddenly on the
answer. Something Marcus had once said brought new
inspiration when Skeeter needed it most. He was still
hung over and hurting, a particularly nasty throb where
Farley had struck the back of his skull. Or whoever it
had been. He was also, however, running out of time.
So he quietly bought up a supply of small glass bottles,
corks, and paper labels from various outfitters, ordering
them over the computer and asking to have them
delivered immediately to his apartment. When
everything arrived, Skeeter got busy, diligently gluing
handwritten labels onto each filled, corked bottle of
tapwater, tinged just slightly with a drop of ink. The
longer he counted the potential profits to be had in
the patent medicine business, the more cheerful he
grew, despite headache and hangover from too much
alcohol combined with too much chloroform. Each
label exclaimed in gorgeous, "antique" script (Skeeter
could, among other odd skills, forge just about any
signature he'd ever seen): MIRACLE WATER—DIRECT FROM
DOWNTIME IMPORTER! FAMOUS SPRINGS OF CAUTERETS! OWN
A BOTTLE OF MYSTIC HISTORY FROM GALLIA COMATA, AD
47! A THOUSAND PASSIONATE NIGHTS GUARANTEED
WITH ANCIENT WORLD'S MOST SOUGHT-AFTER LOVE POTION!
He hadn't spent much and the uptime tourist crowd
was just as gullible as any nineteenth-century Iowa

farmer. The descendants of twentieth-century new-ager crystal mystics, in particular, ought to be "medicine show" pushovers. As Ianira Cassondra's little booth on the Commons had proved, they'd buy anything even moderately wacky—particularly if he hinted that the stuff had not only been bottled in Gallia Comata, but that the water from the famous spring actually bubbled up from the sacred rivers of lost Atlantis. He pasted another label, wondering how much he could get per bottle? Ten? Twenty? Fifty? Shucks, some fools might go as high as a hundred.

Gingerly humming a little ditty Yesukai the Valiant's aged mother had taught him, the tune warlike and lighthearted, Skeeter was as happy as any exiled Yakka tribesman in a *lot* of pain could be. He had several bottles left to label when someone buzzed his doorbell frantically. Curious, he peered through the peephole.

"Huh?" Skeeter opened to the door to find Ianira Cassondra outside his apartment, literally wringing her hands in the folds of a pretty, Ionic-style chiton. "Ianira! What are you doing here?"

He ushered her in, shocked by the tears sparkling on pale cheeks and ashen lips. The door clicked softly behind him, the latch catching, but he was so distracted he didn't bother with the deadbolt. Ianira had clutched at his arm.

"Please, you must help him!"

"Who? Ianira, what's happened?"

"Skeeter, he's going with that terrible man, and I don't trust him, and it's your fault he's going at all—"

"Whoa, slow down. Now. Who's going where?"

"Marcus! To Rome!" The words were torn from her. Skeeter blinked. "Rome? Marcus is going to Rome? That's crazy. Marcus would never go back to Rome."

Her nails dug painfully into his arm. "His cursed *master* came back! You know his pride, his determination to pay that man his purchase cost, to be free of the debt!"

Skeeter nodded, wondering what on earth had happened. "He should've had plenty, I'd think. I mean, I know the new baby was expensive, and all, and what with little Artemisia getting so sick from the fever that idiot tourist brought back they had to quarantine her, but there's that bet money I gave him—"

"That's just it!" she cried. Her nails drew blood. "He found out how you got it and gave it back!"

"He . . . *gave it back?*" Skeeter's voice hit a squeak. "You mean . . . he just *gave it back?*" Then: "Oh, shit, that means he knows how to find that maniac that's been—"

"Yes, yes," Ianira said impatiently, "Lupus had been staying with us, because he needed help and we didn't know it was *you* who had stolen the money he needed to start a new life away from the blood and the killing!" Harsh accusation rasped along Skeeter's nerves. After that fight with Marcus, this new accusation felt like Ianira had just dumped a whole shaker of salt into an open wound.

"Okay, I really screwed up with that gladiator. I've known that a while, Ianira, and I'm sorrier than you know. But, *what does that have to do with Marcus going to Rome?*"

Ianira gave out a strangled sound like a sob. "How can you be so *blind?* That man came back, the one who bought him. Marcus didn't have quite enough money to pay him back. Not after all the medical bills. So Marcus agreed to carry his luggage to Rome to finish paying off the debt."

Skeeter relaxed. "Is that all? He'll be back, then, in a couple of weeks, free and clear."

"*No, he won't!*" Petite little Ianira, snarling like an enraged wolverine, backed Skeeter into a corner. He'd seen that look in a woman's eyes before—more than once and usually when Yesukai's new bride had vented her temper on some hapless victim in her imprisoning bridal yurt.

"Can't you see it, idiot?" Ianira demanded, raising the fine hairs on his neck and arms. "He's made Marcus keep records of certain people who come and go. The man who calls himself Farley, a name which does not match the soul-darkness in his eyes, *steals* things, downtime. Expensive things. Artwork. Some of it sexual and very rare! Once they're in Rome, Marcus will be just another expendable bit of profit to be auctioned off! That horrible Farley man has tricked him. I can *feel* it—and I was trained in such arts nearly three thousand years before you were born!"

A touch of coldness settled in Skeeter's belly. *Chuck Farley was Marcus' old master?* That put a whole, new—and utterly terrifying—wrinkle on the situation. After his own experience with Chuck Farley, Ianira had to be right. Hell, Ianira was never *wrong*. The lump on the back of his head still ached, making rational thought nearly impossible. Torn by helplessness, he asked quietly, "What do you want me to do? I can't afford the price of a ticket to Rome."

Dark eyes flashed rage. "You mean you can't and still save enough to win your horrible wager!"

Skeeter groaned. That damnable wager, again. "Ianira, the man kidnapping Marcus robbed *me*, of almost everything I had left. And Brian Hendrickson is holding every red cent of what I've accumulated for that stupid wager."

"So steal it back! Before it's too late! There are still a few minutes before the Porta Romae opens! Marcus is in line, Skeeter, looking confused and scared, just standing there guarding that miserable man's luggage." Her nails dug even deeper into his arm. Skeeter winced.

"I've got The Found Ones out there, but we don't have the money between us, and he won't listen to them if he can't pay off that debt. Please, Skeeter, he is your friend. *Help him!*

"I—" He stopped. He didn't have many resources at the moment and if he were going to stop Marcus from stepping through the Porta Romae, he'd have to come up with some fast cash to pay off Farley before the gate opened. "Oh, hell!"

He switched on his computer and searched out the listing he needed, then picked up the telephone and dialed. The elderly Nally Mundy answered a bit testily.

"Yes, yes, hello?"

"Dr. Mundy? It's Skeeter Jackson. I—I know you're going to think this is a scam, because of that damned wager I made with Goldie, but a friend of mine, Marcus, the bartender from Rome, he's in trouble and I need money to keep him from doing something stupid. *Dangerous* and stupid. If—if you still want to do that interview with me about Yesukai and the Khan's boyhood," he swallowed hard, "I'll do it. I swear. And Ianira Cassondra's here to witness it."

A long silence at the other end ticked away precious seconds. "Put her on the phone, Skeeter."

Ianira took the instrument and spoke rapidly to the elderly historian—in Archaic Greek. Then she handed the telephone back to Skeeter.

"Very well, young rascal. I should probably be committed to an asylum for such folly, but I'll authorize the transfer. You can pick up the money from a cash machine in five minutes. If you cheat me on this one, Skeeter Jackson, I swear to you I will make *certain* you get tossed off this station into the highest security uptime prison I can land you in!"

Skeeter winced. He'd pledged his word—and besides, the elderly and utterly harmless Dr. Nally

Mundy was an 'eighty-sixer. "Thank you, Dr. Mundy. You don't know what this means."

If he could just get to the Porta Romae departure line with that money in time . . .

The door imploded.

Skeeter swung around, shocked, even as Ianira gasped with fright. Lupus Mortiferus stood in the shattered remains of his door, face flushed with murderous anger.

"Now," he growled in Latin, "*now* we will settle accounts!"

CHAPTER FIFTEEN

The unnatural quiet, broken at regular intervals by a high, beeping sound, convinced Goldie she was neither in her shop nor her apartment. Confused, disoriented, she turned her head and found an IV bottle hanging near her head and a heart monitor beeping softly beside her. The slight movement tugged at monitor leads placed at seeming random about her torso. Then Rachel Eisenstein came into her frame of view and smiled.

"You're awake. How do you feel?"

"I—I'm not sure. What am I doing in the infirmary?"

"You don't remember?"

Goldie frowned, but nothing came back to explain this.

"You collapsed in the library. Brian thought you were dead, started hollering for help." Rachel smiled. "I was afraid you'd had a heart seizure or a stroke, but it seems you simply fainted for some reason."

Fainted? Why in the world would she have—

Memory returned, shocking and brutal. Farley had conned her. There was no such mine—the article had been a fake.

Rachel uttered a little cry and fumbled for something, then injected it into Goldie's IV lead. The room stopped spinning as drowsiness tucked itself around her awareness like a woolly blanket, but memory remained, harsh and inescapable.

Rachel had found a chair. "Goldie?"

She managed to look up.

"Goldie, what is it? What happened?"

She started to laugh, high-pitched and semi-hysterical. Laughter gave way to hiccupping sobs as the reality of her loss sank in. Nearly her entire life's savings, gone. All of it, except for a few coins and the odd gem or three. And, thank God, her precious parakeets, which were safe at her apartment. She'd have to raise cash to live on by selling what little was left—except for her beautiful birds, which she'd sell only after she'd sold everything else she possessed—including her soul. She found herself blurting it all out between sobs, mortified yet strangely comforted when Rachel eased her up and put both arms around her, letting her cry it out. By the time she'd told it all, Goldie realized that whatever Rachel had slipped into that IV line was more potent than she'd realized. Drained of tears and energy, the drug took hold with triumphant strength. The last thing she was aware of was Rachel's hand on hers, comforting. Then she was asleep, face still wet with tears she hadn't shed in many, many years.

Skeeter barely had time to think, *Aw, nuts . . .*

Then the enraged gladiator dove at him. Skeeter lunged across the bed, scattering labelled and corked bottles as he went. He ducked as the gladiator threw something. The mirror above his dresser shattered. Skeeter scooped up a couple of water bottles and hurled them back in the gladiator's general direction. He heard a meaty smack and a roar of pain and anger, but didn't wait to see what damage he'd done. He scrambled for the door, shoving Ianira aside as gently as he could. She shrieked behind him and he heard a loud curse in Latin, then he was around the corner and running hard.

Damn!

Lupus Mortiferus' voice roared out behind him. The chase was still on. A swift glance over one shoulder revealed the gladiator, shirt dark and wet with ink-stained water, face contorted with murderous fury, gaining ground. Skeeter put on a burst of speed and skidded around a corner into the corridor leading toward Commons. He caught his stride and shot into the midst of a packed crowd gathered to watch gate departures. He slithered between tourists and 'eighty-sixers who'd gathered to watch the usual antics of a gate departure unfold.

Cries of dismay and anger in his wake told Skeeter Lupus was still back there, dogged as a cursed snow leopard after its favorite prey. Skeeter vaulted over a cafe table in Victoria Station, startling screams from the diners and scattering glassware and lunches in several directions. A bull's roar and more screams accompanied the crash of the whole table. Skeeter raced and dodged through Victoria station, whipping around iron lamp posts, jumping park benches whether they were occupied or not, flinging himself past gaping tourists and residents while his mind raced in several directions at the same time.

He had to save Marcus. To do that, he had to get that money and stop Farley from taking Marcus through the gate. To get the money, he'd have to stop running. That meant Lupus the Murderous back there would chop him into minced Skeeter. He skidded into Urbs Romae, splashed straight through a shallow goldfish pond—scattering a flock of *Ichthyornises* with a flapping of wings and shrill, toothy screams of protest—and risked a glance back.

Lupus was still coming, inexorable as a Mongolian sandstorm.

Skeeter passed a cash machine without time to stop.

Shit! Now what? Maybe he could sprint around the waiting area, double back somehow, grab the money, and snatch Marcus? Even as the thought formed, the klaxon for a gate departure sounded.

"Your attention, please—"

Skeeter ignored the loudspeakers and concentrated on the crowd waiting to step downtime to Rome. Maybe if he just burst up to the pair of them and offered an IOU? *Yeah, right. Cash deal or nothing, buddy. Your credit's no good.* It was a bitter pill to swallow. The line had already started to move up the long ramp as returning tourists exited the gate. Skeeter caught sight of Marcus, but was too winded to call out. He and Farley were near the front of the line, almost to the portal already.

With no time to stop for cash, no breath to call out anything—much less the deal he'd made with Dr. Mundy—Skeeter did the only thing he *could* do. He jumped the roped-off waiting area's steel fence, caught a ramp girder, swung himself up and around, and landed on his feet next to a Time Tours guide so shocked she actually screamed. More screams behind him told Skeeter that Lupus, curse him, was still back there. He put on a burst of speed, clattering up the steel meshwork ramp, trying to catch up to Marcus before he could step through the portal.

"*Marcus! Wait!*"

His heart plummeted to his toenails.

Just ahead of him, Farley and Marcus vanished into the distortion of the open gate. Skeeter would've sworn in a court of law that Farley had bodily dragged Marcus through after hearing Skeeter's desperate shout.

Skeeter had two choices. He could jump off this platform and elude Lupus yet again, leading him another merry chase through the station, or he could crash the gate and find a way to get Marcus back

through. Time Tours, Inc. was going to fine him
something dreadful—

Skeeter drew a deep breath and threw himself bodily
through the portal. He landed in the familiar wine
shop, momentum hurtling him past shocked tourists.
Skeeter crashed into a rack of stacked amphorae and
knocked the whole thing over. Wine, like foaming
seawater against rocks, spread out in rushing waves
across the entire floor. Tourists screamed and tried
to dive out of the way. He couldn't see Farley anywhere
in the confusion.

"Marcus!"

No familiar voice answered. He grabbed the nearest
guide he spotted and gasped out, "Farley! Where'd
Farley go with Marcus?"

The man shook his head. "They just left, in the first
group. For the inn."

Skeeter laughed semi-hysterically. "If Farley ends
up at the inn, I'll eat your shoes."

He was just about to dodge into the street when a
heavy hand closed on his shoulder. Someone spun him
around with brutal force. Screams of panic rose all
around. Lupus Mortiferus' visage loomed enormous
in Skeeter's vision. He had just enough time to think,
"*Oh, shit—*" before a massive fist and darkness crashed
down.

Sights and smells overwhelmed Marcus from both
past and present the moment the door to the wine
shop's warehouse opened onto the street. A tremble
hit his knees. Farley glanced around.

"Stop dawdling," he said irritably in Latin.

Marcus clutched the man's luggage with sweating
hands and followed the rest of the group toward the
Time Tours inn on the far side of the Aventine Hill
from the great Circus. They headed down the Via Appia

toward the hulking edifice of stone bleachers, rising in tiers to the arches high overhead. When the rest of the group turned left to skirt the Aventine, Farley surprised him by heading the other way, toward the Capitoline Hill.

"Mr. Farley—"

"Be quiet and follow me!" Farley snapped.

Marcus glanced once at the tour group disappearing into the crowd. Then, hesitantly, he followed Farley. He'd given his word. And he needed to clear this debt. But the longer they walked, passing the Capitoline Hill and moving through the great Forum, where the rostrum towered with its glittering trophies of war, the battering rams of ships taken in battle, the greater grew Marcus' sense of wrongness.

"Mr. Farley, where are you going?" he asked in English as they left behind the Forum.

"To a place I've arranged," Farley answered carelessly.

"What place?"

Farley glanced over his shoulder. "You ask too many questions," he said, eyes narrowed.

Marcus stopped dead in the street, setting down the man's bags. "I believe I'm entitled."

Farley's mouth twitched at one corner. "You? Entitled?" He seemed to think this outrageously funny. "Hand me that bag. That one."

Marcus stooped without thinking, handing it over automatically. Farley opened it—

And the next thing Marcus knew, his face had slammed into a brick wall and Farley's fist into his left kidney. He gasped in agony and felt his knees begin to go. Farley held him up with a fist twisted through his tunic. The next moment, Marcus' hands were manacled in iron chains.

"Now listen, boy," Farley hissed in his ear, "you're not in La-La Land any longer. This is *Rome*. And I am your master. I paid good, goddamned gold for you and I intend to do with you as *I* see fit. Is that clear?"

Marcus tried to struggle, knowing even as he did that any fight was hopeless. Farley put him on the ground with another punch to his kidney. He groaned and lay still at the man's feet.

"Get up."

Marcus fought to catch his breath.

"I said get up, slave!"

Marcus glared up at him through a mane of fallen hair across his eyes. "Bastard!"

"Get up, slave, or I'll have you branded as a runaway."

Marcus blanched. The letter *F* burnt into his cheek . . . He struggled and lurched, but finally made it to his feet. Curious onlookers shrugged and returned to their business. Farley fastened a long rope to Marcus' chains, then signalled to a couple of idle fellows at a wine stall, their sedan chair leaning against the wall.

"You, there! Is your chair for hire?"

"It is, noble sir," the broader of the two said eagerly, setting aside a chipped earthenware mug of wine. "You have merely to tell us your destination."

In a daze of disbelief and growing terror, Marcus watched Chuck Farley climb into the sedan chair and accept his luggage, which he balanced on his lap. The porters struggled and grunted to get him airborne and settled onto their shoulders. "Come here, slave!" Farley snapped. "I don't want you getting tangled up in traffic and causing me to fall!"

Marcus stumbled behind the sedan chair, wrists weighted by the heavy cuffs. Chains clanked with a sound of buried nightmare. He remembered being chained . . . chained and worse. *Ianira!* he cried silently. *What have I done, beloved?* If opportunity had presented itself, he would cheerfully have plunged a dagger through Chuck Farley's black heart. But he knew opportunity would *not* present itself.

The porters carried Farley to an imposing villa, where one of them pounded on the door. A slave chained to the interior wall of the entryway opened the door and bowed low, asking their business.

"Tell your master the man he was told to expect has arrived," Farley said, his Latin flawless. "With the goods, as promised."

The slave bowed and passed word to someone deeper in the house. A moment later, the porters had set down their burden, sweating and gasping for breath as though they'd just carried five men, rather than one. Farley paid them and sent them away with a wave of his hand. Then he turned to Marcus, an unpleasant smile lighting his eyes.

"This way, if you please, young Marcus. You are about to meet your new owner."

He wanted to run. Everything in him shouted the need. But in broad daylight, with hundreds of Romans to take up the cry "Runaway!" trying to bolt now was tantamount to suicide. He swallowed down a dry throat. Farley jerked him off balance with the rope, dragging him forward into the villa. He said in an ugly whisper, "You'll have to work a few years to pay off this debt, boy."

Marcus felt sick—sick and trapped. He knew in his soul that no man had the right to own him, but that was in a world two thousand years away. Here, now, to gain his freedom and satisfy the law and his sense of honor, he would have to obtain his purchase price, somehow. Or compromise the values he'd come to believe in so highly and simply run.

It was even money at the moment which he would choose.

Then he was stumbling into the presence of a

wealthy, wealthy man. Marcus actually went down, catching himself on hands and knees. *Gods* . . . He had seen this man many times, at public functions, on the Rostrum, in the law courts. Farley was selling him to . . .

"Farlus, welcome! Come in, come in."

"Your hospitality is gracious, Lucius Honorius Galba. Congratulations, by the way, on your election to *curule aedileship*."

Tremors set in, chattering his teeth. Lucius Honorius Galba had been elected *curule aedile*? As powerful as his hated first master had been, Galba was a thousand times more so. Escape this man? Impossible. Galba glanced down at him.

"This?" the man said, disdain dripping from his voice. "This cowering fool is the valuable scribe you offered for my collection?"

Farley jerked on the rope. "Get up, slave." He said to Galba, "He didn't wish to be sold from my household. And he doubtless knows your illustrious reputation very well." The smile Farley gave Marcus was cool as a lizard's. "I assure you, he knows his job well. I purchased him some years back when the estate of one of the *plebeian aediles* was being disposed of due to the man's death. As to the terror, his desire to make a good impression has left him shaking like a virgin."

Galba chuckled. "Come, boy, there's nothing to fear. I'm a fair man. Get up. I have need of a new scribe and your master, here, has offered a fine trade, a very fine trade. Come, let's see a demonstration of your skills."

Marcus, hands trembling as Farley unlocked the chains, wet his lips, then took the stylus and wax tablet handed him.

"Now," Galba said with a slight smile, "let's see if you can take this down properly."

The stylus jittered against the soft wax, but he did his best to take the dictation, which ranged from a partial letter to a business partner to household accounts to cargoes and trade sums earned at interest. Galba nodded approvingly over the result.

"Not bad," he allowed, "for a man trembling in terror. Not bad at all. In what capacity did you serve your *plebeian aedile*, boy?"

Marcus' voice shook as badly as the rest of him. "I kept records . . . of the races, at the Circus, the inventories of the wild beasts for the bestiary hunts, and the records of gladiators who won victories and those who did not. . . ."

Memory closed in, harsh and immediate despite the time elapsed since those days. He heard Galba say, "I do believe you've brought me a boy who'll settle in nicely. Very well. The bargain is agreed upon."

They retired to a small room off the atrium and its splashing fountain. Chuck Farley and his new master bent over papers, signing their names and exchanging coins for Marcus' life. A moment later, his new owner had called for the steward of his house.

"See to it the new boy is made comfortable, but confined. I want to be certain he doesn't run at the first opportunity. Now, about the pieces you wanted in trade . . ."

Dismissed entirely from the man's awareness, Marcus stumbled dazedly between a burly steward and another thickset man who guided him toward the back of the house. The room they put him in was small and windowless, lit with a lamp dangling from the ceiling. A shout from the steward brought a collared slave girl running with a tray of food and drink. Marcus had to hold back a semi-hysterical laugh. If they thought he could possibly eat now without being sick . . .

They left him and the untouched meal alone in his cell, locking the door from the outside. Marcus sank onto the only piece of furniture, a bed, and closed his hands into the thin mattress until his fingers ached. The blur of the alcohol Farley had plied him with was beginning to wear off, leaving him colder with every passing moment. Light from the oil lamp gleamed against the sweat on his arms. He felt like screaming, cursing, battering down the door with the bed. . . . Instead, with as much calm as he could dredge up from the depths of his soul, Marcus forced himself to eat and drink what he'd been given.

He would need to keep up his strength.

Marcus was aware that it would be ridiculously easy, in a few weeks' time, to simply slip away and run for the Time Tours wine shop on the Via Appia. Everything in him screamed to do just that. Everything except his honor.

And that honor—the only bit of his parents, his family, his whole village and the proud tribe of the Taurusates, kinsmen to the great Aquitani themselves, left to him—demanded he repay the debt of coin his new "master" had paid for him. Somehow, someday, he would find his way back through the Porta Romae and hold Ianira in his arms again. It would take years of work to repay his purchase price and he had no guarantee that beautiful Ianira would wait. Perhaps he could send a message, somehow, with a Time Tours employee? How, he didn't have the faintest idea. But he would. And he *would* get back to her, somehow. Or die trying.

Kit Carson was on his way to a business luncheon he'd rather have avoided—he *hated* the monthly business meeting of TT-86 hoteliers—which was scheduled to take place at the Neo Edo's expensive *and* excellent restaurant this month. 'Eighty-sixers and tourists alike appreciated Kit's kitchen. But these stupid monthly meetings, where everyone talked, no one *did* anything, and Kit invariably sat through, silently fuming . . . he'd accomplish *nothing* except the loss in revenue to the Neo Edo from a group of men and women more interested in the delicacies of his kitchen than they were in Guild business.

Thank God the meetings rotated from one hotel to another, so Kit didn't suffer too often. He was nearly to the doorway of the *Kaiko no Kemushi*, the Silkworm Caterpillar—any form of bug, particularly *caterpillars*, elicited greater disgust from Japanese than even cockroaches did for Americans, so most of his Japanese customers found the restaurant's name hysterically funny. Then *it* happened. The miracle he'd been hoping would rescue him from this interminable luncheon.

His skull began to buzz in the old, familiar way, but he was constitutionally certain that no gate was due to open today. He grinned suddenly, transforming in a blink from serious businessman to imp of mischief ready for some fun.

"Unstable gate!" he crowed, racing into the Commons, even as warning klaxons blared. What would it be this time? Another peek into the late Mesozoic? No, the buzzing of his skull bones wasn't intense enough for a gate that big. The eerie, nonsound told him that this would be a smallish gate, open for who knew how long? Would it cycle several times, then vanish, or set up a steady, long-term pattern? *Where?* Kit wondered, having seen everything from giant pterodactyls to murderous Welsh bowmen stumble through unstable gates.

Kit arrived a few instants earlier than Pest Control, with their innocuous grey uniforms and staunch faces, discontinuity detectors sweeping the whole area. They also carried rifles, shotguns, and capture nets to be ready for *whatever* roared through. Mike Benson and several of his security men raced up next, followed by a puffing Bull Morgan. Mike looked terrible—eyes bloodshot, bags under them so dark a purple they looked nearly black, jawline unshaven. Bull looked sharply at his Chief of Security as well, then snapped out, "Any ideas?"

Pest Control's chief, Sue Fritchey, always had a quiet, almost demure air about her—and it often fooled people. Sue was twice as strong and at least four times as smart as she generally looked. Kit chuckled silently. There she stood, looking exactly like a carbon copy of all the other Pest Control agents. You'd never guess to look at her that she held doctorates in biological/ecological sciences, nematological/entomological sciences, had large- and small-animal veterinary and zoo degrees, and a paleontological science Ph.D to boot: in both flora *and* fauna. With a master's in virology thrown in for good measure.

Sue Fritchey was *very* good at her job.

A shimmering in the air opened ten feet above Time Tours' Porta Romae gate platform—and about four feet to one side of it. The air shimmered through a whole doppler range of colors and indescribable motion, then the dark, ever-shifting edges of an unstable gate slid open. Little yellow-brown things fell through it, all the way to the concrete floor below, where they smacked with a bone-cracking sound. A flood followed them, a tidal wave. Kit widened his eyes when he realized what it was. He laughed aloud. "Lemmings!"

Pest Control tried desperately to stem the flow *at* the gate, using nets to capture and toss back as many as possible while leaning dangerously far over the rail of Porta Romae's gate platform. For every batch of five or six they caught and hurled back, twelve or fifteen more got through, falling messily to their deaths on the now enormous pile of silent, brown-furred bodies. Tourists, aghast at the slaughter, were demanding that Pest Control *do* something, it was cruel, inhuman—

Kit interrupted a group of five women dressed in the latest Paris haute couture, all of them badgering Sue while she tried to direct one group at the gate, tried to get another squad into position from a different angle, and put a third squad to work shovelling the bodies into large bags.

" 'Scuse me, ladies," he smiled engagingly, "I couldn't help overhearing you."

They turned as one, then lost breath and color in the same moment as they recognized him. Kit hid a grin. Sometimes world-famous reputations weren't such a curse, after all.

"Mr.—Mr. Carson?"

He bowed. "As I said, I couldn't help but overhear your conversation." He drew them adroitly away from Sue Fritchey a few steps at a time and was rewarded with Sue's preoccupied smile. "Are you ladies by any chance acquainted with the behavior patterns of the ordinary lemming?"

They shook their heads in time, well-practiced marionettes.

"Ah . . . let me help you understand. Lemmings are rodents. Some live on the Arctic tundra, where predators generally keep their populations in check. But they also live in cold, alpine climates like you'd find in, say, the northern tip of Norway. Without sufficient predators our sweet little rodents breed out of control, until they've destroyed their environment, not to mention their food supply." Five sets of eyes went round. "When that happens—and it does to many a herd of lemmings, I assure you—then something in their genes or maybe in their brain structure kicks in and causes them to leave their environment, sometimes by the thousands. You see, that unknown signal is a warning that their population has become too large for the land to sustain it. It's as unstable as that gate up there."

He pointed, and waited for five sets of shocked eyes to return to him. "So they leave. Now, the herds that live in very rocky country, with lots of cliffs, have the perfect suicide mechanism built right into their habitat. Some of those cliffs drop into deep, jagged valleys. Some shadow a deep, narrow bay. One full of water," he added, not sure that their collective IQ's were above those of a *live* lemming. "And you know what those cute little buggers do? They run straight for those cliffs, almost as though they knew, *wanted*, to throw themselves and their pups over the edge. Those," he pointed to the avalanche of small rodents still falling through the gate, "have jumped off a cliff somewhere. They'd be dead already, even if the gate hadn't opened ten feet over the station floor. You can't change history—or the deep genetics of certain species. Fool about with their genetic structure, get rid of the signal—if you could—that triggers the suicidal migrations, and pretty soon you'd be hip deep in starving lemmings. And there wouldn't be anything green left for thousands of square miles."

Round eyes stared at him from pale, pinched faces. He tipped an imaginary hat and left, humming a delighted tune under his breath. He gave out a short, humorless bark of laughter, wondering what those five would say when they went back uptime?

He then joined the crew sweeping bodies into containers supplied by shopkeepers and other willing 'eighty-sixers. Kit found himself scooping warm, still little bodies into an ornate brass wastebasket that could only have come from the *Epicurean Delight*. Kit grinned, then got to business filling it. He sighed. It *was* a shame; lemmings were so darned . . . cute. But their biology and behaviors were as they were, which meant that on this particular day and time in La-La Land, Kit Carson was shovelling up hundreds of dead rodents, same as everybody else on volunteer duty. Really, anything was better than attending pointless meetings!

Of all people, Goldie Morran appeared in the crowd, sniffing disdainfully but eyeing all those lemmings with speculation. What in God's name was she up to *now*? Hadn't she been in the infirmary recently? Didn't take *her* long to recover. *I sometimes think Goldie's too mean to die.* She turned on a stilt heel and sought out Sue Fritchey, who listened intently for a moment, then nodded impatiently and shook Goldie's hand. The look on Goldie's face as she tried to figure out where to wipe her hand, covered now with blood and lemming hair, was priceless. Then, when she leaned over an intent newsie's vidcammer and cleaned her hand thoroughly while asking him sweet-voiced questions to distract him from the motions she was making against his back, it was almost too much to bear.

In fact, when one film crew caught it on camera, Kit did laugh—but softly enough Goldie couldn't possibly hear him.

Whatever she'd wanted, she'd clearly gotten, as she left with a contented smile on her face. Kit worked his way toward Sue.

"What'd Goldie want?"

"Hmm? Oh, hi, Kit. She wanted the skins. Said she'd pay a downtimer to skin 'em and tan the skins for her, then maybe the big *sternbergi* might take a fancy to lemming meat. God, I hope so. Have you got any idea what it's going to *smell* like, all through the station, if we have to incinerate these little beasts?"

Kit shuddered. "Yeah. I got a real good idea."

She glanced sharply at him. "Oh, damn, I'm sorry, Kit. I was distracted . . . forgot all about that witch's burning you were forced to watch. . . ."

He forced a shrug. "Thanks. I appreciate the apology, but that's one of 'em I sometimes still wake up screaming over. And it's the *smell* that lingers with you, like a spirit as malicious as the goddamned Inquisitors who ordered the burnings in the first place." He cleared his throat and pointed his gaze into the far distance. "Sue, one of those so-called witches was a little girl, curly red-blond hair, couldn't have been above two years old, screaming for her mommy—who was burning on the stake right next to her."

Sue had squeezed shut her eyes. "I will never, ever again complain about my job, Kit Carson."

Kit thumped her on the shoulder. "Go ahead and complain away. Makes me feel good to hear other people's problems. Not my own."

Sue swallowed hard, then managed a shaky smile. "Okay, Kit, one helluva big job complaint, comin' at you. *Why the hell are you just standing there in that bloody three-piece suit? Pick up a goddamned shovel and start shovelin'!*"

Kit laughed, hugged her, then swung his own shovel like a baton, whistling as he returned to work.

At last Pest Control hummers with attached sidecars for hauling whatever needed hauling, pulled up. The cleanup crew dumped their loads into the hoppers. Kit did the same, then turned back for more.

Fortunately, the unstable gate closed before the entire herd of several thousand fell into TT-86, but a final lemming, halfway through as the gate closed shut, was sucked back with an almost startled look in its button-black eyes, the inexorable shutting of the gate sending the animal back into its own time—and a probable fall with its fellows off whatever cliff they'd found. Judging from the size of the piled little bodies, at least a quarter of that herd had ended up on the floor. It took hours of back-breaking work to get them all into hoppers, never mind cleaning bloodstains from the floor. The newsies from uptime covered the whole event, not only for the on-station television network but for the hope of a potential scoop by getting the video through Primary first.

They tried, without success, to interview him where he knelt hip deep at one edge of the miniature mountain, blood all over his expensive three-piece suit and previously immaculate white silk shirt. Despite his absolute, categorical refusals—"I'm busy, can't you see? Talk to someone else."—they hovered around him like hornets, vidcams whirring with the sound of hornets' wings.

Ignoring the newsies as best he could, he continued shoveling bodies into the Pest Control hoppers. While most of the lemmings had landed on concrete, several hundred had splattered against expensive, exquisite mosaics funded by the Urbs Romae merchants and built by a downtimer artisan who had designed and placed mosaics in his native time. Now the beautiful, tiled pictures of grapevines, gods and goddesses, even the portraits of Imperial family members done with astonishing accuracy from memory, had not only to be cleaned, but cleaned with painstaking care to get the blood out of the grout between colored tiles no larger than Kit's pinkie fingernail.

A voice he'd know anywhere growled, "Goddamn mess."

He glanced up into Bull Morgan's face. "Yes, it is."

"Those tiles under there cracked?"

Kit used his hated necktie to scrub away enough blood and intestines to see. " 'Fraid so. Some cracked, some shattered to bits. Damn."

Bull echoed him. Then he shouted, "Sue!"

Sue Fritchey slewed around, then began walking toward him. When she arrived, covered in even more blood than Kit, Bull said, "Show her, Kit."

He pointed out the damage done to the mosaic. Sue groaned. Already news was spreading to the Urbs Romae shopkeepers, hoteliers, and restaurateurs, mostly thanks to newsies who rushed at them to "get their reactions on record." Bull narrowed his eyes. "Sue, when the worst of this mess is gone, get your people to digitally map each damaged mosaic. Station Manager's office will foot the bill for any repairs. Spread the news to 'em and fast, before they start mobbing your people." Sue hurried off to spread the word and instruct her crews to spread it farther—the faster, the better.

Bull grinned abruptly, looking very much like a fire-plug riveted to living human arms, legs, and head. Kit, his shoulders aching almost worse than his knees, took in Bull's grin and muttered, "Want to share the joke? I could use a laugh. Goddamned newsies crawling across me like flies . . ." He shivered. Bull's laugh only deepened as he thumped the taller, slighter man's back. "Never heard of Kit Carson giving in to a newsie."

"And you won't, either," Kit muttered, "unless they doctor the tapes, in which case I can sue. And lose my fortune, my reputation, and my case, all in one fell swoop."

"Yeah," Bull said through narrowed eyes as he watched them pestering anyone they could for a story. "Can't win a case against a newsie, that's for goddamned sure. Gotta think up a reason to toss 'em all up Primary and keep any more from coming in."

Kit's full, blazing grin was seen so rarely, even the

stolid Bull Morgan blinked. "And what, exactly, are you thinking, Kenneth Carson?"

"Oh, nothing too mischievous. I was just thinking you might want to plant a little bug in someone's ear, you know, just a hint about courageous newsies coming to the rescue in a Station Crisis. Get their flunkies to film 'em scooping up busted-open lemmings. Ought to be good for, what, fifteen points on the Nielsons just for the gore content alone?"

Bull Morgan slowly pulled a cigar from one pocket and lit it, sucking until it created clouds of obnoxious blue-grey smoke. His eyes crinkled. "Yeah," he said around the cigar, starting to smile. "Yeah, that's a good, solid idea you got there, Kit. Keep 'em out of our crews' hair, away from the shopowners, 'til they've had their fill and leave to shower someplace where the water's endless and hot enough to wash away the blood, the stink, and their own puke."

Kit chuckled. "You, Bull Morgan, are a wicked judge of human character."

"Hell, Kit, thought you'd figured it out by now: *all* human character is wicked. Just varies in degree is all."

Leaving Kit to ponder that odd, un-Bull-like bit of philosophy, Bull Morgan waded through the slop and bent to murmur into the ear of the nearest newsie. She looked startled, then delighted. Soon, every newsie in the place was down on hands and knees, scooping up dead rodents alongside the Pest Control crews and 'eighty-sixers who'd seen, done, and been through *everything*. Or at least enough to know that a mountain of dead lemmings wasn't exactly a dire crisis, just a massive pain in the butt.

True to Bull's prediction—Kit was glad he hadn't wagered—the newsies didn't last long. They retreated to their hotel rooms with their vidcams and flunkies and were not seen again until much later that evening, when La-La Land's very own in-house TV network ran various tapes and commentaries. Kit didn't bother to watch the broadcast. If it contained anything truly terrible, friends of his would let him know—and probably hand him a recorded copy or six.

Once the dead lemmings had all been carted away, and the blood scrubbed away with toothbrushes and ammonia, Pest Control filmed every cracked or shattered tile in every single mosaic affected. Bull's generous offer settled several upset merchants. Sly cuss, their station manager. He had to be, or he'd watch La-La Land's artificial world crumble apart like dry cake left outside too long in brittle, harsh sunlight, slowly turning to dust.

Yeah, Bull Morgan was just the right man for the job, a man who found the law useful in how far it could occasionally be bent to save a friend. He chuckled aloud, drawing startled stares from the Pest Control crews still filming damaged mosaics. He didn't care. This would make a great story, full of places for artistic embellishment—and Kit Carson knew he could spin a *very* good yarn. He laughed again, anticipating the reactions of his granddaughter and his closest friend, soon-to-be his grandson-in-law.

He grinned like a fool and didn't care about *that*, either. For the first time in years, Kit Carson realized he was genuinely happy. The last of the hummer-trains groaned into motion, then Kit glanced down at himself. His three-piece suit—from the same designer who'd fashioned clothes for that idiotic quintet of rich, empty-headed women—was soaked in blood and thick with yellow-brown fur. And the *smell* was even worse. No wonder Bull had smiled. He sighed. *Maybe* the suit and silk shirt could be salvaged.

Kit returned to the Neo Edo, managed to sneak

past the still-in-progress hoteliers' meeting, and took the elevator to his office. He didn't feel like going home and he *did* feel like putting on the kimono left in the office for the sole purpose of comfort during work. There was a shower, too, hidden away behind a screen that had once been the pride of some ancient Edo nobleman's house.

He stripped, showered, towelled off, then found the kimono. *Ahh . . . much better.* He left the suit on the shower floor, unwilling to touch it; this kimono had cost him a small fortune. More, actually, than the suit. He telephoned the front desk for a runner and soon heard the breathless knock of one of his employees.

"C'mon in, it's not locked!"

"Sir?" the wide-eyed runner gasped, trying to appear that he was *not* staring, awestruck, at Kit's office.

Kit chuckled and said, "Come on in. Stare all you like. It *is* a bit different for an office."

The boy, a downtimer Kit had rescued and employed, stepped into the office.

The boy's gaze drank in Kit's eclectic office, with its wall of television screens, some of which played tapes of views uptime and some of which showed views of various parts of the Neo Edo and the Commons. The sand-and-stone garden, with its artificial skylight, drew his attention so powerfully, he actually bumped right into Kit, who had paused at the edge of the screen hiding his bathroom.

The boy reddened clear down into the neckline of his green-and-gold Neo Edo tunic. "Oh, sir, please forgive me—"

Before the apology could turn into an avalanche thick as those lemmings, Kit smiled and said, "It *is* rather impressive, isn't it? I remember the first time I saw it, after Homako Tani vanished and left this white elephant on my hands. I think I dropped my teeth clear onto the floor."

A hesitant smile passed over the boy's face, revealing as clearly as though his face were made of mountain-stream water, rather than flesh and blood, how unsure he was that he might be taking liberties.

"Through here," Kit smiled. "I, er, rather made a mess of that suit scooping up dead lemmings."

The boy brightened. "I heard about that, sir. Were there really millions and millions of 'em?"

Kit laughed. "No, but sometimes it *seemed* like it. There were probably at least two or three thousand, though."

The boy had gone round-eyed with wonder. "That many? That's a big number, isn't it, sir?"

Kit reminded himself to be sure this youngster was included in orientation and education sessions he held at the Neo Edo for downtimer employees and their families. Many had profited enough from the lessons to leave the Neo Edo and drudgery work behind forever, finding or even making better jobs for themselves. Kit prided himself that none of *his* downtimer employees— current or former—had walked through a gate and shadowed him- or herself, vanishing forever the moment they crossed to the other side.

The boy took the ruined suit and promised he'd take it to the best drycleaner in the station—there were only two—then bowed and ran for the elevator.

Kit chuckled, then sighed and decided he might as well tackle the four stacks of triple-damned government paperwork *every* shop owner on TT-86 was required to file weekly. Sometimes, he pondered as he sat down and began on the first tedious document, Kit wondered if Bull Morgan was seen so rarely because he had locked himself into his office to cope with *his* mountains of paperwork.

CHAPTER SIXTEEN

The pain in Skeeter's head registered first. The next sensation to impinge on his awareness was his nakedness. Except for a cloth at his loins, he'd been stripped clean as a Mongolian sky. He blinked and stirred. That's when he discovered the chains. Skeeter moaned softly, head throbbing savagely, then blinked and focused once again on his wrists. Iron manacles and a short length of chain bound them together. A circlet of iron around his throat caught his adam's apple when he swallowed nausea and fear. Further exploration revealed chains and manacles around his ankles, hobbling him and locking him to an iron ring in a stone wall.

He was alone in a dim, tiny stone cell, iron bars forming a sort of door-cum-fourth wall. Beyond, he could hear distant voices: shouts, cries of pain, screams of terror, pleas for mercy. He managed to sit up. The unmistakable snarl of caged cats—big cats—somewhere nearby brought a shiver to his naked back. He'd seen snow leopards and Mongolian tigers during Yesukai's famous hunt drives. He didn't care to go one-on-one with *anything* feline that even remotely approached *that* size. The claws and teeth would be far too sharp and his death would be far too slow . . .

Despite the iron ring around his throat, Skeeter gagged and voided the contents of his belly onto the cold stone floor.

Footsteps approached his cell with a clatter of hobnailed boots. Skeeter looked up, still feeling sick and dull of mind, and gradually focused on two men grinning in at him. One of them he'd never seen in his life. The other was Lupus Mortiferus. The fear and nausea in his belly turned to sour ice.

"Hello, odds maker," Lupus smiled. "Feeling comfortable?"

Skeeter didn't bother to answer.

"This," Lupus gestured to the other man, a thick-set individual with arms big around as Skeeter's thighs, "is your *lanista*." *My trainer?* "Thieves are condemned men, you know, but you will have a chance." Lupus' eyes twinkled as though this were hilariously funny. "If you survive, you will remain the property of the Emperor and fight for his glory." At least, that's what Skeeter thought he'd said. His Latin wasn't very good. "You and I," Lupus laughed, "will meet again, thief."

That's what I'm afraid of, he groaned silently.

Lupus strode off, a wicked chuckle echoing off stone walls.

The other man smiled coldly and unlocked the door.

Skeeter wanted to fight, to break free and run—

But not only was he chained and hobbled, the *lanista* who unlocked his chains from the wall dragged him around as though he were a mere babe to be dandled in one hand. Skeeter held back a groan of pain and allowed the man to drag him through a confusing maze of corridors. Then, past a set of heavy, iron-bound doors, bright sunlight blinded him. He blinked, overwhelmed by harsh light, the odd clack of what sounded like two-by-fours smashing together, and the screams of wounded men. He balked instinctively and received a terrible buffet to the side of his aching head.

Reeling, Skeeter found himself dragged forward into the middle of a practice session on a sandy floor.

High iron fences and armed soldiers surrounded the area. Gladiators in armor, wielding wooden swords, practiced what looked like set-piece moves, as carefully choreographed as a ballet, while "trainers" called out moves to them. Other men were engaged in calisthenics, jumping low hurdles, wrestling, practicing hand springs and tucked rolls, hacking at straw men or thick wooden posts. Still others sighted along javelins and hurled their weapons at—

Skeeter stumbled as a mortal scream tore the air.

A slave tied to a post at the far edge of the practice ground sagged, a javelin embedded in his bowels. A nearby soldier grunted, stalked over, and yanked the weapon out again, then slit the suffering man's throat with a neat slice from a dagger. Skeeter had seen such casual cruelty before, many times, in Yesukai's camp—but that had been a long time ago. He'd grown more civilized than he'd thought during the intervening years.

Skeeter's *lanista* dragged him past and thrust him into the group doing calisthenics. He was unchained and forcibly prodded into movement with the tip of a long spear. Sweating, head spinning uselessly, Skeeter did what he was forced to do, vaulting low hurdles awkwardly and going through the motions of the calisthenics. Then he was handed a dull-edged wooden sword and a shield and found himself facing his trainer. He swallowed again, dizzy and terrified.

"Shield up!" the man shouted—and lunged with a short wooden sword.

Skeeter's reaction time, dulled by pain and shock, was slow. The wooden sword caught him in the gut, doubling him over with a retching pain. His trainer waited until he'd caught his breath, then dragged him up again and shouted, "Shield up!"

This time, Skeeter managed to drag his arm up to

catch the blow across the wooden shield. The smack and force of the blow drove him to his knees.

"Thrust!"

Over the next two miserable, wretched weeks, his trainer beat the drills into him, until he could at least follow the instructions. He learned the various methods of fighting, tried to use the various types of weapons different classes of gladiators used. His *lanista* spent a great deal of time grumbling, while Lupus Mortiferus stalked the training arena like a god and laughed at him, besting every opponent sent against him with lazy ease.

Disheartened, bruised, Skeeter slept in chains, too exhausted to move once allowed to collapse on his hard bed. He ate the gruel he was given as fast as he could shovel it in. It tasted faintly of beer; barley gone a little too far toward fermentation, perhaps? Occasionally Lupus Mortiferus would visit his cell, grinning and taunting him from beyond the iron bars of his cage. Skeeter returned his gaze steadily and coldly, while his insides quaked with deeper terror than he had ever known, deeper even than his terror at falling through the unstable gate into Yesukai the Valiant's life.

Each night as he drifted into bruised sleep, Skeeter dredged up from memory everything Yesukai had ever taught him, every trick and dirty move he'd ever learned on the plains of Mongolia. Then it occured to him that perhaps he was reviewing the wrong memories. And he thought of his time on the broken, filthy streets of depraved New York, where a boy, even a grown man, could find himself fatally trapped before he knew anything had gone wrong. Certain areas of New York were said to be as deadly as the ancient Roman gladiatorial combats. Looked like he was about to find out.

At the moment, Skeeter would take the concrete-and-glass canyons of New York, even the washed-out ruins of New Orleans, over *this*. He just prayed he had time to come up with some sort of escape plan before Lupus Mortiferus killed him in the arena. Given the diligence of the guards, he didn't hold out much hope.

"QUIET!"

Brian Hendrickson had sufficient command presence to be heard—and obeyed—when he wanted. The babble in the library sliced off like a dagger cut. He glared at Goldie Morran, whose nostrils flared unpleasantly as she breathed hard. Ianira Cassondra, clutching her pretty little children close, glared at Goldie, hatred and possibly even murder in her dark, ancient eyes. This had to be defused, and fast.

"Goldie," he said, speaking as gently as possible, considering her recent release from the infirmary—and the reasons for it, "I know as well as you do the terms of the bet. The most cash at the end of a month. But this evidence about Skeeter's disappearance complicates matters. Considerably."

He glanced at Ianira. "You will swear by all you hold sacred," he asked her gently—in archaic Greek—"that Skeeter Jackson was trying to rescue Marcus when he crashed the Porta Romae?"

"I swear it," she hissed out, with another murderous glance at Goldie.

"Do you have any way to prove that?"

"Dr. Mundy! I spoke with him on the telephone! He arranged for Skeeter to pick up money to pay that man Farley. He will speak the truth for me! And my 'acolytes' were following me. Someone must have taped it!"

"All right." He glanced across the growing crowd,

many of them the loons who followed Ianira wherever she went. "Any of you catch on vid Skeeter Jackson crashing the Porta Romae?"

One timid, mousy little man near the back cleared his throat five times, casting awestruck, terrified glances at Ianira, then managed, "I—I did—"

Brian nodded. "Cue it up, would you, while I place a call?"

The loon began fiddling with his camera as Brian picked up the telephone behind the library counter, placidly ignoring the crowd which grew by fives and tens as word of the argument over the wager's terms spread through La-La Land. The telephone was answered testily by Nally Mundy.

"I'm in the middle of a session, here, so if you'd please call back—"

"Dr. Mundy, Brian Hendrickson here."

"Oh. Yes, Brian? What is it?"

"Ianira Cassondra tells me you offered Skeeter Jackson money to help Marcus the bartender pay off a debt."

A long silence at the other end of the line caused Brian to sigh. Skeeter had ripped off the old man, after all, and vanished downtime—

"Yes, I did. But he never picked up the money. Odd, you know. Heard about that ruckus at the gate. I'd say Ianira's telling the truth. If Skeeter'd had time, he'd have picked up that money and something tells me young Marcus would still be with us. Don't trust that dratted Jackson much, blast him, but he didn't take the money. If I could just get one decent session taped with that boy, the mysteries about Temujin that we could solve—"

"Yes, I know," Brian hastened to interrupt. "You've been very helpful, Dr. Mundy. I know you're busy, so I'll let you get back to your session."

The historian hurrumphed into the phone, which then clicked dead. Brian cradled the receiver. "Well. Have you cued up that camera?"

The little man pushed his way through the crowd and handed over the camera, then knelt and kissed the hem of Ianira's gown. "May my humble camera bring you comfort and victory, Lady."

Brian watched the whole thing unfold, from Lupus Mortiferus kicking down Skeeter's door to Skeeter's desperate lunge up onto the ramp, the hoarse cry he'd uttered for Marcus to wait, the man with Marcus bodily snatching him through—and, finally, Skeeter vanishing through the gate after them. He clicked off the camera thoughtfully, wondering what in the world had possessed Skeeter to such altruistic rashness. Then he roused himself slightly and handed the camera to Ianira, who returned it to the man at her feet. He uttered a tiny cry and pressed lips to her hand, then snatched the camera and scuttled more than a yard away before rising to his feet again, face alight as though he really had touched the hand of Deity.

Odd bunch of folks, Ianira's followers.

Brian cleared his throat. "It seems Ianira is telling the truth. Nally Mundy *and* that videotape prove it, beyond any question in *my* mind." When he glanced up, he wasn't surprised to find a crowd of nearly a hundred 'eighty-sixers pressed as close to the reference desk as they could get, with more peering in through the door.

"Well. As I said, this unexpected gesture of altruism by Skeeter changes everything. I'm afraid, Goldie, I can't declare you winner by default on the grounds that Skeeter will be gone for at least two weeks downtime. Your wager stipulated a month, true, but that doesn't mean the month has to run straight through, uninterrupted. I declare this wager on hold until Skeeter returns. If he returns."

Ianira blanched and blinked back sudden tears. She clutched her children more closely to her breast. Alerted by their mother's sudden fear, communicated in that mysterious way between mothers and their offspring, the two little girls began to whimper.

Goldie sniffed. "*If* he returns, indeed. That maniac who's been chasing him has probably carved out his entrails by now. And it would serve him right!"

A tiny sound broke from Ianira's throat.

Brian caught Goldie's eye. "In the interim, you are hereby barred from scamming, scheming, or accumulating *any* stolen funds toward this bet. I wouldn't dream of interfering with legitimate business, particularly considering your recent loss, but in the interest of fairness, I would suggest placing an impartial witness with you at all times until Skeeter's return."

Goldie let out a sound like an enraged parrot and turned purple. "*A guard!* You'd set a guard on me? Damn you, Brian—"

"Oh, shut up, Goldie," he said tiredly. "You agreed to this idiotic wager and dragged me into refereeing it. Now live by my decisions or default in favor of Skeeter."

She opened and closed her mouth several times, although no sound emerged, then she compressed white lips. "Very well!"

"That's decided, then. Now. Goldie, I have it on good authority you've been selling lemming-fur cloaks down near the Viking Gate."

"And if I have?" Her chin came up several notches.

"Calling them blond mink, I think it was?"

"It seemed appropriate." Her eyes were dark and watchful as a vulture's.

"Yes. Well, that constitutes a scam. All proceeds you've earned up to now and haven't logged in yet, you will hand over in the next fifteen minutes. Oh, and bring along the cloaks. You can sell 'em to your heart's content—*after* this wager is officially over."

"Curse you," Goldie hissed. "And what am I supposed to *live* on?"

"You got into this, Goldie. You're going to have to get yourself out of it. That's it, then, folks. Now, if you all would kindly get the hell out of my library so I can get on with my work?"

Chuckles in the crowd drifted to him, then people began ambling out the door. Brian saw money exchanging hands as multiple, impromptu bets on the outcome of his decision were settled. Brian sighed. What a mess. Then, before the fellow could leave, Brian high-signed Kynan Rhys Gower, who hovered near the edge of the crowd.

"Kynan," he said gently in the man's native Welsh, "I know your integrity is beyond question and I am also aware," he allowed himself a small smile, "that Goldie Morran cannot possibly bribe you. Would you agree to stay with her during the next two weeks, watching to be sure she does not cheat, until the Porta Romae cycles again?"

Kynan's wind-tanned cheeks crinkled into a broad, twinkle-eyed grin. "It would be my honor, should my liege lord give his permission."

Somewhere in the dispersing crowd, Kit Carson's famous laugh rang out. "Not only my permission, Kynan, I'll make up all lost wages from your sweeping job."

Goldie just glowered.

Ianira smiled grimly. "Thank you, *kyrie* Hendrickson. We downtimers have few friends. It is good to know there are honest people here who will champion our cause." She gave Kynan Rhys Gower a swift smile of thanks, then vanished into the dispersing crowd.

Kynan grinned at Goldie, eyes alight with savage mirth.

She said something profoundly unladylike and stalked out of the library. Kynan followed at his ease, winking at Brian on the way out. Brian suppressed a grin of smug satisfaction. With Kynan on the job, Goldie'd stay honest for the next two weeks. She wouldn't have a choice. And if Brian were any judge of solidarity in the downtimer underground community, more than Kynan's pair of eyes would be watching that purple-haired harpy through the days to come.

He allowed himself a soft, wicked chuckle, then waved off the rest of the crowd and got back to work.

After seeing Hendrickson, Ianira went to the top.

Bull Morgan saw himself as a fair man. Tough— God alone knew he had to be, to do this job—but fair. So when Ianira Cassondra walked into his office with her two daughters, he knew he was in serious trouble. There was only one thing she could possibly want from him. He wasn't wrong.

"Mr. Morgan," Ianira said in her beautiful, oddly accented English, which was neither quite Greek nor quite Turkish, but something far more ancient, "I appeal to you for help. Please. The father of my daughters has been taken away. The man who took him has broken the law before, by bringing him here, and now he breaks it again by taking him away. Please, is there nothing you can do to help me find the father of my children?"

Tears trembled on thick, black lashes.

Bull Morgan swore silently and steeled himself. "Ianira, there is nothing I would like more than to find Marcus. Please believe that. But I can't." The tears spilled over, even as her mouth tightened into a thin line of anger. "Let me try to explain. First of all, Marcus went downtime with him willingly. Second, you and Marcus are downtimers. The uptime government can't make up its mind what to do about people like you, so it's a confused mess as to what I can and can't do. Besides, this Farley bastard was smooth. There really isn't anything I can pin on him."

"So you will do nothing to find Marcus!"

"I *can't*," he said quietly. "I have a very small security staff. We're not authorized to go downtime to rescue people who are *from* downtime."

"But you have told us we cannot go back, even if we wanted to, to live downtime in the places of our births! How can you permit Marcus to return permanently to Rome, when your own law says he cannot?"

Bull groaned inwardly. "That's station policy, yes. I'm doing my best to interpret the law. Downtimers can work as porters through the gates, so long as they return. But, Ianira, there just isn't any way I can *enforce* that." Even as he said it, he knew it would have terrible repercussions in the downtimer underground community he knew existed on his station. "If I could," he said as gently as possible, "the next time the gate cycles I'd send in a division of Marines to find him. But the reality is, I can't even send down one security man. Our budget is so tight, I can't afford to lose the man-hours of even one security guard for two entire weeks—with no guarantee he or she could even *find* Marcus."

More tears spilled over, silently. But her head remained high and her eyes flashed dangerous defiance. "So I am just supposed to sit and wait to see if I must put on widow's weeds and weep the death of my children's father aloud?"

Bull shook his head slowly. "The only thing I can do is talk to some of the guides, some of the scouts. They like Marcus. If I can persuade some of them to go downtime to Rome, I can get the necessary paperwork approved quickly. It's the best I can do—and I can't promise that another man will do as I ask."

To Bull's surprise, Ianira nodded slowly. "No one can ever speak for the behavior of another. Only for one's self can you speak, and even then, do we not lie to ourselves far more often than we lie to others?"

"You'd make a damn fine psychological therapist, Ianira. You should talk to Rachel Eisenstein about training with her."

Ianira's laugh was brittle as shale. "I am a Priestess of Artemis, trained at the great Temple of Ephesus where my mother's sister was High Priestess. I do *not* need more *training*!"

Without another word, Ianira Cassondra gathered up her beautiful little girls, both of whom looked scared, and swept out of his office like a primal force, siphoning away every erg of his willpower to continue going through the motions of his job.

It was a long, long time before Bull Morgan answered his phone or moved a single sheet of paper on his desk from the "to do" to the "done" stack.

If he'd been able, he'd have gone downtime himself. But he'd told her nothing except the naked, brutal truth. Manager of the time terminal he might be, but there was absolutely nothing he could do to help her, except call a few guides and scouts who were currently in and ask them for a favor they wouldn't be too wild about granting.

Bull sighed mightily, dislodging several sheets of paper from the "to do" stack, which landed on the floor beside his massive desk. He ignored them completely and reached for the telephone. If he were going to make those calls, he'd better start making them, before Ianira did something stupidly desperate.

As the phone rang on the other end of the line, Ianira Cassondra's ancient, bottomless eyes haunted him like a whiff of perfume diffused through his entire awareness, inescapable and unutterably damning.

"Yeah?" a surly voice on the other end of the line said.

Bull sighed again, dislodging more papers, and said, "Bull Morgan here. I've got a favor to ask . . ."

Malcolm nudged his fiancee. "Margo, that young woman over there. By the exit ramp?"

They were waiting, along with half Shangri-La station for the cycling of the Porta Romae. After Skeeter and Marcus had both disappeared downtime, Malcolm had canceled their reservations for the Wild West Gate, to wait and see if a rescue would need to be mounted.

"Yes," Margo stood on tiptoe to see over taller heads. "Isn't that the woman you introduced me to at the Delight? The Enchantress?"

"Yes. Ianira Cassondra. She'll be waiting to see."

He didn't have to tell Margo *what*—or rather *who*—Ianira was waiting to see. News of Marcus' disappearance downtime with a con man so slick he'd fooled even Goldie Morran was still the talk of the station—particularly since Skeeter Jackson had crashed the gate going after the young bartender.

"I think perhaps," Malcolm murmured, "we ought to get a little closer. Just in case."

Margo glanced up, swallowed once, then just nodded. She'd grown up a very great deal in the past few months. Her hand closed tightly around his, tacit admission that she understood just how close she'd come to losing him forever.

Several downtimers were standing close to Ianira

but gave way with surprise when Malcolm edged through, his hand still tightly gripping Margo's.

"Hello, Ianira," he said quietly.

She flashed a stricken look into his eyes. "Hello, Malcolm. And Margo. It is good of you to wait with me."

He tried to smile reassuringly. "What else are friends for?"

Just then the klaxon sounded, drowning out further conversation as the Gate departure was announced from blaring loudspeakers the length of Commons. The message repeated in three other languages. The line of tourists stirred expectantly, while porters gathered up baggage, fathers snagged unruly sons they'd paid a ransom in extra fare to take downtime, and mothers gripped daughters' hands tightly, admonishing them to be quiet and behave. Elegantly gowned women whose appearance and carriage would have screamed *money* in any society sipped at the last of their wine and tossed paper cups into trash cans in the fenced-off waiting area.

Always the same, Malcolm mused, *the rich ones who've been before, the families who've scraped and saved for the family vacation of a lifetime, the millionaires out for a sightseeing jaunt, the zipper jockeys ready to go brothel hopping.* Always the same, yet always different, with new wrinkles and near-disasters each time.

Then the gate dilated slowly, causing a painful sensation in the bones of his skull as the sound that was not a sound resonated harshly at subsonic level through the station. Gate Six rumbled open, then disgorged the inevitable staggering, pallid tourists, exhausted guides, chattering women comparing their shopping sprees in the bazaars and markets of Rome, and the teenaged kids who'd drunk too much and were that peculiar shade unique to a boy about to puke.

But there was no Marcus. And no Skeeter. Ianira scanned the departing tourists frantically, but they simply weren't there. She did hiss at one point. "Him!" she said viciously. "That's him!"

"You're sure?" Malcolm asked quietly.

The man Ianira pointed toward looked nothing like the man who'd gone downtime as Chuck Farley. Lightly bearded, beard and hair a different color from Farley's, even his eyes were a different shade. Contact lenses, no doubt. Malcolm wondered just how many pairs he owned, as well as how many bottles of hair dye and glue-on beards to match?

"I swear it by Artemis! That is the man who took Marcus to Rome with him. Now I know why his face has always remained hidden to me: he changes his face every few weeks!"

That was good enough for Malcolm. Several of the downtimers near Ianira began to mutter, most of the mutters having to do with violent, slow deaths in the bowels of the terminal.

"No," he said aloud, cutting across bloodthirsty plans. "Let me take care of him. I understand how creatures like *him* think."

"Yeah, leave it to *us*," Margo said darkly, watching the man who'd once been Charles Farley slide a time card through the reader and step off the ramp. She wondered just how many timecards, under how many names, the snake owned. "We'll take care of him, all right." Her eyes flashed that Irish-alleycat glare that did such deadly things to Malcolm's insides.

Malcolm drew a quick, steadying breath. "Everyone spread out, discreetly mind, and follow him. When we've established where he's staying, we'll watch him, day and night. Ianira, you can identify him better than the rest of us, even through the disguises. How long can you hold up, watching?"

Her eyes met his. "As long as it takes."

He didn't pretend to know the ways of her ancient training. She *might* be able to stay awake for days, for all he knew. The fakirs of the Far East could do some amazing things. And if Farley's next destination were somewhere beyond the Philosophers' Gate? Malcolm was a good guide through Athens, but Ianira had spent the bulk of her young life in the fabled city of Ephesus, across the Aegean Sea on the once-beautiful coast that the Balkan Wars had pounded into rubble over the decades. He wasn't even sure if the archeological ruins still existed.

Ephesus . . .

Malcolm really would have to get away on a little vacation of his own, to satisfy his scholarly itch. Purchase a ticket to Athens, arrange downtime transportation on a sailing vessel, and then . . . Ephesus, in all her ancient tragedy and glory. See the city of Artemis, whose magnificent temple, finally pulled down by Christian zealots. Its magnificent porphyry pillars had been transported away to be built into the Haghia Sophia.

He shook himself slightly, to find a faintly puzzled line between Ianira's dark brows. "You point him out and we'll take our vengeance, never you fear that, Ianira. I am *not* fond of people who sell my friends into slavery."

She nodded and strode away purposefully in the wake of Charles Farley.

Malcolm found Margo looking up at him with a glow in her eyes akin to hero-worship. He quite suddenly felt eleven feet tall and more than capable of taking on the dragon, St. George, *and* his horse. "Let's go," he said a bit gruffly.

Margo, clearly as moved by what they'd just witnessed as Malcolm, simply nodded.

As it turned out, following Farley was easier than either of them had expected. He took a modest room in the Time Tripper, then went downstairs to breakfast in the hotel restaurant. This new version of Farley was far quieter than the last. Once he returned to his room, he didn't leave it again, ordering tickets (Margo batted eyelashes and smiled at the Time Tours clerks until she got his new alias and destination) over the phone, eating only through room service—delivered by a downtimer—doing only God knew what up there by himself until the Wild West Gate departure was announced.

Malcolm and Margo repurchased tickets through Malcolm's computer, then scrambled into their "Wild West" duds well in advance of departure. Although the tour was full, Bull Morgan had pulled some strings at Time Tours to let Malcolm and Margo be added to the group. A few hours later, dandied up for what was to have been a celebratory vacation for their engagement, Margo and Malcolm found themselves appointed as the posse, stepping through the Wild West portal, along with the group of pre-dust-coated paleontologists carrying their assorted arsenal (they'd delayed departure to get in more practice with their firearms, one of them had explained diffidently to Margo) in correct period holsters . . . and Chuck Farley, still with blond hair and beard.

Once through the portal, the trick was not to be spotted following him. Denver of 1885 spread out in all its nouveau riche splendor against the backdrop of snow-capped Rockies. The better streets were bricked; many were dirt. Chuck hired a horse at the livery stable, hired a second as pack animal, and tied his baggage to it, trotting away with a clatter, not even bothering to glance back.

Cocksure bastard, Malcolm thought darkly as he paid for hacks for himself and Margo. Spreading out her riding skirt gracefully across the leathers, she gathered up the reins, gave a curt nod, and sent her mount down the street at a brisk trot, riding sidesaddle as though she'd been born in one. Malcolm followed, his heart soaring at the sight of her—and positively burning with fierce, primitive joy when he caught sight of Chuck Farley and his pack animal ahead.

He caught up with Margo. "Not too fast, dearest. We must *not* let the blighter catch on to us."

She nodded. "Quite right. Forgive me." She flashed him a brilliant smile. "In my zeal, I forgot myself."

He wanted to crush her against him and kiss those laughing lips—

But there was work waiting to be done.

What *sort* of work would depend entirely upon Mr. Farley's activities over the next few days.

CHAPTER SEVENTEEN

The day he returned to the great Circus was the most terrifying day of Skeeter Jackson's life. He came in a cage, like one of the big cats trapped so close to his iron box on the long barge. Their snarls of rage beat through him, making him wonder how long it had been since they'd been fed anything except prods from sharpened stakes and taunts from their keepers. Skeeter knew very much how they must feel.

Some of the gladiators on shore walked around freely, some of them still under armed guard, not yet dressed for combat or given the weapons with which they would slaughter one another. Those not under guard were free men who'd taken up the insane game of life or death and glory; those guarded were valuable slave-gladiators who'd earned grand reputations and were proud of their skills—not condemned criminals awaiting a mockery of a fair chance at survival.

The previous night, though he wasn't sure where they'd actually been, he and the other prisoner-gladiators had been paraded into some kind of public banquet hall and feted, given anything they cared to eat—or could hold down. More than a few men said goodbye to family members, clearly expecting never to see them again. Skeeter didn't have even that. All he had were Yesukai's lessons to get him through a last meal under the eyes of jeering, laughing, *betting* Romans.

Now, with the sun high in the sky, and the races at the Circus, which took place in the mornings, just about to end, it was time for the next part of the show. Skeeter's barge halted and the cages were hauled one by one onto shore near the back of the great Circus itself, where the starting gates of the races were. Inside, the crowd was cheering so loudly it startled the raging cats—leopards, lions, sleek cheetahs—into even greater frenzy. Caged antelopes bleated their terror and hurled themselves against narrowly spaced iron bars, unable to escape.

Some of the other prisoners near Skeeter's cage, also doomed to the arena, were crying for mercy to such men as passed, none of whom listened. Skeeter wanted to do a little crying of his own, but he didn't see the good it would do. Yesukai the Valiant had taught him endurance, tenacity. He called on those lessons now with everything in him and managed—just barely—to remain silent. But he could not stop the shakes quite so easily.

Far down the line, some slave with a stack of wax tablets was busy making his way past each cage, noting down contents or checking off his list, something like that. *Inventory clerk*, Skeeter thought with a sudden, near-uncontrollable desire to laugh insanely. Those infuriatingly thorough, meticulous Romans. Keeping their records right down to the last doomed prisoner and bleating antelope.

But when the slave got close enough to hear his voice asking questions of each caged gladiator, such as his name and fighting style, Skeeter gave a sudden start and grabbed the bars, straining to see. *He knew that voice!* He knew . . . but didn't quite believe it until he came face to face with Marcus through the bars of his filthy cage.

Marcus went deathly white in a single instant.

"Marcus, I—"

"Skeeter, what—"

They began, and halted again, simultaneously.

Marcus went to one knee, to be on the same level as Skeeter. His eyes were dark with emotion. "Skeeter!" He swallowed hard, consulted his tablets as though confirming the nightmare, then slowly met Skeeter's eyes. "They have paired you with the Death Wolf." His voice broke a little as he said it.

"Yeah. I know." Skeeter managed a sickly version of his old smile. "Nothing like justice, huh? I'm just— I never meant for this"—he gestured to Marcus' collar—"to happen. Never, *ever*. You . . ." He couldn't finish it. Couldn't say, "You were the only friend I ever had." The enormity of his loss was just now opening inside his mind.

"I am sorry," Marcus whispered. "My master . . . I will be on the balustrade above the stalls, watching the fighting. I . . ." He swallowed hard, tapped the wax tablets he carried. "I have to record who wins."

Skeeter tried, and failed, a bright smile. "Yeah. Well. Maybe I'll surprise everyone, huh? At least you can run away, get to the gate next time it opens."

Marcus was shaking his head, 'eighty-sixer fashion rather than Roman. "No. I have an enormous debt to repay. I know, here," he touched his breast, "that no man has the right to hold me slave. But I must repay the money, Skeeter. The honor of the Taurusates is all I have left, now."

There were tears in his eyes as he said it.

"Taurusates? That your real name?"

Marcus started to laugh, ended up crying. "No," he choked out. "My tribe's name. We . . . we were both betrayed, you know. The moneychanger, Goldie? With the hair of purple? The one against you in the great wager." His voice came out bitter, brittle as the hot sun beating down on them both. The stink of terrified men and the reeking musk of enraged lions engulfed their awareness.

Skeeter narrowed his eyes, trying to drive present reality out of existence at least for the moment. Sweet memories of Time Terminal Eighty-Six were almost too much. "Yeah, Goldie Morran," he managed. "What about her?"

"She told . . . she told Lupus about you. How to find you. This I *heard* her do, right before I returned to the Neo Edo to give Farley what I owed him. As much as I could of it, anyway."

Skeeter winced, writhing inside as he recalled the tears and bitter accusation in Ianira's voice. "So she told him, did she? Too bad I won't get a chance to throttle that old witch by the throat."

Marcus shrugged, very Gallic. "She will not be doing so very well, either. Farley stole a great deal of gold from her, just before we left. He laughed as he told me of it, *after* my sale. I . . . I asked him how he had brought so much gold through Primary. He said he took it from Goldie."

Despite the genuine calamity to Goldie Morran, Skeeter found himself laughing a little too shrilly, even as tears formed in his eyes, tears of helplessness, rage, terror. "So he got her, too, eh?" Marcus' dark eyes widened. "Christ. Both of us. What a couple of suckers we were. So goddamned sure—"

He glanced through the bars at Marcus. "I don't suppose you'd believe me, anyway, if I told you I was trying to stop you from going through the Porta Romae?" Marcus' eyes widened even further. "That's when Lupus crashed the Gate behind me and cracked me across the head."

Marcus' tightly pressed lips came adrift. "But— *why?*"

"I'd . . . I'd arranged to borrow some money, see, do some sessions with Dr. Mundy, to pay Farley the rest of what you owed him."

The look in Marcus' eyes told Skeeter he should've taken pity and kept his mouth shut. Skeeter cleared his throat roughly. "You'd better get on with your job," he said, "before your master gets pissed off and thinks you're loafing."

Marcus swallowed. "I had thought, until the moment I saw you in that cage, that I hated you, Skeeter. But now . . ." He trailed off helplessly. "May the gods fight on your side."

He made a hasty mark on his wax tablet and hurried on to the next cage, and the one beyond it, until he was out of sight and hearing. Skeeter slumped against the bars, feeling the throb of hurt inside him turn slowly to bitter rage. Goldie Morran, curse her, had sent him to this. Skeeter deserved to be punished, that much he could at least admit, but to just sell him out, knowing he'd be murdered, in order to win that accursed wager . . .

Skeeter owed Marcus, owed him his freedom, his family, a debt *he* needed to absolve himself of before he met the gods of the high Mongolian mountains, where the bite of ice in the sharp winds could kill a man in minutes. "If I get out of this alive," he vowed, "I'll get you back to Ianira and your kids. Somehow. And when I do . . ." He thought blackly of Goldie Morran. "When I do, I'll wring that scrawny old buzzard's jewelled *neck*!"

Rage sustained him through the exhibition before the start of the real games. Paired off with Lupus, whose laughing eyes and grinning mouth told of supreme confidence, Skeeter went through the motions he'd been beaten into learning, doing the whole, maddening drill in slow motion to the cheering encouragement of the crowd. Lupus' shield, Skeeter noted as he studied his adversary's every move, every potential weakness, was decorated with an odd, painted motif: a coiled serpent inside a circle of feathers painted a lurid shade of green, like First Officer Spock had bled all over them. Realizing that he was thinking about a television show some fifty years old, Skeeter gave a short bark of laughter that caused shock to detonate in Lupus' eyes for just a second.

Good! Skeeter thought savagely. *Keep the bastard off balance, maybe you'll live through this yet.*

Some of the men near him were literally gibbering with terror. Skeeter *should* have been shaking, too, with fear of what Lupus was about to do to him. But all Skeeter felt was a cold, dark rage at what Goldie had done. A Yakka Mongol knew only too well that death would come sooner or later, pleasantly or in agony, which was why he lived life to the fullest every day he still breathed; but what Goldie had done, had deliberately set in motion—

That could not be forgiven. He prayed to gods he thought he'd forgotten the names of, sky gods and mountain spirits and the demons which drove the great, black storms of sand across the valleys and open plains, and waited to match weapons for real with Lupus Mortiferus.

Lupus just might have a surprise or two in store.

While even in 1885 Denver was a fair sized city, with many stately buildings in brick and stone, most of the streets were dirt. Puffs of dust from their horses' hooves rose behind them as Malcolm set out with Margo on Chuck Farley's trail. Fortunately, that same dust made trailing him very easy. He left town completely, heading out to a spot that would one day become, if Malcolm were correct, a public park in the twenty-first century. He and Margo slowed their horses, which blew quietly as they slipped into the cover of a grove of trees, and watched Chuck dismount. He was whistling cheerfully. The sound carried on the slight breeze, straight toward them. The backdrop of the snowclad Rockies was breathtaking and the air was so clean, it smelt of bright sunshine and clear wind.

Malcolm glanced at Margo and smiled. Clearly she was entranced by the setting, the chase, the whole deadly game they played. Although she rode sidesaddle, a Winchester lever-action Model 76 Centennial rode in a saddle scabbard, and her skirts concealed a beauty of a revolver, one of the Colt .41 Double Actions. *This* time, Malcolm had no qualms at all about her ability to use—with deadly accuracy—any weapon she was forced to bring to bear. Out in the clearing, Chuck had begun to dig with a heavy spade unloaded from his pack horse. If he caught sight of them, they might well have to fight it out. But Malcolm, glancing at his own firearms, hoped it didn't come to that.

At least Margo had set those idiotic paleontologists straight. *They* were now properly armed with rifles and pistols that would arouse no one's curiosity. Malcolm hid a grin. What a way to begin their first adventure together as Smith and Moore, time guides, soon to be Moore and Moore, time *scouts*. He edged his horse just far enough toward hers to catch her hand and squeeze it. She glanced up, startled, then grinned and squeezed back. Malcolm quietly unstrapped the leather satchel holding his computerized log and ATLS, opened the flap, and slipped out a digitizing video camera attached to the log. He turned it on and was gratified when Margo copied his action efficiently, setting up her own digitizing camera and training it on Chuck, still busy digging. The images both cameras captured would feed directly into their individual logs—and could be used as legal evidence, along with the sworn affidavits, in most any uptime court of law.

Chuck's hole was getting larger by the minute. What was he burying, a crate the size of a steamer trunk? Malcolm narrowed his eyes. From the looks of the luggage tied to that pack horse's back, if he intended to bury it all, he'd need a *big* hole.

Chuck finally laid the heavy spade aside and straightened his back, grumbling audibly. Whatever he was burying, he was going to a great deal of personal trouble about it. Antiquities smuggler was Malcolm's private bet with himself. It was the only reasonable explanation he could devise for a man who went downtime with a vast sum of money, and returned with a great deal of clearly precious luggage.

What, Malcolm mused, had he brought back? Manuscripts? The way Chuck grunted when he unstrapped one case quashed that idea. That box was *heavy*. Chuck set it on the ground beside his deep hole, then unpacked several other cases. Then he sat down and opened them one by one. Apparently he had been too careful to examine them while in TT-86.

"Mother-fucking—" Chuck's curse was loud and startling. He was glaring into the first box, which he'd angled enough that Malcolm and both cameras could see its interior—and complete lack of contents. "Goddamned gold must've been used for something else later in history. Shit! After the trouble I went through to get those pieces . . ." He muttered something under his breath, then tossed the case aside. "Just like what happened with those goddamned jewels of Isabella's. How was I supposed to know those rocks would end up in her collection, never mind Chris Columbus' greedy Italian hands? Damn. Wonder if *any* of it managed to come through the goddamned Porta Romae intact?"

Malcolm held back a chuckle at the look of glee on Margo's face. She was absolutely intent on her work, recording Chuck's every move, every savage curse, every case he opened. Another foul expletive cut through the air. "—gold inlay vanished!" He held up a piece that Malcolm at first couldn't identify. Then the shape took on abrupt, crystal-clear meaning. It was an ivory dildo, complete with testes, which were evidently missing a detailed inlay of some sort. Malcolm zoomed in on the piece and thought, *Yes, I do believe there was supposed to be golden "hair" on that thing, and inlay for the veins along the shaft. Good Lord, what's he done, robbed or bribed every brothel in Rome?*

A quick glance at Margo showed him flaming cheeks and even a pinkened throat, but she was still recording as steadily as any pro. *Good girl!* Chuck laid the dildo back in is velvet-lined case and examined the rest of the contents. All of them were sexual in nature, although not all of them were actual sex toys. Each new case brought to light exquisite statuary in marble, ivory, bronze, even—Chuck gloated through the digitizing camera lens—a few surviving golden pieces. A delicate little silver statue of Aphrodite in flagrante delicto with one of her lovers came to light, followed by a marble statue of Hermes with a *very* erect—and removable—phallus.

Very carefully, Chuck re-covered his treasures in their lined cases, dragged out a small, battered notebook and made a few notations in it, then bagged each case in waterproof plastic which he then heat-sealed with a handy little battery operated gadget. He then gently laid them in the deep hole he'd dug, clearly planning to return uptime and reclaim his treasures without having to pay ATF taxes on them. It was a nice little scam. Those pieces would bring a fortune on the black market—even if they hadn't been commissioned by some uptime collector. Chuck filled in his hole again and tamped the dirt down, then carefully replaced the sod he'd cut out and tamped it down, too, pouring water from two entire canteens over it to ensure that it wouldn't die and turn brown, sticking out like a neon sign saying "Somebody buried something here!"

Chuck then pulled out an ATLS, surprising Malcolm considerably, and shot geographic coordinates using lines of magnetism, the position of certain mountain peaks in relation to his treasure trove, and so forth. He'd have gotten a better reading at night, when he could shoot a complete scan, with star-fixes to be completely sure of his location, but Malcolm decided he'd get an accurate enough reading to find his little treasure with minimum difficulty once he'd returned uptime.

Having taken his ATLS reading, Chuck stowed the instrument generally used only by trained time scouts in its leather bag on the pack horse—which now had a *much* lighter burden—and started whistling again. He mounted his saddle horse, glanced back at the watered sod, and said quite distinctly, "Not a bad haul. Not bad at all. Boss is going to be pissed as hell about the lost pieces, but that's the risk you take in this business." He chuckled. "Ah, well. I should've known better than to buy that whole lot from one source. Rotten little Egyptian. Too bad I won't be able to zip back down to Rome and settle the score." With that, he clucked to his horses and set off at a brisk trot toward town.

Malcolm waited until he'd been out of sight for a full fifteen minutes, then signalled Margo to wait. She thinned her lips, clearly seething at the restriction, but this time she stayed put with no arguments. She was learning. Good. Malcolm walked his horse around the clearing several times, but Chuck showed no sign of returning. He filmed a closeup of the tamped down, wet sod, then signalled Margo to join him. She did, grinning like the evil little imp she was.

"Okay," she said, fairly bursting with excitement, "what do we do? We've got him dead to rights—but how do we *catch* him?"

Malcolm chuckled. "We notify the uptime authorities the moment Primary opens to stake out this spot. He'll show up to dig up his booty one nice quiet night and they'll nail him. Meanwhile . . ." He turned off his camera, stowed his log, and said, "Keep filming, would you, Margo? I'm going to leave a nasty little surprise for our dear friend Chuck Farley, or whatever his real name might be. Let's see, now . . ." He sorted through his saddlebags until he found a short-handled camp spade he'd planned to use on a jaunt he'd wanted to take Margo on out into the countryside.

Instead of camping, they had something much more enjoyable lying ahead of them. Malcolm chuckled, carefully laid Chuck's wet sod aside, then began to dig. He uncovered every single plastic-wrapped case, then filled in the hole with rocks while Margo recorded the whole thing. "What I intend to do," he said, puffing for breath as he heaved the final rock into place, "is return these antiquities to the . . . proper authorities. There." He tamped dirt down around the rocks until the entire hole had been filled, then settled the sod back in place, watering it from his own canteen.

Then he glanced into Margo's digitizing camera. "I am Malcolm Moore, freelance time guide, working out of Time Terminal Eighty-Six. I hereby do solemnly swear that a man known to me as Charles 'Chuck' Farley acquired the antiquities in these bags, which we recorded him commenting upon as he buried them;

that said Chuck Farley should be apprehended by uptime authorities for antiquities fraud; for violation of the prime law of time travel; for tax evasion on objects of immense artistic and historical/archaeological value; and potentially for kidnapping, as two residents of TT-86 are missing as a result of his actions.

"I also hereby solemnly swear that as soon as the Wild West Gate reopens, I will turn over each and every antiquity recorded here to the proper, designated representative of IFARTS on TT-86 for cataloging, copying, and return to its point of origin. I freely agree to serve as a witness at any deposition or trial should the man calling himself Charles Farley be apprehended."

He signalled to Margo to hand him her camera. She passed it over and he settled her face in the viewfinder. Her normally vivacious countenance was unusually stern as she repeated approximately the same statement Malcolm had just made, adding only—but significantly:

" . . . and should be charged for murder or manslaughter, should one Skeeter Jackson be determined to have died in an attempt to stop Chuck Farley's intended plans, an attempt witnessed by several hundred individuals in Time Terminal Eighty-Six and recorded by one of the tourists. This can also be corroborated by Time Tours, Inc., as Mr. Jackson 'crashed' the gate in a desperate bid to stop the kidnapping of a TT-86 resident. Should Mr. Jackson's deceased remains be discovered downtime, I strongly urge whatever court may hear this testimony to charge the man known to us as Charles Farley with murder, manslaughter, or whatever charge the prosecution may deem appropriate under the circumstances. Chuck Farley is an evil, ruthless man who will stop at nothing to gain what he wants and if caught should be denied bail and punished accordingly."

Malcolm was nodding silently, pleased that she'd thought of those finishing touches. Jackson was no friend, but his action at the Porta Romae two weeks previously had elevated him in Malcolm's estimation by several notches of respect. Malcolm just hoped that whatever was happening downtime in Rome, Skeeter and Marcus would make it back to La-La Land safely.

Malcolm thought of Ianira and those two beautiful little girls and silently told himself that going after Farley in person and calling him out to a duel here and now in Denver would not only be suicidal, it would put Margo in desperate danger, as well. Nevertheless, his hands itched to line up Farley's bearded face in the sights of the Colt single-action army revolver strapped to his waist and squeeze off as many shots as it held.

Malcolm did *not* like losing friends. If Marcus and Skeeter didn't return by the next cycling of the Porta Romae, Malcolm would be ready to go through the other direction and hunt for them. Rome was a big city, but Malcolm had his sources and so did Time Tours, Inc. Losing two 'eighty-sixers—even if one were a downtimer and the other a gate-crashing con man and thief—would definitely *not* be good for their public image or their business. Malcolm would personally make them see that, if necessary.

Malcolm smiled grimly. Oh, yes, there would eventually be a reckoning with Mr. Chuck Farley, if Malcolm had to go uptime and hunt him down, himself. He just hoped Skeeter Jackson and Marcus were still alive and able to testify when that reckoning finally came.

CHAPTER EIGHTEEN

The sun beat down fierce as any Mongolian desert sky, and the sand underfoot was hot enough that Skeeter could feel it through the thin leather soles of his shoes—sandals that were mostly straps. Heat radiated off the arena sands, boiled off the embossed plaques of the great bronze turning posts, blinded the eye with tier after tier of stone and wooden seats and marble temples built right into the stadium itself. Sound roared down, assaulting his ears until his head ached, with the heart-freezing beat of a hundred thousand voices screaming in one solid mass nearly a mile long on each side.

Skeeter swallowed, briefly closed his eyes, and thought, *If Ianira's right, then I could use a little help here, Artemis. And Athene, Ianira says you even beat the God of War in battle once. I sure could use some assistance.* He even prayed to the Mongolian sky and thunder gods, as well as the singular Trinity of the Methodist church to which his mother had dragged him as a small boy. When it came to prayer, Skeeter wasn't too particular at just this moment Who answered, so long as They helped him get out of this fight alive. He wondered how many other prayers were winging their way heavenward with his.

He counted the pairs: twenty men, fighting in ten pairs, all at the same time. Two pairs of *essedarii* would be fighting from chariots drawn by a couple of horses each. A pair of *laqueatores* would fight one another with throwing slings—he'd seen what they could do during practice and was glad he wasn't fighting one of *them*. Two pairs of *myrmillones* in their weird, Gaulish helmets with the fish soldered on top would slash and stab it out with swords. Two *retiarii* were paired off against their traditional pursuers, the heavily shielded *secutores* with their massive, visored helmets, shields, and short swords. A duo of mounted *andabates* brought a dull, burning anger to Skeeter's gut. Mounted, he could've held his own for at least a little while, by running his horse in circles around the gladiator until Lupus fell down from exhaustion, if nothing else. But he didn't have a horse. The last two pairs were armed the same way he and Lupus were: the underdogs with nets and tridents, like the *retiarii*, with lassos as backup weapons, while they faced seasoned champions who fought nearly naked—but with a wicked sword in each hand.

As a group, they marched stolidly out across the burning arena sands to the Imperial Box, while the slam and *whap* of the starting-gate boxes being closed up reached his ears. A deep water moat at least ten feet across separated the fighters from the crowd, not to mention an iron fence tall and solid enough to keep an elephant from breaking through it. A few massive dents which even blacksmiths hadn't quite been able to unkink caused Skeeter to wonder if injured elephants *had* tried an escape through that fence.

The only hiding place anywhere out here was up on the spine, a collection of long, rectangular pedestals between the racing turns, on which stood statues of various deities, winged Victories that Skeeter hoped were smiling on *him* today, and an enormous Egyptian obelisk right in the center.

Skeeter's *lanista* prodded him. The gladiators were bowing to the Emperor. They shouted as one, "We who are about to die . . . ."

Skeeter stumbled over the words, more because his Latin just wasn't very good than from a shaking voice. Besides, he didn't feel like saluting the Roman emperor. Claudius was sitting up there like a deformed god, gazing coldly down on them like they were insects about to provide some trifling amusement. As a displaced Mongolian *bogda*, that made Skeeter mad. *For five years, I was a god, too, dammit. I was lonely as hell, but I'm just as good as you are, Imperator Claudius*.

Anger was far better than fear. He fed it, cunningly, as a fox fed his craftiness to catch unsuspecting the prey that thought itself safe. The champion of a hundred or more victories, Rome's wildly popular Death Wolf, bowed low and received the adulation of tens of thousands of voices: "Lupus! Lupus! Lupus!"

Skeeter glanced at his trainer who held a whip in one hand and a red-hot branding iron in the other, to encourage him if necessary. He laughed aloud, visibly disconcerting the man, then turned his back. He wouldn't need *that* sort of encouragement. A swift glance at Rome's Death Wolf showed him a grinning, overconfident champion already counting his victory. Skeeter knew he should've been scared to his bones. But the knowledge that Marcus was standing somewhere to his left, watching helplessly because both of them had been betrayed, burned away fear as effectively as the Mongolian desert sun.

The Emperor raised his hand, then dropped it. A monstrous roar beat at him—then he was dancing aside, away from Lupus' flashing double swords. He narrowed his eyes against the glare, wishing for a pair of sunglasses, a suit of chainmail made from titanium links, and an MP-5 submachinegun with about fifty spare magazines of ammo, and began the fight for his life.

The roar of the crowd faded from his awareness. Skeeter's whole concentration narrowed to Lupus Mortiferus and his flashing swords and grinning face. He danced this way and that, feinting and falling back, getting the champion's rhythms down, then made his first net cast. Lupus lunged aside barely in time. The crowd's roar penetrated his concentration even as he danced backward, away from those deadly blades and reeled in the net by the attached string. He held the heavy trident out to block thrusts or slashes and allowed his mind to race ahead with ideas.

The great spine of the Circus wasn't solid. It had gaps in it, wide enough for a man to duck into—or through. Skeeter ducked. Lupus swore hideously, his bulk too large to follow. He ran around the long distance of the spine to catch him on the other side. Skeeter simply ran back the other way. The crowd's roar turned to howls of laughter. Lupus' face, when Skeeter glimpsed it, was almost the color of pickled beets. The gladiator, veins in neck and throat standing out in clear relief, charged back down the long wall of the spine.

Gee, maybe he'll have a stroke and I'll win by default. No such luck, though. Lupus scrambled through sideways this time, grunting and cursing at him as he scraped belly and back on rough stone. Skeeter dodged out into the open, where he most profoundly did not want to be, but avoided a deadly sword thrust aimed at his side. Shouts and cries from the stands indicated that someone had gone down. Skeeter's peripheral vision showed him one of the netmen down, left arm upraised in supplication. The crowd was roaring, thumbs turned up. The Emperor copied their motion, jerking his thumb upward from gut to throat.

The *secutore* who'd hacked his opponent's leg out from under him plunged the sword through his fallen opponent's chest. The crowd roared its approval. Skeeter ran, Lupus chasing him, and dodged around behind one of the racing chariots, drawing curses from its driver as well as from Lupus. Skeeter caught the harness of one of the horses and hung on, letting the horse save his strength while Lupus fought to get past the encumbering chariot. Down where the dead gladiator lay, a man raced out from the starting stalls and smote the poor bastard a skull-cracking blow from an enormous hammer, then dragged the body away.

Okay. Thumbs up means you're a gonner and if the guy you're fighting doesn't do it properly, they'll finish you off. Good things to know, Skeeter, my boy.

He let go of the chariot horse's harness and darted between a pair of circling horsemen, ducking *under* one horse's belly. The startled animal screamed and reared, blocking Lupus' way. The crowd roared its approval with cheers and laughter. Sweat dripped into his eyes, along with a pall of dust—stirred up from the speeding, circling chariots and horsemen—forcing him to blink tears from his eyes. *Not near as bad as a rip-snorting Gobi sandstorm, though,* Skeeter decided. He was quite abruptly very glad Yesukai the Valiant had made him go on that hunt so many years previously.

If I can take a snow leopard with a bow, I can take this bastard.

Maybe.

If I'm really damned careful.

When Lupus closed, Skeeter dove for the ground, rolling under the stabbing swords, and came up with a fistful of sand and a net, both of which he flung at the cursing gladiator. Lupus snarled, swiping at his eyes with the backs of his hands while fighting blindly to free one entangled leg. Skeeter hauled—hard. Lupus went down—harder. The crowd surged to its collective feet, screaming its bloodlust. Lupus hacked at the net, managing to free himself before Skeeter could close with the lethal trident.

Shit! Goddammit, I don't really want to kill this cretin, but what am I supposed to do? Ask him to dance? Skeeter skipped back out of range while Lupus fought to clear sand from his eyes. Skeeter unwound the lasso from his waist. He formed a hasty loop and swung it easily. A lasso, he knew how to use. Skeeter grinned, a taut, fang-bearing grin. During his brutal training he'd deliberately fumbled the lasso exercises, same as he'd tossed the net with awkward casts. They'd thought it a monstrously funny joke, sending him out with the weapons he'd done poorest with.

Bless you, Yesukai, wherever you are, for teaching me a sneaky trick or two.

The crowd roared again, three times in rapid succession as gladiators fell to their opponents and died. The next one was spared and limped bravely from the sands while Skeeter ducked and dodged and felt his own strength ebbing under the cruel sun and Lupus' inexorable stalk.

Gotta do something spectacular, Skeeter, or it's shish-ka-bob a lá Skeeter as the main course.

A charioteer went down, dragged behind his spooked horses. The crowd screamed its decision and the other charioteer pursued, stabbing his opponent to death on the run before collecting his prize and leaving the arena under armed escort.

Okay, so even if you win, a bunch of soldiers are waiting to haul your butt back to barracks. Another good thing to know.

A slice of fire along his ribs sent the breath rushing

out of him in a hiss. He brought up the trident, cursing his momentary lapse of attention, and managed to entangle the bloody sword in the prongs. He gave a heave and a twist and the sword snapped off halfway down. Lupus snarled and lunged forward while the crowd went mad, on its feet and screaming. The cut along his ribs burned like a thousand ant bites. If it'd been a slashing blow instead of a stabbing one, he'd be on his back in the sand, bleeding to death from the deep wound.

Skeeter stumbled away, too tired to dance lightly on his feet any longer. Lupus grinned and closed in for the kill. Skeeter, unable to think of anything else, began to sing, his voice hoarse with pain and fatigue. Lupus' eyes widened. Skeeter sang on, a wild, hair-raising Yakka Mongolian war song, while the crowd nearest them fell silent, as disbelieving as Lupus. Skeeter pressed the slight advantage and whirled the lasso expertly. It settled over Lupus' body and slid down to the knees. Skeeter jerked. Lupus went down with a startled yell.

Skeeter couldn't understand individual words in the immense wall of sound that beat down across him, but he gathered the general gist of it was, "Skewer his belly with the trident, you fool!"

Skeeter didn't. Lupus hadn't asked for quarter, but Skeeter wasn't about to take the man's life unless ordered to do so. And maybe not even then. What happened to a gladiator who refused the express orders of crowd and Emperor? *That maniac with the hammer probably crushes your skull or something.* While Skeeter was thinking such happy thoughts, Lupus hacked at the rope binding his legs. It gave way with a snap, leaving Skeeter with half the length of the original lasso. He took to his heels, fashioning another knot and threading it as he ran—

—and then it happened.

The answer to all those prayers he'd sent heavenward.

A mounted *andabate*, mortally wounded by his opponent, toppled to the sand. While the crowd was cheering and the victor was collecting his prize and the hammer-happy executioner was making damned sure the poor sap was dead, the loose horse ran within lassoing distance. Skeeter flipped the rope expertly and tightened it down. The poor horse reared once, half-heartedly, more confused than ornery. Skeeter ran toward it, leaping into the saddle with old skill he'd never quite forgotten. There were no stirrups, as there had been on Mongolian ponies, but the saddle was a good one and the horse, after one snort, settled down and responded to the hastily gathered reins.

Skeeter whirled the animal's head around and caught a glimpse of Lupus gaping up at him. Skeeter laughed aloud, started his war song again, and charged, trident lowered like a medieval jousting lance. Lupus hurled himself out of the way, barely missing the horse's thundering hooves. The crowd went maniacal. Even the Emperor had straightened in his chair, leaning forward intently.

Wonder if this is a foul or just something they didn't expect?

Skeeter worked Lupus in circles, harried him with the tip of the long trident, tripping him up and letting him rise again, just to let his opponent—and the crowd—know he was toying with a doomed victim. Skeeter's blood sang in his veins. *This* was living! Driving your opponent back against the wall, looking him in the eye and seeing nothing but shock and dawning terror. . . .

Lupus tried to bring up the single remaining blade he carried, but Skeeter caught it in the prongs of the trident and ripped it out of his grasp. A collective gasp went up from the crowd. Unarmed, Lupus snarled up at him, then grabbed the trident. For a few seconds, no more—although it seemed like minutes—they played tug-of-war, Skeeter skillfully backing and turning his mount with legs and reins. Lupus was forced to follow, putting all his weight into the effort of wresting the trident loose.

Skeeter glanced along the barrier wall of the long spine—and felt his heart leap with wicked joy. A long, long hunting spear from an earlier fight had tumbled to the sand at the foot of some enormous, golden goddess in a chariot drawn by lions. Skeeter grinned— and let go of the trident. Lupus staggered backwards and fell, wounding himself inadvertently as he went down, the weight of the trident's barbs cutting one arm and drawing blood on his bare chest.

Under a solid wall of noise from a hundred thousand human throats, Skeeter kicked his mount into a startled gallop and leaned forward and down, his head mere inches from the wall of the spine. A miscalculation at this speed would be death—then he closed his hand around the hunting spear, clutching it solidly in one hand. He whirled his mount around, bringing the long shaft up and around even as he regained his seat in the saddle. Then he charged, spear held like a medieval lance.

Lupus parried awkwardly with the trident, a weapon he was clearly not accustomed to using. Skeeter raced past at full speed, passed the turning post at the far end of the straightaway, then whirled and sent his horse leaping *over* a tiny shrine on a circular pedestal set right down on the track. Another gasp went up from the crowd. *If that was sacrilege, sorry about that, whoever you're dedicated to.*

Whoever it was, they didn't seem to mind.

The crowd started chanting what sounded at first

like "mercy," then resolved into a single word: "Murcia! Murcia! Murcia!"

Skeeter had no idea who or what Murcia was. The only thing of immediate concern to him was the stumbling figure of Lupus Mortiferus ahead, trying to bring the trident around, its tines aimed low this time, to catch his horse. Skeeter windmilled the spear in his grasp, letting it slide butt-first until he gripped it near the lethal tip. At the last second, he jerked his mount's head, sweeping past just out of range of the trident. The solid butt-end of the spear clanged against Lupus' head with such force that it lifted the gladiator off the sands, bent in his helmet, and hurled him at least four feet across the arena floor.

Skeeter whirled his mount for another charge, but there was no need. Lupus didn't stir on the sands. He was—thank all gods—still breathing, but he was clearly down, and out for the count. The crowd had gone absolutely mad, waving colored handkerchiefs, screaming words he couldn't begin to translate, throwing flowers, even coins, through the high fence and across the wide gap of water. Skeeter drew another wild burst of enthusiasm when he dipped from one side to another, scooping up anything that gleamed silver or gold in the sands.

He ended in front of the Emperor, sitting his mount easily, breathing quickly and lightly against the fire in his side where Lupus' sword had grazed him. The Emperor met his gaze for long moments. Skeeter, who had met without flinching the gaze of the man who'd sired Genghis Khan, stared right back at Claudius, neither of them speaking. The Emperor glanced at the crowd, at the fallen champion, then back to the crowd. Then, with a swift gesture, he drove his thumb down, sparing a brave man's life with a single movement.

Skeeter would've sagged with relief and exhaustion had he not faced a yet worse challenge: escaping the Circus alive. He had absolutely no intention of being hauled back to that training camp in chains. The Emperor was beckoning him forward. Skeeter moved his horse closer. A slave ran from the Emperor's box and hurled a laurel crown and a heavy sack down to him. Skeeter caught them, felt the bulge of coins inside, knew the prize was a really *big* one and felt the skin of his face stretching into a savage grin as he donned his honest-to-God victory crown.

All he had to do now was figure out a way to: One, escape the soldiers who were even now galloping toward him from the starting stalls—which had already been shut behind them; Two, figure a way over that high iron fence; Three, somehow rescue Marcus from his so-called master; and Four, hide out until the Porta Romae cycled again.

After what he'd just been through, his impudent mind whispered, *Piece of cake*. The rest of him, aware how close it had been, resumed intense prayers to Anyone who'd listen. Even the mysterious Murcia, with his or her little shrine down in the track itself, next to a scraggly little tree growing from the hard-packed sand.

He caught a thrown handkerchief, which landed on the sands nearly at his horse's hooves, with the tip of his spear and brought it up, snapping bravely in the wind of his horse's canter as he rode *toward* the soldiers, carrying that handkerchief like the pennon of victory it was. He tucked the coins he'd scooped from the sand into the quilted, chain-studded sleeve that protected his net arm, shoved the money pouch's leather thong into his waistband, and sent his horse flying past the soldiers in a sweeping victory lap of the Circus. The crowd was on its feet, hurling money at him which he scooped up as best he could on the gallop, aiming for golden gleams in the sand. And as he rode, Skeeter looked for a way—any way—out of this pit of sand and death. He rounded the far turn, mounted soldiers riding easily behind him, and headed down the long sweep of the straightaway toward the starting stalls, with their wooden doors, metal grills set above into marble, and above that, the open balustrade where officials stood, having doubtless watched with delight the show he'd put on saving his skin.

He measured the height critically, glanced at the long spear in his hand, studied the looming marble wall he and his horse thundered toward—and made the only decision he could. He'd mounted horses that way dozens of times, learning to do what the older boys and warriors could do, earning their grudging respect as he mastered skill after skill. He'd never scaled a fifteen-foot wall off the back of a horse, but with the horse's momentum and the long axis of the spear . . .

It was his only hope. He headed his mount for the starting gates at a rushing gallop, aiming between the tall, semihuman stones that stood on round stone bases between each starting stall. When he was certain the horse wasn't going to shy on him, he stood *up* in the saddle, drawing a gasp and thunderous roar from the crowd. Skeeter narrowed his eyes, timing it, timing it—and planted the butt of the spear solidly on the pavement in front of the starting stalls. Momentum from the galloping horse and the long arm of the spear helped as he leaped and swung his body up, higher and higher as he twisted like an Olympic pole vaulter, up past the heads of the statues, up past the grillwork on the stalls, up and up past the marble facade of the balustrade . . .

Then he was over the top, rolling like a cat across an incredibly hard stone floor. His laurel crown, loose around his head, fluttered back down to the arena sands. Shocked officials simply stood rooted, staring open-mouthed at him as he continued the roll and came to his feet, weaponless but free of the suddenly astonished soldiers in the arena below. Then his eyes met the stunned gaze of his one-time friend.

Marcus, standing behind a richly dressed man who was gaping at Skeeter, ignored everything, even his "master," to stare, jaw slack, even *hands* slack as he completely failed to write down the winner of this particular bout. Obviously, he still couldn't believe it. What had Marcus told him? Honor was all he had left of his tribe? Skeeter's throat closed. The money in the pouch still tucked through his belt seemed to burn him, saying, *I will win your wager. Cut your losses and run, fool!*

Instead, he hurled the heavy prize pouch at Marcus' master. It thumped off his chest and fell to the marble floor with a solid chink of gold. "I'm buying and you're selling," Skeeter snarled in bad Latin. Then, in English, "All debts paid in full, pal. Now *run like hell!*"

Without bothering to see if Marcus followed, Skeeter did just that, bursting down the stairs to the street level before the soldiers down there could recover their wits enough to ride him down. Every stride hurt him, hurt his ribs, hurt with the knowledge that he'd lost his wager for sure—

"This way!" Marcus' voice yelled behind him.

A hand grabbed his iron collar and forcibly jerked him into a narrow alleyway that wound down around the Aventine Hill away from the Circus. The roar from the great arena was deafening, even at this distance.

"We've got to get you out of that gladiator's getup or we're lost!" Marcus yelled practically in his ear.

Skeeter just nodded. The next man they came to, Skeeter simply tackled and stripped, top to toe. The fellow protested loudly until Marcus, showing a ruthlessness Skeeter had never witnessed, simply kicked him in the head until he passed out.

"Hurry!" Marcus urged, scanning the street for any sign of pursuit.

Skeeter wriggled out of his protective sleeve, forming a bag of it with knots at both ends to hold his coins, then skinned into tunic and perniciously awkward toga while Marcus dragged the unconscious man into an alleyway. "Hey, Marcus, know where we might find a blacksmith's shop?"

Marcus laughed, a little shrilly. "Follow me."

Skeeter grinned. "Lead the way."

The blacksmith was close, tucked between a potter's stand and a bakery. Before the blacksmith knew what was up, Skeeter had grabbed a dagger, a sword and a belt, and cutting tools, then he and Marcus were off and running again, dodging into twisting alleyways until Marcus pulled him into a rutted little snaking pathway between tall wooden tenements.

"Here! Give me the cutting tools! Bend your head!"

Skeeter did as he was told, even as he strapped the swordbelt on and hid the sleeve full of money in the awkward folds of his badly draped toga. The lock on his collar snapped.

Skeeter grabbed the tools. "You next."

"But—I can't pass for a citizen!"

"Then pass for a freedman!"

"But I have no freedman's cap or—"

"Shut up and turn around! We'll *get* one! Or would you rather get caught by whoever's been sent after us?"

"The Praetorian Guard?" Marcus shuddered and bent his head. Skeeter went to work on the lock holding his friend's collar in place. The lock gave with a screech, then broke. Marcus jerked the collar loose with a low snarl.

"I have been keeping track of the days. The Porta Romae cycled last night."

Skeeter swore. "Then we hide out for two weeks and make our getaway next cycle. Broad daylight'll work to our benefit, anyway. More chances for a diversion to get *you* back through."

Marcus paused, dark eyes blazing with unspoken emotion.

"Don't mention it. All in the package deal. One combat, two escapes. C'mon, let's make tracks before those guards figure out which alleyway we dodged down."

They waylaid a hapless freedman by simply racing past him and snatching off his peaked cap. They rounded two corners and Marcus jammed it onto his own head.

"Hope he didn't have head lice," Marcus grumbled.

Skeeter laughed aloud. "Rachel Eisenstein will disinfect you nicely, if he did. And I don't think Ianira would give a damn even if Rachel *didn't* disinfect you. Okay, one more block, down that little alley, then we slow down to a nice leisurely walk, a citizen and his freedman out for a stroll. . . ."

About ten minutes later, mounted Praetorian guardsmen tore past them, searching the crowds for a fleeing gladiator and his collared companion. Marcus waited until they were out of sight to sigh in heartfelt relief. Skeeter grinned. "See? Told you it'd be a piece of cake." He didn't mention that his knees were a little weak and his insides shook like gelatin in a blender.

Marcus glared at him. "You did not say any such thing, Skeeter Jackson!"

His grin widened. "No. But I thought it, to give myself the nerve to try pole-vaulting out. And look at us, now; we're alive and we're free. Let's keep it that way, if it's all right by you."

Dark emotion bubbled up in Marcus' eyes again. "It is very much all right by me."

"Good. I think I see an inn up ahead. Know anything about it?"

Marcus peered through the crowd. "No. But this is a good part of town. It should be safe enough and serve food worth eating."

"Sounds good to me." He chuckled. "Nothing like that proverbial purloined letter."

"The *what*?"

"A story I read once. Sherlock Holmes. Best place to hide something is right out in the open, where nobody expects to find it."

Marcus laughed, not from mirth but from sheer amazement.

"Skeeter Jackson, you astonish me more and more the longer I know you."

Skeeter rubbed the side of his nose, feeling heat creep into his face. "Yeah, well, I've had an interesting sorta life. I'd about ten times rather have a great wife and a couple of kids, right about now. Hell, I'd settle for a friend." Marcus cast a glance in his direction, but didn't speak. Skeeter felt the silence like a punch to his gut. He dragged in a deep breath, even *that* hurting, and muttered, "Okay, here we go. Your Latin's better than mine and something tells me rich guys don't do the dickering."

Marcus smiled. "You learn quickly. Keep closed your mouth and no one will be the wiser."

Skeeter grinned, then dutifully closed his mouth, shook loose some coins, and handed several of the silver ones over. "That be enough?"

"I'd say so. Now hush and let me play the hero this time."

They stepped into the cool quiet of the inn and met the bright smile of the proprietor. Marcus launched into Latin too rapid to follow, but it got results. They were taken to a private room and shortly were feasting on chilled wine, roasted duckling, and a pot of boiled beef and cabbage. Skeeter ate until he couldn't hold another bite.

"Gawd, that was heavenly."

Marcus wiped his mouth and nodded. "*Much* better than wheat gruel." He paused, then added awkwardly, "If—if you will take that tunic off, Skeeter, I will wash and bandage your injuries."

Skeeter didn't argue. His wounds stung and burned every time he moved in his stolen garments of wool. Marcus tore up some of the bedding and laved the long slice with clean water, then wound strips of cotton around Skeeter's torso. "There. That should keep the blood from seeping out and giving you away." He cautiously dabbed at the stains on the side of the tunic, which the long toga had hidden. Most of them came out with the application of cold water. Marcus finished that chore and hung up the tunic to dry, then cleared his throat. "If you will give me the sword, I will stand guard. You are exhausted, Skeeter. Sleep. Anyone looking for you will have to kill me."

Skeeter held his gaze for a moment and realized Marcus meant it. He didn't know what to say. Maybe . . . just maybe . . . all those prayers he'd uttered back at the start of the fighting had given him back not only his life, but a chance at winning back the friendship he'd so thoughtlessly shattered?

Because he couldn't have spoken to save his half-wild soul, Skeeter sank back on the denuded mattress without a single word and was asleep before Marcus had finished setting aside the dishes from their meal. His final thought was, *If I do have a second chance, don't let me screw it up. Please.*

Then all was silence and peaceful sleep while Marcus stood guard over him, placing his life between Skeeter and the door.

Goldie Morran spent an unhappy two weeks, waiting with the rest of TT-86 for word of Skeeter Jackson. As she'd discovered already, she didn't want Skeeter dead. Kicked off the station had seemed like a grand idea, but now . . . all she could do was wonder what he was up to downtime. Rescuing Marcus? She snorted. Goldie really couldn't credit that, Dr. Mundy and vidcam evidence notwithstanding. A person could *always* interpret a bit of evidence ten different ways from Sunday. Besides, Skeeter was too much like Goldie to spend his time rescuing a worthless slave when he could be scamming so much gold downtime, she'd never catch up. Of course, Brian might disallow it, on the grounds that the wager was on hold. Or— she shuddered delicately behind her cold, glasstop counters—that dratted librarian might just decide that since Skeeter would have had no way of *knowing* the wager was on hold, his earnings *would* count.

Curse the boy!

She was theoretically ahead, with more than half the bet's term left to run. If Skeeter returned.

What if Skeeter *never* returned? Some people thought Goldie was a heartless sociopath. She wasn't— although she put out considerable effort to seem that way. So if Skeeter Jackson, never mind that nice kid who tended bar at the Down Time never came back, she'd have their fates on her conscience.

And backstabbing cheat that she knew herself to be, that was something she knew she couldn't live with.

Please, she whispered silently, *bring them back. I miss that obnoxious little bastard.* She was discovering she actually missed watching that boy con tourists out of cash, cameras, wristwatches, wallets, and anything else he could lift to turn a buck. She even missed the arguments over whiskey and beer at the Down Time while tourists who wandered in watched, goggle-eyed. . . . *I miss them. Bring them back, please. Whatever I felt before, I never meant for this to happen.*

Goldie didn't realize she was crying until the tears dripped with a soft splash onto her glass counter. When she sniffed and looked around to find a handkerchief, she found a young Asian woman she'd never laid eyes on standing in front of her counter. The girl offered a clean, beautifully embroidered handkerchief.

"Here, Miss Morran, you are hurting. You have much to be sorry for, but we understand."

Without another word, she slipped out of Goldie's shop, moving with the unobtrusive grace of a girl trained in one of the finest geisha houses in Japan. Goldie stared at the embroidered handkerchief, stared at the doorway, then very slowly dried her face and blew her nose. It wasn't easy, facing the fact that if those two boys didn't return, it would be largely her fault.

"All I ask," Goldie muttered, blowing her nose miserably again, "is a chance to tell that miserable, thieving, no-good cheat that I'm sorry—to his face."

A tiny whisper at the back of her mind warned her to be wary of what one asked the gods for, lest they grant it.

Just where was Skeeter Jackson? And what the living hell was he doing down there in ancient Rome? Playing hero? Or playing the cad? She hoped she'd have the chance to find out which.

Goldie sniffed one last time and wadded up the exquisite handkerchief until her hand hurt.

"Come back, damn you!"

Only the chill of her glass cases, filled with cold, rare coins, cool, smooth miniature sculptures in precious stones, and the frozen glitter of a few scattered jewels on shivering velvet heard.

CHAPTER NINETEEN

For the remainder of their stay in Denver, the man calling himself Chuck Farley spent his time visiting one cathouse after another. Margo wrinkled her nose as they watched quietly in the darkness while he entered yet another establishment of ill repute.

"I hope he catches something really nasty!"

"He might, at that," Malcolm muttered. "He's doubtless been inoculated, because smallpox is still rampant in these parts, but he might catch a social disease and be put into quarantine. Dr. Eisenstein could either heal it or recommend permanent quarantine. Uptime, too; Rachel Eisenstein takes her job very seriously, she does. She wants to ensure diseases like that don't get passed on to anyone in the real world." A bitter chuckle issued near her ear. "He would certainly deserve it. But it's more likely he's gathering additional inventory."

"To make up for the pieces that didn't come through the gate with him?"

"Exactly."

Margo flounced as only Margo could do while standing perfectly still. Her dress rustled like wind through aspens at her movement. "He's disgusting," she muttered under her breath. "And he doesn't look or act rich enough to keep those for himself. Wonder who his uptime buyer is?"

Malcolm stared at her with considerable surprise. He hadn't expected her to pick up on that part of it so fast. But there *were* uptime billionaires who paid agents to loot the past for their collections. A tiny number of the agents moving downtime then uptime again had been caught, their stolen antiquities confiscated and turned over to IFARTS for evaluation and return downtime. Disgusting was far too mild a word for the kind of man who'd pay others to take the risks, do the legwork—the dirty, often lethal work. The payoff from the actual client would, of course, be only a fraction of what the antiquities were worth, but enough to keep them busily moving back and forth time and again, to steal even more artwork.

Malcolm realized from Margo's look, she'd like to do murder when Farley exited the house. And with the gun concealed in her fur muff, she probably could have drilled him through whichever eye she chose. As though following his thoughts, she glared at the cathouse Farley had entered. He half expected a Margo-style explosion or an outright attack murderous with pent-up emotion, but all she said was, "Creeps."

The deep silence of the late Denver night was shattered abruptly by the rumbling, squeaking, and groaning Conestoga wagons—a long line of them—which began forming up nose-to-tail on a long, dirt road that led southeastward out of town. "Malcolm," she whispered, "is that what I think it is? A real, honest-to-goodness wagon train?"

With the ease of long practice, Malcolm shifted into his Denver persona.

"Yeah, I s'pect so, ma'am. Lots of prairie schooners in that train."

Malcolm's uncanny ability to mimic local languages, even dialects, always amazed Margo. It was his way of reminding Margo that she, too, would have to master the knack.

"But I thought all the wagon trains were a thing of the past? I mean, I read somewhere that the whole continent had been settled by 1885 or so."

Malcolm shook his head. "Nope. With book learnin' you has to go deep to ferret out truth. Lemme 'splain somethin', ma'am. This here city o' Denver weren't nothin' more'n paper plans, laid out nice and neat, back in '59. Then along comes the Pike's Peak rush— over what?"

Margo's brow furrowed delightfully. Then her whole face lit with an incandescent glow. "Gold! The '59 Gold Rush."

Malcolm chuckled. "Very good. 'Cept nobody could find any. Miners called it the biggest humbug in all history, they did, and left in disgust. But the experienced men, now, the ones who'd sluiced and dug out the big Georgia and California motherlodes, they stayed on. Saw the same signs, they did, same as the signs they'd noticed before. So they stayed on and come late '59 and into '60, made the really big strikes. Caused another rush, o'course," he chuckled.

"Yes, but what's that got to do with that?" She pointed toward the wagons.

"W-e-e-l-l-l, that's another story, now, ain't it? There's still odd bits and pieces o' land rattling around this big country, pieces that're still unclaimed for homesteadin'." He lowered his voice to a nearly inaudible murmur. He whispered into her ear, "In fact, four times as many acres were homesteaded after 1890 than before it, but you'd never guess it from period attitudes about land. It borders on sacredness." Then at a slightly higher volume and a more discreet distance, he said, "Take careful note 'o what those wagons is carryin'. And what they ain't."

Another lesson, even during the very serious duty of watching for sluglike Farley? Malcolm Moore was always so sure of himself, yet so gentle compared to the men in her old life. She studied each wagon in turn, trying to ignore weird shadows thrown against the canvas tops as those departing checked over their equipment. She saw the usual rifles and pistols, bandoliers and boxes of ammunition to hunt game for the table, dozens of tools whose use Margo could only guess at, and a few rough-hewn bits of furniture.

"No women's things," Margo said abruptly. "No trunks for clothing or quilts, no butter churns, no barrels of padded china from back East. And no children. Those men aren't married. No farming equipment, either, and no livestock except the oxen and horses pulling those wagons. Not even a single laying hen—and you can hear them clucking a fair distance away. And believe me, they cluck *loud* when they're upset. Do *you* hear any chickens?"

Malcolm shook his head solemnly.

"No, me neither."

"Very nice, indeed," Malcolm purred. "You've a good eye—and ear—for detail. Now just keep up with the bookwork and you'll make one damned fine time scout."

Margo's fierce blush was, thank God, hidden by the dark night.

"Those," Malcolm continued very quietly, "are hardened frontiersmen, always on the move. They follow the remnants of the buffalo herds for their hides, which are commanding good prices again, now that there are so few buffalo left. They follow hints and whispers of gold found on this creek or that. Or they work for hire as ranch hands, even drovers, although that profession is just about as extinct as the poor buffalo. Now that bunch," he turned Margo's head toward the front wagon in the caravan, "is bound for the Indian Territory, or my name isn't Malcolm Moore."

"Indian Territory?" Margo echoed.

"Later renamed several things, but Oklahoma was generally mixed in there somewhere. Right now men are streaming in by the hundreds to support David Payne, a cutthroat frontiersman leading a band of even more violent frontiersman in a war against the Indians given that land, even against the Federal Government."

"Your accent's slipping,"

"Right you are, ma'am, and thank you it is for the reminder."

"So," Margo concentrated, her brow deeply furrowed as she thought it through, "these men are going to stir up Indian tribes by taking part of their land illegally?"

"Yep. Worse trouble'n anybody thought they'd stir up. But the whole country's clamorin' to kick out the 'savages' and open up Oklahoma for 'decent' folk to settle."

Margo shivered, watching these men pack away their clothes, excess weapons, and whatever they considered valuable enough to take along. The rest, they abandoned along the road, in bundles and boxes, for anyone to salvage. "The more I learn about history, the more savage I find it was. These men are going out to murder as many Indians as they can get into their goddamned sights, aren't they?"

"My dear lady, you shock me! Such language!"

Gentle reprimand, steel-hard warning behind it. Ladies of quality did *not* curse like sailors in 1885, not even in the frontier. Of course, barmaids and whores could be expected to say anything and everything . . . but Margo did most emphatically not wish to be associated with them.

Not Minnesota prudishness this time—she'd lost

a lot of that on a beach in Southeastern Africa—but a cold, calculated decision in the direction of survival. Time scouts, as her grandfather Kit Carson put it, had to be bloody careful anywhere downtime. Especially if scouting an unknown gate. Shaking inside her frontier, multibutton, impossible-to-fasten boots (until Malcolm, shaking with silent laughter, handed her a button hook and explained its use) Margo recalled her formidable but lonely grandfather, a man who'd stepped through a gate to rescue her, not knowing if he'd survive the trip to the other side; then glared at the men in those murder-wagons, at the ones standing outside in little knots, smoking some kind of foul-smelling cigars, their boasts of killing no-account Indians like it was some insane game where they tallied score by the number of people they butchered.

Not that she thought the Indians shoved into that Oklahoma Reservation to be the peaceful, nature revering, squeaky clean role-models the TV ads and movies made them out to be. She'd read with a clinical, removed-from-the-dreadful-scenes detachment as her only defense against descriptions of massacres perpetrated by desperate and enraged young warriors, young men with their blood up, refusing to give up either tribal or manly pride. *Pride!* How much trouble that one little word had caused the world . . . That was new—these insights and connections she'd begun making about all kinds of subjects, to the everlasting astonishment of her professors and the steady rise of her GPA.

She slitted her eyes slightly against the sting of wind-borne cigar smoke, thinking it all through as carefully and thoroughly as possible—as Kit and Malcolm had jointly taught her to do. No, the Native American tribes hadn't been peaceful nature lovers at all, even before the coming of Europeans; before that momentous date, they'd made war on one another in just as savage a fashion as they later made war against the pale invaders of their continent. But what the American government had later done to these people was hideous, unforgivable.

Margo liked getting her facts straight, more and more so the longer she was in college, delving through books she had once abhorred, so she could *understand* the real message behind admittedly biased writing on Native American Indians—contemporary accounts by trappers, traders, settlers, mountain men—as well as modern scholarly research-hero-worship crap about people who—according to several archaeological site-analyses written by the archaeologists themselves—tossed their meal scraps right out of the tepee's front door for weeks, maybe even months on end (at least, that was true of some of the plains tribes, well before the arrival of the European); people who thought nothing of making their immediate surroundings a latrine/cesspit and thought their women attractive in hair dressed in bear-grease applied six months previously. Margo shuddered delicately.

Ultimately, what she had found were two differing stories of two very different peoples, each savage in their own way. Who was to say which was worse? Warriors taking scalps as trophies of victory or men who calmly plotted the obliteration of entire tribes. She finally managed to choke out, "Will they give a damn about shooting women and children, too?" And this time, notably, she received no scolding for her anachronistic manners.

After a look of pain passed through Malcolm's expressive eyes, he said very quietly, "W-e-e-l-l-l, not really. Least, not everywhere. But yeah, ma'am, it happens, here 'n there, all across the whole land. They say the first known record of biological warfare was takin' a load of blankets from a smallpox victim still aboard ship and delib'retly handin' 'em over to a tribe of six-foot Indians down in Florida, men who could put a long, heavy arrow through a man's leg, his horse, and mebbe catch his other leg on the way out again."

Margo nodded silently, letting him know she'd read about that already. "Now, these men," he nodded toward the wagoneers, "they're a tough bunch o' claim-jumping cutthroats with one aim in mind. They'll settle down in parts of the Oklahoma Reservation that don't no one tribe actually own, massacre a bunch from one tribe, just so's another would go on the warpath. Not just for revenge for a fellow tribe. Hell, the poor bastards just figure they're next, anyway, and who wants to be shot in bed, like a fat, lazy cow waitin to be milked?

"It's been gettin' so bad, Fed'ral troopers have done come in to stop it all and toss the Boomers, as they style themselves, out o' Indian land. But shucks, there's always ten, twelve men waiting to replace every corpse or kickin', cursing Boomer tossed out or arrested. That's decent farmland, compared to what was left everywhere else at a cheap price. What them men wanted was decent, *cheap* land to homestead. And the only place left to get it was in Indian land, see? Hell, ma'am, and 'scuse the language, but some o' them Boomers mean to have as much as they can beg, borrow, or steal by murderin' whoever's already there that ain't got a white hide. It's a dirty, rotten land-grab of a business, played like some damned child's game, only a long-sight bloodier."

"And there's nothing we can do to stop it?"

A sigh gusted past her ear. "Nope. Not a goddamned, helpless thing. History cain't be changed. One of the first rules of time travel, and you should know 'em all by heart now."

Margo's sigh echoed Malcolm's. "Rule One: Thou shalt not profit from history nor willfully bring any biological specimens—including downtimer human beings—into a time terminal. Rule Two: Do not attempt to change history—you can't, but you *can* get killed trying it." She halted the rendition of "The Rules" to glare at the wagons. "Too bad. I'm a pretty good shot, these days."

Malcolm, who'd witnessed her performance in the "Lesson for a Few Rattled Paleontologists," silently agreed. "Quite a good one, in fact, at least with modern cartridge guns and most of the black-powder stuff. But we're not here to stop Indian wars. We're here to track Chuck Farley's movements and discover what disguise he'll wear back uptime to the station. Believe me, if it would do any good, Margo, I'd shoot every one of those mother's sons and leave 'em to bleed into the dirt.

"But, Margo," and he placed warm hands on her shoulders, which tingled at the contact through thin cotton calico, "that wouldn't stop the massacres of hundred of millions of innocents since the beginning of human existence, now, would it?" Margo shook her head, trying to hide the grief in her eyes, none too successfully given the look on Malcolm's face. "We can't, Margo. We simply cannot change it. Something *will always go wrong*, leaving you in the delicate position of run like hell or be painfully shot/stabbed/ sliced/burned/scalped/or done in through other, even more gruesome methods. Can you really imagine me just popping in to visit the Pope and saying, 'Hey, I'm an angel of death. God's really pissed over your little crusade against the heretics in France. Ever hear of a thing called Black Death? It's the prize your butchers have earned for themselves.' Or maybe I could wait a few years, let Temujin grow up a good bit, then show up at his yurt one fine evening and change his mind about slaughtering half the population of Asia and Europe." He snorted. "Rotten as he is, if you ever get the chance, ask Skeeter Jackson sometime about that."

Margo blinked, surprised. "Skeeter? He spent time with Temujin?" Then, as no answer was forthcoming, she swallowed a little too hard. "I know nothing important can be changed. It's just so . . . hard." She thought about a certain, terrible fight with this man who wanted to spend the rest of his life with her, thought about a dingy London street that bordered the true, deadly slums where her ignorance had nearly gotten them both killed, and fought a lump in her throat.

"Malcolm?" Her voice was whispery and unsteady as she reached for his hand in the darkness. The security of his strong hand wrapping around hers gave her courage again.

"Yes?" he asked, quite seriously.

"Why is it that whenever I go downtime with you, thinking it'll be a special treat, I end up seeing so much misery?"

Malcolm didn't speak for quite a while. Then he said, "It's just like that bloody wretched day in London, isn't it?"

Margo nodded. "Yes. But only worse, because some of these people have no hope. That's what's going to give me nightmares."

Malcolm squeezed her hand gently. "It's a rare scout who doesn't suffer damned *terrifying* nightmares." Margo, recalling those her grandfather had suffered, simply murmured agreement. "And," he said more gently than before, "it's a very rare man *or* woman who sees past the glitter and romance to the scalded hands of Chinese coolies washing clothing for others.

"It takes . . . I don't know . . . *heart*, something truly alive inside, to possess the wit and courage to grieve for victims of the world's great migrations, to see the scars of rejection in their eyes and hearts. A Chinese, an Indian, a Brit, all of them see the world through vastly different eyes. Do they see the same things? Mere facets of the whole? Or something else entirely? Classic case of the blind men and the elephant." He sighed. "I don't have the answers to that, Margo. But finding them out . . . together . . . is as good a lifetime's work as any I can think of."

Margo squeezed his hand, glad of the deep shadows. She didn't want him to discover the tears on her face. She swallowed hard to avoid snuffling the mess in her nose and sinuses.

"How *do* they manage to make this—" she gestured around them "—so confounding *dull* in school when it's so absorbingly human, so marvelously, tragically interwoven, it makes me ache and want to cheer at the same time?"

Malcolm's only answer was a long, desperate kiss that somehow conveyed the fear that he would lose her to someone else, someone who outshone him, had more money than he did, or an estate and noble lineage longer than many a champion horse's, to a man who was younger and more attractive than he was, or had ever hoped to be. In answer, she crushed herself against him, returning the kiss with such fervor, holding him so tightly that for a moment she thought he meant to join with her right then and there. But being British in his soul, a tumble in the weeds along a dirty Denver roadside was *not* seemly—and it was *her* reputation he so carefully guarded.

"Oh, Malcolm," she sighed against his lips, "my beloved, my silly, insecure Malcolm. Do you honestly think any other man could take the place of a certain person I know who sold eel pies and green glop along the streets of Whitechapel, saving my idiotic life in the process? I almost got us both killed because I hadn't studied enough, hadn't learned my shooting lessons properly, not to mention my sense of when to strike and when to just give 'em what they want. I nearly got us both killed!" She crushed him close. "Don't *ever* let me go, Malcolm! Whatever my role downtime as a scout turns out to be, even if it's a skinny boy—"

"Hey, you're not skinny!"

Appreciative hands ran across curves until Margo flushed in the darkness. "It's all these wretched underthings and bustles and gewgaws that make me look fat. Playing the role of a young boy is *much* more comfortable. No bustles, no corset stays, no drawers, no layers of camisoles and underskirts and no final dress which I have to be literally wedged and *cinched* into just to avoid being called a loose woman—and pursued as such."

"Mmm . . . sounds like romantic illusion number twenty-seven hitting the ground and shattering into zillions of pieces."

"That's not funny!"

"I didn't mean it to be. It's just that being a guide is tough enough. Tackling the job of scout . . . that's scary, Margo. I almost panic when I think about watching you leave me, maybe never to return and I'll never know why or how you vanished from my life—"

"Then come with me."

Malcolm stiffened at her side, then covered her entire face in kisses, paying sweet attention to wet eyelashes and tender, trembling lips. "I've prayed you would ask me that. Yes, I'll go, when and wherever it is. I'll go."

During the clench and flurry of kisses and hasty promises on both sides, Margo's eyes widened.

"Malcolm! It's Farley! Looks like you were right. New inventory."

Malcolm said something truly creative *and* extremely filthy, giving the lie to those brave words earlier about their mission being to follow Farley everywhere. He swore once more beneath his breath, then turned slightly in her arms as Farley left the brothel with a heavy leather satchel which bulged in odd places.

"You don't suppose he'll try to add it to the hole he's already dug and discover our tampering?"

Malcolm chuckled. "Nope. If we'd attempted to change history, something would have stopped us from carting off that prize of erotic loot. He'll make a second treasure hole, all right, near the first. We'll mark its position, then leave it for the uptime authorities as incriminating evidence in his arrest."

Margo grinned. "Malcolm Moore, have I ever said, 'I love you'? Your evil genius is beyond compare."

"Huh," Malcolm muttered, "just a few tricks and pointers I picked up from your grandfather."

She nuzzled his arm. "I like that. Hey, if we're going to follow that lout, we'd better get moving!"

They mounted up, Malcolm giving her a leg up, not because she needed it, but because it was what just about any man in this time period would have done. Cautiously they followed the lone rider into the darkness while shadows raced across a three-quarter moon, bringing with it the taste of ice and waist-deep snow in the high mountains above Denver on a chilly night sometime late in 1885.

It was a good night to be alive. If they hadn't been stalking a criminal to his hoard, Margo would have burst into exuberant song. Instead, she held rigidly quiet, as did the remarkable man at her side, both of them intent on the figure ahead, bathed in the faltering light of a cloud-cocooned moon.

✧   ✧   ✧

Neither the Praetorian Guard nor the city's watch patrol found them. Skeeter's and Marcus' disguises were good—and no Roman would think to look for an escaped gladiator in the fine tunic and toga of a citizen, with his freedman accompanying him. But, just as a precaution, they changed inns often, paying for each night's lodging and meals with the dwindling amount of money Skeeter had picked up from the arena sands.

Late one night, the only time they risked speaking English, Marcus asked in a troubled voice, "Skeeter?"

"Mmm?"

"When you gave over your winnings to pay the debt I owed," his voice faltered a little, "all you had left was the coins you plucked from the sands. I have nothing. Do we have enough money to survive until the gate opens again?"

"Fair question," Skeeter answered. "I've been worrying about that a little, myself."

"May I make a suggestion?"

"Hey, it's me. Skeeter. You're not a slave, Marcus. If you wanna talk, I'll listen. If I'm bored, I'll probably fall asleep. Hell, I might, anyway. I'm bushed and my back and arm muscles are screaming bloody murder."

Marcus was silent for a moment. "That leap you made. I've never seen a thing like that, ever."

Skeeter snorted. "Obviously you've never seen a tape of the Summer Olympic Games. It was just a pole vault, after all. A little higher than most pole vaulters are used to, maybe, but then I had the added advantage of my horse's height. So enough. Wipe that worshipful look off your face and tell me what's on your mind."

"I—at the Neo Edo—what I said—"

Very quietly, Skeeter muttered, "I deserved every word, too. So don't go feeling bad about that, Marcus.

God, I was stupid and selfish to fool you, to force you into a position where you had to decide between honor and your family." For a moment, neither man spoke. Then Skeeter continued, "Your village, the one in France, the men there must've taken honor very seriously if an eight-year-old boy who grew into a man as a Roman slave still puts honor ahead of everything."

Marcus took a long time answering. "I was wrong about that, Skeeter. Since the moment Farley tricked me back here and sold me to the arena master, I have discovered that such honor is cold and empty compared with protecting those of your own blood. I have hurt Ianira terribly, and my children . . ."

It took a moment to realize that Marcus was crying. "Hey. Hey, listen to me, Marcus. We all make mistakes. Even me."

That brought a watery snort of near-laughter.

"Point is, when you fall flat on your backside or put a new dent in your nose from smashing it into the ground, you learn something. From whatever stupid thing you've done wrong this time, file away the lesson learned as a warning against the same mistake, then just keep on going. I'd never have survived in Yesukai's camp if I hadn't been able to learn from the multi-bejillion mistakes I made there. You know, it's funny. I came to feel like that murderous old Yakka Mongol was more of a father to me than my real one. Did I ever tell you he made me Temujin's uncle? Believe me, that's a helluva responsibility and honor in Mongol society: uncle to the Khan's first-born son. And you know, he was a decent little kid, toddling about the yurt, curling up to sleep against his mother, maybe begging "Uncle *Bogda*" to play with him. When I think what he went through as a teenager, what all that did to him, made him into, I sometimes just want to sit down and bawl, 'cause I can't change it."

Marcus' silence puzzled Skeeter. Then, "There is much hurt inside you, Skeeter, a very great much. One day you must let it out or you will never heal yourself."

"Hey, I thought Ianira was the mind-reading wizard of the family?"

Marcus' laugh was thin but genuine this time. "Amongst my people—my family—there were certain . . . talents that passed from generation to generation."

"Oh, God, please don't say you're psychic."

"No," Marcus said, the smile in his voice clear even to Skeeter. "But . . . you have never asked me about my family."

"Thought that was a bit too private, friend."

An indrawn hiss of breath was followed by Marcus' shaking voice. "You can still call me friend? After what I have done to you, can I still be your friend?"

"I dunno. Can you? I got no problem with it."

Dark silence passed. "Yes," Marcus said quietly. "Perhaps I am mad to say it, knowing what you are, but after what you sacrificed to wrench me out of slavery . . . I seldom know what to think about you any longer, Skeeter. You steal from good, ordinary people to make your living, yet you give part of your stolen money to The Found Ones to help us stay active—"

"How'd you find that out?" Skeeter demanded, voice breathless.

Marcus laughed quietly. "You are so certain of your privacy, Skeeter. The Found Ones have many ways to find out things we desperately need to know. In one such search, it became clear to us where some of the money was coming from."

"Oh." Then, "Well, I hope my goddamned ill-gotten gains helped." He turned on the hard bed and groaned as aching muscles sharply called attention to themselves from his shoulders to his thighs and from his biceps down to his wrists.

A stirring of the darkness gave him scant warning. Then, when hands touched his naked shoulder in the darkness, panic hit. "Marcus, what are you doing?" The other man was kneading his sore shoulders as though they were bread dough.

"I am doing what I was trained to do from boyhood. To give my master soothing back- or shoulder- or foot-and-leg rubs when he requested them. Just lie still, Skeeter. I'll work through your tunic cloth, since you do not have the mindset—that is the right word?—of a Roman. Your privacy is a dark shroud you pull about yourself. That is your choice; every man needs his privacy intact."

A certain darkness in Marcus' voice connected quite abruptly with other things he'd said on occasion, leaving the truth about Marcus' boyhood lit by a scathing spotlight. He knew; but he found he had to confirm it to *believe* it. "Marcus?"

"Yes, Skeeter? What is wrong? I have hurt your shoulder?"

"No. No, that's fine. Feels like maybe I'll be able to move it tomorrow after all."

"It would be better with liniment, but we have no coin to buy it."

"Marcus, would you please shut up? I have something really important to ask. You don't have to answer; but I have to ask it. Your old master, the one before that bastard Farley dragged you through the Porta Romae . . . when you gave him rubdowns like this, did he request—order—other things as well?"

The sudden stillness of the hands on his shoulder and the utter silence, broken only by rattling breaths, gave Skeeter all the answer he needed.

Surprisingly enough, Marcus answered anyway, in

a whisper torn from a proud man's soul, leaving it filled with nothing but pain and fear. "Yes. Yes, he did, Skeeter. He was . . . not the first."

Skeeter blurted out, "He wasn't? Then who the hell *did* rape you first?"

Marcus' stilled hands on his shoulder flinched badly. "A man. I never knew his name. It was on the slave ship. He was the first."

It hit Skeeter harder than most, for he'd seen prisoners of the Mongols buggered before being split open from throat to genitals and left to bleed out. "My *God*, Marcus! How can you even bear to touch another person? To father children, to give my aching muscles the rubbing they need. I mean, the rubbing they want?"

He said simply, "Because for whatever foolish reason, I have come to trust you again, Skeeter. My life is literally in your hands. If we are caught, they will take *you* back to the gladiatorial school. You have become famous in the Circus, so you are valuable. I am only a scribe. I've grown too old for the other, thank all gods and goddesses, but even as a scribe, I am worth little compared to you. If we are caught, our faces will be branded with the *F* of a fugitive. That's all that will happen to me, if I'm lucky. My so-called master could well cripple me to keep me from running again, or turn me over to the state for execution, or sell me to the bestiary masters, to be torn apart by ravening wild animals." He drew a deep breath. "So, I stay with you, Skeeter, as my only hope of survival until the gate opens. And . . . I wish to ease your pain because you *are* my friend, and you acquired that pain saving *me* from the arena master's ownership. *I* knew that was wrong, but not another man in Rome would have questioned it, never mind defended me."

"Hey, I wasn't just helping you. As I recall, I had

some pretty selfish reasons to get the hell out of that arena, too, you know."

"Yes, but . . ." He gave up with a sigh, and said instead, "What I said at the Neo Edo, Skeeter . . . I had no right to say it. Any of it. The truth of what happened between you and Lupus Mortiferus I will never know, for I was not present, and I know now the kind of professional killer he is. So . . . who am I to judge?"

"Huh." Skeeter remained silent a moment. "Well, just to set the record straight," he couldn't keep a bitter hoarseness from creeping into his voice as, for once, he told the gods' own truth about what he had done, "I swindled and pickpocketed every bit of the money I brought back from that profitable little trip. Right down to the little copper *asses* and their fractions."

Marcus was silent a long time, kneading muscles along Skeeter's back until they felt like pudding.

"There are many ways of growing up, Skeeter, and I have no right to judge when I, of all people, know your truth—the way *you* were brought up. Your childhood, Skeeter, was far worse than mine."

"*Huh?* How the hell do you figure that—?"

Marcus wasn't listening. He gave out a little, wan laugh just this side of anguish. "Believe me, Skeeter, when I say mine was hell. But yours was far worse. I was every kind of fool for judging you so cruelly."

"The hell you were." Silence fell between them, both of them stilled to the point that the sound of an unknown voice outside their hideaway would have drawn indrawn, ragged screams from them both. Skeeter finally broke the silence with a sigh. "No judging, huh? Is that how your Found Ones operate their business?"

"First," Marcus dug into a muscle under Skeeter's shoulder blade with enough force to wring a yelp of pain from him, "we are not a 'business.' We are a survival necessity for those of us ripped from time and left stranded at TT-86. We serve as what Buddy would call a 'support group.' And we have to accommodate the religious and political beliefs of many, many differing times and nations and kinds of men and women. It is not easy to be a leader of that group."

"And you are?"

"*Me?*" Honest shock filled his voice. "Great Gods, no! I am neither talented nor patient enough for such demands." A brief pause. "I *did* say that the right way, did I not? It is 'either/or' and 'neither/nor' is it not?"

Skeeter knew far better than to chuckle. Marcus was a man with little but battered pride left and Skeeter didn't want to make more mistakes than he felt he already had. "Yes," he said quietly, "you got it right, Marcus. But if you're not a leader, who is? You've adapted better than almost anyone else, you're smart and driven to improve yourself—"

"Skeeter! Please . . . it is some other man you must be speaking of, not I." He drew a deep breath and let it out. "It is Ianira who leads us, with a few others who take responsibility for certain tasks. Things like making sure no downtimer goes hungry." He chuckled, then, clearly over his embarrassment. "Do you have any idea how long it took to convince Kynan Rhys Gower that we were not devil-worshippers damned for all time? Yet now he comes to our meetings and speaks up with ideas that are good."

"Humph. I didn't know you were that organized, or even if you *were* organized, but I figured you needed help. I gamble away most of my money, anyway, you know, a habit I picked up in Yesukai's yurt, so I just take some out first and send it to you, so I can tell myself I'd done *something* decent as judged by *this* world."

His voice caught slightly on the word. Surprising himself immensely, he found himself saying, "Do you have any idea how *my* two worlds tug at me? Some days . . . some days they come near to ripping me apart. In my most secret heart, I still yearn for the honor of riding on raids as a Yakka warrior. But I *lived* in the squalor and deadly dangers under which they live, Marcus—lived in it for five years. It is a perilous life, usually brutally short; yet I still want it. And another part of me is pulled the other way, into the now in which I was born. The now where I hated my father so much for not caring, that I became an accomplished thief and swindler by the age of eight. In that same heart, I know Yesukai would have been proud of me, these past years. But here I am tolerated only because I don't steal from 'eighty-sixers. They don't seem *ever* to understand they're the only family I have left." It was Skeeter's turn to suffer hot, stinging eyes. "What you said, about my lying to myself? Maybe you were right. I just don't know, any more."

Marcus said nothing, just moved magical hands down his spine, kneading burning muscles as he went. "Those were harsh words, I know," Marcus finally said, "and I am sorry I said them the way I did. But I worry about you, Skeeter. If you are caught often enough, Bull Morgan will have you sent uptime for trial and I would lose a friend . . . and not merely a dear friend, but also a Lost One."

Skeeter, puzzled, stopped feeling sorry for himself long enough to ask, "Lost one? That's silly, when you know my apartment number, my phone number—"

"No, Skeeter, you do not understand. A Lost One is a downtimer in need of help, but from fear or terror of being discovered, disguises himself or hides until starvation drives him to action. Until we find them, we cannot help. They are lost to us, to the whole universe, until they make themselves known. And even then, it may take weeks, months, sometimes years before such a one trusts us enough to become a Found One.

"You remember, Skeeter, the Welshman I spoke of, Kynan Rhys Gower? He was such a one. *Weeks* it took to convince him we were not after his soul. Fortunately, one of us was a Christian—an early Christian, true, who had come through the Porta Romae—but he managed to convince Kynan that it would be safe— no, that it would be God's will—to join us." Marcus sighed. "It always brings great pain to know there is a Lost One amongst us and be unable to reach him, through word or action."

Vast astonishment like light pouring into his soul, drove away the vestiges of lingering self-pity. "Are you talking about *me*, Marcus?"

The answer was very soft in the darkness. "Who else?"

It was too much to take in that fast, all at once. Retreat was literally the only course he could take in that moment. "Huh. Well, thanks for the backrub, anyway. I don't think I could move now if I had to. Felt good, Marcus. I'm glad you're my friend again. It gets awful lonely when a man loses his only friend."

And with that statement, he drifted to sleep.

Marcus sat up in his own bedding for a long time, gazing blindly in the direction of Skeeter's sleeping breaths. *At least he is willing to become a friend again.* Marcus was struck with such pain he could scarcely breathe. The words, " . . . only friend" kept battering at him. He didn't know quite how, but if they did manage to get back through the Porta Romae, Marcus would do everything in his power to give Skeeter more than one friend in the world. He swallowed hard, recalling the terms of the wager with Goldie Morran.

They might step through to find Goldie declared the winner in the face of Skeeter's long absence. To go through what Skeeter had gone through already and then be thrown off the station, bag and baggage . . . it was simply not to be borne. Should that happen, Marcus and the other downtimers would make *very* certain that Goldie lost her entire business and was driven, bankrupted, back uptime to the world Marcus would never know first-hand. Somehow, the Council of Found Ones (a very great many of whom were capable of very long-lived blood wars, indeed) would find a way.

Marcus smiled bitterly in the darkness. Very few uptimers took *any* downtimer seriously. Tourists considered them unmannered savages with just brains enough to carry luggage through the time gates. Uptimers didn't even seem to mind that more than a few had vanished through shadowing themselves because no one had thought to warn them of the danger. Time Tours, Inc. took great measures to protect their customers, but no measures at all to protect the men who hauled baggage for them.

Such uptimers were in for a rude shock, very soon, if Marcus had anything to say about it.

If he and Skeeter got back safely through the gate. *If* . . .

Well, he told himself prosaically, *there is not a thing you can do stuck in this inn, waiting for the Porta Romae to cycle. Better get some sleep while you can. Tomorrow may find us in the hands of the slave-catchers, or worse, the Praetorian Guard.* He shivered involuntarily, having heard the tales of what happened to runaways caught by the elite Praetorians. Marcus settled down in his hard bedding—far superior, of course, to the slave cots he'd grown reaccustomed to, but a miserable bed, indeed, compared to the wonderful one in his apartment on TT-86, where Ianira waited with no word of his fate.

Marcus drifted into sleep planning his reunion with his family and plotting either Skeeter's salvation or Goldie's ruin.

One or the other would come to pass as surely as the sun rose and set on a blazing hot Roman day or a crisp and lovely one in Gaul.

One or the other . . .

Marcus finally slept.

When the Wild West Gate dilated open at the back of a Time Tours livery stable, Malcolm and Margo stumbled under the weight of their luggage. Both had managed to get digitized video of Farley burying his Denver haul on their scouting logs. Farley had, as predicted, chosen a site just a few yards away from the original site they'd already dug up and camouflaged. They shot more video with their scout logs when Farley emerged from his hotel sporting blond hair going grey at the temples, a different nose, and an enormous moustache which matched the color of his hair. He carried with him almost no baggage at all.

If they hadn't been tailing him for a week, neither would have known him. This guy was *good*. Too good. A whole lot of uptime money had to be paying for a professional of this caliber. Farley stepped through the Wild West Gate ahead of them, a new man (doubtless with new ID forged to perfection in New York, right down to the retinal scans and med records). Fortunately for Malcolm and Margo, he did not suspect a thing was amiss, even though Malcolm staggered under the weight of the fortune in antiquities they had so carefully unearthed. Margo was having an even worse time. She stumbled and staggered like a teenager who'd drunk one too many beers. Margo was stone

cold sober, but even her luggage was enormously heavy,
despite the fact that Malcolm had packed the heaviest
items in his own bags.

Mike Benson, Chief of Station Security, was nearby,
scrutinizing returning tourists when they emerged,
clearly watching for any signs of illegal activities.
Someone must've tipped him off. Goldie? Couldn't
have been Skeeter—he'd been gone nearly a month,
now. When Benson caught sight of them, his eyes
widened, then narrowed again into angry slits.

"Mike!" Malcolm hissed, aware that Farley was
still near enough to hear. "Need your help! *Official*
help."

Benson, whose biggest excitement came when an
unstable gate broke open inside the station, or when
kids left behind with the station's babysitter got loose
and went on a rampage, clearly recognized An
Important Event about to unfold. His expression
moved through vast, sudden relief to deep curiosity
and a cold anger that built in his eyes. He motioned
curtly for Kit Carson, who'd come to see his
granddaughter and almost son-in-law return. Kit was
looking puzzled, as well, and murmured in Mike's
ear. The relief on *Kit's* face was actually comical. Both
men waited until they'd descended the ramp all the
way, passing their timecards through the automatic
reader at the bottom of the ramp, to be updated in
a Time Tours effort to keep its customers from
shadowing themselves.

"What is it?" Benson asked quietly.

"See that guy up there, greying blond hair, protruding
nose, huge moustache?"

Benson squinted through the crowd. "Yeah, I've got
him. What's so special about him?"

Kit put in quietly, "If I'm not mistaken we've just
seen Chuck Farley in a new face."

Benson glanced sharply at Kit, eyes a bit wide, then nodded abruptly. "Yeah, I expect you're right."

Kit laughed quietly, puzzled eyes still studying their massively heavy luggage. "Mike, you should know by now, I am *always* right." He let that sink in, then forestalled any outburst by adding, "Unless I'm wrong, of course. That's actually happened, oh, eight or nine times, and most of them"—he tickled Margo's chin— "were over this little fire-eater."

Margo blushed to the roots of her hair.

Malcolm broke through their levity with a low-voiced, "Mike, I really think you should have someone tail him until Primary cycles, but not so close that he bolts the second he's gone through."

Mike nodded. "My men are very, very good. Most of 'em got dumped on the street after The Accident when the DEA was torn down and its employees let go. They're good, Malcolm."

He nodded his trusting acquiescence. "I've got this plan, you see, Mike, to catch a member of that gang of notorious 'antiquities acquisition specialists.' A really slick one. We'd appreciate your escort to the IFARTS office. We'll tell you the entire story there."

Kit put in wistfully, "I know this is police business, but could I come, too? After all, my only relative *is* involved."

Mike Benson snorted. "Kit Carson, you could wheedle your way into Buckingham Palace."

Kit laughed. "I already have, Mike. *Long* story." His eyes twinkled.

"Oh, you're impossible. Suit yourself. Hell, you probably know almost as much about antiquities as Robert Li does."

With that, Benson plucked off his belt the in-station radio unit all TT-86 security wore and efficiently set up the undercover tail.

"There. Now lets go find Li, shall we?"

They started toward Robert Li's antiquities shop, which also served as the IFARTS office in La-La Land. Every station had an IFARTS facility, staffed by at least one thoroughly trained expert, and sometimes more than one for the really *big* stations with twenty or thirty active gates. Since carbon dating was now useless, experts had to be relied upon to judge fake from genuine, to assign an approximate date as well as detailed descriptions, photos, the whole bit. Mike noticed Margo's red-faced struggle with her baggage only a few feet closer to their goal. Evidently, so did Kit, because before Mike could call for a baggage cart, Kit took the heaviest bag, earning a dazzling smile from his granddaughter.

Mike sighed, jealous of Malcolm Moore because he'd found her first—and because Kit had asked him to help train her. Given the looks that passed between the two lovebirds, each was as smitten with the other just as surely as Goliath had been smitten by little David. He shook his head over mixed metaphors and quietly herded them toward the IFARTS office.

They were approximately a third of the way there when Kit changed the suitcase to his other hand—again. "Thundering—" Kit cut off the oath midsentence, shaking out his cramped hand. "What the living hell is *in* this thing? Solid gold?"

Margo grinned up at him. "Yep. Mostly. Our Mr. Farley had expensive if disgusting taste in collectibles."

Mike gave her a long, measuring look, but all she did was wink at him. *Damn* that lucky bastard, Moore. That one smile had seriously interfered with the transfer of oxygen-laden blood from his brain to a spot somewhat considerably lower. Grumbling, he grabbed one of Malcolm's bags to hide it, and actually staggered under the weight.

"Warned you," Malcolm laughed. "You're not gonna believe what that rat buried. And we even left the other motherlode intact, so uptime authorities can nail him digging it back up."

"That's . . . great . . . can we just . . . get a move on, please?"

In minutes, he was as red-faced as they were. Margo laughed, Kit chuckled, and Malcolm gave him that irritating smirk-smile that was uniquely his own. From necessity, they stopped chatting and speeded up. Thank God. He wasn't as young as he'd once been and the strain was telling in his heart-rate, painful spasms in arms, shoulders, and bone-deep pain down his back from an old gunshot wound sustained while still working as a cop. *This had better be worth it, Moore, or you're going to find yourself in deep, deep trouble whenever I'm around.*

But when they opened the cases and spread the contents (except dirty clothes) across Robert Li's counter, Li gave out a strangled sound like a cat in orgasm, Kit Carson's eyes widened until his whole face was little more than luminous, shocked eyes, and Mike Benson forgave Malcolm with a low whistle. He glanced from one glittering figurine to the next, open-mouthed, unable to believe *he* had a chance to catch an international thief of this magnitude.

Malcolm explained their whole story, recording it on his guide/scout's log, then sighed and added, "He was really angry that some of the pieces had vanished, obviously because the gold on them or in them was destined for something important. He made quite a haul in Denver's cathouses, too, and buried that a few yards from the hole he'd dug for these." He gestured carelessly at what amounted to an entire room's worth of display cases in some museum that didn't mind putting erotic devices of antiquity on display.

"Well," Robert Li rubbed his hands in anticipation, "shall we begin?"

It took several hours, with Kit occasionally arguing over a date for some weird little piece made of gold or wood where gold inlay hadn't survived stepping through the Porta Romae. Malcolm drew up a stool and watched quietly. Margo leaned against the counter, chin resting on elbows, drinking in every word, every date assigned. She was charming, leaning there like that, still in her Denver getup, so absorbed in the cataloging he doubted she would hear her own name if he said it.

One by one the pieces were examined, determined genuine, and carefully packed away. Occasionally a piece wrung groans and exclamations from Robert Li— and a few times, even from Kit.

"My God, Kit, look at this! It's a solid gold herm, you won't believe the detailing! Look, there, at the back end. The face and attributes of Hermes himself, and look at the expression on his face!"

Kit took what looked like a slightly-larger-than-lifesize phallus, turned it carefully in reverent hands, and held it up to the light. The beautiful art on what should have been the flat "base" was muttered over in tones of ecstasy. "I've read of pieces like this," Kit said with a low moan in his voice, "but to *hold* one . . ."

"Know what you mean," Robert said softly.

"The detailing is incredible. Lost wax?"

"Possibly. Or mold and the mold lines rubbed out."

Kit held it up to the bright light again. "No, I don't think so. That would leave marks and I don't see anything like that."

"Lost wax would leave similar marks," Robert mused. "How the hell did they do it?"

Surprisingly, Margo spoke up. "Well, maybe it's a

real man's, uh, you know, dipped in gold after it had been severed."

All three men stared at her. Then Robert Li managed a strangled-sounding reply. "That's, uh, not a bad guess, Margo," he started, breaking off to cough and get his voice back under control, "particularly considering the detailed veins, ridges, and foreskin, but a phallus dipped in gold wouldn't be nearly as heavy as this. It's solid metal."

"A copy of the original palladium of Athens, perhaps?" Malcolm offered quietly. "I doubt Farley could wrest away the real one. After the Romans stole it, it was used in annual secret rituals which only the Pontifex Maximus was allowed to attend. But a copy, perhaps, carved from an ingot?"

"Carved from an ingot?" Robert echoed. Then, sudden realization hit. "Yes, that must be how it was done. Carve it from a solid piece, polish out any tool marks left over . . . my God, it must have taken a master artisan months to craft this!"

Kit was nodding agreement. He said, grinning slightly, "Sometimes we forget your doctorates, Malcolm."

He bowed slightly in acknowledgement of the compliment. Then said a bit smugly, "Apology accepted. And coming from *you*, Kit, any apology on professional matters is an honor to hold forever."

Kit flushed. "Huh. Ever since you got engaged, you've gone soft-headed and sentimental."

Malcolm just grinned, neither defending himself nor admitting guilt.

"Oh, you're impossible." Kit ignored him in favor of Robert Li. "Bob, do you have that phallus logged in?"

"Yes. And the next piece is . . ." He simply stopped talking. His gaze was rivetted to an exquisite little jade figurine.

Margo gasped. "Why, that's Kali-Ma, dancing on her dying consort, Shiva! But—they're deities of India. However did that little statue end up in Rome? And without breaking any of those delicate little pieces off?" The hands, the feet, the nearly translucent crown, were so fragile light poured through them as though the solid stone had gone transparent.

Kit said slowly, "There were some unsuccessful forays into India. An officer might have plundered it, wrapped it carefully, carried it on his person. Then again, by the time of Claudius there were some trade routes open to the East. Or a slave artisan might have carved it from memory. We'll probably never know."

With reverent hands, Robert Li lifted the little multiarmed, multilegged dancer. "Flawless," he whispered. "Absolutely flawless." A low moan of pleasure escaped him as he turned it around and around in his hands, absorbing details with his dark, quick eyes, caressing it with trembling fingertips. "But why would a man who collected those," he gestured toward the small hoard of sexual implements, representations, and brothel art, "want *this*?"

Margo cleared her throat. "Well, the dance of Kali-Ma and Shiva *is* sexual in nature. Very much so. They dance the dance of life, meant to regenerate the entire universe each year. Shiva *has* to die, so his blood will fertilize Kali-Ma, impregnating her so she can give birth to his reincarnated self, plus all the grain crops, the fruits of the earth, the birds and game animals, the deadly snakes that could kill a man within three dizzy steps . . ." She trailed off, suddenly uncertain under the stares of all three men, each of whom was qualified at least five times more than she was.

Kit spoke first. "Margo, I see you *have* been hitting the books hard." He shook his head. He leaned across the corner of the cabinet and ruffled her hair playfully. "You done good, kid. *Real* good."

Margo's delighted grin brightened the room.

Robert Li smiled, too, then entered the Kali-Ma/ Shiva statue into his computer, carefully wrapped it up, and—with a sigh—moved to the next piece.

CHAPTER TWENTY

Dawn of Gate Day left Marcus and Skeeter in a tense sweat. They intended to remain in hiding until nearly ten-thirty that morning, since this was to be a daylight opening. No games, though, which meant Lupus Mortiferus—a man very much smarter than he looked—would be there in the crowds on the Via Appia.

"We'll *have* to watch out for him. He's got his life back," Skeeter groaned, "but I made a fool of him in sight of practically all Rome. Not to mention the Imperator, Claudius. He's going to want blood, and the more he gets, the more his reputation will be soothed. *If* that happens, blend in with the tourists, offer to carry baggage, anything—just get through that gate!"

"Without you?" Marcus asked in a low voice. "Without the man who has brought me safely this far? No, Skeeter, I cannot in good conscience leave you behind to die."

"You ever *see* Lupus play with his victims?"

Marcus' shudder was his answer.

"You break in, try to stop him from killing me, he'll tear you apart like kindling."

"So we must avoid his notice. Go through carefully, perhaps in disguise?"

Skeeter considered that. "Not a bad idea. With a

quick expedition, I could acquire just the right costume for you. At the market," he added, seeing the stricken look on Marcus' face. "Now . . . I'm going to be a little trickier, since I don't have any of my makeup kit with me."

"Well, we could always ask the innkeeper to send for a barber. With a close shave and a few changes in costume, you could pass for an Egyptian merchant."

"Close shave, hmm. Just how close are we talking about?"

Marcus' face burned. "Well, Skeeter, you would need to, um, buy an Egyptian robe and neck collar—no Egyptian would be seen in public without one—and then, um . . ."

"Yes?" Skeeter, having guessed the reason for the barber and the stalling tactics. He just wanted it confirmed, so no misunderstandings loused up their chances.

Resignation darkening his eyes, Marcus met Skeeter's gaze. "You would need to shave your head bald."

"Bald," Skeeter echoed aloud, his guess confirmed, while to himself he thought, *Poor Marcus. He thinks I'll be shocked. He never saw me in Mongolia, thank all the gods of the air.* "Very well, I'll go and fetch what we need and when I come back, you can ask the innkeeper to send in a barber."

Marcus hesitated. "Can we afford this?"

Skeeter snorted. "We can't afford *not* to. Besides, I thought you knew. Several gold *aurii* were amongst the coins I scooped out of the sand on my victory lap. Quite a few silver *denarii* and *sestercii*, too. We can't afford to waste it, but these purchases are *necessary*."

Marcus nodded. Skeeter rose to his feet and squeezed Marcus' shoulder. "Lock the door, Marcus. If it won't lock, push a couple of chests in front of it, and pray Lupus doesn't trace us here. When I come back, if I say, 'The weather's going to change,' you'll know I'm being held hostage to catch the other runaway. Get out through that little back window, if you can."

Marcus glanced at it, nodded. He could probably squeeze through. He was no longer as thin as he'd been as a slave, but the time spent in the arena master's household had taken a few pounds off his frame. He could still taste the gruel that had been his only meal for so much of his life. "And if you are alone?"

"I won't say the code words." With that, Skeeter departed, leaving Marcus to move furniture around with deep, scraping sounds and more than a few grunts.

Skeeter was genuinely in his element at the market place, an enormously long colonnaded building which sat right behind the wharves and warehouses along the river's edge, busy with the cargoes from ships that had sailed from gods-only-knew what part of the empire, only to unload at Ostia's deep-water harbor and send their goods upriver on heavy, shallow-water barges. It was just like a mall. He recalled it fondly from the trip here with the unfortunate Agnes. The roofed-over portico ensured a wild babble of voices rising to a roar in the market itself, crowded with slaves running errands for their masters, merchants looking over goods with resale—and profit—in mind, and everywhere the haggling, shouting, ear-bending roar of voices engaged in bargaining with merchants for a better price.

Skeeter ignored the cacophony. He'd lived in New York, after all, mostly on the streets for several years; by comparison, the market seemed almost quiet: no sirens screaming in the distance, no semi–trailer truck horns blaring at smaller cars to get out of the way, not even the screech and roar of taxicabs dodging through the perpetual traffic with the nimble, reckless grace of a gazelle with a leopard snarling hungrily at its heels.

Intent on his errand, the displayed goods he shouldered his way past did nothing to attract him. A glance here and there showed fine cloth, imported wines, bulging sacks of wheat for making bread (the staple of a poor man's diet), delicately hand-blown glass vases, baskets, cups, even glass amphorae which rested in wrought-iron tripod stands.

Skeeter dragged his attention back to concentrating on his job. He figured Lupus was going to be skulking around the Via Appia wineshop, so he should be perfectly safe here in his disguise as a toga-wrapped citizen, but he wanted to take no chances whatsoever. It took some time to find what he wanted, not only for his own disguise, but one for Marcus, too. He hoped Marcus didn't mind losing *his* hair, as well. Frustrated, he skillfully lifted a couple of heavy money purses from distracted Roman men and continued shoving his way through the throng of eager shoppers snapping up the goods that every conquered province was required to send to the capitol. Skeeter looked wistfully at some of the more primitive pieces, reminded of the time spent in a yurt and wanting them, just to remember. But he wasn't here for souvenirs.

He finally discovered what he wanted: a whole booth devoted to Egyptian wares, all of it dreadfully expensive. *Good thing I lifted those extra money pouches and dumped them into mine.* He bargained with the shopkeeper in his slowly improving Latin, fighting to bring down the prices. He succeeded on two exquisite linen robes, the pleats sewn down and neatly pressed where they weren't sewn. The shopkeeper moaned, "You have robbed me, Roman," and put on a mournful face that neither of them believed for a single second.

Skeeter said, "Wrap them."

The shopkeeper bowed and did as told.

"What else may I offer to interest your Eminence? Collars? Rings? Ear-bobs?"

Skeeter, who did not have pierced ears—and even if he had, the hole in his earlobes wouldn't be nearly large enough to wear those earrings—declined the latter with an air of distaste, then perused the collars and rings.

"How much?" he pointed to two collars and several rings.

"Ah, a man of perfect, exquisite taste. For you, only ten thousand *sestercii*."

"Who is the robber now?" Skeeter demanded, carefully choosing his words from his limited Latin vocabulary.

The bargaining began in earnest, delighting Skeeter, who had spent five years watching—and occasionally taking part in—haggling over the price of a pony, a bauble for Yesukai's wife, a strong, new bow. He talked the shopkeeper down by seven thousand, quite an accomplishment. Glowing inside with pride, Skeeter maintained a polite smile for the shopkeeper, instructing him with the simple words, "Wrap them."

The shopkeeper, who seemed nearly in tears—conjured by who knew what method—wrapped the new items, put them with the parcels containing the robes, and added a small basket for nothing, so Skeeter could carry his purchases. *Should've haggled even lower,* Skeeter realized, glaring at that innocent basket. Despite the mournful face, Skeeter caught the satisfied gleam in the back of the trader's eyes. Skeeter gestured and his purchases were carefully piled into the basket. Skeeter hefted it, moving and watching carefully lest some pickpocket steal one of his parcels, then left the shopping district.

He returned cautiously to the cramped upper room of the inn where they'd taken refuge, taking great care to ensure he was not followed, then finally knocked on the door. "Marcus, it's me. Shopping's done."

Inside, Marcus waited for the code phrase. When it was not forthcoming, Skeeter heard the scrape of heavy furniture. Then the door opened, barely wide enough for Skeeter to peel himself and his purchases through the slit. He shoved the door closed again and said with a relieved smile. "Did it. Not a tail, not a hint of pursuit."

Marcus was shoving the furniture back into place. "While you were gone, I slipped downstairs and told the innkeeper that my patron was in need of a haircut and shave and could he please send a barber up. The man should be here momentarily."

"If that's the case," Skeeter mused thoughtfully, "this room has got to look normal." He started shoving furniture away from the door, returning each piece to its correct place. Marcus, eyes dark with fear, did the same. Not five minutes later, a knock on the door startled Marcus to his feet.

"Easy. It'll be the barber."

Marcus swallowed, nodded, and went to the door like a man on his way to the executioner. It *was* the barber. Marcus actually had to lean against the doorjamb to keep his knees from shaking.

"I was told to come," the barber said uncertainly.

"Yes," Marcus said in a good, steady voice, "my patron wishes a haircut." He gestured toward Skeeter, seated regally in one of the better chairs.

"Patron, eh?" the barber asked, glancing from Marcus' peaked, freedman's cap to Skeeter. "Looks like you didn't take that cap too seriously, if you ask me."

Marcus' face burned at the insinuation, but then the barber was moving toward Skeeter. Marcus managed to shut the door.

"Better if we had sunlight," the barber complained.

"Lamplight will do," Skeeter said shortly. "Marcus, explain what I want."

"My patron wishes you to shave his head."

The barber's eyes widened. "Shave it? All of it?"

Skeeter nodded solemnly. "And Marcus' hair must come off, as well."

Behind the barber, Marcus' eyes widened and he put involuntary hands to his longish brown hair.

"But—*why?*" the barber stammered.

"Vermin picked up accidentally."

Marcus, picking up on the cue, added, "I believe we have found most of them and their filthy egg sacs, but to be safe, the patron wants you to shave our heads."

The barber nodded, then, in perfect understanding. "Let me get my things."

In a very short time, neither of them recognized themselves in the polished bronze mirror the barber held up. Nearly bald, the barber having carefully scraped away most of the stubble left over, Skeeter nodded and paid the man. The barber bowed, murmured, "I thank you for the business," then left the room.

"Unless I miss my guess," Skeeter said quietly, while unconsciously running one hand across his bare pate, "we have about half an hour to reach the gate. Here." He tossed a couple of parcels to Marcus, who caught them with a numb, clumsy motion.

Skeeter ripped open his own, glanced up, and said impatiently, "Come on. We haven't much time."

Marcus opened the packages slowly, then gasped. "Skeeter! This . . . this must have cost you thousands. How could you pay for such things?" He shucked out of his rough tunic and freedman's cap and slipped on the exquisite robe.

"Lifted a couple of heavy purses. And don't give me that look. Our goddamned lives are at stake."

Marcus only shook his head, regretfully. He slipped on the collar and glittering rings, set with precious gems. Skeeter was already dressed in similar getup when he finished.

"Ready?" Skeeter asked with a grin for the way they looked.

Marcus managed a snort of laughter. "No. But I will come with you, anyway. I want to be rid of Rome forever."

Skeeter nodded and opened the door.

Stepping through it was harder, this time, with his head bare and vulnerable, and wearing enough jewelry to look like a New York drag queen. Marcus closed the door softly behind them, then caught up at the bottom of the staircase. "Let's go," he said roughly.

Skeeter nodded sharply, and led the way to the Via Appia, eyes alert for any sign of Lupus Mortiferus in shadowed streets no bigger than alleyways, in the dark interiors of wine shops, in the crowd pushing its way past the vast facade of the great Circus. He repressed a shiver, and found the Time Tours wine shop. Men, women, and a fair number of children converged slowly on the shop. Street urchins, their faces filthy, their hollow eyes screaming their hunger, lined both sides of the great road, begging for a few small copper coins from Romans and rich Greeks and Egyptians and others Skeeter didn't recognize. A rich litter carried by sweating slaves approached from the side away from the Circus.

Skeeter narrowed his eyes; then smiled, a chilled, savage smile that caused Marcus, standing courageously straight and alert at his side, to shiver.

"What is it?" Marcus asked in Latin.

Skeeter shook his head, the movement feeling strange without hair to shift about around his ears. "We wait. It is almost time."

The street urchins continued begging in pitiful tones. Some had lost limbs, or were—or pretended to be— crippled, to increase the sense of pity in those who might give them coins. Skeeter averted his face, judging the timing of the approaching litter. Just as it neared the wine shop, the familiar sound-that-was-not-a-sound began buzzing inside his bald skull.

Now!

Skeeter tossed an entire handful of glittering, gold coins into the center of the street. Begging children scrambled for them, creating a mass of limbs that was impassable. The slaves bearing the litter were caught dead in the center of the miniature storm. The litter swayed dangerously. One slave lost his footing and the litter crashed to the street, accompanied by a high, feminine scream.

"*Move!*" Skeeter snarled. He dodged around the confusion, Marcus at his heels, and dove into the Time Tours wine shop. He cold-cocked the guard at the sound-proofed door, then yanked it open and ran inside, a juggernaut that no one in the room could stop. He was aware of Marcus at his heels. New arrivals were already pushing their way into the shop, creating confusion, but Skeeter plowed right through them, as well. Cries of protest rose behind him, some of them from Time Tours guides, then he glanced around, making sure of Marcus, grabbed him by the arm just to be sure, and dove headfirst through the gate. The sensation of falling was genuine: the moment his body hurtled through the portal, he fell flat on the steel grid and rolled violently into the solid railing with leftover momentum.

Marcus slammed into him in much the same manner. Sirens were already sounding. Skeeter didn't care.

"We did it!"

Then he gulped. He'd have an *awful* fine to pay, crashing the monumentally expensive Porta Romae *twice*, plus Marcus' fine, which Skeeter had already decided was his own responsibility to pay for having let him down so badly earlier.

"C'mon," Skeeter said more quietly. "Might as well go down and confess to Mike Benson and take our punishment, 'fore they come and slap us in handcuffs."

Marcus' eyes showed fear for just a moment—fear, Skeeter realized, that was focused on *him*, not for his own sake—then he nodded and pushed himself painfully up while Skeeter grabbed for the railing and hauled himself to his own feet. In the crowd below, Mike Benson stood out like an angry beacon. Security men were converging on all the ramps. Skeeter sighed, then started down the one closest to Benson. Marcus followed silently.

The return of Marcus and Skeeter was a nine-day wonder, even for TT-86, which always had *something* exotically strange to gossip about. But their return, together—that was something unheard of in the station's annals. An uptimer crashing a gate, remaining missing for a whole month, then crashing the gate again, *with* the missing downtimer? It was a thing to twist and turn and talk and argue over endlessly, late into the station's night and on into the early morning hours, the passage of time hardly noticed under the eternal glow of the Commons' lights. Everyone wondered—and laid bets on—how long Marcus and

Skeeter would be quarantined in one of Mike Benson's unpleasant cells.

Many another wager was laid on how soon Benson would kick Skeeter's backside through Primary into the waiting arms of prison guards.

The 'eighty-sixers waited, laid their bets, and talked the subject to death with one theory after another to explain the inexplicable *why*.

And just outside Benson's office door, a gathering of silent downtimers, including Ianira Cassondra and her beautiful little daughters, sat blocking the door, waiting for news or sitting in protest, nobody was quite certain. Many an 'eighty-sixer had been shocked that the downtimers, previously regarded as nonentities, had managed to organize themselves enough to hold a silent but well-orchestrated "sit-in" vigil that Gandhi himself would've been proud to claim.

More than a few bets were wagered on that, alone.

Inside Benson's interrogation room, an exhausted, pain-riddled Skeeter Jackson went through the whole story again, aching from the cut in his side, bruises sustained in the arena and their flight from the Circus, even from rough scrapes and tiny, stinging nicks along his scalp. Bronze razors were not particularly kind to the skin. Skeeter was so tired, he wasn't even certain how many times Benson had forced him to repeat his story. A *bunch*, anyway. Hours and hours of it. His body cried out for sleep: healing, heavenly sleep. How long he'd been here, he didn't know, but Skeeter's bleary vision spotted the strain in *Benson's* bloodshot eyes, on his sagging cheek muscles. He, too, was clearly fighting sleep.

Marcus, defiant to the last, had submitted under protest to the drugged-interrogation method Benson felt necessary to get at the truth. Skeeter, as an uptimer, was safe from such tactics, but Marcus *had* no such protection, no rights to keep the needles out of his arms. He, too, repeated his story again and again, including his re-enslavement, his discovery of Skeeter amongst the caged men and beasts he was inventorying, then the rest of it, which matched Skeeter's so closely, that despite the grueling hours of interrogation, Skeeter *knew* Benson had found not a single discrepancy. When his final, drug-induced, mumbled story ended, Marcus collapsed, boneless and silent, across the table, perhaps into a coma or a foetal withdrawal to escape this unexpected torture instead of the joyful celebration of homecoming they'd both longed for.

Skeeter managed through a slurred, furred tongue, to get out the question, "What now? Hot boiling goddamned oil?" He would cheerfully have killed Benson if he'd been able to move. But he knew if he tried to stand up, he'd crash to the floor.

"Lookit him." Skeeter more or less nodded toward Marcus, who still lay collapsed across the interrogation table, oblivious to everything— including Skeeter's continued suffering.

"Gonna kill us both, Benson, to get your goddamned truth out of us? You'd like killing me, wouldn't you? *Wouldn't you, Benson?*"

An odd flicker ran through Mike Benson's exhausted eyes.

"Before *this*," he, too, gestured awkwardly toward Marcus' inert figure, "I . . . I just dunno. You're a thieving rat. Put a lot of rats like you in jail, while I still wore a City badge. Nothin' but scum of the earth, those bastards." He sat and looked unblinkingly at Skeeter. "But this . . ." He gestured toward Marcus. "This changes the whole thing, doesn't it?"

"Does it?" Skeeter asked, exhaustion causing his voice to quiver. "Aren't I still just a thieving rat, Benson? Can't have it both goddamned ways. Either I'm a worthless scoundrel or I finally managed to do something decent—something *you're* ripping to fucking *shreds*."

Mike Benson scrubbed his face and eyes with both hands. "Not thinkin' straight," he muttered, to which Skeeter added a silent, snarled *Amen, you stinking pig*. Benson said through his hands, "Yeah. It does make a difference, Jackson. To me, anyway. Can't figure why you did it, what was in it for you, but your story's consistent and airtight with his." He nodded toward Marcus.

Benson sat back in his chair, letting both hands fall to his lap. "All right, Skeeter. You can go now. Your pal, too. I'll, uh, speak to Time Tours about the fines for crashing the gate, seeing as how it really was a mission of mercy."

Skeeter just looked at him. Benson's face flushed. He refused to meet Skeeter's eyes. "Can't promise anything, you realize; it's *their* gate and Granville Baxter . . . well, Bax is under tremendous pressure during the holiday season and Time Tours has laid down some new rules he's going to have to enforce, despite the fact they're just not enforceable." He sighed, evidently gathering from Skeeter's closed, set expression that Skeeter didn't give a damn *what* Bax's management problems were.

"Anyway, Skeeter, I can be pretty persuasive. And so can Bull—and I expect he will be *very* persuasive when I make my report." Again, Skeeter simply blinked and looked at him. *Does he honestly think this bullshit makes up for the last God-knows-how-many hours?*

"Huh," was all he could find to say. Short, derisive, and abrasive.

Benson had the good grace to flush. He looked away and muttered, "Need help getting home?"

Skeeter desperately wanted to grab Benson's shirt collar and shout, "No, you stinking bully!" Pride alone demanded it. But his strength was shot and he knew it. And there was poor Marcus to consider. "Yeah," he finally muttered. "Yeah, I could use some help." He continued without a hint of a smile anywhere in him. "Don't think I could walk across this room on my own, thanks to your hospitality."

Benson flushed again, darker this time. He dropped his eyes to his own hands, knotted on his side of the tabletop.

"Marcus is gonna need help, too." Skeeter jerked a thumb at his friend then dropped his arm abruptly, shaking all over. "I could cheerfully murder you, Benson, over what you did to him. He sure as hell didn't deserve needles and drugs and hours of questioning."

Benson was staring at him oddly, as though he wasn't quite sure what he was seeing, then he finally nodded. "All right, Jackson. Some of my men will drive you. If," he added dully, "we can get a hummer in through that bunch of protesters out there."

Skeeter drew a blank. "Protesters?"

Benson said slowly, "Downtimers, all of 'em, organized in a sit-in protest. They're blocking the goddamned door twelve deep."

Skeeter didn't know what to think until Benson added, "His, uh, wife and kids are out there, center stage. If looks could kill, I'd be a stone statue right now."

A hollow emptiness in Skeeter's belly froze his breath into ice. *A welcome home for Marcus. But not for me. Never for the stinkin' rat of a thief.* He tried to shrug it off, knowing what they must think of him after betraying their faith, as it were, by causing Marcus to step through that portal with Chuck Farley. Skeeter wondered absently, thoughts drifting, what had become of that rat. *Prob'ly never know.*

Mike Benson prodded the still-unconscious Marcus' shoulder with astonishing gentleness, considering what he'd just put the young bartender through. Slowly, Marcus swam toward the surface, moving small bits of himself one at a time. He finally opened his eyes. The sight of Benson stooping over him brought a terrible flinch, both in body and eyes.

"It's all right, Marcus," Benson said quietly—and in pretty damned good Latin. "I believe your story. Both your stories. You can go home, now. I have a hummer and driver on the way to take you there. But I'd better warn you, just so the shock won't kill you, there's a bunch of downtimers outside, blocking the door, waiting for news, I guess, and what else, I can't guess. Your family's in the crowd, right near the door.

Marcus sat up straighter. "Ianira?" he choked out. "My daughters?"

Benson nodded. Marcus surged to his feet, swayed badly, shrugged off Benson's hand, which the Chief Security Officer had held out in an offering to help, then finally steadied. "I will go to my family, now. Thank you for my freedom," he said, irony heavy in his voice. Skeeter and Benson both knew who was genuinely responsible for that.

He made it to the door, then vanished into the corridor, back stiff, knees a bit unsteady.

Well, hell. If he can, I can. A straight back was agony to maintain, a fact he hid from Benson with a light, "Thanks for *my* freedom, too." Benson looked uncomfortable. Then it was over and he finally managed to stand completely straight. The pain in his body was bearable. Maybe. Benson said nothing as Skeeter limped his way out, teary-eyed from a stab of knife-hot, pinched nerves down his sciatic channel.

The pain stabbed all the way to his left foot. But he made it to the door, too, moving woodenly. By the time he gained the outer door, he was gasping, *gulping* for breath. His vision kept going dark, fading back in again to show him the way out, then straying dizzily back into darkness.

When he opened the door, he glimpsed Ianira and Marcus clutched together, their daughters holding tight to Marcus' unsteady legs. Neither of them even noticed him. Skeeter felt abruptly empty, defeated. All he had left were a few of the coins he'd scraped from the arena sands. Benson hadn't searched either of them, it being clear through the semitransparent Egyptian linen that neither of them carried anything. So it wasn't really Benson's fault, because he didn't know about Skeeter's injuries, but when he stumbled in a drugged haze against one of the downtimers fading back into whatever they called home or job, the jostle was too much. Overbalanced, Skeeter tried to compensate, but exhausted, bruised, fire stinging along his ribcage, and a pain like torn muscles down his side from that pole vault, rendered him abruptly helpless. Not a single, abused muscle in his back and legs obeyed his commands.

He went down hard. As complete darkness settled over him, he realized the downtimers would simply leave him here, after what he'd done to Marcus, involving him in that gods-cursed scam of Farley's. Promising himself to hunt down Farley and kill him, Skeeter's face connected with a cold, rock-hard cement floor. The settling darkness became complete in that instant and he knew nothing more.

Skeeter woke slowly, with bits of his body making themselves known by varying degrees of screaming pain. The headache alone thundered through his skull like a Gobi lightning storm. He lay very still, trying to breathe around the pain, hoping it would lessen just a bit if he remained perfectly frozen in place.

It didn't work.

Gradually, Skeeter realized he was not lying face-first on the Commons' concrete floor. *Someone*—probably Benson's gang—had moved him. He thought bitterly, *Probably didn't want the tourists to see a passed-out con man apparently drunk out of his mind on the Commons floor. Bad for business.*

For a moment, he wondered if Benson had put him in one of the private detention cells of La-La Land's little jail. Then, startling him beyond all measure, came the incongruity of a child's voice. *Mike Benson does not lock up children. Not one that young.* He moved his head slightly on the pillow to hear better and gasped at the pain in his neck and the sensation of a hairless skull sliding across the pillowcase. He dealt with those startling facts each in turn, finally recalling the reasons.

The child's voice spoke again. He couldn't understand the kid's words; but they flowed like music. A female voice answered in the same liquid language. Skeeter blinked. He knew that voice. Deep, throaty, as beautiful as its owner. *What am I doing in Ianira Cassondra's apartment?*

Not that he minded, so long as Marcus didn't— *Where's Marcus?*

He strained to hear, but didn't catch a single syllable of Marcus' voice. Then he strained to remember, but Mike Benson's interrogation blended into one, long stream of ruthless, sleepless, pain-filled questions. He vaguely remembered being told he could go, vaguely recalled collapsing outside Benson's office . . . but he did *not* remember what had become of Marcus.

Somehow, that was intolerable. He tried to swing his legs over the edge of the bed, shove covers aside, and get up. He really tried. Instead, he got about halfway between horizontal and vertical, blacked out, and fell back with a faint cry of pain, which exploded through the whole of him like an electric shock prod wired to his insides and left set on full charge—one whose existence he'd completely forgotten. The next thing of which he was clearly aware was a soft touch on his brow, a hot towel that brought ecstasy when it soothed the throbbing behind his eyes, and a murmuring voice he'd last heard raised in desperation, begging help from *him*.

"Skeeter?" Her voice came like rich, deep bell tones. "Don't worry, Skeeter, you're safe now. Marcus has gone to fetch Dr. Eisenstein for you."

Skeeter was really glad the wet towel on his brow leaked water down his face, because quite suddenly his eyes filled and spilled over, completely out of his control. No one but Yesukai had *ever* treated him so kindly. As though she had divined the source of his greatest pain—and maybe she had, at that; everyone called her the Enchantress—she touched his face in various places, featherlight, drying tears on his cheeks, pressing against places he'd never realized would feel so . . . so warm, so comforting.

"It is all right to weep out the pain, Skeeter. A man can go only so long alone, untouched, unloved. You miss your fierce Khan, I know that, but you cannot go back, Skeeter." Her words tore something inside him, something he'd realized but not acknowledged for a long, long time. "From here," she murmured, still touching his face gently, "the road unwinds in only one of two directions for you, Skeeter Jackson. Either you will remain on the road you have been traveling all your life and your loneliness will destroy you, or you may choose the other road, into the light. It is a choice neither I nor Marcus can make for you. Only you can decide such a profound question. But we will be travelling beside you, trying to help and support as best we can, whatever road you choose."

He fought a thickening in his throat.

"Oh, Skeeter, Cherished One, you risked everything, even life's blood in the test of the gods' arena, to save Marcus."

Then, when the deep emotions her words evoked wrenched him impossibly in too many directions, she massaged his temples and crooned a song, or perhaps an ancient incantation, while he turned his head as far away from her as he could and cried as he hadn't since the age of eight. The words she'd whispered kept reverberating through his whole being: *Cherished One. . . .*

Then Marcus' worried voice rang out and a moment later, Rachel Eisenstein bent over him, ignoring his tears or taking them as a reaction to pain. She turned him with clinical, gentle expertise, examining the damage front and back, the scars of the lash across ribs and spine, the muscles strained and knotted from shoulder to shank from that tremendous vault from his horse's back, the slash across his side.

He was eased back down and covered warmly. "Skeeter? Can you hear me? It's Rachel."

Rather than nodding, he managed to croak past the tightness in his throat. "Yeah." It was a sound of defeat and even he knew it. He hoped Ianira and Marcus understood. He was simply too exhausted, in too much pain to struggle any longer.

"Skeeter, I need to take you to the infirmary. Nothing that won't mend, but there's more of it than I like to see in one patient. Do you understand, Skeeter?"

Again, the thick-throated, "Yeah."

He closed his eyes, praying Ianira would understand his need to escape for just a little while the intense, soul-cracking emotions she'd roused with so few words. That portion of himself needed healing, too. Maybe he'd go see Dr. Mundy, after all, tell him everything, get all the secrets and the pain and the memories of good times and terrifying ones out of his system.

Someone removed the cooling towel from his brow, then Ianira's voice came low and velvety: "Remember, we will always be here, ready to help."

Then the metallic clanging of a gurney came to his ears and he was lifted and slid with professional gentleness by two orderlies. He only bit his lip once during the entire process. Then the gurney was moving and he thought he heard the sound of a woman weeping, but he wasn't sure of much in this state.

They slid him neatly into the miniature ambulance used on station and moved away with lights flashing, evidently taking back ways down, since their speed didn't slow for the throng of holiday party-goers jamming the station just now. In the cramped quarters of the little ambulance, Rachel Eisenstein deftly lashed his gurney to tie-downs on the ambulance wall. Then, before he knew it, she'd threaded an IV into his arm. "Dehydration," she explained, "plus a mild painkiller. You need it."

That's for goddamned sure. But he had no voice left to say it.

Then, almost conversationally, she added, "Spoke to Mike Benson earlier today." Skeeter pricked up his attention. "Let him have it between the eyes, I did." She chuckled. "Should've seen the expression on his face. By the time I was done, I do believe he understood clearly that when injured people fall through a gate—regardless of who they are—they are to be brought directly to *me*, not abused for nearly a whole day in a sham investigation."

She touched his brow. "You can mop up the floor

with him as soon as you're back on your feet with all your muscles working properly again."

Skeeter tried to smile, grateful she understood. "Promise?" he croaked hoarsely.

"Promise."

He might spend time behind bars, but by all the gods, he had a score to settle with Mr. Michael Benson.

"Easy, now. We're nearly there. Just hang on, Skeeter. Soon you'll be asleep again, mending faster than you realize." When he furrowed his brow, worried about money, she correctly guessed the cause. "Don't worry about the bill, Skeeter. Someone's already agreed to pay it."

"Who?" he croaked through his still-tight voice.

Rachel chuckled and tickled his nose. "Kit Carson."

Skeeter's eyes widened. "*Kit?* But . . . but *why?*"

Rachel laughed warmly this time. "Who ever understands why Kit does *any* of the things he does? He's an original. Like you."

Then the back doors opened and his gurney was untied, slid backwards, and the wheels lowered. Skeeter closed his eyes against the dizziness of the moving ceiling overhead and pondered Rachel's revelation. Why would Kit Carson, of all people, agree to pay for Skeeter's medical bills? He couldn't understand it. Still didn't when they injected something incredibly potent into his IV's heplock. The room swam in dizzy circles for just a second or two, then darkness closed around him.

CHAPTER TWENTY-ONE

When Skeeter, aware of a new inner strength, cold-cocked and then mopped up the floor with Mike Benson, the big cop didn't even press charges. "Rotten bastard," Skeeter growled. "Bad enough you tortured *me* for hours—I might actually have deserved it, given my reputation—" another punch sent Benson reeling into the wall, whereupon he slid comically to the floor like a wrung out cartoon, "—but no, you had to do the same thing to *Marcus*, who's never done a goddamned thing wrong in his life. This one's for Marcus." And he slammed the flat of his hand against Benson's nose, with just enough force to break it, but not enough to drive a sliver of bone fatally back into the brain. Blood poured in streams. His eyes lost all focus. He was still sitting there, unable to move so much as one arm, as Skeeter stormed through the astonished crowd of onlookers.

He'd found the Security Chief near Primary, which was due to cycle soon. Montgomery Wilkes, with his red hair, black uniform, and steel-cold eyes, routinely prowled the whole area. When Wilkes deliberately put himself in Skeeter's way, growling out, "You are under arrest, you filthy little rat," a collective gasp went up.

Skeeter said dangerously, "No way, Herr Hitler. *Way* outside your jurisdiction."

"Nothing's outside my jurisdiction. And people like you are a danger to peace in our time. And I'm the one who's going to take you off the streets." When Wilkes actually grabbed Skeeter by the arm, he slammed his other fist into Monty's solar plexus. Monty doubled over with a gasp of shock, letting go of Skeeter's arm to hold his middle. Skeeter, coldly enraged, took advantage of Wilkes' doubled-up condition and added a nice chop to the back of his neck. Skeeter then kicked him to the floor. That felt good. Wilkes had been begging it for years. He said loudly enough for Wilkes to hear, "Look, I haven't broken any of your laws. And you just assaulted me. Just remember, I'm hell and gone outside *your* jurisdiction, Nazi. Or do you really want to spend another couple of weeks in Mike Benson's lockup?"

Wilkes, too winded to reply, glared coldly up at him, eyes promising retaliation.

Skeeter gave out a harsh bark of laughter that startled Wilkes into widening his eyes. "Forget it, Monty. You do and I'll press charges so serious, you'll end rotting in a cell forever. *I* grew up as a living god in the yurt of Genghis Khan. I could kill you in so many different ways, not even *your* lurid imagination could come up with all of 'em. So take some advice. Go hassle taxes out of honest tourists who can't or won't fight back."

He spat, the wad of saliva landing right next to Monty's chin. The head ATF agent didn't bat so much as an eyelash. "Face it, Wilkes. You're no better than I am. You've just got a badge to hide behind when you swindle people and pocket the stuff you skim off the top, before it's ever recorded where government accountants might find it. So cut the Mr.-Upholding-Law-and-Order-Good-Guy crap. I ain't buyin' it and I ain't scared of you or any of your underhanded tricks. Got that, Monty?"

Monty looked cold and pale on the floor. He nodded stiffly, his face nearly cracking with the movement. Skeeter had him dead-to-rights and they both knew it.

"Good. You leave me the hell alone and I'll leave *you* the hell alone."

God, that felt good.

When he stalked away, anger palpably radiating from him, *everyone* got out of his way. Even ATF agents. It reminded Skeeter of that Charlton Heston movie, where the sea had peeled back for the Israelites to flee Pharaoh's wrath.

So far, so good. Two thrashings down, one yelling match to come. Next stop: Kit Carson's office.

He shoved impatiently past the Neo Edo's front desk, grabbed an elevator, pressed the unmarked button, and rose swiftly upward into Kit's private domain. When he stormed into the office, not bothering to remove his shoes, Kit's brows knotted above a deeply disapproving frown. Skeeter didn't care. He knew Kit would put him down in about two seconds if he started anything physical, so he gritted his teeth, leaned his palms on the enormous desk, and said, "All, right, Carson. Let's hear it. *Why?*"

Kit hadn't moved. The stillness scared Skeeter, despite his momentum and the fire in his blood.

"Sit down, Skeeter." It was not an invitation. It was an order and a fairly forceful one at that.

Skeeter sat.

Kit finally moved, leaning back slightly in his chair and observing Skeeter closely for several silent moments. His clothes were disarranged slightly from the knock-down, drag-out with Benson and his knuckles were a scraped-up mess from bringing Monty the Monster down a peg or two. Kit finally pointed to the wall-sized rank of monitors to Skeeter's right. He turned cautiously, wondering why Kit wanted him to look at them, then understood in a single flash of understanding. One of the screens showed live feed directly from a security camera at Primary. He saw Mike Benson staggering to his feet, still bleeding, with the help of two of his men. The sway in his knees warmed Skeeter's heart. Yesukai would have approved: honor avenged.

"That, Skeeter, was quite a performance." Kit's voice came out dry as a Mongolian sandstorm.

"I wasn't performing," Skeeter growled. "And you haven't answered me yet." He ignored the monitors and glared at Kit, whose abrupt bark of laughter startled him so deeply he almost forgot why he'd come up here. "Do you have any idea," Kit said, actually wiping tears, "how long I've wanted *someone* to put that overbearing ass on the floor so hard his brains rattled? Of course, this *is* going to start another round of battle between ATF and Station Management. Oh, don't look so scared, boy. I just got off the phone with Bull Morgan, who was laughing so hard he just about couldn't talk." That world-famous grin came and went. "No need to worry about charges being pressed or getting thrown off station. Both of those idiots got what they richly deserved."

Word travelled fast in La-La Land. Skeeter sighed. "Okay. So everybody's cheering my fight of honor. Big deal. But you *still* haven't answered my question."

Kit studied him some more. Then rose and walked barefooted except for black tabi socks to a sumptuous bar. He chose an ancient-looking bottle, handled it with the greatest reverence, and found two shot glasses. He poured carefully, not wasting a drop, then put the bottle cautiously back into the depths of the bar. Skeeter realized he was being granted some special privilege and didn't know why.

Kit returned and set a shot glass in front of him

then resumed his chair. His brown eyes were steady as they met Skeeter's. "Marcus is a friend," he said softly. "I *couldn't* go after him, which damn near broke my heart. I've watched that boy grow from a terrified slave into a strong and self-confident young man. I've offered him jobs dozens of times, but he always shakes his head and says he prefers friendship over charity."

Kit paused a moment, shot glass steady in his hand. "You and I haven't had much love for one another over the years, Skeeter. The way you make your living, what you tried to do to my granddaughter . . ." He shook his head. "Believe me, I understand all too well the fear behind your eyes, Skeeter Jackson. But four weeks ago you did something so out of character, it shook me up. Badly. You tried to save Marcus from that bastard Farley, or whatever his real name is. Word is, you suffered some pretty rough treatment downtime before both of you escaped."

Skeeter felt heat in his cheeks. He shrugged. "Gladiator school wasn't so bad, if you didn't piss off the slave master enough for him to rake your hide with the whip. And I beat Lupus, hands down, in the Circus. No big deal."

Kit said quietly, "Yes, very big deal. Remember, I've fought for my life in that arena, too." Skeeter *had* forgotten in his anger. "So far as I can tell, that fight was an important first in your life. First time you put somebody else's life ahead of your own."

Skeeter felt uncomfortable again.

Kit lifted his glass. Clumsily, Skeeter took hold of his.

"To honor," Kit said quietly.

Skeeter's throat closed. An 'eighty-sixer had finally understood. He gulped the bourbon, astonished by the smooth flavor of it. Where, he wondered, had Kit acquired it? And why share it with Skeeter?

Kit set his shot glass upside-down on the desk; Skeeter did the same.

"I offered to pay the hospital bill," Kit finally said, "because you acquired those injuries in a desperate fight to get Marcus back where he belonged—with his wife and children. And I *know* exactly how much money you don't have."

"There's the wager money Brian's holding—hey, what *about* that wager? Do you know anything?"

A smile came and went. "Goldie screamed and kicked for a whole week when Brian put the wager on hold until you returned. It's still on hold until you officially visit Brian in the library."

Skeeter thought that one out. The wager seemed almost irrelevant, now. But he could use the money Brian was holding. He *did* rather enjoy the mental image of Goldie purple-faced enraged. Then he sighed and startled himself by admitting, "Wish I'd never made that goddamned wager."

Kit nodded slowly. "Good. That's one of the reasons for the bourbon." He chuckled. "It's illegal, you know. Brought a few bottles back with me from a scouting trip."

Skeeter couldn't believe it. Not only was *the* Kit Carson speaking to him man-to-man, but he'd shared a chink in his squeaky clean honor, shared it knowing it made him vulnerable.

He rose slowly to leave. "Thanks, Kit. More than you know. And thanks for the 'vodka,' too. It was bracing and I needed that." It was the only way Skeeter knew to tell Kit he would keep his mouth shut about the wonderful, illegal bourbon.

Kit's lips twitched and a wicked gleam touched his eyes, but he said only, "Any time. I think Brian's waiting for you."

Skeeter nodded, headed for the door, then turned

and said, "Sorry about the shoes. Won't happen again."
Provided, that was, if Skeeter were ever invited back
to Kit's sanctuary, which he deemed improbable at
best. He closed the door, stood in the corridor for a
moment, a little unsure just *what* he felt, then he
sighed, found the elevator, and left the Neo Edo,
heading toward the library. The few coins left from
his victory lap jangled in his pocket. If the wager was
still on, he was still in very hot water. Any tiny bit of
coin he could scrape up would help.

When he entered the library, Brian Hendrickson
looked up and said in his impossible accent, "Ah,
heard you were up and about again. Glad to see rumor
true, for once. I've been waiting, you know, for a
month."

Skeeter, his mind and blood cooled by the time spent
in Kit's office, pulled the coins out of his pocket and
set them on the counter.

"Mmm . . . very, very nice. And a gold *aurii* amongst
the lot." Brian looked up. "However did you come
into possession of these?"

Skeeter wanted to tell him they'd come from the
purses he'd stolen; but that wasn't the truth. He'd spent
every last copper *uncia* of that money getting Marcus
and him through the gate. All that remained were a
few coins from the arena sands. So he said, very quietly,
"I snatched them from the sand when the crowd at
the Circus Maximus started throwing coins to me on
my victory lap. I'd, uh, beaten the favorite champion
in Rome, and, uh, things got pretty wild for a few
minutes."

Curiously, "Did you kill him?"

"No," Skeeter bit out. "But I beat the hell out of
him and Claudius spared him."

Brian Hendrickson gazed at nothing for a moment.
"That," he said, "would have been something to witness.

Claudius spared very few." Then he shook himself slightly and a mournful look appeared on his face. "I'm afraid these *cannot* count toward your wager, Skeeter. You earned them honestly."

He'd half expected that answer, anyway, so he just nodded and scooped up the coins.

"Going to exchange them somewhere?"

"No." They represented a pivotal moment in his life, when—for just a few minutes—the crowd really had treated him as the god Yesukai the Valiant had once called him. He stuffed the coins back into his pocket. *Some god.* All the years he'd spent fooling himself into thinking that what he did was correct was simply time wasted from his life, on delusions and fantasies that kept him from seeing what he was and where he was inevitably headed with genuine clarity. Thank God for Marcus. Without him, Skeeter might never have woken up.

"Thanks, Brian."

He stalked out of the library, unsure what to do next, or where to go. Surprisingly, he ended up at Dr. Mundy's door. A few minutes later, relaxed in a deep, easy-on-the-back chair with the whir of a tape recorder in the background, Skeeter started spilling all of it out, every single thing he could recall about Yesukai, Temujin, and the yurt he'd lived in as *bogda* and then as uncle of the Khan's firstborn son. Then, under Dr. Mundy's gentle persuasion, he let out the rest of it, as well. When he'd finished, he knew the hurt and fear weren't gone, but much of it now inhabited that whirring strand of metallic recording tape rather than Skeeter's belly and nightmares.

He refused the usual payment, startling Mundy into stutters, then left quietly and closed the door on that part of his life forever.

❖　　　❖　　　❖

Margo and Malcolm got word from Primary just about the time Skeeter Jackson was punching Mike Benson into the ground. A sealed letter with official letterhead and stamps arrived for them.

"Open it!" Margo demanded.

"Patience," Malcolm laughed.

"You know I haven't got any!"

"Ah, yet another lesson to explore."

The Irish alley-cat glare, at least, had not changed since she'd begun college. Malcolm carefully slit the envelope with his pocketknife, replaced the little folder in his pocket, then slid out a crisp, official reply.

"Re: William Hunter, a.k.a. Charles Farley. Above was apprehended while digging up an illegal hoard of downtime artwork from Denver. Your recordings were most helpful in getting his cooperation and should serve very nicely at trial. I know you're wondering, and ordinarily I wouldn't commit words to paper before a trial, but you are, after all, on TT-86, many, many years in 'our' past. He was, indeed an agent, collecting unusual pieces of art from the past and returning with them to his employer." Malcolm's eyes bugged when he saw that employer's world-famous name.

"We'll have a separate trial for him, of course. Seems he and another rich gentleman, on whom we have not a shred of evidence beyond Mr. Hunter's statements, had several years ago engaged in a little wager as to which of them could smuggle uptime for their private collections the most, ah, aforementioned artwork. We've already seized one collection and will be turning it over to an IFARTS office as soon as the trials are completed. No one expects either trial to be long. I thought you should know, as you went far beyond the extra mile—and citizens, not law enforcement, at that—to bring this temporal criminal to justice. Good luck to you and thank you most sincerely for your incalculable help in cracking this illegal wager wide open."

The signature block caused even Margo's eyes to pop. "Wow! The actual Justice Minister, not one of his flunkies!"

Malcolm chortled and folded up the slip of paper, sliding it back into the envelope. "I'd like to have seen old Chuckie's face when they caught him with the goods. He'll get life for the illegal trafficking alone and probably a death sentence for the people he killed along the way." He sighed slightly. "I always did fancy happy endings," he mused, smiling down at Margo.

She leaned up and kissed him, not caring who was watching, then breathed against his mouth, "Let's go make a few copies, eh? Give one to what's left of Benson's carcass, another to Bull Morgan, maybe even one to that horrid Montgomery Wilkes. Tax evasion is, after all, in *his* jurisdiction."

Malcolm laughed hard enough to draw stares, then brushed a kiss across her lips. "Sounds good to me, fire-eater."

"Huh. Fire-eater. You just wait until I get you alone, you prudish, staid old Brit, you."

They set out toward Bull Morgan's aerie of an office, grinning like a couple of Cheshire Cats.

Wandering aimlessly, Skeeter finally ended up inside the Down Time Bar & Grill, where—of all people—Marcus was on duty at the bar. He flushed and nearly walked out again, but Marcus was pouring his favorite brew and saying, "Skeeter, have a beer with me, eh?"

He halted, then turned. "No money, Marcus."

"So what?" Marcus said a shade too seriously. He came around the end of the bar, handed Skeeter a foaming mug, then sat down with his own. They drank in silence for a few minutes, popping peanuts in between sips and longer pulls at the beer.

"Been wanting to thank you," Marcus said quietly.

"Huh. Been wanting to do the same."

Another long silence reigned, filled with peanuts and beer.

"Just returning the favor," Marcus said at last. "Isn't nearly enough, but it's a start."

"Now look here, Marcus, I'm not going to put up with any more of your honor is sacred bullshi—"

Goldie Morran appeared at the entrance.

Marcus winked once at Skeeter and resumed his place behind the bar. Goldie walked over and, to Skeeter's dismay, took a chair at his table. "Marcus, good to see you back," she said, with every evidence of sincerity. He just nodded his thanks. "Would you get me a tall bourbon with a touch of soda, please?"

Back in his bartender role, Marcus made the drink to Goldie's specifications, then delivered it on a tray with another beer for Skeeter.

"Well," Goldie said. "You have been through it, haven't you? I didn't expect you to survive."

Skeeter narrowed his eyes. "Not survive?" he asked, his tone low and dangerous. "Five years in the yurt of Genghis Khan's father, and you didn't think I'd survive?"

Goldie's eyes widened innocently; then, for some reason, the mask shattered and fell away, leaving her old, tired, and oddly vulnerable. She snatched at her drink the way Skeeter had snatched at that hunting spear in the stinking sands of the Circus.

He wondered which of them would say it first.

Before either of them could summon up the nerve, Mike Benson—both eyes blacked, limping a little— entered the bar a bit gingerly and sat down very carefully at their table. He looked from one to the other, then said, "Got a copy of a communique from the Minister of Justice today." Skeeter's belly hollowed. "I, uh, just wanted to ask for the record if either of you had run into a professional antiquities thief by the name of William Hunter during these last few weeks? He's one of the best in the world. Steals ancient pornography for an uptime collector as part of a wager with another collector. Oh, by the way, one of his aliases was Farley. Chuck Farley."

Skeeter and Goldie exchanged glances. Neither of them spoke.

"Well, do let me know if either of you've seen the bastard. They'll be needing witnesses for the trial next month."

With that, Benson left them.

Goldie glanced at her drink, then at Skeeter. "Professional, huh? Guess we were a couple of damned amateurs, compared to that."

"Yeah." Skeeter pulled at his beer while Goldie gulped numbing bourbon. "Funny, isn't it? We were trying to win our stupid little wager and he cleaned us both out to win his boss's wager. Feel a little like a heel, you know?"

Very quietly, Goldie said, "Yes, I know." She stared into her drink for several seconds, then met his gaze, her eyes troubled and dark. "I, uh, I thought I really needed to apologize. I told that gladiator where to find you."

Skeeter snorted. "Thanks, Goldie. But I already knew."

Goldie's eyes widened.

"Marcus told me, right before I went into the arena to fight Lupus Mortiferus."

Goldie paled. "I never meant things to go so far."

"Me, neither," Skeeter muttered. "You should feel what *I* feel every time I move my back and shoulders.

Got a bottle of pain pills this big." He measured the length and diameter of the prescription bottle. "Not to mention the antibiotics, the muscle relaxants, and whatever it is Rachel shoots into my butt every few hours. Feel like a goddamned pincushion. One that's been run over by all *twelve* racing chariots in a match."

Goldie cleared her throat. "I don't suppose . . ." She stopped, visibly searching for the right words and the courage to say them. "That stupid wager of ours—" She gulped a little bourbon for bravery. "I think we ought to call it off, seeing as how it's done nothing but hurt a lot of people." Her eyes flickered to Marcus, then back. "Some of them *good* people."

Skeeter just nodded. "Terms accepted, Goldie."

They shook hands on it, with Marcus a silent witness.

"Suppose we ought to go tell Brian," Skeeter muttered.

"Yes. Let's do that, shall we, before I run out of bourbon courage."

Skeeter slid his chair back and took Goldie's chair, assisting her up. She shot a startled glance into his face, then fumbled for money.

"Goldie," Marcus called from the bar, "forget it. You're money's no good for that one."

She stared at the young former slave for a long time. Then turned abruptly and headed for the door.

"Thanks, Marcus," Skeeter said.

"Any time, friend."

Skeeter followed Goldie out into Urbs Romae where workmen were busy patching broken mosaics. They stepped past as carefully as possible, then headed for the library.

Word travelled far faster than they did. Telephones, word-of-mouth, however it happened, the alchemy proved itself once again, because by the time they reached Brian Hendrickson's desk, an enormous crowd of 'eighty-sixers and newsies holding their vidcams aloft and trying to shove closer, all but filled the library. Goldie faltered. Skeeter muttered, "Hey, it's only 'eighty-sixers and some lousy newsies. Isn't like you're facing a champion gladiator or anything."

The color came back into her face, two bright, hot spots of it on her cheekbones. She strode into the crowd, muttering imperiously, "Get out of the way, clod. Move over, idiot."

Skeeter grinned to himself and followed her through the path she plowed. When he caught sight of Kit Carson, Kit's grin and wink shook him badly enough he stumbled a couple of steps. But he was glad Kit was there, on his side for once.

Then, too soon, they both faced Brian Hendrickson. Voice flat, Goldie said, "We're calling off the bet, Brian."

A complete hush fell as every eye and vidcam lens focused on Skeeter. He shrugged. "Yeah. Stupid wager in the first place. We're calling it quits."

A wave of sound rolled over them as minor wagers were paid off, vidcam reporters talked into their microphones, and *everyone* pondered the reason. Skeeter didn't care. He signed the paper Brian shoved at him, watched while Goldie signed it, too, then collected his earnings, stuffed them into every pocket he possessed, borrowed an envelope from Brian to hold the arena coins, then moved woodenly through the crowd, holding mute as questions were hurled in his direction. *Let Goldie cope with it*, he thought emptily. *I don't want any part of it.*

A fair percentage of the crowd followed him up to Commons and down its length, whispering wagers as to what he'd do next. He ignored the mob, including at least two persistent newsies, and stalked through Castletown, Frontier Town, and into Urbs Romae.

The only warning he received was the flash of light on a sharp metal blade. Then Lupus Mortiferus—*how the hell did he slip though the gate again?*—charged, sword and dagger in classic killing position. Skeeter did the only thing he *could* do, while unarmed. He turned, shot through the startled crowd, and *ran*. The coins and bills in his pockets slowed him down, but not by much. Lupus remained behind him, running flat out, but the gladiator wasn't gaining. At least, not yet. A quick over-the-shoulder glance showed Lupus and, incongruously, two newsies in hot pursuit, vidcams capturing every bit of the lethal race.

Skeeter cursed them, catskinned over a railing— and howled at the pain which made itself abruptly known all over again—then charged up a ramp, shouting at tourists to get out of the way. Startled women lunged for children or shop doorways as Skeeter pelted past. His shirt pockets were lighter by a fair percentage, having dumped money to the floor while in the middle of that catskinning move. *Damn.* He kept running, aware from the screams that Lupus was still back there. *Doesn't this guy ever give up?* Then he had to admit, *C'mon Skeeter, you robbed him then humiliated him in front of the Imperator himself, never mind all his fans. Either you outrun him, or he's gonna chop you into deli-sized slices of Skeeter. And you'd deserve it.*

With Lupus and both panting newsies in pursuit, Skeeter whipped around a corner, grabbed an overhead girder, and swung himself up and around, then dropped to the catwalk the moment Lupus and the confused newsies rounded the corner. He sped back the way he'd come, hearing a roar of rage far behind. The next roar was much closer. Skeeter knew he was getting winded, and cramps the length of his body slowed him even further. He dropped to the Commons floor and headed for Residential, hoping to lose the man in the maze of corridors and elevators. Maybe, if he were lucky, he could grab an elevator for the gym and find a weapon. Preferably one of those fully automatic machine guns Ann kept in her little office, with a full belt of ammo in it.

Lupus charged down the corridor, shouting obscenities at him in Latin and gaining ground. Winded, aching from wrenched muscles that hadn't quite healed yet from the arena, Skeeter didn't notice it at first. Then, as he fell against an elevator door and frantically pressed the button, a shimmer dopplered wildly and a gate opened up between him and the enraged gladiator. The gate's edges pulsed raggedly in the typical configuration of a very unstable gate. It grew, shrank to a pinhole, then engulfed the entire hallway. Through the intense vibration of his skullbones, Skeeter thought he heard a startled yell. He peered hard at the pulsing, black opening, wondering if anyone had ever studied the *back* side of a gate, or could see what was on the other side.

Before he could make out any details, the gate shuddered closed. Skeeter slid to the floor, panting, when he realized there was no sign of Lupus, just two gaping newsies. One of the stammered, "D-did you see what I think I saw?"

"I think I did. Our vidcams should've caught it."

They exchanged glances, ignored Skeeter completely, and dashed down the corridor the other way. Wearily, Skeeter found a stubby pencil in one pocket, and pushed himself to trembling legs, marking out the gate's position and size as best he could, dragging the pencil down walls and across the floor, with arrows pointing toward the ceiling, since he couldn't reach it.

Unstable gates were nothing to mess with. Whenever

possible, their location and duration were logged. He'd call Bull Morgan as soon as he got home. Exhausted, he dug for keys that the slave master must've taken away from him at least a month ago, then remembered that Lupus had shattered his door a long time ago. He hadn't needed a key since his return. Eventually, he might even have enough money to have the door fixed. He stumbled in the direction of his apartment and found it exactly as he'd left it earlier in the day. The bottles of water he'd planned to sell as a con he'd already shoved angrily into the wastebasket. Skeeter hunted a little desperately for the pill bottle he'd described to Goldie. He shook out two tablets, reconsidered, and shook a third into his palm.

He swallowed them dry, then tumbled into bed. By some odd chance, he'd left his small television on this morning. The television, even his apartment still looked and felt alien. He was about to shut it off by remote when a newsflash came on, showing Skeeter running from Lupus, with a breathless commentary on the long-standing feud. Skeeter grunted and reached again for the remote. Then froze, hand in midair.

"This, as you can see, is a blowup of what our vidcam lenses picked up through the unstable gate. Rumor is, it has already started a heated debate among on-station scholars." Skeeter stared at the screen as Lupus, larger than life, plunged into the gate with a startled yell, then stumbled on a stone step. One of a huge number of stone steps, leading to the crest of a flat-topped pyramid. Lupus, grasping sword and knife, was staring down at an enormous crowd of feather-clad Indians. They were prostrate on the ground.

"Clearly," the voiceover said as Lupus just swayed there, stupefied, "this will begin an intense scholarly debate over the legendary origins of the god-like Viracocha, who came to Central America wearing a pale skin, taught the people a great deal of knowledge they didn't possess, then vanished across the ocean to the west, vowing to return. Speculation about the classic legend should fuel debate for years to come. Whatever the truth, this tape represents a scholarly as well as journalistic victory in the search for knowledge of our past."

Skeeter finished the motion he'd started with the remote and turned off the television with a deep sigh. He was almost sorry Lupus had suffered such a fate. He knew in his bones the shock of dissonance caused by plunging accidentally through an unstable gate, with no way home again. But in his inner soul, he was even gladder that he was still alive. *Still selfish, aren't we, Skeeter?* He realized sadly he probably always would be. But the painkillers had already begun to hit his system, so that he couldn't quite raise enough anxiety to worry about it now. Within moments, he drowsed into blissful oblivion.

"Marcus?"

Her voice came drowsily in the darkness. He'd been lying quietly, wrapped up in the miracle of holding her again and wondering if the gods would bless them with a son this time.

"Yes, beloved?"

Ianira's tiny movement told her how the endearment, new to his lips, had startled and pleased her. "Oh, Marcus," she breathed huskily into his ear, "what would I have done if—"

He placed gentle fingertips across her lips. "Let us not tempt the Fates, beloved. It did not happen. Let us not speak of it again."

Her arms tightened around his ribcage and for a moment she buried her face in his shoulder. A marvel of sensation, of need ... but she wanted to discuss something, so he willed it back, ran his fingers through her silken black hair and murmured, "You had something to say?"

She turned just enough to kiss his wrist, then sighed and said, "Yes. That telephone call you were so angry about earlier?"

Marcus felt the chuckle build deep inside. "Not angry, love. Impatient."

His reward was another brush of her lips across his. Then she settled back into his arms, wrapped around him as warmly and contentedly as any cat. He'd had a kitten, as a child, tamed from the wild as the only survivor of its litter. Perhaps they should ask permission to get a kitten for their children? It would be a delightful surprise—

"Marcus, you haven't heard a word I've said!"

"I'm sorry, beloved. I was just thinking of asking the Station Manager for permission to get a kitten. For the girls."

It was Ianira's turn to chuckle. "Always my romantic dreamer. I would never have you be otherwise."

"What were you saying, beloved?" Strange, how the endearment he'd never been able to say before *now* came so easily to his lips.

"The phone call. It was Council business. They were taking votes over the phone, to move as quickly as possible."

Marcus turned his head slightly. "What could possibly be so urgent?"

She said very softly, "Skeeter."

Ahh . . .

"He is no longer Lost. He must therefore be given the chance to become Found."

Marcus nodded. "And your answer?"

"Yes, of course. Who do you think started the round of calls in the first place?"

Marcus laughed, softly enough not to waken their sleeping children, then turned until Ianira was beneath him, both arms still wrapped around him. This time, he could not hold back the love in him. Ianira cried out softly, moaned his name and sought his mouth. Marcus moved slowly, dreamily, thinking of kittens and sons and the miracle of this moment in whatever time Fate gave them together.

EPILOGUE

Skeeter was dreaming again. He'd dreamed often, these last few weeks, all of them terrible and strange, so at first he felt no great alarm, only a frisson of fear and a great deal of resignation as to what horrors his unconscious mind would put him through this time.

The dream began with dark figures, faces masked in black, bodies sheathed in black, hair covered with black, sinister figures which touched and lifted him, began to wind strips of black around his feet and lower legs so tightly he couldn't move even his toes. Then he realized he wasn't sleeping anymore. He began to fight—was subdued thoroughly and expertly. Sweat started along his back and chest and face as the black strips rose higher, covering thighs, hips, lower belly, like some monstrous black mummy casing. But they wouldn't get his arms. He had to have his arms free, to struggle, to plant a fist in *someone's* face before his strength ran out.

He fought savagely. He thought he heard a faint curse from one of the figures holding him and fought even harder. But his other fights, never mind that final run from Lupus, had taken nearly everything left in him. Eventually, his strength began to wane. And then, before he could react, an unknown person grabbed his shaved head and bent his head back until the pain was so deep all he could do was blink tears down an

441

open mouth and fight for air through the strain on his windpipe.

When they let him go, black wrappings swathed arms, chest, and neck. He could not move.

Coming slightly out of shock, Skeeter thought to use the other major skill he possessed: language. "Hey," Skeeter began, "look, whoever you are—not that I care, really, that's your business—but what're you doing? With me, I mean? Kidnapping's illegal on TT-86." At least, he thought it was. He hadn't ever gotten around to actually *reading* the rulebook they'd given him at Primary. "Look, have a heart. You can see I'm helpless, here. What could it possibly hurt to just *tell* me?"

Then, terrified as a new set of wrappings dug into his brow, covered his head and brow, wound around his eyes in one gauze-thin layer after another, Skeeter fought a whimper that had been building since childhood. "Please," he said while his mouth, at least, was still free, "what harm have I done to you? Just tell me, please, and I'll make it up to you, I swear it—"

His eyesight disappeared completely, both eyes covered in layer after layer of thin black cloth until there *was* no light. He struggled again, far too late. He could not move *anything* beneath the wrappings more than a quarter inch. Genuinely terrified now, a one-time Mongol battling claustrophobia, his breath came in ragged gasps. They left his nose clear—small comfort—then forcibly closed his jaw over a thick gag and tightly wrapped his mouth closed until the loudest sound he could utter was a faint, muffled, "Mmmmf" which even *he* had difficulty hearing. Getting enough air through his nose to fuel the mindless terror ripping through him proved futile. As he was lifted and carried toward his shattered apartment door, Skeeter blacked out.

✧   ✧   ✧

He came to in ragged bits and pieces, aware of movement, of jostling as those carrying him grew tired and rearranged his weight in their grasp. He saw no light whatsoever and could catch no scent that might tell him where he was. He drifted out of consciousness again, then faded back into it, pondering this time *who* had him? ATF? Benson's men, intent on wresting whatever "unofficial" confessions they could beat and starve out of him? Or maybe Goldie Morran's henchmen, hired to do only the gods knew what— kill him, cripple him, send him uptime as luggage through Primary . . . Despite her capitulation on the bet, she must still hate him with all her greedy, cold little heart. Or perhaps it was simply a tourist with a taste for revenge, who'd hired enough men to do this, maybe dump him down the garbage incinerator. . . .

A chill shook him inside the wrappings. Burned alive, like so many captives over the centuries. He'd heard the crazy stories about Kit's grandkid and that crazy Welsh bowman, both of whom had nearly been burned alive. His skin crawled already, anticipating the suffocating heat and the flames searing him while he writhed inside his black bindings and screamed himself to death.

He finally was set down on a cold, hard surface, unable to move. Someone unfastened the wrappings from his eyes, allowing him sight. At first, he thought he must've gone blind during that semiconscious trip, for whatever room he'd been brought to was black-dark. Then he noticed specks of light as his eyes adjusted. Candles. Candles? He blinked a few times, clearing his eyes of dried tears and grit, and noticed shimmering golden draperies which formed a quiet, snug little room filled with candles—hundreds of 'em— and with warmth beyond any possible heat those

candles could've given off and . . . he felt a fool for
saying it even to himself . . . welcome.

*Some welcome, Skeeter, wrapped up tight so's you
can't move, in black mummy bandages.*

He noticed a dais, then, low and right in front of
him. It was wide enough to hold seven people
comfortably. Currently six stood on it, with a gap in
the center for someone unknown. The six were men
of various builds and heights, robed in black, faces
masked in black, but unmistakably male. *The ones who
brought me here, then.* A shuffling of many feet and
the sound of dozens of lungs in the utter silence told
Skeeter that a crowd had gathered to witness . . . what?

He shivered inside his imprisoning layers of cloth
and looked up. He'd never gone lower in the terminal
than the basement where the gym and weapons ranges
were, having a Mongol's fear of tightly closed-in places.
This must be the level beneath the basement, nothing
but steam pipes, sewage drains, electrical conduits,
and computer cables strung everywhere, festooning
the girdered ceiling like the web of a very large and
completely insane spider.

Skeeter shuddered again.

He didn't much like spiders.

Being caught in one's web was even worse.

At just that moment, the golden draperies stirred
behind the dais, admitting darkness in the guise of a
slim figure also robed and masked in black. *Looks like
it's showtime.* Skeeter swallowed hard around the thick
wad of cloth in his mouth. The gag forced every sound
he tried to make shrivel and die in a parched throat.
He gazed up at the seven robed figures, aware of
dozens of figures still crowding into the already
claustrophobic little space.

It's a court, Skeeter realized with a tremor. *It's a
court and they're the judges and prob'ly the jury, too.*

Probability that he'd be sentenced without defense was decidedly high—but for what crime? And what would that sentence be? Skeeter had come through so much over the past few days, he couldn't credit the evidence of his eyes: robed, silent judges, a rack of what looked like knives and instruments of torture just visible at the edge of his restricted gaze, a neat, terrifying coil of rope, just the right diameter and heft for hanging a man.

Skeeter, claustrophobic twice over, struggled in vain while the back of his brain whispered that any one of those ducts, pipes, and concrete supports overhead would make a great platform for a hangman's rope. And even if he hadn't been gagged, who would've heard him screaming, anyway, down in the bowels of the terminal where concrete met native Himalayan rock and merged with it?

Well, Skeeter'd survived a bloodbath, giving the spectators their money's worth; he'd won the damned laurel crown and the money prize fair and square. He'd even managed to rescue Marcus, alive and uninjured, except for the desperation in his dark eyes that spoke eloquently of how much his one-time friend wanted simply to go home and forget everything that had happened.

Skeeter hadn't expected elaborate thanks from the former slave and he certainly couldn't blame Marcus for wanting to forget those few weeks when circumstance and his stubborn, Gallic pride had forced him to pick up the burden of slavery again. True to his expectations, Marcus had not offered an elaborate, embarrassing demonstration of gratitude. A couple of beers; but no elaborate show of gratitude. Yes, Skeeter had predicted that and it had come true.

A little bitterly, Skeeter wished he possessed a quarter of his former friend's character.

But in of all his long musings over Marcus' eventual reaction, Skeeter had not predicted *this*. Not in his wildest, most terrifying nightmares.

Before he was ready, a deep, male voice began speaking in a language so archaic Skeeter didn't understand a single syllable. When the robed judge had made his statement and retired to his place, another stepped forward. At least *he* spoke English. Sort of, anyway.

"I will speak the words of our most learned colleague, Chenzira Umi, a scribe of pharaohnic Egypt, in English to you, for that is our common language now, necessary for survival; then will I add my own thoughts for your consideration."

Skeeter didn't recognize either of those voices; his tummy did inverted spins like a dying aircraft.

"Chenzira Umi speaks against this man, who is nothing more than a common thief and cutpurse. He should have both hands cut off to end his career of thievery and blasphemous conduct such as we might expect of a worshiper of Set himself, the dark one who murders even our very Lord, wise and all-knowing Osiris. These are the words of Chenzira Umi."

Beneath his wrappings, Skeeter had turned whiter than his bindings were black. *Cut off his hands?* Who were these people? And what gave them the bloody, arrogant gall to pass such judgment on him? He was far from perfect, a scoundrel since earliest childhood— but that did not justify such torture! Did it? *Well, the guy is from Egypt and people from the Middle East have funny ideas about crime and punishment. And there are six more to go. Surely reason would prevail?*

He wasn't so sure when the man who'd done the translating said in a scathing, late-Elizabethan-sounding voice, "If it were my choice, I'd say hang him, then draw and quarter the whoreson on yon wall, for the

children to see as an example before he bled out and
died."

Skeeter closed his eyes, queasy to his soul and losing
hope fast.

One by one, the five male members spoke. Another
one for violent retribution. One for mercy, because
he'd never stolen from *them*, whoever the hell *they*
were, although Skeeter was beginning to form a pretty
good guess. Then, surprisingly, another vote for mercy
for the sake of the children Skeeter had saved over
the years with his large donations. Skeeter narrowed
his eyes. *How's he know I've been donating, never
mind why?* Dimly, Marcus' voice came back to him,
explaining how The Found Ones had known about
his gifts of money for a long time. Based on that alone,
Skeeter knew he ought to know the man, but the
voice was completely strange to him. Maybe they
wore voice synthesizers under those masks? The sixth
vote was also, astonishingly, for mercy, leaving the
vote at a tie.

Then the seventh, small-statured person stepped
forward.

Skeeter knew her voice in an instant. He stared,
aghast that she could be a part of such a bloodthirsty
organization, but there she stood, her voice as clear
as ancient temple bells.

Ianira Cassondra's voice, issuing from the black mask,
said, "The voting of the Council of Seven stands at
three against, three for. Should I vote either way . . .
well, either decision's outcome would be obvious,
would it not? I will not, *cannot* break a tie in this vote.
As head of this Council, I may vote to create a tie,
for some things must be considered very cautiously.
But I may not cast the deciding vote. All of us having
given reasons for our vote, I will speak as a special
witness, then we will poll the Committee members

again, lest any have changed their minds, hearing others' testimony."

Skeeter felt like what's-his-name, that ancient Greek guy the Athenian city fathers had forced to drink poison. Ianira herself had spoken of it to him one time over dessert in the apartment she and Marcus shared, when Skeeter himself was the guest of honor. *So fare the fortunes of men,* Skeeter thought bitterly, *when seven wolves and a sheep decide what's for lunch. Perfect democracy: everybody got to vote. Even the lunch.*

He wondered if this crowd would even bother *asking* this lunch before they devoured it, metaphorically speaking?

Ianira Cassondra's voice, so soft she might have been whispering her children to sleep, yet so well projected Skeeter was certain even the back row of listeners could hear her perfectly, began to speak. *Must've picked up that little trick in that big temple of hers.* He waited for the betrayal to come.

It didn't. Instead, disbelieving, Skeeter listened while she wove a thread that became the yarn of a great tale of evil and danger, with Skeeter caught at the center of it, Skeeter who had, indeed, donated large sums of his earnings to them, donations which had saved many a child's life—and many an adult's, as well.

Then, as he was beginning to squirm with embarrassment, she launched hypnotically into the tale of Skeeter's run for life—Marcus' life—all the way from the back of Residential to the Porta Romae gate, already open with tourists filing through, while he dodged a man determined to kill him. How Skeeter had at last been forced to crash the Porta Romae to try and save his friend from the evil clutches of the man who'd planned all along to kidnap and sell Marcus back into slavery.

A craning, strained glance backwards showed Skeeter a roomful of people leaning forward, intent on her every word.

Damn, I'll bet she was impressive in that temple. In her flowing robes and flowing hair and that voice . . . Many a man would've thought she was whatever equivalent to angel he knew.

Ianira's magic voice then softened in horror at the fate of each man: one sold to the master of the games and ordered to keep track of inventory—men and beasts. Beside that, she wove the story of the other man, kidnapped and sold to be a gladiator, hardly able to communicate with his captors, beaten and tortured into learning the art of butchering others to stay alive, when his own presence in Rome spoke eloquently of the fact that he could be no killer, that he had come here because he had promised to save Marcus, whatever it took. In trying to keep that promise, he had lost his freedom and was slated to die in the arena on the end of a grand champion's sword.

By this time, there were murmurs in the back rows, murmurs that sounded angry. Skeeter didn't dare hope that note of anger was for *him* and the foul treatment he'd received.

"And then," Ianira Cassondra cried out, raising both arms in a graceful, possibly symbolic motion, "our Skeeter defeated the champion *and refused to kill his opponent!* The Caesar—" she pronounced it Kai-sar "—gave him both laurel crown and purse as rightfully his. Aware that only more slavery awaited him, victory and prize notwithstanding; aware also that he had not yet freed his friend, who stood with his evil master on the great balustrade above the starting boxes for the races, Skeeter did what only a man with the smiles of the gods at his back could possibly have done."

She deliberately stretched out the tense silence.

Then, all but whispering, as if in holy awe herself, "He galloped his horse for the starting-gate wall. Leapt to his *feet* on the galloping horse's back—" a number of people, men from the sound of it, gasped in shock— "then dug the butt of his spear into the blood-drenched sand and spun himself up and over the balustrade. While every guard on the balustrade gawked just to *see* him there, instead of fifteen feet down in the arena, Skeeter tossed the heavy purse that was his well-earned prize to Marcus' new master as payment for his friend's freedom."

Somewhere behind them, a ragged cheer broke out. Skeeter began to pray with the tiniest smidgen of hope that he might yet live through this.

"And then?" Ianira's voice demanded of her audience. "Then our resourceful Skeeter arranged for them to impersonate more highly placed persons than they were, to throw off the slave trackers after them. They hid. They changed disguises and hiding places, again and again. And when gate time came for the Porta Romae, Skeeter caused a great diversion so that he and Marcus could win through to the time gate and come safely home.

"Now," and her voice turned abruptly hard as diamond and angry as a rattlesnake stirred up in the rocks, "I ask you, members of The Found Ones, what was his reward for this? A monstrous fine from that evil group calling itself Time Tours whose employees use us badly and care not a bit for our health, our dependents left behind should we die, our very lives squandered like spare change without anyone ever warning us of the dangers! They actually had the gall to *fine him*! *Both directions!* And what followed that? Imprisonment by Station Security—during which he was starved, beaten, humiliated!

"I ask!" she cried, sweeping off her mask, shaking

out her hair, revealing her face, alight now with startling holiness—it was the only way Skeeter could find to describe the light that seemed to flow outward from her—"I ask you, each of you, is this any *fair* way to treat a man who has risked his very life, not once, but many times, for *one of us?*"

The roar echoed in the confined space like a Mongolian thunderstorm trapped in the confines of a canyon deep in the high, sharp mountains.

Very, very slowly, Ianira allowed her head to fall forward as though infinitely wearied by the gruesome story of treachery, courage, and betrayal she'd just been forced to reveal. When her head rose again, the mask was back in place. *Symbolic, then,* Skeeter realized. But of what?

Voice carefully neutral again, Ianira said, "He has the qualifications. All of you know already the story of this man's childhood, lost in a time not his own. He has faced all that we have faced—and worse. Yet he has survived, prospered, remained generous in his heart to those in greater need than he. I now ask for a new and final poll of the Seven. Do we Punish? Or Accept?"

One by one the answers came to Skeeter's sweating ears.

In thick-accented English came the single word, "Punish," from the ever-condemning voice of the Egyptian.

A pause ensued. The man who had previously translated the Egyptian's longer speech said very quietly, "Accept."

The next man refused to be swayed, which, if Skeeter were reading the body language under the robe correctly, deeply irritated Ianira Cassondra.

Down the line it went, skipping over Ianira: "Punish." "Accept." "Accept." "Accept."

Skeeter wasn't certain he'd heard—or counted—

correctly. *Was that really four versus two? Now what?*

Ianira stepped forward, the final member of the Seven to cast her vote. Skeeter waited to hear her confirm what he thought he'd just heard. "The vote stands at four to accept, two to punish. As there is no chance for a tie, I may cast my vote freely." She looked down at Skeeter, lying helpless on the concrete floor at her feet. "I cannot deny that Skeeter Jackson is a scoundrel, a thief, and a man who charms people out of their money and belongings, to his own benefit.

"Yet I must also repeat that he has saved the lives of many in this very room through donations he thought anonymous. And then, on nothing more than a promise, this *scoundrel* and thief risked his life to save a downtimer, a member of The Found Ones. I admit difficulty in putting aside personal feelings, for Marcus is the father of my children, but this is a thing in which I was trained at the Temple of Artemis at Ephesus: to look beyond personal feelings to the heart of the truth.

"And that is why, peering as we have into this man's heart, his soul, judging him by his actions—*all* his actions—I *must* vote to Accept."

Another thunderous roar went up while Skeeter stared, wide-eyed, at Ianira. He still didn't quite believe it. Ianira approached from the dais, a sharp knife in her hands. Skeeter swallowed hard.

"Do not fear, beloved friend." She cut loose the clinging, confining gauze wrappings, freeing him to stand up and beat his thighs with equally leaden arms to restore circulation. Then he was swept away, buffeted, occasionally kissed—and the kissers were not always female—his back pounded until he was certain the well-wishers would leave bruises the size of dinner plates. He wasn't precisely sure just what the vote to Accept meant.

Apparently Ianira sensed this, as she sensed so much else out of thin air, for she called a halt to the merrymaking and restored order to The Found Ones' chamber.

"Skeeter Jackson, please approach the dais."

He did so slowly, filing down a sudden double line of grinning Found Ones, curiosity and uncertainty wavering within him still. He *hated* not knowing precisely what was about to unfold. He wondered what he should do when he got there? *Show respect*, his mind told him, somewhat dry with disgust that he hadn't thought of it sooner. So when he arrived, he went down on one knee and kissed the hem of her robe. When he dared glance up, her mask was gone and she was actually blushing—furiously.

Regaining her composure quickly, however, she said to him, "There are things we must explain to you, Skeeter Jackson, for although you are now one of us, it is through accident only. Born an uptimer, you spent formative years of your life downtime, with a group of men as harsh as the summer's noonday sun on the marble steps at Ephesus. You have suffered, lived, and learned from every misfortune you have encountered. You might have become a creature like the gems dealer, Goldie Morran, who has no true heart anywhere in her.

"But you did not. You gave to others, not once but many times. Your . . . misadventure . . . down the Porta Romae only cinched your right to hold this honor, Skeeter Jackson. From this day until the end of your life and beyond, you shall be known as a Found One, for although you have been Lost all your life and took great pains to hide it, Marcus was able to discover the truth. You are one of us," she swept the room with one arm, taking in what must have been more than a hundred women, men, and children of all ages, dozens of societies and time periods—some having come through a tourist gate, more through an unstable one.

"You are one of us, Skeeter Jackson, and we are now your Family."

And then, as people filed past, many giving him gifts of welcome—plain, simple gifts made to be cherished over a lifetime: a flower, a handmade handkerchief bearing an embroidered logo which must stand for The Found Ones, a box of food, a new pair of bluejeans—*it* happened. Skeeter Jackson began to cry. It started as a tickle at the back of his throat. Worked its way up to a tight throat, then to wetness welling up in his eyes. Before he knew it, he was crying so hard, each indrawn breath shook his slender frame. Eventually he found himself alone on the dais with Ianira and Marcus and the many, many gifts left for him.

"Why?" Marcus asked quietly.

Ianira rolled her eyes. "Men," she said tiredly. "It is so obvious, Marcus. He has a *family* now."

Skeeter nodded vehemently, still unable to speak. He had a real Clan again! One that accepted him on his own terms, knowing his worst faults, yet took him in anyway and made something of him more than an outcast kid shivering in the Mongolian nights and trying desperately not to waken Yesukai the Valiant, lest he waken the man's formidable temper—and worse punishments.

"I swear," he whispered, voice still choked with tears, "I swear to you, Ianira, Marcus, I will *never* betray your faith. I have a Clan again. And I *never* break faith with the people who are of my Clan. There . . . there were times I believed I was not worthy of finding another to accept me, other than one I adopted from necessity's sake."

"The 'eighty-sixers?" Marcus asked.

Skeeter nodded. "Not that I'll start stealing from them now. I *did* adopt *them*, after all. And . . . and it sounds crazy, but . . . I don't know what to do. I haven't any skills worthy of The Found Ones."

Ianira and Marcus exchanged glances, obviously having given this careful thought. Then Ianira bent close and murmured in his ear. "We have a few ideas you might find . . . intriguing." She then proceeded to describe three of them, just to tantalize his imagination.

Skeeter started; then grinned and began to laugh like a newly freed imp. Not only would he be *useful*, it sounded like *fun*!

"Lady," he shook her hand formally, "you just got yourself a twenty-four-carat deal!"

He had difficulty, still, imagining himself an honest man. But what the hell? Ianira's ideas were fabulous.

An entire new life stretched out before him.

All he had to do was grasp it.

"Yeah," he repeated softly, to himself, "a genuine twenty-four-carat deal."

That said, he dried his face with the heels of his hands and let Marcus and Ianira carry some of his gifts while he carried the lion's share. They escorted him away from the dim-lit Council Chamber (blowing out candles as they went) up to the bright lights and holiday cheer of Commons.

Skeeter Jackson stopped and just *looked*. Today, for the first time in his life, all he saw were happy people making merry during the happiest time of year. "Say, how about we dump these things at my apartment and go celebrate somewhere out there?"

Marcus and Ianira exchanged glances, then smiled.

That was exactly what they did.

To Read About Great Characters Having Incredible Adventures You Should Try 🖐 🖐 🖐

BAEN

IF YOU LIKE . . .	YOU SHOULD TRY . . .
Arthurian Legend...	*The Winter Prince* by Elizabeth E. Wein
Computers...	Rick Cook's *Wizard's Bane* series
Cats...	Larry Niven's *Man-Kzin Wars* series
	Cats in Space ed. by Bill Fawcett
Horses...	*Hunting Party* and *Sporting Chance* by Elizabeth Moon
	Dun Lady's Jess by Doranna Durgin
Fantasy Role Playing Games...	*The Bard's Tale* ™ Novels by Mercedes Lackey et al.
	The Rose Sea by S.M. Stirling & Holly Lisle
	Harry Turtledove's *Werenight* and *Prince of the North*
Computer Games...	*The Bard's Tale* ™ Novels by Mercedes Lackey et al.
	The *Wing Commander* ™ Novels by Mercedes Lackey, William R. Forstchen, et al.

IF YOU LIKE... YOU SHOULD TRY...

Norse Mythology...   *The Mask of Loki* by
Roger Zelazny & Thomas T. Thomas

The Iron Thane by Jason Henderson

Sleipnir by Linda Evans

Puns...   *Mall Purchase Night* by Rick Cook

The Case of the Toxic Spell Dump
by Harry Turtledove

Quests...   *Pigs Don't Fly* and *The Unlikely Ones*
by Mary Brown

The Deed of Paksenarrion by Elizabeth Moon

Through the Ice by Piers Anthony & Robert Kornwise

Vampires...   *Tomorrow Sucks*
by Greg Cox & T.K.F. Weisskopf

Hard SF is Good to Find

CHARLES SHEFFIELD

Proteus Combined
Proteus in the Underworld
In the 22nd century, technology gives man the power to alter his shape at will. Behrooz Wolf invented the process—now he will have to tame it....

The Mind Pool
A revised and expanded version of the author's 1986 novel *The Nimrod Hunt*. "A considerable feat of both imagination and storytelling." —*Chicago Sun-Times*

Brother to Dragons
Sometimes one man *can* make a difference. A Dickensian novel of the near future by a master of hard SF.

Between the Strokes of Night
None dared challenge the Immortals' control of the galaxy—until one man learned their secret....

Dancing with Myself
Sheffield explains the universe in nonfiction and story.

ROBERT L. FORWARD

Rocheworld
"This superior hard-science novel of an interstellar expedition is a substantially revised and expanded version of *The Flight of the Dragonfly*.... Thoroughly recommended." —*Booklist*

Indistinguishable from Magic
A virtuoso mixture of science fiction and science fact, including: antigravity machines—six kinds! And all the known ways to build real starships.

→

ROBERT A. HEINLEIN